"We sleep peaceably in our beds at night only because rough men stand ready to do violence on our behalf."

- Attributed to George Orwell

MY FATHER'S SON

Mascot Books
560 Herndon Parkway #120
Herndon, VA 20170
info@mascotbooks.com

PRBVG0615A

Library of Congress Control Number: 2015906547

ISBN-13: 978-1-63177-041-8

Printed in the United States

www.mascotbooks.com

MY
FATHER'S
SON

ANDY
SYMONDS

Dedicated not only to the men and women who put their safety on the line defending our country, but also to the people who love them.

Chapter 1

MOST PEOPLE CAN'T PINPOINT an exact moment when their life changed to such an extent that they effectively became a new person. It's a rare privilege, or great burden, to have cognizant memory of what amounts to a re-birth.

For better or worse, I am in that terrifying fraternity.

I suppose that morning would be the obvious place to start. And the obvious thing to say would be that it had started as ordinarily as any other. With something as innocent as the ringing of our doorbell.

Mom had woken me with a gentle hand that morning, clearing the hair from my face as she so often did. I wiped the sleep from my eyes and felt her petite frame on the edge of my bed, her worried yet calming smile the first thing to greet me.

In those days her smile had always hinted at an uncomfortable anxiety, one that was even more apparent during my dad's frequent deployments. I imagine that vague concern is present in all women whose husbands volunteer to be in harm's way – police officers, firemen, soldiers. Those rare souls who run towards danger instead of from it. But overpowering the discomfort was a tangible strength in her face, especially in her eyes. They glinted with confidence, like she knew something you didn't. In hindsight maybe she did; that the beacon behind her eyes was actually a shield to the inevitable truth realized on the day it happened. And it *was* inevitable, I now know. Because by definition, anything that happens was at one point inevitable.

I remember the lethargic fall sun was especially bright that morning – even now as I close my eyes, I can still see warm streaks of light tearing through tiny openings in the window shade. They played and danced on Mom's auburn hair, working with the remnants of sleep to force me into a squint as I looked up at her.

Her nose was pointy in an elegant, almost noble manner. The skin around her eyes and mouth may have showed just the beginnings of creases, but dignified-like. The rest, milky smooth. It glowed then, but doesn't anymore.

I can still smell the pancakes that had been cooking that morning, unmistakable even in my grogginess. I must have smelled them in my sleep, because I had been dreaming it was Saturday, normally the only day we had pancakes. But it wasn't a Saturday, and I haven't eaten a pancake since.

Although still half-asleep I heard her tell me that it was time to get up and get ready for church. "And," she murmured, "I made pancakes," whispering it like a secret shared between friends. But I didn't eat breakfast that morning and we didn't go to church.

You'll forgive me if what happened next, at least the exact sequence of events, is a little unclear. Time seemed to alternately speed up and slow down for the rest of the morning, to the point of near dizziness, leaving me with a vertigo's sense of tunnel vision.

And it was the doorbell that started it all.

That sudden, unannounced report was what sent my mom sliding stiffly off the bed. Its shrill note briefly paused time. As she left my room she paused at the door, looking back at me with what I can only describe as resigned dread. Our eyes met, and at that moment we were equals. Both vulnerable and helpless, searching in each other for strength.

It's an easy stipulation that a military family with a loved one in war is always leery of unexpected visitors. So it probably won't be a surprise that the intrusion that morning automatically triggered our worst fears. The significance of that chime had sunk in for both of us even before its echo had faded. We hadn't yet had time to admit it to ourselves, but we also hadn't had time to deny it.

As I clench my eyes tight now, pulling that memory, I see the image of her face that morning. Frozen with the reception of that sound, a defeated look boring a hole into me. She knew then, like she must have always known. The smile was the same, but the protective, gleaming eyes went suddenly dull, and I never saw that shine again.

I was thirteen at the time, and can say without hesitation that every experience I have been through since bears the smudged fingerprints of that day.

Chapter 2

"POP UP!" My dad's booming voice rises above the churn of the surf, words of encouragement that always give me a quiet confidence no matter what I'm doing. If he said it, if he believed I could do it, then who was I to disagree?

With those words steadying me like a strong hand, I paddle one last time, feeling the wave connect with my surfboard, grabbing it in a harmony of kinetic energy. I leap to my feet, wobbly arms extended, with only air and salt water spray to steady them. I am standing, I am riding. My body feels outside itself, my joy expounded by the exhilaration and fulfillment I feel as I ride the wave past my father, the proud look on his face the most nerve-inducing gratification I know. There are few things in this world matched by a father's adoration and the knowledge that you have met his expectations.

The wave carries me past him straddling his board, bobbing on the same wave I am riding. Our eyes meet. It's a moment that can only be shared by a boy and his father. I am honored to be his son, as he is proud to be my father.

The wave falls out; I tumble over the front of my board, and grin as I churn under the water. A surfer has been born.

"So whadcha think, Nate?" We are toweling off on the sand, eyes not

meeting, a quiet commonality now co-existing between us. Feeling closer to equals than we actually are. "I knew you could do it. Pays to be a winner."

"It was awesome," I calmly tell him, trying to suppress my excitement. Stoic, confident, composed. I am ten, and I just caught my first wave, and I will have my dad for another three years.

Chapter 3

IT WAS MY MOM'S SCREAM from downstairs that finally shook me out of bed that morning. It couldn't have been more than a moment after the doorbell rang and she left my room, but somehow I had managed to drift back into a protective sleep.

Suddenly I found myself standing at that sunny window in my bedroom, shades ripped back, my short breaths fogging the panes that just minutes before had brought light into the room. Now, through that same lens, my panicked eyes focused on a dark blue sedan parked in the driveway. Two ashen sailors were adjusting their covers as they respectfully stood at attention on the front porch. One appeared to be a chaplain while the other was wearing standard Navy Dress Blues – with one difference. My eyes instinctively went to the large gold pin on the stockier man's uniform. It rested proudly on his upper left breast and blazed brightly, like it had a life of its own. The anchor, trident, eagle, and pistol. A relatively small object that told a much bigger story. That signified its wearer as a warrior elite. A U.S. Navy SEAL. It was the same pin that I had looked upon with fascination on my dad's uniform. The same pin that when he let me hold it, under his direct supervision, I cradled in my cupped palms like the treasure it was. My eyes ignored the other ribbons and medals on the man's uniform, the white collar on the chaplain's dark suit. I stayed focused on that symbol of strength, drawing solace from the Trident. Not crying, barely breathing, but knowing what their presence meant.

I watched their faces register devastation as a second shriek echoed throughout the house. She must have been standing at the large plate glass window in our living room. From that window she would have a clear view of these nervous sailors standing on our stoop, bouncing on the balls of their feet. I knew she was hoping that if she didn't open the door, didn't invite them into her home, didn't hear their message, then the inevitable wouldn't have happened. I knew better.

Looking back, I gravely wish that I had walked down those stairs to comfort my mother and stand with her to face the notification team. As a matter of reason but not excuse, I can only say I was frozen in my confusion and rising heartbreak, which lead me to merely observe the scene from the distance of my bedroom window. My inaction that day is one of the great regrets of my life, and something I reflect on often.

While I watched them wait for someone to answer the door, I tried to pause time. No, I tried to rewind it. Not to reverse what had happened – I knew that was asking too much. But just to bring it back a few minutes, back to before the doorbell rang, before my mother retreated from my bed, before these two men came to the house that I lived in with my sister, my mother, my father. I knew that if I could just go back to that minute, to those precious seconds before I knew, back to when my mom's cool hand was on my forehead, when everything was still fine – if I could just feel that peace and security one more time, I would never let it go. I scrunched my eyes as tightly as I could that morning, willing myself back to that place, as even now I still occasionally do. Sometimes, I almost get there. Almost. But as I unclenched my eyes that day, I knew nothing would ever be as it had.

What had been a sluggish swirl of motion quickly sped up, sending a rush of blood and adrenaline to my face. For a moment I thought I was going to barf, right there on the damn window. I was frozen to it, watching the chaplain and SEAL walk through the front door, my muscles contracted and tight. My stomach finally quieted and the sourness subsided. Time and sound seemed to pause, nonexistent for how long?

"Nathan, what's going on?" Cheyenne's tiny voice cut through cluttered chunks of broken time, finally moving me to action.

She was standing in my doorway in her favorite Hello Kitty pajamas, sporting untidy pigtails, disordered, rubbing her eyes. There was a sudden realization that at thirteen, I was now the man of the house. As Dad had always told me I was when he was gone. And now, he was.

"I'm not sure, Chey," I told her truthfully. "Some guys that work with Dad are downstairs talking to Mom."

"Someone screamed."

"I know. Mom's upset."

"Is everything okay?"

"I don't think so."

"Is it Daddy? Did something happen to him?" Even at seven, the realities of having a father at war were not lost on her.

"I think so. I-I'm not sure exactly," I stammered, feeling my chin quiver and neck flex. Determined to stay strong for my sister, I gritted my teeth. Again, bile rose to my throat. Deep breaths pushed it down, deep breaths slowed my heart, deep breaths deep breaths deep breaths.

I walked toward her.

Her face was angelic; innocent and clean. She had these really intelligent eyes, like a good teacher's, and they tore into me, reading my body language. Eventually a tear formed, slowly falling onto the bridge of her nose, picking up steam as it slid down her cheek. Now she knew.

I reached her just as the complete sadness and realization hit her little body. I wrapped her in my arms, feeling wet on my shoulder, her sobs uncontrollable.

"I want Daddy, I want Daddy," she slurred over and over, too many times to count. Her breaths quickened and came in shorter and shorter bursts. I worried that she would hyperventilate.

I closed my eyes, pulled her tighter, but still not crying myself.

I thought back to the last time I saw my dad. We had dropped him off on base at Little Creek a few months earlier for another deployment to Afghanistan. Mom had been sitting in the passenger's seat of our brand new Ford Explorer, Cheyenne asleep in the back. Dad's big, calloused hand securely enveloped my neck as he led me across the gravel parking lot ringing the headquarters of SEAL Team 2.

The drab, prefabricated building carried no identifying markings. Bright exterior lights buzzed – it was still hours before daylight. They gave off a murky glow, humming animatedly while imposing a lulling effect on moths and young boys alike.

I had never before been inside Dad's "office," but had certainly spent many an afternoon daydreaming about what the SEAL compound looked like and what went on inside. He nodded at the uniformed guard standing at the gate, showed his ID, and we were soon on the other side of the chain link fence. Four hopeful eyes looked back to Mom, not sure if we were allowed to do this. A complicit look gave us all the permission we needed. This was between the men, or at least that's how I interpreted it. The next thing I knew the heavy metal door swung open and we were inside.

The business-like bustle and energy inside was a stark contrast from the early morning stillness. A quiet confidence radiated among the few dozen tough, serious men walking the Spartan halls, sipping coffee, assembling weapons, reviewing documents. Their green duffle bags and assault kits littered every open area. An organized clutter. Most acknowledged my father with a tight smile or raise of the eyebrows. A lot of them were men I knew, some well. The guys who came over for summer barbeques and home-cooked meals. The few months out of the year when their platoon wasn't deployed or training, these were the men who came to my house for Thanksgiving dinner, who went to the boardwalk restaurants with my parents and played golf with my dad. The guys who had taught me curse words and how to play poker. The guys who treated me one way when my mom was around and tried to choke me out when she wasn't. One of whom – I still wasn't sure who – had covered my toilet bowl in clear plastic wrap last year. I saw Mr. Vaughn, Bull, LT Hagen, all making their final preparations for war.

"Mo." Uncle Spencer walked over, shaking my dad's hand and placing his free one on my head. Like most of them, he was either spitting into or sipping from a Styrofoam cup. It was difficult to tell which.

Spencer Detse was one of the youngest men on my dad's team, a single guy from Nebraska who was like a younger brother to my father and a fun uncle to me.

He had joined the Navy soon after high school and had made it through BUD/S, the legendary SEAL training program, soon after. Spencer was short, especially for a SEAL, and made up for that by resembling chiseled stone. He loved Cornhusker football and playing practical jokes, often on me. He had once pinned my pinky finger into my palm for the entire halftime show of the Super Bowl, telling me he wouldn't let go until I said "uncle." Despite my mom's pleas (if it wasn't for her I'd probably still be curled under the coffee table, arm contorted above my head) and the excruciating pain, I'm proud to say I didn't give in.

"Hey there, Little Warrior." That's what he had called me since then, and I thought it was the greatest nickname in the world. "What are you doing in here?"

"Hi, Uncle Spence. Dunno, Dad brought me in. We came to see you guys off." We *always* came to see my dad off and pick him up from every deployment and training exercise, no matter what time he had to report.

"You know this is top secret stuff in here, make sure you don't give the enemy any intel."

"Ah, it's just you guys and your guns. I've seen it all before."

He cracked a smile before threatening me with a wedgie. I expertly dodged his half-hearted attempt, not bothering to look to Dad for help. I knew he expected me to defend myself.

"Don't even think about it, Napoleon," I said as menacingly as I could muster, using his Team nickname. I tried my best to sneer, and even balled my fists. Then, really going out on a limb: "Don't make me kick your ass."

His eyebrows shot up in surprise and mock-anger, but I hardly noticed. My focus was on Dad, his reaction. To my relief, there was none. Maybe an accepting acquiescence? Grudging respect?

"You win this round Little Warrior, but I'll be back for you."

I knew he would. I'd probably have to "pay the man" at a later date, but that was okay with me.

He left us, passing by Bull as he waddled down the hallway.

"The hell's the matter with you?" Dad asked.

Bull, as his name belied, was a hulk of a Southern gentlemen, ul-tra-proud to be from Arkansas. Although a religious man, his team-mates appreciated the fact that he wasn't a Bible-thumper. Dad told me that before every mission Bull was the one who said the prayer and even the non-religious guys would partake. I guess they figured they'd cover themselves. You know, just in case. I always thought how interesting it was for such a devout man to be a trained killer.

"Too much coffee and protein bars," he replied, barely slowing or glancing in our direction. "Gotta use the head. Nate. Mo, see you on the quarterdeck."

"Going to take a shit?" my dad called after him. I looked up, sur-prised and flattered he felt comfortable using the four-letter word in front of me.

Bull's gait slowed, shoulders clenched. While his snarl may have scared me, it didn't have the same effect on his platoon mates. To me, his nose alone was tough to look at. Broken who knows how many times, it was flat and jutted out in at least three different directions. There was a smattering of laughter from Dad and a few of the other SEALs in earshot. The thing was, Bull endured a rare affliction, par-ticularly painful for a SEAL, and one that he suffered for often. You see, he didn't curse. And worse, cringed when others did. Needless to say, the standard foulness common in special operations was often exaggerated for his benefit.

"That's like a lawyer who can't tell a lie," LT Hagen, their OIC, once explained to me.

I watched Bull saunter down the hall before feeling Dad's hand on my neck once again. I looked up at his rugged, newly-bearded face, and smiled. He returned it, leading me towards a wall with a huge blue circle painted on it. The circle had a black seal hovering over the number "2" and the words "SEAL TEAM" on the top.

Off to the right was the ready room. It housed a pool table, some worn couches, an old big-screen TV, and a wobbly conference table. A few laptops were sprinkled around the room, sitting on ugly and mismatched government furniture. Poking my head in, I recognized a few of the burly guys lounging in front of Fox News, checking and re-checking gear. Several had cleaning supplies out, disassembled guns in their hands. I recognized M4 assault rifles, MP7 submachine guns, a Heckler & Koch PSG-2, which I knew was a sniper rifle, and some standard SEAL issued Sig Sauer P226 pistols.

I acted nonchalant as I looked over the men's hardware, but inside my heart raced with excitement. Dad had showed me most of these weapons before, and I had even helped him clean his guns after deployments and trips to the range. But it was still a huge rush to see up close the powerful tools these warriors would take into battle. If there was one thing I had learned at an early age, it was to respect firepower.

The walls in the room were covered with framed pictures of men in uniform, wooden plaques and other awards. There was a photograph of President Bush shaking hands with a large, unidentified SEAL in the Oval Office. I saw a dartboard with Osama Bin Laden's picture on it, covered with tiny holes. The far right wall featured photos of girls, some naked, pinned haphazardly under a hand-written sign reading *"Wall of Shame."* I let a giggle escape before quickly looking up at my father, embarrassed by my reaction, hoping he hadn't heard me. He shook his head understandingly, and led me back outside into the cool morning.

Twilight's gray soupiness was a stark difference from the glaring florescent lights burning inside the building. I blinked several times, finally getting my bearings. Gravel crunching under our feet was the only sound, seemingly muted by the haze. We exited through the same gate we had entered only minutes before. I could make out my mom standing at the back of the Explorer, Cheyenne sleeping on her chest.

"Here, let me take her," my dad offered, extending his arms. Cheyenne barely stirred while being transferred to our father, and quickly had her head resting peacefully on his large shoulder.

"You didn't sign anything, did you, Nathan?" my mom asked, mock-worry on her face.

"Nah, not for five more years," I told her.

"In five years you'll be starting college," Dad stated firmly. I shrugged, knowing now wasn't the time to make my argument.

"Alright baby, it's that time," my father said. He put a groggy Cheyenne on her feet, placed both hands on Mom's cheeks.

"You're my light, my life, and my inspiration. Everything I do is for you."

She gave him a brave smile, and said the same thing she always did:

"You know the rules. Come home."

"I promise," he replied.

As far as I know, it was the only promise he ever broke.

He wiped away a tear with his thumb before leaning in to kiss her. Their embrace lingered. Cheyenne held my hand. The combination of holding back tears and the immense pride I felt made my chest feel like it would burst. It was an honor to be his son. He was the toughest, most honorable man I knew, and it gave me great pleasure knowing what he did for a living. But also great trepidation, even if I hadn't recognized it at the time. To me, war had just been a part of life, a part of my family. We'd been in it ever since I could remember.

Then he knelt down in front of Cheyenne, tickling her armpits. She squirmed sleepily, letting him lift her high in the air and kiss her belly.

"You be a good girl for Mommy, okay, Munchkin?" he said, setting her back down before turning to me. He looked me right in the eye, and I didn't look away, just like he taught me.

"Nathan, make me proud. Remember, integrity is doing the right thing even if no one is watching. I trust you more than you can know, and can't tell you what a comfort it is knowing that my son is here to look after the family when I'm away."

I nodded, remaining stoic. He shook my hand, and told me what he always did: "See you on the other side."

As I stood at my window it occurred to me that would be the last time I would ever speak to my father. The realization made me rack my brain, searching for that memory, needing to save every sound and scent of it. With a wash of anxiety I feared that some parts of it had already slipped away. Did I walk out of the gate first that night, or had he? Did he tell Mom he loved her? I panicked, not remembering if he had been wearing a hat and wondering what else I could have forgotten.

I was looking at the top of Cheyenne's head, feeling her tears on my arms, when I sensed someone else in the room. I spun around and saw a uniformed SEAL standing uncomfortably in my bedroom doorway.

"Hey guys. Can I come in?"

I think his name was Mike. Just Mike, no last name, no nickname. And that suited him perfectly. Short blond hair, tall, thin, unremarkable save for the fact that he was a United States Navy SEAL.

"Free country," I said, and immediately felt stupid.

He nodded understandingly and came closer.

"Hi Cheyenne," he said, kneeling gingerly in front of her. It reminded me of my father's goodbye two months earlier, and irritated me. I didn't want to share that with anyone.

"It's my dad, right?" I challenged, looking him dead in the eyes. He turned to me, not breaking eye contact, and took us both into his arms. I quickly escaped, having no interest in his embrace.

"I wanted to let your mom be the one to tell you, but she's lying down right now. Yes, it's your dad. There was an accident, and he's gone."

"Where did he go?" Cheyenne asked, wriggling out of his grip. He struggled with her for a minute, words eluding him. It was clear that a lifetime of expected and constant success left few people on the planet worse equipped to deal with loss.

"He went to be with the angels, Cheyenne. Daddy's in Heaven now," I explained, staring at Mike. "Right?"

"He died for his country and teammates, for his brothers. He died for his family, his kids and his kids' kids. Your dad was a true warrior and hero," he said.

So as to not confuse Chey, I didn't say "no shit," even though that's exactly what I was thinking.

Chapter 4

THE NEXT DAY Uncle Spencer, Bull and LT Hagen arrived. They had been with him on the mission and hadn't left his side since he had been hit. They had been the ones to carry him down the mountain. Who had loaded him on the medevac. The ones who had applied tourniquets to his wounds, whose words had surely soothed him as he bled. These men believed they were invincible, and at no time did any of them think he wouldn't make it. When the worst had happened, they controlled what they could, if only to maintain their sanity. Then they escorted him home proudly.

He was now in Dover, Delaware, with another SEAL standing watch over his casket. He wouldn't be left alone before the funeral, not even for a minute. There was no real comfort in a time like that, but knowing this was the closest thing I had.

The pieces that remained of Spencer were at our house by noon. It was clear his physical injuries paled in comparison to what he was grappling with inside.

Spencer eased into Cheyenne's room like a shadow. His right arm was in a sling. Two black eyes rested hollow above a bandaged and swollen nose. His fair hair meant he never could grow much of a beard, but the stubborn scruff was thicker than it had been the last time I had seen him, in the Team 2 compound. The weather-beaten face was now darker and he seemed like an older man than before.

Cheyenne and I had been sitting on her bed reading one of her *Frog and Toad* books. I, for one, was trying to slow the river of thoughts gushing through my brain when I heard his tap at the door.

Excited, Cheyenne dropped the book on my lap and jumped up. Her hug landed at 100 miles an hour, causing a stifled grunt. I was hoping she didn't expect Dad to follow him into the room.

Holding her and watching me, he asked to come in. I didn't speak, emotions pinning tongue and mind.

Gingerly, he limped into the room. A Navy sweatshirt and sweatpants hid his muscular frame. I felt a rage begin to build inside me, and my face flushed.

"Where were you!?" I yelled. "How could you let this happen? You say he was your brother, you guys were there to protect each other! And you let him die!"

Cheyenne immediately started wailing, and Uncle Spencer lifted her with a noticeable wince. My rage was misdirected, I knew that, and the pain in his face made me realize how bad he was hurting. Breaths came in hurried gasps as I seethed. Still, I didn't cry. I stared at my father's teammate, one of the top warriors on the planet, and for some reason found myself taking solace in his pain. I knew that he had done everything he could to save my father, more than likely risking his own life while doing so. I immediately felt guilty for my reaction.

I calmed myself, asked, "How did it happen, Uncle Spencer? Where were you guys?"

His eyes were sorrowful.

"You know I can't tell you that, buddy. On a mission."

I could tell he wanted to tell me the truth. But I also knew about the sacredness of mission secrecy that SEALs lived by. I looked into his eyes, searching for answers, finding only hurt and sadness.

There was movement behind Spencer, and my mom entered the room.

She looked surprisingly calm, her thin arms reaching out for Cheyenne. The room was silent; even Chey's whimpers had dissolved into quiet sobs as she buried herself into our mother's chest. For a moment, no one spoke. We stood wide-eyed, not knowing what to do.

"Gayle, the CACO needs to speak with you about arrangements," Uncle Spencer finally said, holding out his arm as a guide. "He's waiting downstairs."

I lunged forward, grabbing his arm before he could follow. Since the second I had seen the notification team the day before, there was one question I had to get answered.

"Did you guys get them? Did you get whoever killed my dad?" I asked him urgently, my expression pleading for a truthful answer.

He stared at me for what seemed like forever, before responding with an almost imperceptible nod. "We got 'em buddy. We got 'em all. If it wasn't for your dad, me and a lot of other guys wouldn't be here. He'd never admit it, but he died a hero, Nathan."

I nodded, and followed him out of the room. I never had a doubt.

Slowly walking down the stairs allowed me a few seconds of alone time. Below me, the house was bustling. The scene of hyperfrenetic activity made Mom's frozen pose at the kitchen table that much more jarring.

She was sitting with the chaplain and officer from the day before, looking like a child being coached through geometry problems. Cheyenne was on her lap, sucking her thumb, a habit she had been bribed with stickers to quit a couple of years ago. Mom listened blankly to whatever the officer was telling her.

I stopped on the landing, unseen, taking in the landscape. Back in the living room Bull's wife, Ms. Dotty, sat on the love seat, whispering with a woman I didn't recognize. Three or four other sailors stood uncomfortably behind them. The doorbell rang, its ominous chime stopping all conversation. Ms. Dotty got up to answer it.

Bull and LT Hagen walked through the door. They were wearing their Dress Blues, and of course my stare went directly to the gold Tridents. They had regulation haircuts and were clean shaven, which was rare for immediately after a deployment. SEALs did not have to follow the same grooming standards as the rest of the Navy, or "spit and shine" as my dad calls it. Had called it.

Still unseen, I watched Ms. Dotty kiss her husband on the cheek. Bull was 6'6", and as result a got a ton of grief from his teammates about slow times on the obstacle course and his posture in the SEAL Delivery Vehicles. Most of the jokes came from afar, because even fellow SEALs avoided doing battle with Bull if they could help it. He had been a heavyweight boxer at Duke, and fought professionally for a short time before joining the Navy. He had a standing bet that no man in the Teams could last a full minute against him without getting knocked down, and had a perfect record against both SEAL groups. Until my dad had given the problem some thought.

Right after SQT, Dad had made the large Chief Petty Officer a bet. As an FNG, Dad was responsible for keeping the team compound spick-and-span to SEAL standards, which wasn't always easy with established SEALs clogging toilets and emptying trashcans on the quarterdeck. He bet Bull that if he could last a minute on his feet, Bull would have to clean the heads for a month. If Bull won, my dad would be shaved from head to toe.

That Friday after colors, the platoons who were not deployed followed the combatants to a large field outside the compound. Bull and

Dad strapped on old boxing gloves, no headgear. Their Senior Chief took out a stopwatch. And as soon as he yelled "fight," Dad took off as fast as he could in the opposite direction, zig-zagging up a hill and eventually climbing a tree. By the time Bull realized what had happened and pulled him out of the tree, the minute was up.

To be clear, Bull knocked him out with a single punch, but it was almost a full two minutes after the fight had begun. And that's the story of how my dad saved his eyebrows, and a veteran Team guy ended up scrubbing toilets. Bull swears my Dad brought in Taco Bell for the guys every day that month.

Still undetected on the landing, I thought about that story and watched the mourning play out before me. It was evident these battle-hardened warriors did not know how to process the pain. One at a time they approached my mother, anger and sorrow plastered across their faces. They offered condolences until I heard Bull quietly ask, "Where's Nathan?"

As if they already knew the answer, everyone's head immediately snapped towards the stairs. Busted. My face was pressed between the railing posts as if in a jail cell. I felt like a caged animal.

Bull appeared to be near tears. His massive bald head and one side of his face were sprinkled with tiny cuts, the dried blood making him look un-human. Bull had always scared me, but I couldn't show that now. I stood, and completed my march down the stairs.

"Come here, baby, sit with your mama," my mother said to me, reaching out with the arm that wasn't balancing Cheyenne. "Come say hi to your uncles."

She was right – they were like uncles to me and Cheyenne. They always had been, ever since I was a kid, and I found relief in their presence. The SEAL community was stronger than most real families, and I knew that these men would be there for mine. Not just now, but forever.

"Nathan, why don't you and Cheyenne come with me and Bull into the backyard? Let's let her talk to the CACO."

I turned towards the living room, where Spencer's voice had come from. He was standing ramrod straight, emotionless, watching us at the kitchen table. I looked his wounds over again, then turned to Bull. The cuts on his face were tiny and deep, and I wondered how they had happened. Shrapnel from an IED? Shards of glass blown out from a window in a sniper hide? There was no way of knowing, and they would never say.

Uncle Spencer motioned towards my sister. I took her hand. My mother didn't want to let her go, and squeezed her tightly. I had never seen her face so pale, and hoped she wasn't going to pass out in front of all these people. Her shell-shocked eyes met Spencer's before she finally let Cheyenne go.

The fall air was brisk on my face, and had a purifying effect on my thoughts. If nothing else, it slowed them down enough so that it no longer felt like I was sleep walking.

Cheyenne was still in her pajamas, already shivering. The morning was cold for November in Virginia Beach. Faint wisps of fog marched forth with each breath.

"Cheyenne, stay with Uncle Spencer for a minute, I'm going to get your jacket."

Bull moved away from the door, and I went back into the kitchen. I could hear the gentle words of the CACO, almost too soothing for comfort. He had the serene disposition of a funeral director, and I wondered how many times he'd had to do this. Was this his full time job? If it was, I felt sorry for him.

Mom's eyes didn't leave me while I walked to the coat closet. I knew she was worried about me, but I also knew it was my responsibility to make this easier on her. I held my head high and shoulders back as I walked, like Dad had taught me to, hoping I would appear strong and take at least one worry off her shoulders.

I found the pink coat buried in the back of the closet. That day had been the first cold one of the season, and holding the tiny jacket in my hand, I realized how much Cheyenne had grown since last winter. And that made me think of how he would never see either of us grow in future seasons.

See you on the other side, I thought, choking back tears again. I was still facing the open closet, but could feel my mom's gaze from the dining room. Determined to stay strong, I swallowed the pain, and turned back into the hallway. She stared through me, eyes shiny, gripping the chaplain's hand. I presented my most comforting smile, eyes still dry, hoping the tiny token would offer even a fraction of relief. I slipped out the back door.

Uncle Spencer, Cheyenne and Bull were standing quietly on the back deck, staring into the changing trees that specked our tiny patch of grass. The yard was still green and mowed neatly, with only a few recently fallen leaves validating the passing of time and season. One of the jobs my dad had taught me to do before one of his deployments, and one I took great pride in completing every Saturday morning, was mowing the lawn. Checking the oil, filling the mower with gas, priming it twice, making sure I wiped any fuel off the engine with a rag before starting it. Emptying the clippings in the compost pile behind our swing set. Trimming the lawn's edges, sweeping the sidewalks and driveway. Hosing down the mower and putting it back in its spot in the garage. I wanted to make sure that when he got home, the first thing he saw was how well I had taken care of the yard.

"Here Cheyenne, put your jacket on," I said, holding the sleeves wide so she could slip her arms into it.

"It's okay if you want to talk about it," Bull said to me without taking his eyes off the tree line. "It's also okay if you don't."

I knew that, but also wasn't sure if I felt like it or not. "Were you guys there? Were you with him?"

They looked at each other, balancing operational security with my right to know. They had always treated me like a man, but now they would have to even more so.

Cheyenne's voice gave them a respite, at least temporarily.

"Look, Nathan." She was holding a yellow sticky note, pulled from her jacket pocket. I knew immediately what it was, and my heart skipped a beat.

"It's from Daddy," she said, wrapping her tiny fingers around it and holding it towards me.

"What does it say, honey?" Bull asked her.

She looked at me, then back at Bull, deciding if she wanted to share. Finally she took a breath, and opened her mouth importantly.

"It says, 'Hi, Munchkin, I hope you are keeping warm. Your daddy loves and misses you.'"

We stayed silent, letting the words sink in.

"See that, even now, your daddy is watching over you from heaven, Chey. He probably just heard you read his note," said Bull.

"Because he's with Jesus now, right?"

"That's right."

I turned towards him sharply.

"Don't tell her that. You don't know that. If Jesus was watching over him, where was He that day? Why did He let him die?"

"Nathan, I know you're angry. We're all angry. But Jesus works in mysterious ways. We can't know His will."

"That's crap. I don't believe it. If there was a Jesus, why would there be wars at all? Why would you have to kill people? Why would my dad have killed people?"

Uncle Spencer stepped towards me suddenly, firmer than I would have expected.

"Nathan, there is a time and a place. This is no way to be talking in front of your sister. Cool it."

I looked at Cheyenne, saw the confusion in her eyes. He was right.

"Chey, why don't you go in and show Mommy Daddy's note," I told her, walking her to the door. A hurricane of emotions was wreaking havoc in me and the need for answers had leapfrogged decorum.

When I came back outside, Uncle Spencer and Bull were sitting on the picnic table, the slow rumble of their voices just audible. They paused before motioning for me to sit with them.

Spencer started.

"Son, this is going to be the most difficult time you will ever go through in your life. I'm not telling you that as a warning, I'm telling you because I know you can handle it. Your father was a great man, and he raised a great son. He never had any concerns about putting his life in harm's way, because he knew that even at thirteen, you were well on your way to becoming a man and could take care of your mother and sister. That's a lot of responsibility, but one he had no doubt you could handle. 'My boy was twice the man I was at half the age,' he'd always brag, in that Southern drawl I can hear in you. And Nate, I don't need to tell you, I'd be proud to call anyone a brother or son who was half the man your father was."

I accepted the words for what they were but took no pride in them. That's the way it was supposed to be.

"What happened? Can you tell me that?"

Another shared look between warriors, another recognition of obligation. To me, to secrecy.

Bull exhaled. "All I can tell you is that Spencer and I were with him the whole time. We never left his side..." he trailed off, still unsure how much to divulge.

"Left his side where, doing what!?" I demanded, surprised at my tone but not sorry for it.

Again they shared uncomfortable looks. A crow cawed. The wind blew. It was Spencer's turn.

"It was a standard direct-action mission, same as we do almost every night. A high-value Taliban bomb maker. This was a bad dude, his IED's directly responsible for killing our Army brothers. We were going to make sure that stopped. That's all I'll say. During the mission your dad was hit several times by small arms fire.

"You should know that he was helping evac another soldier when he was killed. A Ranger. The guy was badly wounded by an RPG and needed an immediate medevac. Your dad fireman-carried him for a few clicks, most of the time at a dead sprint in the middle of a fire fight, firing back the whole way. The word 'hero' gets thrown around a lot, I know, but if it ever fit..."

I could picture my father carrying the wounded soldier over his shoulder, firing his M4 or H&K 416 assault rifle one handed, taking out scores of terrorists. What was most interesting to me about this vision was that it wasn't hyperbole, that if anything, my father's exploits were probably being undersold. That was the way SEALs were. Humble and unassuming. The quiet professionals. And I knew that I wouldn't hear anything from Uncle Spencer or Bull about their part in the mission.

"It's important you know that he was never alone, Nate. We never left his side. Not from the first time he was hit until we reached the

States this morning. He was with his brothers the entire time."

It was both surprising and terrifying to hear their level of candor. These warriors didn't usually speak to anyone outside of their brotherhood about what they did in battle, and I was grateful and honored they were speaking to me like an equal. But there was one more thing I had to know.

"Did he make it?"

Bull looked confused, wounded. "Nathan?"

Impatient, I shook my head. "Not my dad. The Ranger. The Army guy that my dad got out. Did he die too?"

Slowly, sadly, he nodded. "KIA."

I slammed my fist on the picnic table, causing it to shake violently. I couldn't accept that he had died for nothing. It was incomprehensible that they hadn't succeeded in saving the Ranger.

As if reading my thoughts, Spencer spoke. "Listen, Nathan, your father saved a lot of people that night. Don't ever think he didn't die for something bigger than himself."

My thoughts raced, my breath quickened. Again, I thought I might be sick. What was I doing when he died? Was I at school? Playing basketball? Complaining about homework?

"What time did it happen? When did he die, exactly?" I asked, frantic.

Uncle Spencer looked at his watch, thinking. "Early Sunday morning, Afghanistan time."

My mind spun, doing the math in my head that I did dozens of times every day. If it happened at 4:30 in the morning Afghanistan time, that would be 7:00 pm our time, Saturday night.

Dirty and exhausted, I had whined about having to take a shower before dinner, and had pushed Cheyenne because she was sitting in my chair. Then I complained about having spaghetti for dinner, even though it was usually my favorite. A sharp pain dug into my chest when I thought back to that night, only days before. It felt like a lifetime ago.

Saturday at 7:00. I had been watching Florida State beat Maryland Saturday night. I was lying on the couch, watching football, while he was at war. While he was dying. I wondered if he had lived until the end of the game, when his beloved Seminoles had taken a knee on the final snap. I wondered if I had been eating popcorn, or had been in the bathroom, or flipping channels when the shots ripped through him.

I closed my eyes, trying to go back two nights, to what I had been feeling when my father was lying in a helicopter somewhere over Afghanistan, thinking about the family he was leaving behind while bleeding and dying. It would be the last good night's sleep I would have for some time.

It occurred to me that it was Veteran's Day.

Chapter 5

I'M LAZILY WALKING *back from chow when LT Hagen comes hustling around a HESCO barrier. The sun is just starting to disappear behind the craggy mountains ringing our base, and like most of my platoon, I woke up about an hour ago. I'm casually working a toothpick, digesting my breakfast, and trying to decide if I want to grab another cup of coffee before I take a shit. But first things first: As soon as LT's within range I let fly, stifle a chuckle. The reaction doesn't disappoint.*

"Good God Mo, what the hell is wrong with you? Your asshole has to be rotted out!" His hand goes his face, a sleeve in digital camo covering his nose.

Laughing, I try to force another one out. Carefully – I do my own laundry out here.

He doesn't seem particularly amused, which surprises (and disappoints) me. Something must be up. Our mission for the night isn't scheduled to be a go until 0130, so it's a surprise to see he already has his uniform and game face on. Something tells me that emailing home and studying for the GMATs isn't going to happen tonight.

"Pucker up," he tells me. "Just got an update from the JOC, standby for an HVT mission. Wheels up in twenty. Gear check in ten." His voice is steady and even, naturally; he has given hundreds of these briefings over nearly a dozen combat deployments. Rank be damned – there are

some officers I wouldn't follow into a titty bar if they had a pocket full of singles. But there is no man I would rather lead me into battle than LT. I don't blink or think, just get my ass in gear. These last minute missions are commonplace for us. That's why they have SEALs in Indian Country – for the hard operations that require our special touch.

"Roger that, sir."

"Warning Order and brief on the tarmac, mission plan en route."

I nod again. The switch has been flicked.

By the time I reach my ten-by-twelve plywood hut the rest of my squad is at full alert. We each stand in front of our assault kits, carefully selecting gear, balancing the need to be light with the unpredictability that each mission presents. "Light is Right." A mission might call for a four-man recon team to be dropped at the top of a mountain to scout an Al Qaeda camp, or a full platoon stealthily hiking fifteen miles through God's imagination's worst terrain to assault a Taliban compound in a blizzard. The gear differs for each mission, but since we rarely know what to expect, we improvise. Something we are damn good at.

As I dress and prep my loadout, I remember that the Under Armour camo-colored long-sleeve shirt I'm wearing under my tactical vest is new, just sent in Gayle's latest care package. I turn to Darby, an enormous Hawaiian and amazing opera singer to ask him for a felt tip marker. Darby was Marine recon before joining the Navy and becoming a SEAL, and is our top sniper. He's currently finishing cleaning, for approximately the thirtieth time in the past 24 hours, his MK11 Mod 0 Sniper Weapon System. He grunts, turns to me with black marker extended, and writes a big "O+" on my sleeve. I nod in appreciation. He goes back to his weapon, the mechanized clicks, swooshes and snaps the soothing music he needs to find his peace before battle.

Within minutes we are jocked up. I check the batteries in my night vision goggles and radios one final time. My gloved hands skim over my vest, inspecting armor plates, explosive charges, extra magazines, blowout kit, cash for bribes, IR lights. I tighten my helmet just as LT arrives on the special operations airfield. No time for a briefing in the ready room. He quickly explains to the men assembled that this will be a squad-sized operation, meaning eight SEALs plus support. We're part of a QRF for a Ranger platoon tied down in the Hindu Kush Mountain Range by Taliban fighters. A quick rescue and recovery, in and out. As the squad chief, I go over the objective and tasks one more time with my men as we swiftly board the MH-60 Black Hawk, simultaneously squinting and yelling through the rotor wash. They don't need to be instructed twice, but it's what we do. Every man recites his responsibility like the professional he is – we've been on hundreds of these missions in both real world and training ops. At this point it's a masterfully choreographed dance. Muscle memory.

Bull, who has more combat experience than anyone in the squad, gives me a wink as we strap in. He's a sniper and our corpsman on this op. Bull and Darby will pull overwatch as the helo hovers at the LZ and we fast-rope in. I have no doubt he will take out any enemy fighters who dare take a pop shot at the helo with an RPG or small-arms fire.

The chopper bolts upwards with pilots from Army's 160th SOAR Nightstalkers at the controls. Within adrenaline-soaked seconds I am looking down through the open door as the rugged terrain of J'bad rises into focus. It's what I imagine Mars would look like; a beautiful wasteland of pockmarks and jagged boulders, sitting majestically in the space assigned to them during the Creation. That is, if Mars had thousands of hardened religious zealots intent on forcing their crazed version of Islam on their planet's inhabitants. I stare at this scene, feeling tiny. A familiar calm descends over me. It's always like this, mission after mission. We are just under an hour from our target, and after doing a run *through of my sixty pounds of gear and checking my safety one last time, I start to nod off. Next to me in the tight cabin, Spencer is already dozing on my shoulder. After much internal debate I decide not to stick a wet finger in his ear.*

I am surprised to see how late it is when I finally roll over to check my alarm clock – 10:30. Then I remember that it's Saturday. Pancake day. I'm starving.

When I get to the kitchen, Mom is standing over the stove and Cheyenne is seated at the kitchen table. Her chin barely rises above it, and she is in full concentration trying to guide a dripping piece of French toast to her mouth. She clutches the fork like a primitive tool, too entranced to take notice of me.

"French toast?" I whine. "Why aren't we having pancakes?"

Mom turns to me, hands on hips, making a face.

The co-pilot's "five minutes" call crackles through my headset, flicking that switch again. I stretch, stomp my feet to get the blood circulating, check the safety on my H&K 416. Even though it's pitch black I know everyone around me is doing the same. When the one-minute call comes I look out the door, but with only the ambient red light from the cockpit I can't make out the ground below. I flick down my NVGs, although on this moonless night it's hard to make out much more than semi-solid green forms. Bull situates himself beside me, scanning the mountain through the scope of his MK-12, looking for targets. The chopper's blades thump, thump, thump, rhythmically, the sound familiar and comforting. When we get the word, I grip the rope, throw it out of the chopper, and swiftly descend, dimly aware of the cold hard ground coming up at me. I sense movement to my left and instantly hear the soothing thwak of Bull's suppressed rifle evenly dispensing rounds into the darkness. There's no time to figure out what's going on, so I follow the plan and fast-rope out of the helo, setting up a security perimeter.

I don't want to admit it, but the French toast is great. After I eat, Mom advises me that the yard could use a mow. I tell her I'm well ahead of her, and that's the very reason why I got up so early. I know that if I mow today, it will clear most of the leaves and there will only be touch-up work to do before Dad gets home, scheduled for next week. Even so, I make sure to complain a little, lest the chore seem too easy and due credit not received. I throw on a sweatshirt and head outside with a jump, suddenly energized by the thought of his pending return. On the way I give Cheyenne a playful flick on the ear. When she cries out in exaggerated pain I raise my hands and shrug at Mom.

"I didn't do anything!"

Normal kid stuff: Truth be told, I'd be more worried if he didn't give his kid sister a hard time. I know it's tough on him, having his dad, this larger than life figure, away nine months out of the year. But I don't worry about him, not really. We knew early on he could handle it. Even as a baby he seemed to cry less when his dad was deployed, like he knew he needed to be better behaved for me. Lately there have been more shows of rebellion and a few behavior problems, but both Steve and I agree they are just active-boy escapades. The kids don't know it yet, but this is going to be Steve's last deployment. After years cycling between training and war, we have orders to San Diego in the spring. He's going to be an instructor at BUD/S for the last year of his contract in the Navy. It makes me a special kind of nervous as the time gets closer, knowing we are almost out of the woods. I can't wait to have him back safe and sound, for good this time.

At first I'm not sure exactly what happened, but I know it hurts like a motherfucker. When we drop at the LZ we're immediately in the shit. It's like the enemy was waiting for us. The cold air takes my breath, but the bullets flying overhead leave no time for recovery. The eight of us spread out quickly and instinctively to pull security until we're all in position and the helo can take off, its wheels never touching the ground. To the east of our ridge is a steep drop-off, and we leapfrog four at a time, returning fire at the thin tree line we're taking fire from until we're all hugging shale and dust behind the embankment.

"Fuck," I say, almost in a whisper, to no one other than myself. "I think I'm hit."

I'm pissed, and embarrassed, but my left side hurts like shit and I can feel wetness. I roll on my right to let Bull take a look. He pulls the blowout kit from my front right cargo pocket and starts to dress the bullet wound. It's just a nick, in and out, not too much blood.

"I'm fine!" I yell over the enemy gunfire, which I can tell is effective because of the high-pitched ZING sound the bullets make as they fly by, rather than the nondescript and more full-bodied CRACK when they are distant and harmless. "Just patch it the fuck up and let's move out!" On each side my teammates are calmly popping regular, rhythmic shots at the mostly unseen enemy combatants. All around us the sporadic blasts of undisciplined AK-47 fire sizzle across the sky, with some lucky shots spitting up rock and dirt around us. Every once in a while a desperate "Allahu Akbar," rings out, followed immediately by a grunt when one of our rounds cuts the shouter down. The THUD of enemy rounds regularly impacts the scraggly trees rising at our six, which, despite all odds, have somehow grown in this unforgiving environment. We need to get moving, and I'll be damned if I'm going to be the reason we don't accomplish this mission. I crouch and tap Blade, the operator to my left. "Moving." He lowers his M4 and follows as I fall more than slide down the mountain, where somewhere a platoon of Rangers needs our help.

"Looks good," I tell him, truthfully. It always does, and I'm proud at the pride Nate takes in our yard. He gives me a half-smile, no big deal. Just like Steve does, their way of showing me that it's just part of their duty. After handing him a lemonade I decide to ruffle his hair because I know it will get a reaction, and I'm not disappointed. There's a chill in the air and I go back into the house, counting down the days until my family is whole again.

It's a crisp morning, and the smell of fall is in the air. A cool sweat coats my body underneath the sweatshirt. Although warm I still shiver, sipping lemonade on our front steps. I am content, happy with a job well done, enjoying the glow brought on by endorphins and manual labor.

I can't believe it. I'm hit again, in the shoulder this time. I am a United States Navy SEAL. I am bulletproof. Invincible. I don't get shot, I do the shooting. At no point do I panic or consider the possibility I could be mortally wounded. More than anything I am pissed, and I grunt angrily while turning back up the mountain. I hope my teammates don't notice. Through my earpiece LT's calm voice tells me that the Taliban fighters are moving south over the ridge, trying to flank us. I swing my rifle up to my good shoulder (and off shot), picking targets through the scope. The green lasers of my teammates' weapons, visible only to us through our NVGs, intersect each other in a disciplined pattern, calmly acquiring and neutralizing enemy targets. Green blobs get bigger, many fall, the suppressed THUMP of our silenced rifles finding their targets more often than not. To my right, LT Hagen is unemotionally calling in CAS, and I hear the words "danger close." He's directing *fire from an Apache circling 2,500 feet overhead. Death from above, one of our many battlefield equalizers. We are eight against twenty, fifty, a hundred, fighting on their terrain, yet with our technology and training we have the upper hand. We always do. We continue our methodical and choreographed dance, leap-frogging down the mountain in two groups. We slide and tumble in as controlled a manner as possible, but in reality most of us are just falling off the side as elegantly as the landscape allows. I take a moment to communicate with my teammates and notice that we all have ripped uniforms, missing equipment, and numerous injuries. I'm the only one shot. No one is anything but calm and businesslike. No one is worried or doubts that we will be anything but victorious, myself included.*

Magicseaweed.com tells me what I already suspected – the jetty is flat and not even long-boardable. I had really hoped to go surfing today, but it appears that's not going to happen. Bored, I take a bike ride through the neighborhood and wonder what my dad is doing right now. I wouldn't admit it to anyone, but I sometimes try to channel him, to telepathically contact him. It's just a game I play; one that as far as I know hasn't yet worked.

Over by the park a few kids are playing basketball in the dusk, but no one I recognize. Doug should be back from soccer practice, so I pedal towards his house. Maybe Tammy will be there too.

I am preparing dinner when a pain suddenly jolts my side. I gasp and straighten up, my breath taken away by a strange panic. It is neither a physical nor emotional pain, rather a combination of the two and then some. I shake the cobwebs and take a few deep breaths, unsure of what just happened. Instinctively I turn on the evening news, seeing what, if any, updates I can get from Afghanistan. Surprisingly, they are talking about the surge, and how Afghan forces are leading the charge. I snicker, knowing the truth, and stir the tomato sauce.

I can't ignore the pain anymore, but that sure as hell doesn't mean I have to give in to it. Adrenaline helps. I just have to suck it up, which I do. We keep scrambling down the mountain, taking heavy fire from three sides, while continuing to professionally and methodically do our job – namely, kill the enemy and reach the Rangers. I open comms, trying to change our LZ, when a thunderous screech screams through the air from the top of the mountain. In a violent explosion that shakes the ground, a giant boulder takes a direct shot from an Apache Hellfire missile, sending shrapnel of rock, tree and dirt raining down upon us. We cover up, hugging earth. The smell of cordite, soot and death makes the silence that much more jarring.

No Tammy, no Doug. With nothing left to do I bike home, watching the hazy sky darken and feeling the air grow cooler. The neighborhood is quiet. No one walking dogs, no cars pulling out for one of the season's last evenings on the boardwalk. Garage and living room lights flick on as I pedal past small, proud homes. I ride into our open garage, pop my kickstand. I feel isolated but not lonely. It's actually an exhilarating feeling, being completely alone in the middle of population. I pause, watching the last of the light fade before hitting the garage door opener and bounding into the house.

"Just in time. Dinner's in five, wash up and get your sister, please," I call out, thankful I don't have to go searching for Nate. I flick off the TV, already worried about the amount of time he spends listening to war reports and researching them online. We'll give ourselves as much of a reprieve as we can during dinner. Afterwards I know I'll spend the

night alternating between worrying and checking for an email, or better, a Skype call from Steve. Since they always conduct their ops at night, he'll often check in when they get back, usually between 7-9 am our time, or when he wakes up, which is late afternoon here.

The squad comes to a screeching halt in a large cutout on the side of the mountain, about the size of a football field. LT calls for us to spread out, giving 360 degrees of coverage. A live feed from a drone circling overhead lets him know that Taliban fighters are approaching from our six, essentially meaning we are on the verge of being surrounded. I chuckle out loud, drawing a sideways look from Bull.

"They have us surrounded – good, they can't get away from us this time," I tell him, raising my voice to be heard over the AK and mortar fire.

"Roger that, Chesty," he mouths back, grinning, shaking his head.

We do have the upper ground on the fighters climbing the mountain towards our position. A fire team sends a steady stream of SAW fire in their direction. Spencer is doing his best to slow the Taliban advance with an M-32 grenade launcher, while the rest of us pick off the targets trying to flank our sides.

I take up position behind a scraggly tree that has grown in a V-shape. I'm able to get into a prone sniper's position behind it, my barrel pointing to the west, facing up the mountain. Just as I get settled I see two men bounding down the mountain, toward my position. One is barefooted and wearing two ammo belts while holding his AK-47 in one hand, racing down the slope as fast as he can. Idiot. I line up the red dot from my scope on his chest, slowing my breathing and watching the dot bounce slowly as it follows him towards me. He's closer now, less than a hundred yards. Inhale. Hold it. I slowly squeeze the trigger and the burst hits him at center mass, ripping his chest open and launching *him into the air. I immediately turn to his young buddy, who can't yet grow a beard but just saw his friend get cut in half. He spins around, and although he doesn't know exactly where I am, he raises his RPG and points it pretty damn close to my direction. I fire before he can, a head shot that spins his whole body with such force it lifts his robe over his head, exposing a gaunt, hairless chest. A brief period of silence before another strike from the Apache above, sending a fireball shooting into the air on the mountain above us.*

In my earpiece I hear, "Fall back, fall back!" We're outta here, and won't be able to enjoy the flat fighting ground for much longer. We're tumbling down the mountain again, heading towards the Taliban fighters advancing from the valley and closer to the pinned-down Rangers. I've forgotten that I've been shot twice.

Mom and Cheyenne want to play Chutes and Ladders after dinner. I'm not interested. Florida State is playing, so I sneak into my parent's room and find one of Dad's Seminoles shirts in his bureau. It smells like him and is so big on me only my hands stick out of the sleeves and it makes me sad and soothes me at the same time. I sit on the couch in the dark and put the game on. At halftime I ask Mom if I can make popcorn – she helps me, knowing it makes me think of him. He always eats popcorn when watching football.

"The Rangers are holed up at the base of this valley." The squad is crowded around LT. He's yelling, but only to be heard over the scattered small arms fire and random mortars. "A second QRF is inserting three clicks to our east on a ridgeline just above the valley. We're going to fight our way to the rear of the Rangers while the QRF clears us a path to the LZ. We've got to move fast, we're about an hour from daylight and I don't need to tell you, once that sun rises we're on our own. The

drone is showing squirters heading south, so smoke check anyone you see heading in that direction."

"Roger that, sir," we reply, and gear up. We don't want to know what this shithole looks like during the day. It goes without saying that there is no way the Army would try to land a helo to evac our asses in the daylight. But that knowledge doesn't faze us, par for the course. Everyone conducts another gear check, taking ammunition and injury inventories. Amazingly, I am still the only one shot, and as I keep telling Bull, it's just a nick and to shut the hell up. We jock up and move out, Spencer on point. As far as we know, the fire from the Apache has slowed the advance of the Taliban fighters chasing us down this fucking mountain. We fucking hope.

Mo looks white. Or gray. I guess he looks more gray than white, and that's not good. He keeps hissing at me, telling me to shut the fuck up, so I do. I patch him up the best I can and we move out. He insists on carrying the wounded Ranger as we hightail it to the LZ. I want to keep an eye on him, but I have my sector to patrol and keep my focus where it belongs. Do your job. Mo's a big boy. The operator at my 3 o'clock lets out a burst from his MP5 then falls back, giving me a squeeze on the shoulder once he's past. Moving.

The sledgehammer of the next bullet is not as jarring as the sudden realization that I am in serious trouble. Without choice I fall, unable to brace myself or my load. It is the first time I've truly acknowledged that I very well may die on this fucking mountain. That I may never again kiss Gayle's lips, feel Cheyenne's hug or surf with Nate. It's a leg shot, and if I know anything I would say it hit my femoral artery. I'm lightheaded watching the blood gush, more than I would have imagined. Self-aid before buddy-aid. Certainly not the first time I've patched a *bullet wound, but the first time it's my own. Black fuzziness starts to intrude on the corners of my vision. I reach to a cargo pocket, tingling fingers just barely able to grip the rubber tourniquet in my blowout kit. I pull it out. What had I been reaching for? My mind starts to wander, back to a vision from a few years before. Neil Bourgeois stepped on a land mine mentor of mine from BUD/S the first operator my first friend killed death land mine had hit me hard many evenings Baghdad Green Zone dip strong coffee discussing Seminole football surf spots in Northern Florida religion's place in war land mine CACO checking service records Dress Blues funeral Taps bronze stars purple hearts land mine escort land mine*

It's heating up now. Not that it wasn't before, but it really is now. We're used to being outnumbered, but surrounded is another thing. Not that we aren't prepared for it. We are; we've trained for every scenario, every contingency. I hear in my earpiece "man down," which does make me pause, slightly. Who, I wonder, while systematically returning fire in my sector. A drab olive coat darts past a tree to my twelve o'clock. Through my scope I can make out the tip of an RPG, the bad guy's do-rag. He's facing west, hugging a tree. I site my red dot a foot in that direction, clear my mind, slow my breathing, inhale, slowly exhale, inhale, feel the breath, taste the oxygen, relish the connection pulsating between us. He has to feel it too, his nerves stink like rotted flesh, I smell them like pungent waste spritzed into the air. I embrace the interaction, strong in my patience. He feints once, twice; I don't flinch. As if in slow motion, he wheels from behind the tree, taking up a knee into a firing position. The RPG doesn't get to his shoulder before the black rag on his head snaps back, falls gently over his forehead. He's still sitting up, propped against the tree. He looks like he is sleeping. I remember someone is hit, and again, I wonder who it is. The injured Ranger we are evac'ing is sprawled on the ground, so I sprint over to him, ready to fireman-carry him as we move out.

I jerk up suddenly in bed, caught in the purgatory between slumber and reality. A dream or thought or vision attacks my mind, and I am brought back to that terrible day in 2005 when Neil had been killed. The only thing worse than the pain of his death was the guilt I felt over the relief that it had not been my Steve.

Steve had escorted the body back from Iraq and had been part of the notification team. He had stayed at Michelle's side for days, doing all he could to ease her pain while she held Matt, just a newborn. We talked about how hard it was going to be for Matt, growing up without a daddy, and how he would need us to be there for him as he grew into a man.

On the morning of Neil's funeral we stood facing the mirror, he double-checking ribbons on his Dress Blues, my cheeks glistened by tears. I had felt an unimaginable pain and despair that day, and now alone in bed I feel it again in spades.

"Mo. Mo!" The yells seem to come from out of a tube, far and distant. "Mo, stay with me!" I can't tell if my eyes are open. Suddenly the veil is lifted, I see Bull above me. He's working on something below my waist, and I remember that I'm shot. My eyes flicker through the scene, trying to get enough information to my brain that will remind me what it is that's happening. Next to me, a cold mass lies alone.

"Gayle – tell Gayle," I stammer, not positive the words are coming out. "Tell Nate -," I start again.

"Don't start with that shit Chief," someone says before the veil is lowered again. I hear the word morphine, but it's fuzzy, drowned out by wind, strong wind.

"Bird's here Chief, we're getting you out of here!" someone else yells over agitated air. My body starts to rise, floats through the wind, so strong so powerful so...

Higher I float now. The wind is less but the noise is not. Again I survey my surroundings. New faces, tubes, blackness...

I jolt awake, confused, unsure of where I am. The television still flickers, the remote on my chest, popcorn at my feet. I yawn, then the horror of my dreams come back to me. I'm awake now, and terrified to go back to sleep.

I see my babies, my babies and my wife. I see David, my parents. Mom Mom and Pop Pop. I see everyone and no one. It's calm, it's okay. I know where I'm going. Sounds are far away, sights are, are, where? I take one last gasp, and then

Chapter 6

THE NEXT FEW DAYS were a whirlwind. There were more visitors at the house than we could see and more food than we could eat. Mom took the phone off the hook. A couple of times Cheyenne asked me when Daddy would be home. She had either forgotten, didn't understand, or was just hoping.

The night before leaving for the funeral we laid together on her bed. She sobbed into a pillow, her outline just visible in the nightlight's glow.

She and Dad had painted the room lime green earlier that summer, per her request. Cartoon frogs were plastered haphazardly across the walls. Her idea, after she learned that SEALs were called "Frogmen."

Dad had laughed when she had unpeeled the first frog and stuck it crookedly in the middle of the wall.

"That's not where it goes," he'd told her. "It's crooked."

She shrugged her shoulders and informed him that frogs don't jump straight out, they jump crooked! And if he *really* was a Frogman, he should know that.

His deep, overpowering laugh had boomed out again, and he had lifted her carefully but easily so she could reach the high spots and plaster the rest of the frogs across the room.

I looked at those frogs now, and tried to remember that day. Tried to remember him, hear his laugh.

What was a memory? Could a sound be a memory? Can you miss something you never had?

I wondered how much Cheyenne would remember of him. When it came down to it, they had had precious little time together. And now, for the fourth night in a row she was crying herself to sleep, saddened by those fleeting memories, clenching them as tightly as she knew how. Each night since it had happened both my mom and I had joined her in bed until she fell asleep.

"Tuckered out, isn't she?" Mom's voice came from the doorway. She tried her best to smile.

I nodded, sad.

"How about you? Ready for bed? We're leaving early tomorrow."

I nodded again.

"Are you ready to say goodbye to Daddy?"

I didn't know how to respond, and was afraid speaking would allow the tears, trying as they always seemed to be, to force their way out. I managed to bob my head, chin quivering. She walked over, sat next to me. Her hand instinctively went to my head, slid the bangs out of my eyes.

"I want you to know how proud I am of you, Nathan. How proud Uncle Spencer, Grandma and Grandpa, Nana and Papa, and everyone is of how you've handled this. I just know your daddy is looking down on you, comforted by watching how strong his son is." She paused here, struggling to find the words.

"But I also want you to know that it's okay to cry. It's okay to be sad and to get upset and even be angry. You need to get those feelings out. I haven't seen you cry once."

"I haven't seen you cry either, not since that first day," I whispered, choking on the words. I wanted to tell her that I was proud of her too, that I heard the other wives whispering about her strength, even through the pain she must be going through. That in her own way, she was as strong as Dad had been. She was the one who kept the family intact when he was gone. Dad always said her job was tougher than his.

"Oh, baby, I cry every night. And I wake up crying every morning. I don't know if that will ever stop. Your daddy was my other half, and I'll never stop crying for him. But I also cry for the other men, the other SEALs and soldiers who are still in harm's way. For all the men who have died in this war, on both sides."

I was confused.

"You cry for the terrorists? For the men who killed Daddy?" I asked her in shock.

"Of course I do, honey. Of course I do. Those men have wives, they have little boys and girls who will grow up without fathers also. The fact that we are on the just side doesn't make their pain any less than ours. And that's what we're fighting for. That's what Daddy died for – so that we can keep our country safe and bring peace to that region, so that no more families will have to feel this pain."

I thought about it for a minute, surprised at my mom's words. Knowing that in a sense, she was right, but not willing to concede my hatred.

"Well, I don't. I'm glad Dad and Uncle Spencer and Bull killed those terrorists. I hope they kill them all."

"That's understandable, Nathan, and we can't help feeling that way. There's nothing wrong with that. But what about their families? Are you glad they feel the same pain we do?"

Again, I paused to think. I didn't like what she was saying. I didn't want to give my sympathy to the enemy. I slid off the bed, leaving the room without answering.

The dark hallway was eerily quiet. It was as if I could hear the walls breathing. My deliberate steps made no sound on the carpet runner. I turned into my room. Curiously, the desk lamp burned brightly, although I couldn't remember turning it on. I stopped, staring at the light. The lamp was rarely used, usually when Dad sat at the desk dispensing life lessons or helping with homework. It was where he had always sat when in my room. I spun around, sensing something behind me. Of course only space and time met me. Exhausted, I closed the door, flopping onto my stomach across the bed. My face extended over the edge, stopping just short of my catcher's mitt. Usually the mitt was far underneath my bed, but for some reason that night it was sticking out just enough to get my attention. I slowly reached for it, and stuck my hand into the leather.

No surprise registered when I heard a crinkle and my finger touched a piece of paper. Somehow, I had been expecting it. I pulled the paper out, knowing what it was.

NATE, GET YOUR WHOLE BODY IN FRONT OF THE BALL WHEN BLOCKING A PITCH IN THE DIRT. – DAD

Nothing earth-shattering, nothing that would change my perspective on life, but at that moment the most impactful sentence I had ever read. I traced his letters with my index finger. Firm, steady block letters, all capitals. I pulled the note to my face, and I cried.

Chapter 7

THE NEXT MORNING we flew to Pensacola, where my dad had been born, had grown up, and was to be buried. Nana and Papa picked us up from the airport, and we went straight to their home in Pleasant Grove.

My dad had grown up in this house, and it occurred to me that part of me had too. We'd been coming here for vacations and holidays since I was born, and the familiarity of the neighborhood enveloped me as soon we turned the corner onto Little Pond Road. As a military family used to frequent moves, this home was an established anchor for us. Stunted palm trees, orange groves and banana trees dotted the luscious green lawns in the neighborhood, each modest house sitting off the quiet street like patches on a quilt. Similar but different.

Theirs was a simple, one-story rambler. Gray with white shutters, the perfectly landscaped lawn and front door, painted a dark red, welcomed us like inviting, open arms. I noticed that Papa had re-paved the driveway since the last time we had been down. For some reason I mentioned it to him, but he just grunted. Papa was a man of few words, and he was grieving badly for his youngest son.

My dad's brother, David, eased through the screen door to greet us after we had exited the car. Cheyenne ran to him, receiving a bear hug for her hustle.

"Chey, Chey, sweeter than pie, too bad your room is filthy as a sty," he sang, the words getting lost on the top of her blond head.

Then, holding her at arm's length: "You've gotten so big, what are they feeding you?" Uncle Dave was barely a year older than my dad, and had never looked so much like him. Irish twins, my mom called them, and the similarity was especially jarring now.

He was bigger than my dad, both in height and girth. The light brown hair was starting to thin, but he had the same block head and concrete chin as my dad. His bright blue eyes were identical to not just his brother's but also to their father's. And in turn there was no doubt where Cheyenne and I had inherited ours from, the same yellow highlight ringing pale blue. Mom always said those eyes were what had first drawn her to him. He always joked with me that the Butler eyes were our ticket to the ladies.

"Gayle, how are you holding up?" he asked my mom, embracing her.

She exhaled strongly. "I don't know Dave, sometimes it seems like we're going to get through this, other times it feels like the world is crashing down around us. I just never know if it's going to be a good day or bad. Heck, minute or hour."

"The days will get easier. The pain will never fully go away, but it will get easier." Uncle Dave's wife, my Aunt Jeannie, had passed away from leukemia. That had been my first experience with relatable death.

"Nathan, David, give me a hand with these bags," came Papa's gruff voice, his head buried in the open trunk. When he turned to hand me a suitcase, his eyes sparkled in the sun. I lugged the suitcase inside.

The familiar smell registered warmly the second I walked in. I'm not really sure how else to describe it, except that it smelled like my grandparents' house always did. I suppose that everyone's grandparents' home has its own special scent; I know both of mine did, and it gave me a welcome semblance of peace. This was the smell that my father had known growing up, although he had probably never noticed it. What he had come home to after surfing before school. Where he had jumped off the roof when he was seven and broken his arm. Where he and his brother had countless fights. The yard where David had hit him with a rock that left him with nine stitches and a scar above his upper lip.

I took my suitcase into the extra bedroom that Cheyenne and I stayed in when we visited: my dad's room as a kid. It looked like the set of a fifties sitcom, down to pennants on the wall. Two simple twin beds, an old dresser, and beat up desk took up most of the room. There were still pictures everywhere of my dad playing football, surfing, in cap and gown. One of him with my mom and grandparents at Great Lakes after boot camp. Young as could be. A photo of him speaking to his BUD/S class as the Honor Man. And of course numerous family pictures, from before Cheyenne was born up until a recent shot of the four of us on the boardwalk. His hand covered Chey from shoulder to tiny bicep in that photo, bringing a smile to my face. He looked different in each photograph, but in each one how I still pictured him.

I remembered the one on the boardwalk well. The previous summer. It had been brutally hot, humid too. One of those days where the sweat ran unabated. He had just gotten back from Iraq, cheeks still browned from the desert wind and sun. Pale white chin and forehead were a stark contrast to the rest of his face. He said the ritual of each post-deployment shave made him feel civilized again.

He had smoked a cigar that day while winning Cheyenne a

stuffed pink elephant at the shooting gallery. Time and time again the *DING* of a bull's eye had rang out. He won so many animals he was passing them out like candy, until the shrunken operator had asked us to move on. I was the only one who recognized the change in his face after the request, before a deep belly laugh of self-assurance quickly covered it and no one was the wiser. But I noticed. It scared me, even as there was no choice but to respect it.

On the wall next to that picture hung one from Afghanistan. Posing with a group of Afghan children, their frail bodies and nervous smiles playing off his looming shape and larger than life presence. During his first winter deployment he had noticed that most of the kids in a village his platoon had been patrolling were wearing nothing but tattered sandals on their feet. He told my mom that instead of sending care packages to him and his teammates, as so many Virginia Beach residents did, she should organize the purchase of cheap boots and socks for the village children. That winter, with Mom's help back home, my dad's unit gave those young villagers over 300 pairs of warm shoes and socks. Even while fighting a war he was still improving the living conditions of the civilians. And of course he never wanted any recognition for any of it.

"We are fortunate to have been born into the most progressive and honest democracy this world has ever known," he once told me when I asked why he spent so much effort on helping the locals, many of whom were sheltering the terrorists trying to kill him and his teammates. "It's not perfect, not by a long shot. But neither is human nature. And our structure is set up as fairly as an imperfect system can be. It's easy for us to take that for granted, until the alternative is thrust onto us. And when you see how these people have grown up generation after generation, you can see why there is so much hatred and despair. There are two ways to dispel that hatred.

You can kill them with kindness, or you can kill them. It takes a strong man to know when to use which one."

That night we went to our favorite seafood restaurant on the pier. I rode with Uncle Dave and Papa, while Mom and Cheyenne went with Nana. As we pulled into the parking lot of Jaco's Bar and Grille, I saw a familiar form walking towards the entrance.

It was Uncle Spencer, holding the door for LT Hagen. Excited, I bolted out of the car and ran up to them, discretion ignored.

"What are you guys doing here?" I said, giving Uncle Spencer a friendly shove. His close haircut and shave made me realize just how young he was. Jeans and a white V-neck revealed powerful shoulders, chest and arms, as well as a full sleeve of tattoos. LT Hagen was dressed similarly but in a black polo. To most people, they probably looked no different than other young, fit guys out to get a bite on a pleasant evening. If you didn't know to look for the quiet confidence, the reserved air and barely noticeable omnipotence, the fact that they were the best-trained fighters in the world would escape you. And that's the way they wanted it.

"Hey, bud, you here with your grandparents?" Uncle Spencer asked, looking around. LT Hagen scratched his head uncomfortably. I could tell this was a chance encounter.

"Yeah, the whole family. This was dad's favorite restaurant, so we decided to come for dinner."

A hand rested on my head. Uncle Dave stood behind me, grimly taking in Uncle Spencer's bruises and cast, knowing who they were.

"Uncle Dave, this is Spencer and LT Hagen. They're in the Teams with Dad," I said as way of introduction.

They all stuck out their hands, somberly shaking.

"Very sorry for your loss, sir," LT Hagen offered as the rest of my family reached the restaurant's entrance.

"Gayle, we didn't mean to intrude. A few of us got into town early, and…"

She smiled, as best she could.

"Spencer, you're family. You're more than welcome to join us."

"We couldn't, thank you. We're actually meeting some of the guys, sounds like doing the same thing you are. Steve took a few of us here over the years, and we thought it would be a fitting send-off."

She nodded, understanding. The guys needed to say goodbye to their fallen brother in their own way. They held the door for us before following us in, headed to the bar where similar tough-looking men already had a line of shots spread out. We picked our way towards the back, into the dining room, but I wasn't paying attention to my steps. I was watching them embrace each other, curse each other, hit each other.

I wondered what it was like to be that close to someone. I wondered what Spencer listened to while he worked out. Who cut LT Hagen's hair? Was he close to his mother?

We ordered. My eyes and thoughts didn't leave the SEALs at the bar. Where did they shop for clothes? How many siblings did they have? Did they stay in touch with high school friends? I looked on while they backslapped, hugged, raised glasses then slammed them down. There were more than a dozen of them, and as our dinner went on, their toasts and chants reached our table.

I watched Papa try to ignore them, but I could tell their behavior bothered him. I wasn't sure if he felt they didn't have a right to mourn in such a public display, or if he just didn't want to be reminded so viscerally of the death of his son. He was sipping from his water glass over a plate of snapper he had hardly touched when I stood up.

"I need to use the restroom," I said to no one, stepping away from the table.

The bathroom was at the far end of the restaurant, and I took the path that would lead me by the bar. I recognized about half of the guys celebrating my dad, three or four I knew well. I stared at them in awe as I passed.

"Lil' Warrior!" someone called out, motioning me over. Westhead, a newer guy in the Teams. The guys called him Pig. I had heard stories about him, that back in Texas the Navy had been his last chance before jail. He was holding a beer bottle and waving at me. I froze, not sure what to do.

He stood on wobbly legs, flashing me a conspiratorial grin. I craned my neck to get a look my family's table, worried I was doing something wrong. As far as I could tell they weren't paying me any attention, so hesitantly I walked over, curious as to what he wanted with me.

Colorful tattoos shot out from under his shirt sleeves, blond hair flopped over a narrow, angular face. He barely looked out of high school, save for *it*. To this day I still couldn't tell you exactly what *it* was, but they all had it. His dark eyes scanned the room behind me, astutely observing everything, even in his current state.

He put his arm around my shoulders, face close, getting suddenly serious. He raised his beer bottle overhead, and I could feel heat and smell alcohol as he leaned into me.

"Mo – your old man – was an exemplary SEAL and a true American Patriot. You lost your father, and we lost a brother," he breathed. "But as strong a warrior as he was, you know what that sumbitch could do better than anyone in the Teams? East Coast or West?"

He was expecting an answer. My face still only inches from his, I finally shook my head no. He then leaned back, letting me go, and raised one leg off his barstool. Closely studying my face, he let fly a terrific fart that seemed to rip through his jeans. It was loud enough to echo across the bar, and his teammates joined me in unapologetic laughter.

Then he raised his beer, yelled: "To Mo! The rottenest-ass, most decayed colon SOB in the entire armed forces of the U.S. of A!"

"Hooyah Chief Butler!" came the loud refrain from twenty or so over-served, thick-necked, cocky, type-A aggressors. I watched with awe as these men banged glasses and pounded shots, disregarding the rest of the crowded restaurant. No one considered chastising this group of unruly combatants as they entered deeper into the throes of mourning their own. Whether that was out of fear or respect I did not know, or if there was even a difference. But it was clear these men lived above normal societal rules.

As if to cement this point home, one of the SEALs stood on his barstool and bellowed: "I don't wanna be no Green Beret..."

Instinctively, the group replied in unison, "They only PT once a day!"

"I don't wanna be no Airborne Ranger," called out LT Hagen, staring into a shot of brown liquor.

"I wanna live a life of danger!" was the reply, louder now.

"I don't wanna be no fag recon!"

"I wanna stay till the job is done!" The responses continued to escalate in volume and passion until the whole restaurant was looking at these crazed SEALs, hopped up on violence, sorrow, and booze.

"I wanna be a SEAL team member/I wanna swim the deep blue sea/I wanna live a life of danger/Pick up your swim fins and run with me!"

They finished the cadence together; loud, emotional and terrifying. I was awestruck, and stared wide-eyed upon these super-humans. As soon as they finished, a palatable grief swallowed the room, like all the air had been sucked out of it. I was dizzy. It got silent just as quickly as it had erupted in song. Now I was numb, frozen in space. I felt as small as a speck of dust. To a man, each stared into his drink, dealing with their own feelings and sensations. Much like war, the violent outburst was followed by a lull of reflection.

The manager of the restaurant began a slow approach towards the group. He had to. He looked like a nice enough guy – pudgy, a dark goatee trying to hide a double chin. I felt sorry for him. He looked like he was walking the Green Mile, slowly going behind the bar for a private word with LT Hagen, the obvious leader. He did so timidly, hoping against hope that the wooden top would be enough of a barrier to protect him from these wild men should they decide to attack.

"Sir, I thank you and your men for your service, and am deeply sorry for your loss. But I am going to have to ask you to keep it down. This is a family restaurant, and we can't have this type of behavior. There are several other bars on the boardwalk that you might be more comfortable in," he said, or rather murmured, uncomfortably. You could tell he didn't want everyone to hear his words and was hoping that LT Hagen would be the voice of reason. I knew the Lieutenant as a sensible, peaceful, and quiet man, so what he did next surprised even me.

His eyes flashed black, and he slowly looked from his drink to the manager. Suddenly he popped off his bar stool, extending his athletic frame and rolling broad shoulders. LT Hagen was tall, and while somewhat thin he had a huge head that sat on an equally large neck. I had heard that when he was in BUD/S the instructors had called him "Pumpkinhead." He turned away from the manager and faced the dining room. I was somewhat relieved and somewhat disappointed to see he wasn't going to knock out the manager.

I had heard him recite poetry from memory on many occasions, taking special pride in Faulkner or Keats at the times most unlikely to require prose. "If you can keep your head when all about you…" In fact, he had been a debater at Harvard and written for the Lampoon before getting his commission. Which is why I expected the forthcoming elocution to be of that variety. I would have guessed that his men, veterans of his recitals, were of the same mind.

But he surprised us all.

"Who in here has ripped open MREs in the middle of a sand storm and eaten more dirt than Pork Patty because it's the only food available to them for a month? Who hasn't been able stop and take a piss because they've been in a firefight for fourteen straight hours? Been frozen in a sniper hide unable to move a muscle while fire ants crawl in your armpits? Swam twenty miles in 60-degree water with twenty pounds of gear? Gone without sleep in a war zone for four straight days? Picked up pieces of your buddy mixed with suicide bomber?"

He paused, making eye contact with his hushed audience. Isolated sounds from the kitchen rushed across the space like miniature sonic booms, until even they fell silent.

"I don't ask you these questions because I don't know the answers. And I certainly don't ask them to brag about what we do. I only ask to make the point that you can't have it both ways. We go do what we do for our own reasons. I'm not claiming patriotism, and I'm not saying these men are better Americans than you are. But don't ask them to act like house cats after being raised in the jungle. It goes against the laws of biology."

The lieutenant slammed his glass on the bar to a chorus of "hooyahs" before making his way through the restaurant. Chin raised, eyes straight ahead, ignoring the looks of shock on the women and admiration on the men. I turned back and could see my grandfather's glare. Ignoring it, I followed LT Hagen and the rest of the SEALs as they marched single file to the back of the restaurant and its patio. We all stepped outside into the night air together. The wind off the ocean was brisk and you could taste the salt on the air. Pensacola's Pier Park boardwalk stood in front of us and immediately I knew what they were going to do.

During the period of adolescence when he could constructively be described as "energetic," my father had developed quite a local reputation for jumping off the structure, despite its illegality. The pier was the second highest on the East Coast, and the city had finished its construction at just about the time he realized anything elevated was worth jumping off. It was only natural then, when he was about my age, he had darted through the crowd attending the new pier's ribbon-cutting ceremony. One hundred and ten feet below the Gulf of Mexico's clear, translucent water licked the shoreline. As the story goes, Dad climbed onto the ledge of the pier just as the mayor was finishing his speech. He let loose a "Geronimoooo!" before taking a head-first gainer into the clear green surf below. The crowd of hundreds rushed to the edge of the pier to watch him fall, at just about the same time as the mayor had blurted "Holy shit!" into the microphone. It was said that if it had been low tide he most certainly would have broken his neck.

That story followed him into the Navy, where he would always call out "Geronimo!" before leaping out the back of a C-17 during HAHO jumps or diving into a river from a Mark V.

Now his teammates were jogging down that same pier on the night before his funeral, leaving a trail of shirts and shoes as they went. Startled diners and stargazers watched the haphazard line of men with shock, until finally they reached the edge. I was sprinting now, trying to keep up with the last man, running in just his skivvies.

When they reached the end, LT Hagen stopped suddenly, turned to the group. The normal-Joe pier patrons had, for the most part, frozen, focusing voyeuristically on this strange crew of half-naked, short-haired, muscular, tattooed men who must have looked to them like a crazed professional sports team. Even two wide-eyed cops allowed themselves to remain placid witnesses. In fact, as I remember it, they looked as puzzled as the rest of the crowd, which watched not only with curiosity but also a respect, the origination of which they probably weren't sure of.

LT Hagen hopped up on the wooden railing and stood over the water. I wondered if he could see the crashing waves, the bottom in the dark, or if it was just nothingness from his perspective. The rest of his teammates joined, arms linked. They looked at each other with a sense of camaraderie, emotion in every face. Then, together, in a booming expression of brotherhood and love he led them:

"If I should die on the silver stretch,"

"Bury me in an old beer can."

"Place my fins upon my chest,"

"Bury me in the lean and rest!"

I looked up at the line of men as they chanted. With a banshee shriek, LT Hagen leapt head first off the pier, his linked brothers in his wake. The echoes of "Geronimo!" followed them into the night air, the sea eventually swallowing both man and war cry. I sprinted over to the railing, grinning, hoping it wasn't low tide.

Chapter 8

AS SOON AS I OPENED MY EYES the next morning, the realization of how hard the day was going to be washed over me. I hadn't slept well at all. Maybe it was the unfamiliar bed, maybe it was the hard comprehension of what we were in Florida to do. Both had certainly contributed to the restlessness. My eyes burned and head felt heavy even as my toes were still pointed at the ceiling.

I had dreamt that night. They were the first dreams that I could remember since – well, since I could remember. They weren't clear or even memorable, but they were there. I had dreamed that I was with my dad. Where we were, or even what we were doing, I was unsure of. I couldn't tell if it was before or after he was killed. But I felt him in my dreams that night, and it was a sobering realization when I woke. That recurrent vision would become a hallmark of my nights for years to come.

Cheyenne was still sleeping in the bed next to me, thumb planted firmly in mouth. Her tiny fist stuck out defiantly above her chin, eyes scrunched tightly. I wondered what she dreamed about, what she really processed about our loss.

The clock radio on the desk said 7:19. Thursday morning, 7:19 am. Four days and eleven hours since it had happened. Since my father had taken five rounds from terrorist AK-47s. The first two, flesh wounds that barely slowed him down. The next just missed his body armor and penetrated vital organs, fragments exploding inside his chest and piercing his lungs, heart, and kidney. One that crashed into his night vision goggles and ricocheted off, catching a teammate in the foot. And one that directly hit his femoral artery, causing massive and immediate blood loss.

His teammates had carried him four miles to the LZ, taking turns giving CPR while returning firing at the insurgents. Together they loaded him on the medevac. The Black Hawk had quickly taken off, the pilots able to do little more than pray a lucky RPG didn't take out the rotors. Bull had tightened the tourniquet on his leg while a PJ started a blood transfusion. Nothing could be done. He bled out somewhere over the desolation of that country while his brothers in arms pounded on his chest, screaming at him to hold on, until eventually they slumped against the helicopter's iron walls, heads in hands, lost in their excruciating thoughts.

They had escorted his body to Bagram, where the SEAL family had been waiting to conduct their sacred ramp ceremony. Hundreds of operators lined up in the dark. They stood at rigid attention at the rear of the C-130 as the American-flag draped coffin was carried to the back of the plane. Each with their own goodbye, whether they had known him personally or not. Each to offer respect for the fallen operator's sacrifice while privately acknowledging their own impermanence.

From Bagram he had a brief stop in Germany, then on to Dover, Delaware before making his way here, Barrancas National Cemetery on the Naval Air Station Pensacola. This was his last stop, his final resting spot.

Four days and eleven hours ago. I did the math in my head: 107 hours since it happened. My dad had been dead for 107 hours, and had traveled the world in that time. The same amount of time it takes to complete a school week or bring a newborn home from the hospital. A familiar period of time normally repeated without awareness, over and over during the course of a lifetime. Evidence that time is not a constant, that it is as subjective as happiness or beauty.

Now he was back where he belonged, by the beach in northwestern Florida, close to the surf, swamps, and people he loved so much. I sighed sadly, looked once more at the clock. 7:25. Another six minutes.

Papa stood in the kitchen, holding a cup of coffee and gazing out the window above the sink. Blood orange trees and some sad-looking ivy lined the chain link fence in the backyard. Any fruit that had grown was long gone, or at the least shriveled up for fall. The withered plants sat morosely, monuments of time and seasons passing. A faded snapshot of better days.

I cleared my throat in the manner one does when announcing their presence. Papa didn't turn, but his shoulders flexed in acknowledgement. Guilt for interrupting his solitude clenched me and I started back towards the living room.

"Nathan." His gravelly voice rumbled through the kitchen, stopping me in my tracks. I faced him. I realized that my father would have looked exactly like him one day. The gray wispy hair, cut short, parted to the side. Sharp blue eyes. The strong, square chin and wide neck. Papa had been a medical logistics officer in the Navy for thirty-three years, and that discipline and attention to detail was still evident in everything he did.

"How many SEALs does it take to screw in a light bulb?" he asked, the joke a familiar one in our family.

I looked to him, unsure if I should answer. His mouth started to open, then quivered before closing abruptly. With a sudden tremor his balance waned and his arm shot out, just catching the counter in time to steady himself. But the mug fell from his grip, bounced once on the floor, the handle breaking off and skidding across the room. Dark liquid slowly spread across the white tiles, oozing outward from the mug's opening until it reached his feet. He was hunched over at the waist, and as I rushed toward him, he made a guttural sound. I feared he might be having a heart attack or stroke, but once I reached him I realized he was sobbing.

It broke my heart seeing Papa like this. I had certainly never seen him cry; in fact, it had never occurred to me he was capable of tears.

Finally: "None. They just stand there holding it and the world revolves around them."

We shared a quiet laugh before he straightened up.

"Joe, are you okay?" Mom's voice came from behind us, worried. Papa and I both turned. Tears may have been clouding his eyes, but he was laughing his ass off anyway. He turned and placed an elbow on the counter, leaning on his forearm. He made no sound, but his back heaved slowly up and down. Mom took me by the wrist and led me out of the kitchen, through sliding glass doors and into the Florida room. I couldn't tell if he was laughing or crying when we left.

The morning sun shone brightly, and it was warm through the glass. A special kind of quiet. Peaceful. I focused on the patch of fruit trees my grandfather had just been staring into. Remembering the stories of my dad and uncle playing amongst these trees as children brought them to life – you could see them sitting in the shade, red juice from the blood oranges running down their chins. Wrestling matches and water balloon fights. The makeshift baseball field at one end of the yard with a stunted banana tree acting as home base. It was now overgrown and brown, with yellowing leaves scattered at its base. I was surprised Papa had let the yard go like that.

A lump began to rise in my throat and my cheeks sunk as I imagined Dad, my age, playing in this yard. I reached out for my mom, only to find her crying. She took my hand, I pulled her close. We hugged, the top of my head damp after we separated. I took a strange pride in her meltdown.

After a suitable amount of time and a few deep breaths, I swallowed, determined again to stay strong. We untangled, she took a step back. Collected now.

"Guess I should get into the shower and start getting ready. Can you wake up Cheyenne?"

I tilted my head towards the living room, and she turned. Cheyenne was standing there awkwardly, watching us. She looked half asleep, unsure of what to do. My mother turned to her. As soon as Cheyenne saw what was left of her tears, her face contorted into a grimace, and in turn she started wailing.

I think the display was a welcome one. In a single motion, Mom rushed to her and wrapped her tightly in her arms. She twirled her around, whispered in her ear. I couldn't hear the words, but Cheyenne responded emphatically.

"Uh huh. I'm ready to say goodbye to Daddy. I want to tell him I love him and I miss him and I hope he's in heaven with the angels."

I watched them embrace, not sure if I felt sadder about my dad or about the pain my family was experiencing. Or if there was a difference. A coldness suddenly ran through me, making the hair on my neck stand up. Goose bumps formed on my arms. The sensation was followed by a soothing warmth that rushed from the hair on my head down to my toes. Something made me spin towards the backyard and those fruit trees. Out of the corner of my eye I swore I saw a figure crouching in the glass. I opened my eyes wider, straining, only to see three leaves fall off the banana tree that used to be home plate.

Chapter 9

"GOOD MORNING MA'AM. I can't tell you how sorry I am for your loss."

A Navy Captain (without a Trident on his uniform) opened the door of the limo, offering my mother his hand. Sunlight poured in the opening, making the day seem suddenly real. We emptied out of the car, steely faces around.

I wondered how many times I had heard that phrase in the past week. "If I had a nickel…" was another of my father's favorite, corny sayings. We numbly followed the officer across the pavement and into a small chapel.

I was dressed in my only suit, purchased for my aunt's funeral two years before. Even with the hem let out and the waist opened, the tightness made me squirm. My shirt sleeves stuck out from the jacket farther than they should, while the tie that Uncle Dave had to knot for me did its best to cover strained buttons.

I took time to drink in the scene. Bright air streaming through painted glass, the smell of soil and holy water and despair. My naked eyes withdrew then widened, unsure of their place in all this.

Driving into the cemetery I had been amazed at the volume of short, white markers lined up in even rows throughout the complex's rolling hills. They shot out like thousands of shining teeth, a gaping mouth filled with the dead of America's wars.

The day was bright, and those headstones jutted out in rhythmical, maybe mathematical patterns. They glistened clearly on their emerald carpet, hypnotizing me as I rested my chin on the edge of the window. The rows had blurred past while I had stared into the day. Tinted windows mercifully muted the scene, giving the sensation of a darkened theater. We parked. Before us, my dad's teammates stood around awkwardly.

Several years ago Dad and I had played golf with Uncle Spencer and LT Hagen. It had been the first time I met them. Dad had recently been promoted and initiated as a Chief Petty Officer on Team 2. LT Hagen was their new OIC, and Uncle Spencer had just joined the Teams, fresh out of BUD/S.

I remember how excited I had been that morning. I was around eight years old, and thought of myself as a burgeoning adult and young man. The fact that my father thought the same was a huge source of pride for me.

He had woken me early, the morning air quiet and dark. I still remember the coffee on his breath and the scratchiness of his voice when he called my name in the lightless bedroom. For such a rough man, he could have a gentle way about him.

I hadn't wanted him to think I was still asleep, even though it wasn't yet 0600 on a Sunday morning, so I popped out of bed with a start. He was shirtless and sweaty, having just returned from a run.

"I'm up," I'd told him, rubbing my head. I could see his grin in the shadow from my doorway. He always knew what everyone's motives were: it was one of his great qualities that he didn't let it on.

"I know, bud. T-minus twenty minutes. Brush your teeth, grab some midrats, and load your gear. We're gonna show these newbies what the Butlers of Team 2 can do on a golf course."

"Hooyah," I replied, feet already on the floor.

Dad had gotten back from Iraq the previous week, a full month before he was scheduled to return, and I was thrilled he finally seemed to be in a good mood that morning. Since getting home, he hadn't spent much time with us, and when he had he was cold and detached.

That been his first combat deployment, and he hadn't returned the same person I remembered. He never spoke about what he had been through over there; all I knew was that he had lost teammates.

Those six months he was gone had been about six percent of my lifetime, and a lot changes in that amount of time. His face looked older. It was the first time I had seen him with a beard. His eyes were darker, more alert. They seemed distant, and for long seconds would drift somewhere far away. The first few days home he had barely slept, and when he did it was mostly during the day. Once, when I had woken up in the middle of the night, I could hear him pacing downstairs. He explained that he had to get acclimated to being back home. It was his readjustment period.

"We're on vampire hours over there," he explained, forcing a cracked smile.

I could also tell that things were not exactly right between him and my mom. He would get angry easily. She was hesitant to let him set rules, or discipline me or Cheyenne. We had fallen into a pattern when he was gone, my mom, Cheyenne and I, and I think in some way she felt he was disrupting that.

So I was extra excited that morning when we jumped into his pickup, our clubs rattling in the bed behind us. Mine had been a birthday present, and this would be the first time he would see me play with them. I had spent time on the driving range with a few guys in his sister platoon when he had been deployed and I couldn't wait to surprise him with my improved swing.

After a quick breakfast we approached the Eagle Haven Golf Club, the new sun spreading a hazy pink across the sky. A single road lined by swampland led us to the nearly empty parking lot on the edge of base.

As we pulled into the lot, the morning stillness was suddenly broken by a loud metallic crash erupting in the bed of the truck. Dad's eyes flashed alertly to the rearview mirror while he abruptly downshifted. I wheeled my head to see what had happened, but instead found my body flying across the seat.

"Son of a bitch," he muttered, swerving the truck violently again.

I tried to collect myself while twisting around to see what had happened. Once again I was flung against the door as Dad hit the gas and cut a sharp figure eight. The seatbelt cut into my chest. I frantically reached for something solid to hold on to.

Cool air began to tickle my neck, and I noticed that the rear window to the pickup bed had slid open. From behind me a shriek penetrated the cab: "Geronimo, Chief!"

The holler, which was about a foot from my head, took me by total surprise. I looked up to find a crazed, open mouth crammed through the window. Who was this lunatic and where had he come from?

Without missing a beat Dad used both feet to slam on the brakes. The truck was still screeching to a stop when his right arm shot out behind him, instantly making the contact he was looking for. The howling face was then viciously yanked through the tiny window, clenched in a chokehold. I looked up as he squeezed, the young, pale face slowly but surely going purple. It slumped with a soft thud into the bed of the truck, and without looking back, my father casually put the truck in gear and eased into a parking spot.

That was the first time I had laid eyes on Spencer, and I was pretty sure my dad had just killed him.

It also was the first time (but certainly not the last) I watched a SEAL choke out one of his teammates. It also turned out to be the day I had my first sip of beer, sitting in Spencer's cart later that morning when I thought he wasn't looking. I had stealthily grabbed his can from the cup holder, pinched my nose and threw back a small swig. I grimaced, taken aback by the sourness.

"It's an acquired taste."

I spun around to find the demented SEAL grinning at me. I quickly put the can back, terrified he would tell my father. He just winked, and pulled out a club.

"Think I can hit your old man from here?" he had asked, squinting in order to line up the cart sitting on the right fairway, 200 yards away.

At the funeral, he gave me a nod while walking towards the hearse. I thought back to that day. It was fitting that the first time I had met him he had been unconscious. After what had felt like the longest minute of my life, he popped back up, shaking the cobwebs with that shit-eating grin I would come to know so well.

Spencer wasn't wearing that familiar expression now. He was lined up with Uncle Dave, Bull, LT Hagen and two other SEALs at the back of the hearse. They seemed awkward, clumsy, no one speaking or acknowledging the others. Tight, unflinching faces. LT Hagen and Bull looked starched and immaculate in their Dress Blues. Spencer and the other SEALs wore Cracker Jacks, which was somewhat amusing since Dad had hated that uniform. He always had trouble with the scarf knot and front flap buttons. I can remember the few times I had seen him putting on the uniform before his promotion to

Chief, cursing in the mirror, fumbling with a roll of pennies. Dad would be the first to admit he was a warrior, not a fashion model. Maybe the second, after his wife.

It was the chaplain from the notification team who escorted us without word into the quiet chapel. Small and wooden, the structure gave the impression of a cabin in the forest. We allowed ourselves to be led down the aisle, incense singeing my nose along the way. The standing-room crowd gave us our distance, softly murmuring as we were led to the area that no one wants reserved for them – the front row.

My mother went first. She wore a plain black dress and dark sunglasses. Pearl earrings and a necklace that Dad had bought her with money he made cutting trees on the weekends when he was home. Even in the subdued attire, her beauty was obvious. My dad always said he was the luckiest man in the world.

A throat cleared through tinny speakers. Words were spoken that I didn't hear. The service began. Cheyenne gripped my hand with ferocity when we sat, Papa and Nana taking the spots beside her.

An empty, rectangular stand waited on the altar. The metal rollers on top glistened, anticipating its charge. My eyes lowered to the light granite of the chapel floors before I purposefully raised them, stared through the wall-sized plate glass window that overlooked the rows of graying markers outside. The sun caught my mother's hair, and I thought it unbecoming for the day to be fitted with such beauty. Likewise, it seemed unfair for all of these people to be here as part of their normal lives and routines. I watched them talk amongst themselves. After the service they would go on about their lives, worrying about washing their cars or taxes or what to do for dinner. In reality, I was jealous of them. I'm sure they were all sad about his death, but did they have a spot in their chest missing like my family did?

Wouldn't they eventually get over it? I knew we never would.

The room hushed. A slight shuffle and restlessness grew louder, moving like a wave down the aisles from the rear. The room couldn't wait to get a glimpse of the slow, pained march of six men. Everyone except me. I knew what that murmuring was and I needed a minute to steel myself. I turned.

They carried my father in a stained wooden casket, a fresh American flag draped across it. The load was heavy; their shuffling slow, step after slow step. Struggling, physically and emotionally.

LT Hagen had the front right position. His dark uniform shone in the sunlight. The gold bars on his sleeves seemed to match perfectly the handles gripped by white gloves. And of course the Trident. Across from him was Uncle Dave, looking out of place in his dark suit and tie. His face contorted in pain, we avoided each other's eyes. The frog that had been residing in my throat made a leap towards daylight. I was just able to push it back down.

Upon sight of the casket, a barely-audible gasp escaped from my mother, leading to a tighter squeeze on my hand and sniffle from Cheyenne. I looked straight ahead, unblinking, afraid any movement would trigger a breakdown. The casket passed slowly by my family, my father's body only inches from me. I wondered what he felt right now. If he really was in Heaven, if he really could look down on us. The uncertainty distracted me from my mission, and before I could remember to hold them, warm tears rolled down my cheeks. I felt woozy. There rose such a deep sadness that I nearly had to stand, overtaken by a need for movement.

After the casket was positioned, the priest stood before us. His words arrived as if from a tunnel.

"We are gathered here to say farewell to Senior Chief Petty Officer Stephen B. Butler and to commit him into the hands of God. Lord our God, you are the source of life. In you we live and move and have our being. Keep us in life and death in your love, and, by your grace, lead us to your kingdom, through your Son, Jesus Christ, our Lord."

There was a ringing in my ears and my head felt light. Everything moved slowly around me, and I was unable to concentrate on what was being said. I slurped air, trying to find enough oxygen. To my side, I could see Mom embracing Cheyenne, my Grandpa Peter kneeling at her side. Somewhere inside me there was still an irrational hope that this wasn't happening. I felt a cool hand on my temple, and realized I had my head in Nana's lap. I sobbed into her dress before a jolt of embarrassment struck me. This was not being a man, staying strong for my family. I pulled my head up, looking at Papa. His face was stone; eyes bulging, lips pursed, staring straight ahead. I saw Uncle Spencer move back over to the casket and lift with the other men. He looked at me sadly, and I could tell he wanted to do something, anything, for us.

The pallbearers carried the casket out a side door. Not far, a blue tarp covered fresh dirt. With a shock, I realized that was where the hole was; *that* was where my dad would spend eternity. The idea was mind-numbing. I stood up and winded my way through the crowd as it exited the chapel, getting as close to the casket as possible. I couldn't help but be dimly aware of the eyes on me, the only son, strong and handsome in his suit and tie.

Again, we were led to the front row. Metal folding chairs, seated in the same order as in the chapel. Mom not as steady for this walk, her grip tight on Grandpa's arm. Her focus didn't leave the coffin as it made its march to another metal stand, next to that deep hole. She looked down at me through the tears, and we tried to give each other a smile.

"Are you doing okay, honey?" she whispered, then reached for my hand.

"Mhm," I breathed, barely nodding. I knew my voice would betray me if I tried to use it. She put one arm around me, the other around Cheyenne. We sat and watched as a line of uniformed sailors started their slow walk towards the casket. They lined up on either side, seeming going on as anonymously into the distance as the tombstones framing them. A wall of white and blue and black, facing the casket and my family. LT Hagen stepped forward first.

"Stephen Butler did not die a hero. Stephen Butler did not die a warrior. Stephen Butler *lived* as a hero. He *lived* as a warrior.

"Before you stand dozens of decorated operators, some of the best this nation has ever seen. Steve was proud to call them brothers, and they likewise him. He had no reservation about following any of them into battle, and I can say many times over we were honored to follow him.

"But where Steve excelled, where he was one of the best among the best, was not only in battle. It was in life – it was when he organized a drive to provide soccer balls for Iraqi children. It was when he volunteered to dig irrigation wells for villagers when the Taliban would shoot them for doing so. It was the love that he showered on Gayle, the affection he showed to Nathan and Cheyenne. It was the time he would take to council a young sailor on maintaining his moral compass, the leadership and selflessness he exemplified every single day to not only his teammates, but to everyone he came in contact with. It was said you couldn't share an elevator with Mo without him bestowing one of his nuggets of wisdom before the doors opened. And in the Navy, we don't have many tall buildings.

"Chief gave me something on the ride over to the Sandbox this last deployment. Something he wanted everyone to hear, should he make the ultimate sacrifice. A 'just in case' letter."

LT Hagen reached into his coat pocket, unfolding a weathered piece of yellow legal paper. I recognized it as the type of paper Dad had often used to write me notes. The breeze fluttered the paper, allowing me to make out familiar block handwriting.

To me, that letter was a gift from beyond. My heart raced with the anticipation of something from my father that I hadn't yet experienced. It was like a new memory, when I had only been worried about cherishing, and remembering, the old ones.

LT Hagen's calm, even voice carried my father's words across the wind.

"LT, if you're reading this, then I'm pretty pissed, because either you're making fun of me, or attending my funeral.

"If it's the latter, then first off let me apologize to my family. Ma, Pop, you were the best parents a boy could ask for. If the company a man keeps is any indication of the quality of his character, then look around you now and realize what a great job you have done.

"To my beautiful wife: you made me the luckiest man alive. The greatest complement a man can receive is being told that he out-kicked his coverage, and darling, I'm not even on the same field as you. But the greatest gifts you ever gave me were our two perfect children. Nathan, I see more of me in you every day. You're becoming a man, and a damn good one. I can't think of a better legacy to leave than you. Chey, you're the apple of my eye, and I love you more than you can know.

"Team 2, and the rest of you Green Faces, you know how I feel about you. You just better have gotten the sons of bitches for me. And I have no doubt you will.

"LT, you can give me back this letter to burn after the last shot has been fired, the last terrorist is buried, and the USA is safe and sound from all threats. Or when I retire, whichever comes first. If you are reading this at my funeral, know that I died for a good, just cause, and that I'm with God. That every second of it was worth it, and I wouldn't change a minute of it. Until then, see you on the other side. Geronimo."

LT Hagen slowly lowered the note, re-folded it, and put it back in his breast pocket. I stared straight ahead, soaking in my father's words, trying to comprehend. They were a true representation of how he felt about God, family and country, and were all things I had heard him say before. But I couldn't believe that he wouldn't change anything. I couldn't accept that he would really do it all exactly the same. I understood he wasn't afraid to die, that he was confident in where he would go and in the cause he gave his life for. But what about the things he was leaving? Would he really choose to leave his wife, his kids, if he could do it all again? Wouldn't he rather be an accountant or a lawyer if it meant Cheyenne and I would have our father attend our high school graduations, our weddings? Wouldn't he rather die in bed fifty years from now after spending each night kissing his wife goodnight, even if it meant a quiet, "normal" life?

Deep down I knew the answer, even if I didn't like it. Dad was always crystal clear about his philosophy on duty. I just wasn't sure why it was his.

Several more SEALs spoke. They talked about his morality, his selflessness, his abilities as a warrior, father, and friend. The words began to blend together. I pondered his sacrifice, realizing that it was my sacrifice too. Was I selfish if I thought that I would happily trade that burden if it meant one more day with him? Was I a traitor for wishing it had been someone else? I understood why we were fighting these wars, at least I thought I did. But I didn't know why it had to be *my* family who gave everything while everyone else got to cheer for vets at ballgames and post their appreciation for long weekends on Facebook. They liked the *idea* of sacrifice. Especially when it wasn't theirs.

Then it occurred to me that it wasn't just my dad who had given all. It had been thousands at the embassies in Africa, in Beirut, the USS Cole, the World Trade Center, the Pentagon, Shanksville, and the troops overseas now.

And then I thought about the Iraqi and Afghan dads. I didn't want to, but I couldn't help it. The ones that my dad and his teammates had killed. They had kids too. And funerals, and legacies, and lives to lead. They were the enemy and I was glad my dad's teammates had killed the terrorists who had killed him. Were their families having funerals for them right now? Many of them had died the same day in the same battle my father had. A wash of anxiety rushed over me as I thought about that possibility. Did I hate them? I hated what they had done to my family. But I didn't think I hated their children, who were probably just as sad as I was. Sitting before a grave in the desert, saying goodbye to the man who had raised them, who had taught them their prayers, just as my dad had taught me mine.

I took solace, as those residing on the just side of a conflict have always done, in knowing mine was the side of righteousness, and the enemy's evil. I had no doubt which side was right, I just wished being right didn't hurt so much.

Adam, a team leader on Team 4, my dad's old team, finished speaking. Adam was a short, wiry New Yorker with a heavy Brooklyn accent and a thick black mustache that moved when he talked. I was pretty sure the phrase "swear like a sailor" had originated with him. He had once appeared on Jeopardy and supposedly was an actual genius, in MENSA and everything. "Stub," as the guys called him, had started in BUD/S as my dad's swim buddy before getting rolled back a class after fracturing his ankle. He had finished Hell Week on that broken ankle, refusing to quit. My dad always said that Adam felt no pain. He joked that when God had been handing out thresholds for pain, he had accidentally given him two other men's allotment, and then a family of rhinos'. But the pain was evident in Adam's face as he approached the casket that day, the soles of his shined shoes crunching on the fresh dirt just in front of me.

His hands moved slowly, methodically, to his left breast. The breeze was the only other movement. He removed the Trident from his blouse, delicately positioning it at the head of the coffin. With a sudden, violent motion, his right fist flew out, and slammed the pin into the wood. A hollow THUD tumbled loudly, its echo racing the wind, accelerating across the sky and trees – the slam as final as a closing door. Gold shined lonely in the sun, until another THUD rang out, then another and another until a quorum was reached. The rows of SEALs walked solemnly by either side of the casket, each rhythmic THUD shaking me until dozens of gold Tridents blurred in my tears and my weary head rested on Mom's shoulder.

Clearing throats and muted sniffles interrupted the peace as two sailors in Dress Blues stood facing each other, several feet apart. Each smartly held the end of an American flag, the same one that had earlier adorned the casket. A light wind fluttered through it, the material rolling in waves against the blue sky. Resolutely they stared into each other's faces, snapping and creasing the flag as my mother stoically waited to receive her donation from the United States which would mark her sacrifice.

"On behalf of a grateful nation and a proud Navy, I present this flag to you in recognition of your husband's years of honorable and faithful service to his country."

The CACO officer then took a knee before my mother, offering her the flag. She pulled it to her chest. He held his position. Suddenly,

I just wished this would be over. I looked behind me at the hundreds of people milling around, some whispering quietly, some looking sadly at the spectacle. I gritted my teeth and turned my gaze towards Uncle Spencer. He looked equally as impatient, and met my stare. I fidgeted in my chair until my grandparents had received their flag, and then stood, the urge to move overwhelming.

A volley of shots rang out, making me flinch yet again. I turned towards them, startled as the rest of the attendees. The distraction gave me an opportunity to move away and I took advantage, wincing slightly each time the Honor Guard fired into an uncaring sky.

I slinked behind the gravesite and wall of SEALs, finding shade under a tree. As soon as the gunshots stopped, a single bugler began to play Taps – a hollow, mournful sound that seemed to come from nowhere and everywhere all at once. I was pretty sure I'd never heard anything as lonely and sorrowful in all my life. The notes rang out slowly and crisply, gripping my mind and pulling on my soul. My view of the casket was blocked, and I craned my neck to get one last look before it was too late. I leaned against my tree, sobbing against the rough bark, supported by its trunk.

"Nate." It was Spencer, approaching me gingerly, a look of uncertainty on his face.

I raised my eyes, contemplating him. He reached into his back pocket, removed something, offered it to me.

I took it, looked down at it. It was a photograph, one I immediately recognized. The four of us at Disney World, taken just a couple of weeks before the final deployment to Afghanistan. It was weathered, dirty in a manner that can only come from heavy usage.

"I thought you should have that. Your father kept that in his helmet on every mission. Changed the picture every deployment too. Said you and Chey grew so fast he needed an updated one every day.

Anyway, thought you should have it."

I didn't look up from the photo, only sobbed harder into it. He took me in his arms, squeezing me awkwardly.

"I don't know what to say to you, son. I just don't know what to say."

"Why him, why did it have to be him?" I choked.

"I would give anything to trade places, Nate, anything. I wish it had been me."

I looked up at him, shaken by his words. He meant it.

I shook my head, horrified. "No, not you either. Why anyone?"

"We don't look at it that way, bud. The world has a lot of evil in it. And you have to know that it has a lot less in it because of your father. I know it's hard to hear now, and damn near impossible to understand, but your dad died doing good and doing what he loved, for what he loved."

With the anger rising in me once more, I told him, "Save that 'for a good cause' bullshit. He said he would do it again if he had the choice. You heard his letter. He would leave us again."

He sighed loudly, crouched before me.

"It's not that simple, Nathan. And that's not what he meant in that letter. No one ever has a second chance at life, it's never worthwhile to play what-if. What he was saying was that he understood the risks, and knew it was a real possibility he could be killed doing what he did. But that he was willing to take those risks to make the world a better place for his family."

"The same risks you're willing to take."

"The same risks every one of us is willing to take. Someone has to do it. How many times did you hear him say 'Next man up'?"

"About a million."

"That's right. There are some people in this world content to be a part of their environment, and some who are destined to change it. I don't have to tell you which type of person your old man was."

"And you."

"And you, Little Warrior."

Chapter 10

MY HEART IS POUNDING, yet I barely notice since catching my breath is such a struggle. I'm vaguely aware of being on the ground, laying on my side, arms and fists tucked under my chin. Eventually my focus transitions to holding back tears, as wheezing gulps of air make it clear I am able to breathe again. The neighbor – I never got his name – is nowhere to be found. Just a sideways view of the world with magnified blades of grass, a perpendicular oak and rising fear. No football.

I pull myself up as slowly as self-pity allows, feeling dusk's shadows descend around me. I enter the house just as slowly, imagining I'm the only person left in the world. That illusion is shattered immediately by Grandpa's inquiry.

"What happened?"

I turn deliberately, unsure of how to respond. Slightly hunched over and still holding my stomach, I am intermittently sniffling despite previous efforts.

"The boy next door punched me," I sob, finally letting go. The despair crescendos. I am now a sniveling mess. "I didn't even do anything to him!" I wail, collapsing to the floor.

"Nathan." My father's balanced voice lifts my face from the cool linoleum like gravity reversing itself. "Get off the floor. And tell me what happened."

His face is a calming influence, and suddenly I am back in the present. And where there had been pain and fear, a rage is building.

"That boy who lives next door to Grandma and Grandpa punched me in the stomach because the football went in his yard!" I seethe. "I went to get it and he hit me! FOR NO REASON!"

"Did you hit him back?"

Convinced I am on the side of the righteous, I proudly answer with an emphatic head shake that no sir, I hadn't.

"Why not?" To my shock, the question sounds accusatory.

"Sir?"

"Why didn't you hit him back?"

"I, uh, don't know. I didn't want to get in trouble."

He takes a quick, definitive step towards me. He crouches down, eye level. Dad's hand, now on my shoulder, feels like a boulder.

"Nathan, you will never get in trouble for defending yourself or anyone who can't defend themself. If someone hits you FIRST, you are allowed to respond in kind. Do you understand?"

I nod, timidly at first, then with increased vigor. How dare this bully make me look weak in my father's eyes! I'll get him back! *The anger grows, widening my eyes and flaring my nostrils. I dart toward the door.*

"Whoa, not so fast buddy." Dad has me by the shirt collar, but I'm so worked up I struggle mightily to free myself.

"Lemme go!"

"One caveat to that pal. You gotta do it right away."

Chapter 11

BACK IN THE LIMO, I decided I was done mourning. Not done being sad, not done missing him, but done mourning. I didn't want to hear Amazing Grace any more, didn't want to listen to men speak of my father's dependability and decisiveness, and didn't want to see hundreds of tiny American flags everywhere I looked.

The procession made its way back through the windy road transecting the cemetery, ringed on either side by those very flags. I wasn't crazy about the crowds of people lining the road in their dark suits and cocktail dresses. They mustered their most-solemn faces and clasped their hands respectfully in front of them as we passed. Not one of them took their eyes off the lead car carrying the widow, parents and young children of the fallen hero. I could see them at home that morning, reading the story in the Pensacola News Journal about the local SEAL who had been killed defending his country.

"What do you think, should we go pay our respects?" Bob had asked Jane.

"Sure. You know Carol was two grades above his brother in middle school, before she went to Blessed Star."

They were more interested in an idea, satisfied with the closeness of sacrifice without actually losing anything.

We turned out of the cemetery onto the main street. Several police cars were blocking the road as people milled around. But what caught my attention were the hundreds of bikers lined up on the far side of the road. I looked on with wonderment at row after row of burly, bearded men. They were dressed in various forms of leather and denim, dirty jeans and long hair. While their personal hygiene may have been lacking, the gleaming motorcycles that stood next to each gave an indication of their priorities. Huge American and dark MIA flags billowed from the back of most.

"Whoa, Hell's Angels," I muttered.

Papa looked over at me, then at my mother. Something about this scene concerned them, which made me take a closer look out the window.

The Hell's Angels seemed to be blocking another, smaller group, who were holding up homemade signs and chanting. Some of the bikers revved their engines loudly as we passed. The throaty bursts from aftermarket tailpipes drowned out the smaller group, leaving me unsure what they were yelling. The cops standing in the street holding up traffic waved us through hurriedly, and the limo sped up as it took the corner. I spun in the leather seat to get a better look out the back window, but could only make out a jumble of chrome, posters and limbs.

"What was that?" I asked Papa.

"Savages," he mumbled.

I looked over at Mom, then back to him, still unsure of what I had witnessed. I could tell by their expressions that it wasn't good, and that they weren't going to tell me.

Chapter 12

IT WAS STRANGE, once we got back to Virginia Beach. Things almost seemed normal. We were used to having Dad gone, and in a way we fell back into our same routine. At least a version of that routine. One day, the FedEx man came to the door. The next, my mother had Uncle Spencer come over and remove the doorbell.

But for the most part, we moved forward. Cheyenne and I went back to school, Mom made us dinner, tucked us in each night, and we said our prayers.

It was the little things about those activities that changed, that made all the difference. At school, the kids and teachers were extra nice. I could tell they felt sorry for us, which irritated me. I didn't want anyone's pity, and I told them so. When Connor Rhodes, who I had never liked and was pretty sure had put gum in my hair in the sixth grade, told me he was sorry about my dad getting killed, I promptly gave him a bloody nose. It was the first time I'd ever gotten detention, and Ms. Spiller, the vice president, told my mother she should have suspended me. Guess she felt sorry for me too.

Dinnertime also was different, and not only because the women in Mom's Navy Wives Club filled our freezer with enough casseroles to feed us until Cheyenne left for college. It was quieter, more subdued. Conversation seemed forced, scripted.

The first couple of nights back I didn't want to say my prayers. I was mad at God, and the silent treatment was the only way I knew to get back at him. But Mom made it clear that was a bad example to set for my sister, and I knew she was right. When I was ready, I said my piece.

Mom sat on the edge of my bed, eyes closed, hands in a perfect steeple. I was positioned similarly, but with one eye open. I had to get this off my chest.

"And everyone keeps praying to you and asking you to watch over Chief Stephen Butler, but I know he doesn't need you to. If anything he's probably watching over you."

"Nathan!" my mom said, opening her eyes and giving me a slight slap on the leg. "Don't say that!"

I opened my eyes and looked at her innocently.

"Why not? You know it's true."

"Just say the Our Father and Hail Mary and go to sleep," she told me, standing up.

I smiled into the dark.

And so the days continued to move forward, with little regard for whether or not we were ready for them to. Christmas came, then went. It didn't feel like Christmas. If I remember correctly, we didn't even get a tree that year.

Before I knew it, it was springtime, and six months had passed since that day. It was a Tuesday night, and the kitchen clock read 8:19.

"It's been six months."

Mom was at the sink washing some other wife's Tupperware when I made the realization. I thought back to that night, when unaware, we had carried on our normal lives. College football, phone calls with friends, arguments. It seemed so long ago. And yet I still wasn't even sure it had actually happened.

Her back tensed and she sighed. "Feels like ten years sometimes. Other times, like yesterday."

"Exactly six months ago. I was watching the Florida State/Maryland game. Remember when I spilled the bowl of popcorn, and you told me I'd better get every last kernel…"

"…because your father can smell popcorn from down the street? I remember," she said. "He loved popcorn. I think he could have eaten it morning, noon, and night. In college, he sometimes did. That man ate like a child. When I would let him."

"What do you think he was doing?"

"When?"

"When I spilled the popcorn. Do you think he was already shot? He wasn't dead yet, because they had a thirty-five minute helo ride back to the FOB, and he died on the medevac to Bagram. I wonder if he had already been shot the first time. I wonder if the Ranger he was trying to rescue was still alive."

"I don't know, honey. I guess it really doesn't matter."

"It does to me."

She looked at me, drying her hands. Then, "Why does the timing matter so much to you, Nate?"

I shrugged, grabbed an apple from the counter.

"Doug wanted to know if we can go surfing tomorrow morning. There's a decent swell and off-shore winds all weekend."

"It's practically still winter!"

"So? That's what wet suits are for. Besides, it's going to be 70 degrees out this weekend."

"Is his father going?"

"No, he's TAD," I told her. "But there will be tons of people at the jetty, you don't have to worry."

"I always worry, kiddo," she said, smiling. "That's my job. How about I take you guys – I haven't watched you surf in a while."

"It's going to be cold."

"I'm a tough gal. Wife of a SEAL, right?"

I almost said "widow," and was glad I didn't. The insinuation hung in the air, and her face contorted into a pained expression. It made me sad too, and the stabbing feeling in my chest returned. It came and went, but was never far.

"Okay. I'll call Doug and let him know. Sunrise is at 6:42. I'll tell him we'll pick him up at 0600."

"You mean oh-dark thirty."

"On time is late. Early is on time."

She groaned. "You are your father's son, Nathan. Thank God for that."

"I thank Dad for that," I said, leaving the kitchen while crunching my apple, headed for the computer. I'd stay up Bing'ing his name and reading what I could about the wars online until she forced me to bed.

Chapter 13

IT WASN'T A SURPRISE when I woke before the alarm went off the next morning. While I hadn't had much trouble falling asleep since it happened, I had been jolted awake each morning before I was ready to.

On that particular morning I had awoken with a sense of confusion. Out of habit I found myself scanning the bedroom door and searching for a telltale crack of light. But then I remembered, and knew that there would be no wake-up call to beat this morning. I was on my own.

Early morning surf sessions had been our thing. Whenever he wasn't deployed or training, we'd hit the First Street Jetty, or if there was a nice swell we'd go north of 31st Street. We were both goofy-footed and there was a mellow left break on a sandbar there that we considered the Butlers' spot. Before school or on summer mornings we'd often be the first in the water.

We'd grab smoothies, load the pickup with our boards and wet-suits, trying to time our first paddle with sunrise. He would shoot out in front of me, his powerful strokes clearing the break while I duck-dived waves behind him, struggling to keep up. He never turned to check on me, but I never had a doubt he was there if I needed him.

The sky would hang a wispy azure shroud as we parked on those mornings. We'd take our time carrying our boards out to the beach, relishing the peace, the gentle sounds of rejuvenation. He'd sip his coffee while we observed the waves, plotting our course before making our way onto the sand. You could always hear the ocean before you could see it, and even in summer the sand would be cold on bare feet that early in the morning. After stopping to stretch and put on our wetsuits or wax the boards, he'd look at me, nod, and we'd ease into the water. On clear mornings, if we timed it just right, the sky would be morphing to pink as we approached the water's edge. We'd pick our path through the break, paddling towards infinity. There would always be that last wave to duck dive under, when you'd return to a different surface than you had left. Somehow in those few seconds underwater, the day would arrive. Fresh brightness would break the twilight as the sun made its daily entrance before us and welcomed us to its pleasures.

We didn't talk much while we surfed. He would offer some sparse encouragement and a high five after particularly good rides, but we didn't need much conversation when we were in the water. It wasn't hard to know where you stood with him, explanations unnecessary.

It was depressing to know I would not be on the receiving end of those proud looks this morning. Enough so to take my breath, suddenly accelerate my heart. Again. And still it surprised me. I realized that would probably never cease. Now, six months after it had happened, I would still intermittently get smacked with sudden waves of pain and sadness, usually when least expecting it.

I paused, collecting myself, and rolled out of bed, not feeling the rush of adrenaline that usually gripped me before morning sessions. It wouldn't be the same, but that was a sentiment I was getting used to.

I tiptoed out of my room but Mom was already up, Cheyenne

curled in her lap on the couch, half asleep.

She gave me a soft "Good morning," looking up with a warm smile.

"I didn't think you'd be up yet," I told her. I slid into the kitchen, grabbed a banana, a blueberry muffin, and orange Gatorade before sitting at the kitchen table.

"Chey was up, so I figured we'd sit in here until you were ready to go."

"Nightmares?"

She nodded, looking down at my sleeping sister.

"It's hard on her," I said.

"It's hard on all of us, Nate. That's to be expected."

"I know, but especially on her. I don't know if she fully understands. She asked me again the other day when Dad was coming home."

"She forgets."

"Lucky her," I replied, throwing the banana peel in the wastebasket. "Don't want to miss sunrise. We need to leave if we're going to make first light."

She nodded and carried Cheyenne into the garage. I followed closely, until she stopped suddenly in front of me. Something in the garage had piqued her interest. We both stood frozen, looking from her Explorer to my dad's pickup truck, where his longboard was still sticking out of the bed.

The truck hadn't been moved since. My surfboard and wetsuit were still in the back from summer, but separately we were both questioning whether or not it was appropriate to take it. Then, like an important decision had been reached, she moved decisively and opened the truck's side door, buckling Cheyenne in.

"We have to drive it sometime," she said matter-of-factly.

"Do you even know how to drive stick?'

"You'd be surprised what your ol' Mom can do."

Shrugging, I quickly found my legs and hopped in the front seat.

We drove the four blocks to Doug's house in a comfortable silence, listening to Cheyenne's deep breathing in the backseat. It was unbelievable how loudly she breathed when sleeping. The only little kid I knew who snored. Mom and I shared a smile over it and she jokingly pushed her nose up like a pig.

Doug's dad was, like most of the fathers in my neighborhood, in the Navy. He was a corpsman, but not in the Teams, and had been deployed to Iraq when the Simmons' first got stationed in Virginia Beach. Doug had been one of the new kids in my class at the beginning of sixth grade. We became close friends – at least as close as military-brat friendships can be. It was a good policy to remain guarded, knowing any friendship had a shelf life. Most families moved every three years, and then you start all over again. Luckily, for the most part SEALs are stationed in only two places, which limited our moves.

But living in a military town, we were used to new kids, and we were used to our friends moving. Someone would be coming or going pretty much every week. I never thought it strange, that's just the way it was. To us, what was strange were the kids who grew up in the same town their whole lives, who had the same bedroom until they left for college and then their parents turned it into an exercise room. Neither lifestyle was necessarily better or worse, just different.

A whisper from Mom greeted Doug after he had loaded his surfboard and wetsuit and squeezed into the back seat. "Good morning, Doug. Shhh, Cheyenne is sleeping."

He squinted his eyes in the dark at the seat next to him, noticing Cheyenne's head slumped on her chest. After a second, he looked at us.

"Is she – *snoring?*" he asked incredulously. We both immediately cracked up.

"Shhh, don't wake her!" Mom stifled a laugh before pulling away from his house with a jerk. I could just make out her profile and was amused by her convulsions. I couldn't remember the last time I had seen her laugh like that.

She tried to regain her composure, still swallowing giggles. "She's our little piggy, don't you laugh at her. You don't want to deal with those consequences."

He looked at me, then Mom, and could tell she was serious.

Doug shook his head. "Who's laughing?"

"So where's your dad?"

"Twentynine Palms."

"Well, I hope you're going to mow that lawn for your mother while he's gone. I saw her struggling with it last time."

He shrugged. "She usually does it. She doesn't mind."

Her head snapped to the rearview mirror. "You need to step up, Douglas. You should be helping out while your father is gone. Nathan always does – did – our yard when Steve was deployed."

He yawned, rubbed his eyes.

"Dunno." Then: "You're nuts, Nate, this is way too early to go surfing. Water's still freezing. Shoulda stayed in bed."

"Nate and his father used to do this all the time. I always thought it was crazy, too," Mom said.

"That's what wetsuits are for, Nancy. Just wait until you see the sunrise over the break. Then tell me who's crazy."

My words quickly proved true: the sun was just starting to poke its head out as we pulled into the First Street parking lot, working its magic on the endlessness where horizon meets water. I rushed Doug out of the truck, jogging onto the beach.

Not surprisingly, the coast was nearly empty. We paused at the top of the dunes to watch the slow rollers ease towards shore. No words were spoken, but I know we both felt the same adrenaline. A quiet wind and inviting waves mutely affirmed our intended activity.

I had always been mesmerized by the path of waves, and standing there I tried to pick one up on the horizon as it formed. I followed its movement as it bobbed and bowled elegantly towards land, completing the last leg of a boundless trip. White spray kicked up, spewing water upwards, until it was pulled back out to sea to begin the journey again. How many waves had that water been a part of?

Anxious and cold, we struggled into our wetsuits as fast as we could. I had grown since the last time I had worn mine, so it took some effort pulling it over my waist. When I stuck my right arm through the spongy material, I felt a comforting and familiar crinkle of paper. I gripped it knowingly and pushed my fist through the armhole. The same yellow paper, the same block handwriting:

AS YOU SHOULD WITH ALL OF GOD'S CREATIONS, RESPECT AND ENJOY THE OCEAN. I'M ALWAYS WITH YOU NATE, EVEN IF I'M NOT RIGHT NOW. SEE YOU ON THE OTHER SIDE. - DAD.

I read it a second time before folding it into quarters, the paper fitting perfectly in the palm of my hand. Doug, too busy shivering, hadn't even noticed. I jogged over to my mom, handing her the note for safekeeping. She just smiled. No explanation needed.

We attached our leashes and dove into the water. Cold slapped my face, but my body was insulated and felt warm, disconnected. The icy spray was a sudden wake-up call, giving me a jolt of energy.

Doug had cried out at the chill, but I was already past the first set of waves, too far ahead of him to have to respond.

My birthday was six months after Doug's, but he always seemed like the younger one. It was I who devised our neighborhood schemes, who decided whether we'd play baseball or football. When getting in trouble for wrestling at school he'd always cower inconspicuously in a corner while the teacher placed the blame on me. He was a lot smaller than I was, and didn't yet have the scratch in his voice that I had recently developed. I could sense his apprehension when we coasted across the whitewash, but I turned away from him anyway and began paddling harder. I could hear him thrashing behind me, trying to keep up, but I pulled away, duck diving under the first breaker. After paddling over a smaller wave I was through the break easily.

Stillness washed over both me and ocean as I pulled into the dark, calmer water. I shook beads of wetness from my head, shivered, checked the zipper on my wetsuit. The rip tide was stronger than I expected, already pulling me south towards the Rudee inlet and its rocks. I turned my board to paddle into the current. Behind me, chest-high waves were breaking in quick succession, blocking any view I had of Doug. I wasn't worried, knowing that another surfer could be just a few feet from you when a big set rolled in and be missed in the churn.

I sat up, straddling my board, craning my neck towards shore. There was now enough light to outline my mom and sister huddled on the beach, sharing a blanket. A nervous lull came over the water, the ocean's declaration of an incoming set. I turned, watching a left develop at my feet. Figuring there would be at least three good waves in the set, I bobbed over it, banking on something bigger. It looked like I would be rewarded for my patience. An over-head giant was rising just behind it. I turned 90 degrees, easing myself to my stomach in preparation. I stared at the nose of my board in subdued anticipation, waiting to feel the pull signaling that it was time to start paddling.

After a long count I turned. The wave had fizzled out. I cursed quietly. I should have ridden the first one. Greedy. Just then I felt that powerful pull sucking me out to sea, low into the surf. I turned in the nick of time, a head-high monster rising at my heels. Pulling my chest up, I started paddling as fast as I could. With only a few quick strokes, the wave caught me, grabbing me and pulling me into its power. I struggled to gain my balance and after finding an equilibrium, placed my hands on the edge of the board. I raised myself and quickly leapt to my feat. It was another left, and I knew that if I didn't angle in that direction the wave would break over me and I would fall out head first over my board, slamming. I bent my knees into a crouch, following the curl, almost getting under the lip. A sense of joy flew through me as I rode the barrel perfectly; one of the best rides of my life.

The sensation one has when in the grips of a perfect ride is of weightlessness, of power, of symbiosis with one's environment. It is effortless and exhilarating, impossible even as it occurs. All that I had in that wave.

I continued to ride its face down the line until out of nowhere, Doug appeared, bobbing in its wash. To my shock, he tumbled under the break directly in front of me. I had no choice but to bail out or crash straight into him. I jumped off clumsily, my board going one way, me the other. As I submerged, the leash pulled, jerking hard. I rolled and rolled, tossed underwater by the powerful sea. Sound ceased to exist; there was only foam and blue water in all directions. Instinctively, I raised my arms over my head to shield it from the board, but soon realized I didn't know which way was up. Still, I didn't panic. I knew I could hold my breath for at least forty-five seconds, twenty to thirty if I was under duress like I was now. I consciously told myself, *stay calm*. After a strong breaststroke I was just able to make out the clearing water above me. The surface! But to my shock, that stroke didn't get me to the top. The expected refresh of oxygen never came. Frantic, I pulled myself towards the clear water, that blurred surface, once again. My fingers felt cold as they touch air, but my head was still underwater. Now, finally, terror took hold – I had a lucid thought: *Could this be it?* My lungs urged my mouth to open, to take a breath; my mind knew better. I grabbed a hold of the leash, walking my arm up it until I felt the edge of the board. I struggled to get a grip, until finally I was able to use the board to pull myself above the waterline. I sucked air greedily, but the relief of breath did not last long. I managed to get a good, deep pull, only to have another wave crash on top of me, forcing me under again. The leash was still in my right hand; again I followed it to the board. Spent, I crawled on top of it, finally able to breathe.

I paused, content to drift for a moment, trying to collect myself while scanning the water for Doug. The last set had been huge, and I soon realized that while I had been struggling, the fierce rip had dragged me towards the jetty. There was no time to rest if I didn't want to crash onto the rocks. Exhausted, I started paddling toward shore, using the white water as if I were riding a boogie board.

When I saw Doug's head pop up a short ways away it was clear he was caught in the rip. Each time he would scramble to climb on his board it would shoot away, knocking him back into the surf. Even as wiped as I was, I decided to change paths and paddle towards him, and the rocks. I made it quickly and with little effort, aided by the fierce current.

"Nate! Nate! My leash came off!" he sputtered once I was within earshot, his head dipping under the water. "I can't get my board!"

I instantly saw what had happened, and why he couldn't get control of his board. The leash was no longer attached to his foot, and each retreating wave sucked the board farther from him, towards the rocks. He was struggling to tread water in the break, his head going under for a longer period each time.

All I could think about was how mad his mom would be at me if something happened to him.

"Grab on!" I yelled before popping into a seated position where he could reach my board. The second he took a hold of mine, his board shot off again, sucked directly into the current. Now what? I knew it would be next to impossible for both of us to get to shore on just one board.

"Do you have a good grip?" I shouted, locking onto his saucer-shaped eyes. Blue lips quivered when he nodded, but I could tell he was with me and understood the importance of what I was telling him. "Don't let go!"

I reached for my left foot, pulling at the Velcro that held the leash to my ankle. Once free, I looked one more time at Doug, took as deep a breath as I could, and dove into the chop. A composure and focus seemed to take over me. I started a steady swim towards his board, now at least twenty feet down the surf line and distancing itself quickly. I navigated through the constant breakers, diving under them and re-starting my swim each time I returned to the surface. But every time I looked up, the surfboard didn't seem to be any closer. It was being sucked towards shore and the rocky inlet faster than I anticipated. With a brief wash of panic, I realized I would be hard pressed to fight this current and swim back to shore without the aid of Doug's surfboard. I had done ocean swims with my dad all the time, but never in surf like this and with these stakes. Already my arms felt like they had weights attached to them, my eyes and lungs burning. I knew I had to push the panic down, digging deep if I was going to reach the board before it crashed onto the rocks. An unanticipated wave belted me from behind, sucking me under, and once again, I wasn't sure which way was up or down. I dove deep to escape the rip, my tired arms pulling water behind me as swiftly and efficiently as they could, in the direction I hoped was bringing me closer to my goal.

"Hope is not a strategy"– another one of Dad's familiar phrases – entered my mind. He was also fond of one about preparation that I figured applicable here, but didn't have the energy to conjure at the moment.

As often happens in life, just as all appeared lost and I thought I couldn't fight the ocean a minute longer, I felt a cord cross my face. I grasped at it, and with elation found I was holding Doug's leash. Treading water as best I could, I finally got it Velcro'd to my ankle. With a well-earned wash of relief, I hauled myself onto the board, completely spent. But again, rest would have to wait. Not more than twenty yards in front of me, waist-high waves were smashing into the rocks. I quickly turned 90 degrees towards shore, aiming for the beach.

As I approached the coastline, I sort of groaned to myself. I knew what Mom's reaction was going to be. She was standing with Doug and Cheyenne at the edge of the water, more or less freaking out. She had that look on her face that only mothers have – the petrified-while-furious-while-relieved look.

"I'm fine!" I yelled out as soon as I thought she would be able to hear me. I tried to wave and extend a toothy smile, but ended up getting a face full of salt water instead. I gagged, falling to a knee. That really sent her into a panic, even though I was in waist-deep water by then.

When I finally trudged out of the ocean I wasn't sure if she was going to hit me or hug me. I guess it ended up being a combination of the two. Mostly she just seemed happy I was on dry land, and quickly covered my wet head in kisses. I, of course, squirmed out of her grip, although not as quickly as I could have. Anyway, she couldn't be *too* upset with me, I didn't *try* to wipe out or anything. I did my best to explain that I was never really in danger, but I don't think she agreed.

Doug never thanked me.

Chapter 14

THE REST OF THE SCHOOL YEAR flew by. Mom asked if I wanted to stay in Virginia Beach for my freshman year. I told her I did.

When I asked her preference, she said she liked the area, and was grateful for the wives' club and support groups she was a part of. Unfortunately, there was no shortage of war widows in Little Creek. So with Cheyenne's blessing – "I don't want to leave my froggies" – our family of three made the decision to stay in Virginia Beach.

I had another reason for wanting to attend Landstown High that fall.

I had decided I would follow in my father's footsteps. I planned on becoming a starting safety on the JV football team, being the fearless, reckless player my dad had been known for while growing up in Pensacola. I had gained fifteen pounds and three inches since the fall, and had started lifting weights. Dad's team was deployed to Iraq, but I had been emailing with Uncle Spencer for workout advice while he was gone. He told me that when they were back, he was going to put me through PT that would make the upcoming August two-a-days for football seem like Jazzercise (his phrase).

I was excited to work out with him. I knew he could be a medieval son of a bitch, but with his help I would be prepared, and not just for football.

I also had been spending less time with Doug and more time with his twin sister, Tammy. I may not have been actively trying to keep that from him, but I sure wasn't advertising it. Doug could be strange about those types of things, so I figured I'd avoid his judgment and passive aggressiveness if possible. I didn't think she was my girlfriend or anything, but I also couldn't say for sure that she wasn't. I mean, we didn't kiss or hold hands or anything, but we sure spent a lot of time together. What makes someone a girlfriend? We usually just went to the movies or lounged around in my basement, playing cards or some stupid board game. She wouldn't let me watch war coverage when she was over, or even read about it online. She told me I was obsessed. I asked her how could I not be? How everyone could not be? That we could be fighting two wars and the American public barely gave a shit was beyond me. Sometimes I'd let Cheyenne hang out with us when Mom gave me enough grief, but usually not.

On one of those afternoons I was watching videos on YouTube of soldiers coming home and surprising their families. It was all the rage – the dad would dress up as the school mascot and when his kid ran on the field he'd see that it's really his dad, home from war, safe and sound. Or he'd be wrapped like a present, or just show up at the kid's dance recital. Must be nice, I thought.

Of course once Tammy came over she made me stop watching. Truth be told I was sick of the videos, but wasn't crazy about being told what to do.

"Again?"

I hoped my glare was all the response she required.

"I don't get it – you bitch about the exploitation, yet you watch every single video. If your philosophy is that these are just propaganda, then why do you watch them?"

"I never said that's my *philosophy*. If anything, it's *yours*. What *I* said was that while it may be glorifying specific individuals, at least it gets some emotions flowing in Suzy Q Homemaker. You know, so they can feel for the cause."

"Sounds like a philosophy to me."

"I don't have a philosophy, Tammy. I wish I did, but I don't. I respect those who do, but I'm not one of them. Not yet. Too many people think they have philosophies, when they're really just ideas."

"What most people haven't figured out is that they should make every place they are the best it can be. I know you haven't figured that out yet.

"Quite a philosophy."

"Thanks."

"It was sarcastic."

"I'm aware."

"Hippy."

"'Murica."

"Fuck you," I told her. She started dealing a game of gin rummy.

"You have any root beer?"

Later, her brother called. He explained that he was with Toby, and Toby was looking for Nitin. Apparently Toby was going to beat up Nitin because he had heard that he had called him a fat-ass.

"Toby *is* a fat-ass," I told Doug, catching a look from Tammy over her cards. She rolled her eyes, a habit I had discovered girls seemed to enjoy immensely. Tammy wasn't the biggest fan of Toby Barton, and for good reason. He had followed her around school like a lost puppy dog for a couple of weeks last year. When she politely explained that she wasn't interested in him, he had called her a bitch in front of the whole class, teacher and all. Tammy was the type of girl that could laugh that off. Toby had gotten suspended.

"Maybe so, but he's gonna whoop Nitin. Mike is going to Nitin's house now to get him, and is going to bring him to the park. You gotta meet us there, man."

"Why would Nitin go to the park if he knows Toby's gonna kick his ass? And why would I want to watch that? Toby's twice his size and a year older."

"Mike's not gonna *tell* him Toby's there, he's gonna say that they found a snake on the basketball court. And why wouldn't you want to see it? It's gonna be a blood bath! Toby knocked out some black kid's tooth in the middle of an AYA basketball game last week. He doesn't give a *shit!*"

I looked over at Tammy, twisting her hair around her index finger again. Another habit that she had picked up. I usually told her that she was going to go bald if she kept it up. Truth be told, I thought it was about the cutest thing I'd ever seen. It must have been some sort of nervous habit, although I didn't know what she had to be nervous about. But if I'm being honest, it killed me when she did it. She would purse her lips out, as if in deep concentration, and just twirl and pull away. It cracked me up, it really did. I just wanted to know what she could be thinking so hard about. How many worries could a fourteen-year-old girl have?

"I dunno Doug, I gotta go. Maybe I'll stop by."

I hung up the phone and turned back to Tammy.

"Your brother has a real taste for blood," I told her.

She rolled her eyes again.

"Yeah, when it's not his."

She was always saying things like that. They weren't particularly smart or poetic or anything, they just made perfect sense. The right thing to say at the right time. I don't really know how to explain it, but I knew it when I heard it.

"I should probably go over there."

"Why? Now you have a taste for blood? War videos aren't enough?"

"Not a taste for it. I'm thinking maybe I should stop it. Nitin didn't say anything about Toby. And he's a good guy. When I had strep earlier this year he walked Cheyenne to the bus stop for the whole week. He told her that his dad had known our dad, that they had been in Iraq together a couple of years ago and that his dad always said what a great guy my dad was, and not just because he got killed."

"He was," she said matter-of-factly.

"Well, I'm not going to let Nitin get beat up for something he didn't say," I told her, standing up. "Wait here, I'll be back."

She immediately rose off the couch, reaching for her sneakers.

"You're crazy if you think I'm not coming."

I could tell she was serious, and knew from the look on her face that it was pointless to argue. I had been on the receiving end of a very similar expression from my mother many times.

I shouted to Mom that we were headed to the park, and we hopped on our bikes. The sun was hot and the day muggy, as to be expected for July in Virginia Beach. I pedaled fast, the exercise and adrenaline soaking me in sweat before we even reached the end of the block. I paused at the stop sign, noticing where someone had placed a "caring" sticker on it.

Tammy quickly fell behind, which was fine with me. I didn't turn around to gauge her progress. I knew she wouldn't ask me to wait and I didn't really want her to see what I was going to do. Especially since I didn't even know what I was going to do.

When I pulled up to the park, it looked like I might already be too late. I jumped the curb and rode up the incline past the jungle gym and swing sets, where a crowd was gathered around the basketball court.

I jumped off my bike, letting it fall where it lay, and squeezed through the dozen or so neighborhood kids who had gathered to see Toby dole out his latest punishment. His family had transferred in a couple of years ago, and he had harassed and bullied half of Great Neck Middle School since then. I had had a few run-ins with him before, but nothing too serious, luckily.

The blacktop on the basketball court was faded and cracked, pockets of inconsiderate weeds sprouting up randomly. The orange rims of the hoops were spotted with rust, nets long gone. In the middle of this stage Toby stood towering over Nitin, clearly enjoying his audience.

I think that was what appalled me the most. It wasn't the venom or foul words he was spewing, or even the threat of physical violence that everyone watching knew was right around the corner. I could understand anger and violence. My family's history, its very roots, were steeped in a controlled and necessary violence. Growing up in a military family, on military bases during a time of war, my dad who he was, I understood the need for forceful action. But I couldn't understand taking pleasure in it, and I couldn't accept inflicting it just for the sake of it.

A seagull landed along the edge of the crowd, catching my eye. I thought it strange for it to be this far from the ocean. Head up, he picked his way through the crowd, not a care in the world. Ignored, and in turn oblivious to the drama playing out around him.

"Leave him alone."

The words had left my mouth, but I didn't recognize the voice. I felt the crowed turn in my direction, but was only aware of Nitin and Toby. One foot stepped off the curb onto the blacktop. Then the other. Slowly. I was surprised at how calm I felt, how in control. Toby was bigger than I was, my recent growth spurt notwithstanding, but it was something much more than his size that painted the menacing picture. His willingness for violence, and even more so his desire for it, made him seem larger than his actual stature. I'm not sure what made me think he wouldn't stomp my head in and go about his day. Maybe it hadn't yet occurred.

The seagull strutted confidently in my peripheral. Pecking. I wondered what he thought of us.

Toby turned in my direction, sneering. But I thought I sensed a slight hesitation in his reaction, maybe an internal check of nerves. Predictably, he said something along the lines of, "Whatchu gonna to do about it?" If I hadn't been a participant, I'd have said the whole scene was comically reminiscent of an after-school special.

In fact, I almost laughed out loud, I really did. An actual thought that ran through my head: *Hey, maybe this is going to be alright. Maybe I'm not committing suicide.* It was then that I realized I was actually going to fight Toby Barton. And I was okay with it.

For his part, Nitin looked like a death row prisoner who had just received the governor's phone call. Obvious relief, mixed with a healthy amount of appreciation. He slowly backed away, extricating himself from the scene, more than content to find the shadows. Just me and Toby, eye to eye.

Beside me, the seagull flew away. I wondered if I'd ever see him again. Even if I did, I wouldn't know it.

I wish I had the dirty details, the blow by blow of what happened next. I do remember that Toby pushed me, hard, two-handed to the chest. Whether I flew backwards through the air or just lost my footing and fell, well, I guess that depends on who is telling the story. I was told afterwards that I reacted quickly, tackling him, but to me it was just an adrenaline soaked struggle, one long reel with no defined actions or movements. Arms flying, taking as good as you got. I do know it was the biggest and most legit fight I had ever been a part of; I had had my share of wrestling and shoving matches, but other than giving Connor that bloody nose, I had never really even punched someone in the face. And I had always felt terrible about that.

But here I was, in a knock-down, kick-ass fight with Toby Barton. Rolling around on the neighborhood basketball court, throwing my fists as hard and wildly as they would allow me. I could hear the crowd, but they were distant, a slow roar playing over the scene. And then everything suddenly sped back up to real time. Powerful arms grabbed me from behind. An adult's voice boomed with authority, and just like that, it was over.

Panting and wild-eyed, I looked across Mr. Simmons at Toby, feeling my adrenaline drain, wondering if he was as relieved as I was it was all over. He didn't appear to be. Toby was bouncing up and down, screaming curse words, trying to climb around Mr. Simmons to get back at me. That was when I realized that Toby was not wired like I was, and it had been a mistake to assume he was. It was like the religious zealots that we were fighting in Iraq and Afghanistan. I remember that after 9/11, I had asked Dad why they actually *wanted* to die in order to kill other people. He had told me that he didn't waste his time trying to figure out the thought processes of crazy people, that it was an exercise in futility. He said it was a mistake to assume everyone thought as rationally as we do. It was a form of underestimation, and something that you had to be careful not to get trapped into. Toby Barton, I realized, was not a rational being like I was, and shouldn't be treated as such.

I, on the other hand, was most definitely happy the fight was over. After a quick inventory, I accounted for all my teeth, but could feel some welts forming. The whole thing had probably lasted a grand total of a minute, maybe two. Which, of course, felt like a veritable eternity. I was able to take some pride in seeing blood dripping from Toby's bottom lip and a growing mouse under his left eye. The nerves that had been absent pre-fight were now popping like fireworks. The adrenaline was wearing off, and I found my hands were shaking. I stuffed them in my pocket, steadied my chin.

Then I saw Tammy standing at the back of the crowd. She tried to break eye contact with me and I realized what she had done.

I was relieved and angry at the same time. I now fully understood that Toby was a lunatic, and who knows how the fight would have ended without her father's intervention. But I also was hurt that she didn't trust me enough to take care of this on my own. And of course there was the whole aspect of getting caught. A vision of Mr. Simmons walking me to my front door and telling my mom what had happened was enough to make me cringe.

And that was exactly what happened. "Let's go, Nate. Now," he growled. "I'm guessing your mother is going to want to know about this."

So, with Tammy and Doug in tow, the four of us started the journey to my house, the very image of a perp walk.

No one spoke for those blocks, the only sound a loose spoke on my bike. I walked it next to me, in no rush to meet my fate – *click, click, click* – the rhythmic pattern calling out, *dead man walking, dead man walking*. Mr. Simmons did not look happy, but I swore I could sense an air of joy radiating from Doug. He kept turning around to look at me – yes, there was a definite gleam in his eye. Was that a smile he was trying to suppress? What the hell was he so happy about? I pushed the thought from my head, heeding Dad's words about that old exercise in futility.

At that moment, a longing for my father washed over me, grabbing at me fiercely in the gut. *God, no, not now, do not start crying*

right now, walking down the street towards a punishment, fresh from a
fight and in front of Doug and Tammy.

But it didn't help. I felt my lips harden and throat tighten. I just
knew that he would understand. That I had fought for *something*, to
protect someone. Wasn't that what he gave his life for?

I could see his stern look, his insightful eyes. He would probably
have given me a light punishment, but somehow would have let me
know that what I did had been right. A wink, a swipe across the head,
something to let me know he wasn't mad, wasn't disappointed. To me,
that was the most important thing. I didn't care what they did to me.
Throw me to the gallows – I just hoped that somewhere, he wasn't
disappointed in me.

The next few minutes went as expected. Mr. Simmons told my
mother what he had seen, but also what Tammy had told him. She
thanked Mr. Simmons before quickly leading me inside. Tammy's
pleading look caught my eye when she turned to leave. I ignored the
silent request for forgiveness.

"Toby Barton, huh?" my mom said, once we sat down on the
couch.

I just nodded, still thinking of Dad, still afraid any spoken words
would break the dam.

"I've heard things about him. He's pretty big, isn't he? Kind of a
bully?"

I nodded again.

"And he was picking on that Noton boy, the small boy that lives at
the end of the block?

"Nitin," I corrected.

"Nitin. Right, sorry. Well, go get a bag of frozen peas and let's ice
that eye. Don't want everyone thinking he got a good shot on you."

I stood up, slowly. I reached to my right eye, felt the puffiness. My hand moved up to my head, where at least three or four bumps were starting to form. Between the adrenaline of the fight and the fear of punishment at home, I hadn't realized how sore I was.

After I returned to the couch, she watched me with sorrowful eyes.

"There was barely a day that your daddy was home that I wasn't icing some part of him. Ever wonder why we always had a freezer full of frozen vegetables but never ate them for dinner? Looks like we'll be continuing that tradition with the next generation, huh?"

I shook my head violently, despite the headache I was just then noticing.

"No, Ma, I promise, I won't get in any more fights. I'm sorry."

She nodded, and we stayed silent for some time.

"Remember when you asked me what we had been doing?" she finally asked me.

Confused, I looked over at her.

"The day it happened. You wanted to know what we had been do-ing at the exact time he was in that firefight. And I thought about it, a lot. It took some time, but I remembered. I was praying. Cheyenne was in the bath, you were watching the game, and I was in the bed-room, on my knees, praying. Not my normal prayer, not for him to come home safely. I was praying for my family that night, for their peace. At the time I didn't know why I was praying for that. I do now."

The tears had started, for both of us, and my mother took me in her arms. She tried to soothe me, but I was inconsolable.

"I miss him Ma, I really miss him. Why did it have to be him? Why did he leave us?"

I blubbered, heaving with sobs. She just held me. I knew she didn't have the answers I was looking for, and that was okay. There were none. I rested my head in her lap, and we cried together.

I didn't get grounded for that fight, and after a few days of thinking on it, I decided that wherever my dad was, he was probably proud of me.

Chapter 15

"HIT IT BUTLER, hit it like you got a pair!"

It felt like the bright red sled was pushing back, but I wasn't going to give in. My shoulder was raw, thighs burning. I could feel the dirt on my face mix with sweat and run into my eyes. It felt great.

It's kind of strange to admit, but somewhere along the way, without ever really noticing it, the momentum of life moved us forward. Things like dentist appointments and holidays happened, not that we had a choice. And so did football practice. I am happy to report that I had not only made the Landstown High JV football team, but was the starting free safety.

The guys' deployment had been extended, and while Spencer wouldn't specifically say so, I got the feeling they had been re-assigned to Afghanistan as part of the president's troop surge. I had read about capture/kill missions that had reportedly taken place ahead of the surge, and figured that SEALs had to be involved.

So while he hadn't been home to help me prepare for August's two-a-days, Spencer emailed me PT evolutions and criticized my times. Starting early that summer, I would set the alarm for 6:00 most mornings. I would knock out 200 pushups in sets of twenty-five while drinking a smoothie Mom had prepared the night before. Then I'd run three miles through the neighborhood, hopefully finishing before the sun was too high and the oppressive humidity had fully kicked in. Sit-ups, pull-ups, flutter kicks and planks would be followed by Mom making a big breakfast, usually eggs with bacon or sausage, sometimes waffles. Never pancakes.

After breakfast, I would either take a nap, or if a swell was in, head to the jetty to surf. It was a relief that after the scare of last winter Mom still let me go. I liked to think that she trusted me enough not to worry. Or at least she had enough faith in me to know that I wouldn't kill myself out there. She certainly didn't come watch me anymore.

Thanks to Spencer's workouts, which were in addition to team organized weightlifting sessions three afternoons a week, I crushed the two-a-days. Don't tell Coach Tapper, but I actually enjoyed them, seeing how hard I could push myself, testing body and mind.

Now we were finishing practice the day before our first game of the season, and this barely-cushioned steel-tackling sled was all that stood before forty-two freshmen and sophomore players and the end of practice. When Coach had told the team we could hit the showers if someone could push the dummy twenty yards in ten seconds, I immediately stepped forward, the SEAL adage, "It pays to be a winner" echoing in my head.

While I refused to question the wisdom of my enthusiasm, I had a feeling my teammates were. As my feet pushed wildly against turf, the sled groaned forward slower than any of us would have liked. I had stepped in front of much bigger, stronger players who probably had a better shot of meeting the time, and my ass was on the line. Gharun Reed, our sophomore running back, was one of them. The only reason he wasn't on varsity was because there were already two all-state seniors at the position. Heck, he already looked like a SEAL. He must have gone through puberty when he was about eight years old. He had grabbed me by my shoulder pads, trying to pull me back when I had volunteered. Too late.

"You better make it," he breathed through my facemask before pushing me forward.

I made the twenty yards, but knew it had taken more than ten seconds. When the sled crossed the goal line, my teammates didn't hide their disappointment. Most had already taken a knee with water bottles, helmets on the ground. A chorus of groans made their position clear.

"Helmets on, line up!" hollered Coach. "Suicides!"

Threats in the form of curses were liberally hurled in my direction as we lined up on the goal line. My back screamed, my lungs burned from the sled run, but there was no way I wasn't going to complete this last painful drill at full speed. Peer pressure and embarrassment are great motivators.

The whistle blew, and we were off. Some running hard, most just going through the motions. Bend down, touch the 20-yard line, back to the goal line. Mid-field, back to the goal line. The far 20, goal line. A final 100-yard dash. Despite my best efforts, I finished third, behind Gharun and Darren Montgomery, our quarterback and an athletic freak. Each player collapsed in the end zone as they finished, waiting for the rest of the team to complete the drill.

Walt Breuer was an offensive lineman, a huge kid. Well over 200 pounds, he was notoriously slow. While the rest of the team was sucking down water in the end zone, he was just reaching the far goal line before starting the final 100. We cheered him on before noticing something was wrong. As he lurched forward, he double clutched, and quickly moved his hand to his butt. He then fell on his face, and we saw what the problem was.

Walt's pants had split right up his backside, revealing his bare ass.

You can imagine our reaction while he scrambled to cover his butt and hold his torn pants up. But they fell to his knees, tripping him, and he went ass over tea kettle once again.

We, of course, were now rolling with unrestrained laughter in the end zone, watching the debacle with pleasure. Coaches too. Walt, not so much. Holding his pants (for the most part) up with one hand, he finally lumbered across the finish line. The extended middle finger on his free hand only amplified our amusement.

"Dammit, Nate, that may have been worth it," Gharun said, loudly enough for the rest of the team to hear. "I just want to know why he wasn't wearing any drawers." I gave him an appreciative half smile. Everyone headed to the locker room.

I had trouble sleeping that night. Thoughts of our game against Princess Anne the next day ran in a continuous loop, singeing my already-ragged nerves. I stared at the ceiling. I had always dreamed about what my first high school game would be like. Now that vision had changed and a sadness settled over the event.

Dad had always made fun of himself for being like Al Bundy and basking in the glory of his high school football days. He would get a child-like look in his eyes when talking about those Friday night games and said the next best thing to playing in them would be watching me play in them. Now that they were here, he wasn't.

I dressed slowly that morning, taking my time donning the black and silver jersey. Number 24. Dad's old number. Mom had neatly pressed it the night before, humming over the ironing board like she had with his uniforms. It sucked that everything reminded us of him. Without thinking I punched a hole in the wall, surprising myself. I groaned when I saw the concave knuckle marks. The senseless destruction was depressing.

"What are you doing in there?"

The tiny but authoritative voice came through the closed door. To its credit, it made me smile.

"Come on in, Chey," I said, plopping down on my bed, shaking my right hand.

She breezed in, dressed cutely in pink corduroy pants and a white turtleneck.

"Naathan," Cheyenne crooned in a mock English accent, "whatever is the problem?"

Following suit, I attempted my best English butler imitation.

"Whatever do you mean, my dear? Everything is peachy in here."

"Marvelous," she warbled, twirling elegantly back towards the hallway. "Just marvelous, my lad. See to it that you are ready to depart for university in a jiffy."

"Likewise, madam, likewise."

She curtsied, before noticing something on my desk.

"What are those?"

I looked over to where her fully extended arm and index finger were directed. A small pile of yellow papers was sitting out.

"Daddy's notes. I was just re-reading them."

"I want to see them."

"You've seen most of them."

"But not all?"

I shook my head.

"Not all. I found a couple more over the past few months. He was a good hider."

"I know," she said, matter-of-factly. "I never know when another note will pop up. I just found one in my doll house. Can you believe that? *In my doll house!*"

I laughed, and grabbed her around the waist.

"You're getting to be too big for me to pick you up anymore, you know that?"

"That's 'cause you're a wimp! I would think a big bad football player would have no trouble lifting a tiny eight-year-old."

I acted like I was going to drop her, but she wasn't fooled.

"You would never drop me," she said, suddenly serious, staring me in the face.

"You are right about that, Chey."

We won that game against Princess Anne, and the next one, and the next. In fact, we kept winning and finished the season undefeated, the first time Landstown JV had done that since anyone could remember.

"Just wait until we all get to varsity next year," Gharun said. "We're going to win state."

The twenty-five or so kids gathered at Darren's house were both celebrating the season and taking advantage of a parentless opportunity. It was your typical high school party, the air uncomfortable but hopeful, brimming with possibilities. While still early in the night and thus far uneventful, not one of us didn't have hopes that someone would at least lean on – if not obliterate – accepted propriety.

"*If* we all make varsity," Darren said. He scanned the group of players casually eating pizza in his kitchen. A group of girls listening to music in the living room went largely ignored – most of us were in that awkward stage where if we did realize we wanted to interact with them, we were even less aware of how to go about it.

It wasn't entirely clear whether Darren was talking about himself or the rest of us. I felt his eyes on me, focused too heavily in my direction. I grinded my teeth, had to force myself to hold his look. Darren, quarterback, unquestioned star of the team, and arrogant bastard. Coach Monsoor already had him earmarked as the starting varsity quarterback next year as a sophomore. He had nothing to worry about. I, for one, never knew where I stood with Darren, or for that matter, the rest of the team. I definitely wasn't part of the inner circle, the uber-aggressive jock crowd that dominated our high school. Whether by choice or circumstance was immaterial.

"We'll make it," Gharun said. He leapt up, putting Darren in a headlock. "And, QB 1, we'll be depending on that golden right arm to take us to the Promised Land."

"States or bust," he said, sliding out of the hold. He performed an exaggerated head shake, his way of flaunting long blond locks. "I just hope everyone else is on the same page and can pull their weight. Because I plan on at least two state titles before I graduate."

Again, real or imagined, the comment felt directed at me. I was undersized, and everyone knew the six-foot burners populating the wide receiver position in our district could run right past me. I heard the jabs in practice, and certainly the trash talk in games, but hadn't let them bother me. Or at least tried not to. My dad always said that the strong turned negatives into positives. I could fold, or I could use them as fuel, as motivation.

I slid off my stool and walked into the living room. Mostly freshmen girls whispering amongst themselves, nervously nibbling on chips. Some trying to make eye contact with us. Mostly with Darren. Brittany Spears played on the stereo while a few of the braver girls did their best to entice the football players to dance.

I had invited Tammy, but she wasn't the biggest fan of football parties. Even JV ones. She had made clear, several times, her feelings about jocks. I considered calling her and trying to change her mind, but eventually put the phone back in my pocket. For the most part, the girls here looked through me. I made my way through the crowd and faded into a love seat in the corner.

Biggy came on. I made a concerted effort to nod my head with the beat, "...*birfdays was the worst days*..." but quickly realized why effort was the antithesis of cool. I sunk lower into the cushions, wondering if I should be embarrassed by my display.

"I stove these fogs!"

The voice surprised me, from behind. I wheeled around, hoping it would be Tammy, knowing it wasn't. Laura Hind smiled down at me, dancing with a Solo cup.

"Huh?" was all I could muster.

She leaned into my ear, screaming. "I said, I *love* this song!"

I nodded amicably, agreement being the path of least resistance.

"Me too."

"Laura!"

She stuck her hand out.

"Nate."

"I know, we have Spanish together! You're on the football team!"

Again, I agreed.

She said some more things, most of which I couldn't make out due to volume and apathy. Don't get me wrong: I was aware of social responsibilities, I just didn't always have the energy to adhere to them. Eventually I stood up and walked away in the middle of her conversation without even the common courtesy of a bullshit excuse.

The guys were still in the kitchen, huddled closer now, whispering. I sat unnoticed in the corner. Suddenly they all stood up, following Darren to the basement door. Gharun motioned to me. I followed.

"Hurry, shut the door," someone hissed. I was the last one to reach the basement stairs, and quickly closed the door behind me. I was now part of the plan, even if I didn't know what it was. Darren stood at the bottom of the steps, looking up at me impatiently.

"Coming?"

I bounded down the stairs and followed everyone into the adjacent room. The sudden lack of noise was disconcerting, with only soft bumps of bass from upstairs reverberating softly. A worn, wraparound sofa sat in the middle of the space, framing a wooden coffee table and old entertainment center. The drop ceilings were old and low, making me feel tall. A musty smell told me that the basement had flooded before.

"What's going on?" I whispered to Gharun, but he just smiled and told me to wait.

Darren reached behind the entertainment center, coming back with a plastic bottle. There was no label on it. He swirled the clear liquid tantalizingly, grinning.

"Bottom's up, boys," Darren said, taking a small swig from the bottle. He grimaced painfully and suppressed a gag, but once he got it down the grin returned.

He held the bottle out. "Who's next?"

Gharun stepped forward, grabbed it.

"Shit, I'll show you how to drink that. Gimme the bottle."

He grabbed it out of Darren's hands, confidently putting it to his lips. His throat visibly contracted as the liquid flowed out of the bottle. A murmur went through us, and we looked on, awe-struck as Gharun chugged.

"Ah," he smacked when he finally pulled the bottle back.

I still didn't know exactly what was in it, but instinctively reached out anyway.

"Let me hit that," I said bravely.

A disbelieving groan went through the crowd when I grabbed the bottle. That made me even more determined to drink longer than Gharun and Darren had. I took a quick breath, and raised the bottle for my first taste of hard alcohol.

The liquid immediately burned my lips in a not-unpleasant way, with the sting following through to my tongue, down my throat, and landing warm in my stomach. My brain turned off, numb to the taste and scorching pain, allowing me to chug until I felt a hand pull the bottle away. I realized my eyes had been closed, and I had no idea how much I had drank. My brain turned back on, a little slower than before. More numb. My throat and stomach ached in a good way.

"Damn, Nate, save some for us," someone said. I wasn't sure who.

I felt dizzy, warm, and a little sick. I didn't feel like myself. I didn't feel like anything, really. That's the thought that came to mind. It felt good, it just didn't feel like me.

I watched with interested eyes as the rest of the guys took swigs, laughing loudly and making fun of those who couldn't keep it down. When the bottle came back to me I took an equally long drink, and immediately had to sit down. After a few minutes, it seemed that the room was not quite stable. Now I wasn't sure if I liked this feeling or not.

"Darren. DARREN." I tried to get his attention, but wasn't sure if I was whispering or yelling. He stood above me, laughing at someone's joke. I pulled on his sleeve. A little kid getting an adult's attention.

"DARREN!" I called out, definitely loud this time. He finally looked down, annoyed.

"Darren, how do you get outside? I think I need some fresh air." The words were difficult, slow and foreign.

"Jesus, Butler, you better not puke in my house. There's a side door over there," he said, pointing towards an alcove next to the washer and dryer. "Just go out there to the backyard."

I'm pretty sure I nodded at him, then picked my way as steadily as I could towards the door.

Once outside, I gulped the fresh, cool air and my head immediately felt better. In fact, I felt pretty damn good. I looked around the large yard, dark except for the light coming from the kitchen window, just barely illuminating the back deck. It was silent, peaceful here. Soft bass and distant laughs made my spot in the dark that much more isolated. I liked it that way.

I soon realized I had a pretty interesting vantage point out here in the pitch black. I could see in, but no one could see me.

I shivered, burped, burped again. For whatever reason that struck me as hilarious, so I sat in the cool grass, laughing at my growling stomach while watching a high school party unfold.

Claudia Silko was trying, unsuccessfully, to not look at Matt Karpos from across the room. But Matt was watching Julia Gaither, which elicited a dirty look from Claudia. She rolled her eyes towards Laura, motioning to Julia's back. That really cracked me up; I rolled on my side, laughing hysterically. After a moment I had forgotten what was so funny, but gave up trying to remember when a great idea hit me. Tammy!

I would go to Tammy's house! I knew she was home. I looked at my watch. Squinted. Closed one eye. Rubbed them both. Dancing digits made it hard to read, but it seemed to be 10:25. I pulled myself up from the lawn, no easy feat, and started searching the dark for an exit.

I certainly gave it a good effort, but for the life of me couldn't find a damn gate. I don't know, maybe the fence didn't even *have* a gate. But I knew I wasn't going back through the house and exiting through the front door, so I decided the only reasonable thing to do would be to jump the fence.

The fence was wooden and old and didn't seem to be in the best shape. I did my best to get a grip on the top, but it kept splintering in my hand. Soon I was pulling large chunks of the fence down and getting no closer to the other side. I decided I would run at it, jump, and scramble over the top. I walked off a good fifteen paces before turning around, eyeballing my target. With a deep breath I took off, imagining I was lining up a hit on that damn tackle dummy. CRACK! I couldn't tell you if I jumped at all, but if I did it was way too late. I basically crashed straight into the fence. A whole section of it bent forward with the collision between body and wood. I figured, what the hell, it's already broken, I might as well keep going. So I put my shoulder into the fence, bringing the whole section down in a clap of splintering lumber, allowing me to make my escape at full speed.

I sprinted through the front yard into the street. The moon shone brighter than usual, the stars more numerous. I pondered their distance, their meaning, as I ran through the night. A side path cut through the park to Tammy's house.

I was quickly out of breath and slightly dizzy. Once at the park my thoughts went back to my fight there over the summer. The reflection was a positive one, and I threw a few hard jabs into the night. It seemed like so long ago.

I needed to sit down, so I did, in the middle of the basketball court. A cool wind whistled, and I groaned, remembering that I had left my jacket at Darren's. Something else for Mom to bitch about. I watched the tops of the trees shudder, bending from the right and making their way across my peripheral, moving like a wave. The wind called me, it spoke to me. Blades of grass danced, weaving and chattering. Mocking my pain, telling me to get over it.

"*Be a man*," they said to me. "*How long are you going to mourn?*" they mocked.

"I told, you, I'm done mourning!" I yelled out, slapping the weeds at my feet.

Defiantly, the wind picked up, howling now, taunting me. I thought of the dead Ranger, I thought of Spencer and Bull and LT Hagen and SEAL Team 2 and dead Iraqis and fatherless children and IED's and I thought of my dad, and I wondered where he was, if he was a part of this wind, if his energy lived on in it.

"Then why are you so angry?" a voice called out. It was hollow and soulful. I spun around to find its owner.

A silver haired man emerged from the dark.

"Who are you?" I asked.

"You know who I am. Who are you?"

The man's clothes were in tatters, his grey, unkempt beard matching the mat on his head.

"I'm Nathan."

"I know who you are."

"Then why did you ask?"

"What are you so angry about, Nathan?"

"Who said I was angry?"

"One doesn't get to say whether one is angry or not. It's in the eyes, in the position of your shoulders. In how you carry your chin. It's who you are."

"Anger isn't so bad. What's wrong with anger? I'll take anger over sadness or embarrassment any day of the week. What the hell do you know? You're just a bum."

"Just a bum," he answered, laughing a toothless grin. "I'm not a bum, I'm the truth."

"Whoever you are, leave me the hell alone."

He laughed once more.

"That's all up to you, Nathan."

The wind picked up again, and I fell back against the blacktop, eyes closed. I pulled long funnels of air through my nose, out again.

Inhale, exhale.

When I opened my eyes some time later, the visitor was not even a memory. My temples ached. I shivered, not from the cold air. Although dizzy, I suddenly remembered my mission, a renewed motivation to see Tammy. I scraped myself off the ground, standing in a fighter's stance as I had done on this same spot months earlier. I swung my fists again, faster, faster, harder, harder, at an unseen enemy. At the wind, at the silver-haired man, at Toby, Darren, Doug, Uncle Spencer; I swung and I swung and I swung until I was too tired to swing any longer and the tears and snot wet my face and I was ready to go see Tammy.

"Tammy... Tammy..." I tapped on her bedroom window again, willing her to wake up, waiting for a light to invite me into her warmth.

"Tammy!" I rapped the window harder, desperate. Finally, the blinds came alive, and I crouched in the dark, waiting.

A hiss came through the cracked window.

"Nate? What the hell are you doing? Do you know how loud you are? What time it is?"

"I called you," I tried to explain. "I called your cell phone but didn't call the house phone because I didn't want to wake your dad up."

"You damn near broke my window. Do you think that might wake him up? What's wrong with you anyway? You seem... stranger than normal."

"Tammy, it's been the strangest night ever. We drank something at Darren's party that made me feel – I don't know, but it made me feel."

"You're not making sense, Nate. Shhh – hold on."

She pulled back from the window sharply, and I could see her looking back into her bedroom. She was wearing lacrosse shorts and a tank top, and it occurred to me that I had never seen anyone look so good before in my life.

"You look amazing, Tammy," I told her through the window. "I mean it. I should have said it a long time ago, but you do."

She turned back to me, but didn't have time to respond. The window next to hers lit up, quickly followed by an angry knock on her bedroom door.

"Get out of here!" she hissed, and I took off alone, towards home, smiling like an idiot the whole way.

I managed to make it back into my bedroom without breaking my neck or waking my mother. It struck me how dark, how quiet the house was this time of night. Peaceful. I turned on my desk lamp, sat down, the single dusty bulb casting shadows on the walls.

I looked around. My home; my familiar, comforting bedroom. Posters of bands, girls, my JV letter and trophies on the bureau. Dirty clothes on the floor, clean ones on the bed. Just the way I liked it.

Instinctively I went for the bottom desk drawer, feeling for the shoebox. I took it out, placed it carefully on the floor. I sat cross-legged in front of it, hearing echoes as I stared.

Finally, I lifted the cardboard lid and reached my hand in. It was like touching my own face. I could tell by feel where everything was, which ribbon was attached to which medal. The familiar textures were soothing, each shape with its own story.

The first one I pulled out was his Purple Heart. The wide, thick ribbon. The raised heart, the engraving on the back. "For Military Merit."

The circular, coin-like feel of the Iraq Campaign Medal and the Afghanistan Campaign medal. His Bronze Star with the V-device, numerous Good Conduct Medals, a Marksmanship Medal, Presidential Unit Commendation Ribbon, Combat Action Ribbon, Joint Service Commendation Medals, and the Silver Star, awarded posthumously.

I laid them out in a line, all sixteen of them. He had other commendations, awards, and ribbons that he had rated. I took those out too. None of which we had known about when he was alive.

Then I reached back in, and took out the last pin. To me, the one with the most weight. His gold Trident, the only tangible symbol of achievement he ever talked about. The one badge he wore every day, on every uniform. He rated many ribbons that he didn't wear, even on his Dress Blues. The Trident was different.

I ran my hands along the sharp edges. The glow off its gold plating was beyond the levels afforded by that 40-watt desk lamp. It radiated, pulsed in my hands. It felt like 100 pounds, 1,000 pounds. I placed it back in the bottom of the box, knowing I didn't deserve to hold that pin. That was to be earned.

There were other items in the box that I ignored. Not for lack of interest or importance, but for modesty's sake. Newspaper articles about him, about his death. Some tried to be about his life, but they were all about his death.

The public loved a story about a hero getting killed, especially a SEAL. They weren't quite as concerned when they were alive, but they sure cared when they were dead.

They loved the story. They loved a badass, especially when the badasses were fighting, and dying, for them. It made them feel like they had something in common. Gave them a sense of closeness, of similarity. That they were on the same side.

I carefully filled the shoebox back up and put it back in its place in the drawer. I then flicked off the light, tiptoed through the hallway into the bathroom and puked.

Chapter 16

I WAS ONLY SUPPOSED to be the lookout. For Cameron. He said he took stuff from the Exchange all the time and never got caught. But just to be safe, he told me to watch the clerk, make sure he wasn't looking.

And I did. Watch out. But when I saw Cameron filling his pockets with gum and candy, the temptation became too great. No one was looking anyway, I had already made sure of that.

The hand reaching out didn't seem like mine. Didn't seem to be connected to my body, didn't seem to be controlled by my mind. Before I knew it, it was gripping a pack of Lick-A-Maid Fun Dip and shoving it in my coat pocket.

And now that pack of Lick-A-Maid is sitting on our coffee table while Mom stands over it, not saying a word. When the MP finally releases his grip on the hood of that very coat, I throw myself on the couch, mid-tantrum. Over my hysterics he starts to explain to my mother what happened, but she quickly cuts him off, uttering a sentence that shakes me to my core.

"Please Officer, if you don't mind waiting a minute. My husband will home any minute and I know he will want to hear this directly from you."

From the rear of the house the baby cries. Mom excuses herself. I continue to bury my head in the cushion and wail. The sound of car tires suddenly becomes audible. It grows louder, stopping outside the front door. The thud of the driver's side door closing is followed by quick but unhurried steps. A key rattles the front door. Both mine and the MP's eyes flash to that door, watching the knob slowly rotate, the outside coming in. I sit up sharply, wiping my face frantically, hoping my heart won't explode.

Chapter 17

THE NEXT MORNING a none-too gentle rap jolted me from sleep. Wow, what a headache! Saliva seemed hard to come by – a sticky tongue struggled to wet my lips, and my eyelids were crusted over. I groaned, pulling the comforter over my head. My first hangover.

"Nathan, someone is here to see you," Mom said, standing dispassionately in the doorway. She spoke coldly and with more volume than I figured necessary.

I pulled my head up look at her. Her glare reflected back at me, shadowy. We paused, aware of the déjà vu.

"Who is it?"

She came closer, throwing the comforter back over my head.

"My goodness, Nathan, your breath is terrible!" she said. "Brush your teeth and come downstairs!"

"I just woke up, Mom! Your breath smells like flowers first thing in the morning?"

"I can't say if it's flowers or perfume, but I know it doesn't smell like a decaying animal. What did you do last night?" Then, not wanting the answer: "We'll be downstairs, waiting."

I groaned, and let her leave my room. Wait a minute, "we'll?" Could it be Tammy?

That thought got me out of bed and into the bathroom. After brushing and Scoping vigorously, I tossed back two Advil, wet my hair, threw on jeans and a button down shirt, and scrambled downstairs.

"You didn't have to get dressed up for me."

I turned to the slow, Mid-western voice. There was Spencer, sitting at the kitchen table, sipping from a coffee mug.

"Uncle Spencer!" I called out, more enthusiastically than I would have liked.

"Hey there, Little Warrior. Looks like we're going to have to drop that 'Little' soon."

He stood up, and I ran over to him. We shook hands, and he clasped his free one on my shoulder.

"You look like you've been on the Grinder. Been doing those workouts I sent you?"

Any effort at suppressing my grin was useless, although it dissipated as soon as I got a better look at him.

They always came back from a deployment different from when they left. I noticed it the very first time my dad had returned from war. It was more than a red face, scorched by desert sun and wind, or the even leaner, more muscular build from a constant routine of missions, gym time, and inconsistent food. It was in their body language, in their eyes. Fear, pride, sorrow, duty, righteousness, horror, death. It was all there, written in their faces if you knew how to look for it.

"You look different too."

He leaned back, forced his serious face to turn light, and patted his belly.

"MREs, Gatorade, and sand, that's about all I've put in my belly in the past six months," he said. "Those FOB's don't have kitchens."

"And that's why I'm cooking a proper dinner tonight," said my mom. "And the whole platoon is invited."

"When did you get back?" I asked. "Did they move you to Afghanistan to support the surge?"

"Couple of days ago. Did my normal decompress-thing, trying to get off vampire hours."

"Afghanistan?"

"Training mission."

"Bullshit."

"Nathan!"

"It's alright, Gayle. I'll tell you this, Nate. Our 'training mission' was a success. We did our job, and no good guys got hurt."

"No 'training accidents'?" I asked, sarcastically using air quotes.

He shook his head. "Not for us."

Turning to my mom, he asked, "If Nate's OK with it, you mind if I take him for some boys time today?"

She looked at me. I tried to hide my excitement. Not very well.

"I think that's a yes," she said. Her smile was sad but honest. The pain was there, but hope was too. She stood up and placed her mug in the sink. "I'm sure it will be good for him. He didn't come home until after midnight last night. God only knows what he was up to."

Spencer's neck snapped in my direction. "We'll have a talk about that," he said.

A half hour later we had eaten a big breakfast that Mom had all-too-happily prepared, I had changed into more appropriate clothes, and we were speeding up Princess Anne Road in Spencer's Jeep. We drove towards the Naval Amphibious Base, Little Creek, chatting about football and Michael Jackson for the first ten minutes. I kept sneaking glances at Spencer, again realizing how young he was. Somehow the experience and age that had crept into his face over the past year had actually made him seem even younger to me.

"Reach behind your seat," he finally said, not taking his eyes off the road.

I did what I was told, and felt a large wooden object. I pulled it onto my lap, confused. It was a paddle, carved out of stained wood, with small, golden letters across it. I looked back at Spencer, waiting for an explanation.

"Read it."

I did.

Senior Chief Stephen B. Butler,
You gave your life so that others

Could live to fight another day,
Your sacrifice won't be in vain

We'll kill those bastards, every last one,
We won't go home until the job is done

Who knows how many lives you did save,
But the ultimate sacrifice you willingly gave

We know what your Team and Family already do,
That Geronimo's got nothing on you.

Fair Winds and Following Seas,
From your brothers at 3rd PLT, B Co. 3/75th RGRRGT "Currahee"

I let it sink in.

"What is it?"

"Ran into the Ranger platoon we were supporting the night your father was killed. They made that in his honor."

"Nice of them."

"They asked about you. I don't need to tell you the hero stuff they asked me to pass along," he said.

"Yeah, I've heard it all before."

"Doesn't make it not true."

"Never said it wasn't true. Doesn't bring him back either."

Spencer shook head.

"No, it doesn't. Him neither."

He was referring to the Ranger that was killed the same night my father was.

"Did he have any kids?"

"Dunno, they didn't say. Just crossed paths in Kuwait. We weren't too chatty."

"Can you find out for me?"

"Sure. Or you can find out yourself. They're stationed at Ft. Benning. His name was Sgt. Kristoffer Hawkins. Write the CO a letter. I'm sure they'd like to hear from you."

I contemplated the plaque, felt the rough wood. I didn't know what to think. My mind raced. A nice sentiment, I supposed, but it didn't make it any easier on me, my family. The dead Ranger's family. I never doubted the extent of his heroics. It was everyone else that was suspect to me.

"Okay," I said.

"We were going to hang it in the Team 2 compound, but I thought maybe you would like to have it."

I shrugged. "I don't need it. Hang it next to Bin Laden and the nudie pics."

He looked at me, gauging. He understood.

"Roger that."

We didn't speak again until he pulled the Jeep into a large parking lot. We were in a remote corner of the base that I had never seen before. There were no identifying signs and only a few other cars in the lot. In front of us stood a wide wooden overhang facing a long field. Rusted Humvees and tanks with massive bullet holes stretched across the field. This wasn't your run of the mill, civilian target-practice shooting range.

"Cool," I murmured.

"Yeah," Spencer responded. "I know your old man took you to indoor shooting ranges from time to time, but this is going to be more like a SEAL experience."

We got out of the Jeep, and he lifted a long black case out of the back.

"Please tell me you have an M-4 for me to shoot in there."

He gave me a wink.

"Better. An H&K 416."

My eyes lit up. The 416 was now the weapon of choice for most SEAL operators, and was one of my dad's favorite assault rifles. I had held his, but never shot it.

We made our way to the entrance, and I could barely contain my excitement. Any residual fog from last night was gone; I was focused on what was ahead of me.

An older man greeted us. He was missing at least one tooth, and had stringy, gray hair and beard. He smiled when he saw Spencer, but went right for me.

"I know who this sonuvabitch is," he said, the hole in his mouth staring right at me. "This is Mo's boy, rest his soul. Look at those eyes. You look just like your pops, son."

He clasped my hand, shaking it vigorously while Spencer looked on, amused.

"Capt. Fay, Nathan Butler. Nate, this mean old salty dog is an original Naval Special Warfare Operator. A UDT man. He was running around 'Nam wearing nothing but war paint and scalping Gooks while I was just a gleam in my mother's eye."

"And I got my share of scalps." The old man laughed, rearing his head back and opening that shocking mouth. I could smell his breath from several feet away. "But you lucky bastards might have us beat. Of course, if we had the weaponry during our little conflict that you have today, well then..."

"I know, Cap'n, I know. We don't need to compare wieners, at least not right now."

"Good idea, Napoleon. You know they didn't call me Tripod when I was in the Teams because I liked photography." He cackled again.

I was shocked. This was Cap'n? THE Cap'n?

Since I could remember, I had heard stories about this guy. The SEALs I knew spoke with a reverence about him that they didn't afford many men inside the Teams or otherwise.

"Wait. You're the guy that took an upper decker in a senator's private bathroom?"

The wild-eyed look on Cap'n got even crazier, and I thought I had gone too far. Finally he doubled over, howling.

"Once upon a time it is true, I did take a shit in the top tank of some bleeding heart liberal's crapper." He looked at Spencer. "How the hell you guys even know that story? Must have been in '73. Just got back from the shit. We had been sent on some suicide mission to kill an NVA general, even though every swinging dick in the jungle on both sides knew that a treaty had already been negotiated. The war was basically over, the ink just had to dry and we were on our way home. But no, the head shed's got a hard on for this guy, so they send us in after him. After we got our balls shot off and lost two Frogmen there was a formal inquiry in Washington. I was hauled in front of some private sub-committee bullshit 'cause I was the team leader, and got drilled by those candy-ass draft-dodging pansies. Well, my CO had made it very clear before the hearing that if I spoke my mind, as I've been known to do, that I'd be held in contempt of Congress and thrown in the brig. A career-ender. But no way was I going to leave without saying my piece. So, when opportunity knocked, I dropped a steamer in the most thoughtful place I could think of."

Spencer shook his head while locking a magazine in the automatic weapon in his hand. "That's saying your piece, I suppose. But Cap'n, as much as I'd love to, if we stayed here and told stories about your crazy ass, we wouldn't get any shooting done today."

"Well you're right about that, you stodgy little bastard. You sure you're gonna be able to see over the top of that rifle?" He winked at me, pulling greasy hair back over his head into a ponytail. "I could talk a dog off a meat wagon, no doubt about that. But I only tell war stories with fellow warriors, so I take advantage of the opportunity on the rare occasions I am afforded."

I smiled, honored.

"You know what a 'vacuum' is, son?" he asked me.

Unsure, I looked over at Spencer. He shook his head, apparently knowing what was coming.

"Well I'll tell you. When your old man was in BUD/S, first phase now, his class was at parade rest on the quarter deck, waiting for inspection. The instructors were circling like sharks looking for blood in the water. Gig line crooked, speck of sand on your boots? Get wet and sandy. Missed a spot shaving? Drop. And you know what that smelly bastard did in the middle of inspection? He let one fly that was so bad the instructors had no choice but to stop what they were doing. Couldn't be ignored. They screamed and threatened and tried to find out who did it, but no one would fess up, and sure as shit no one would rat. They ran around sniffing the air, trying to find its source. They couldn't find out who did it, so they told everyone to 'turn on the vacuum' – suck air as fast and hard as they could until they could taste the fart."

He shook his head. "Never met a man with a worse intestinal track than your father."

"Adam told me about that," Spencer laughed. "Said after they got done inhaling his gas, the whole class had to be sugar cookies and have an hour of surf torture. As payback his classmates tied him up that night and stuck him in a trash can full of ice water. When they finally pulled him out, despite blue lips and glass nipples, he was blowing bubbles in the water and belting out 'Singing in the Rain' at the top of his lungs."

A dark silence moved over us while each man fell into his own personal thoughts of loss.

The pity party ended as abruptly as it had started with a steady, confident voice.

"So are we gonna shoot or gossip all day? You ready, Nate?" Spencer didn't wait for a response. He hoisted his gun case and started moving.

"Good to go," I told him. Cap'n's wiry frame trudged towards the covered shooting stand. We followed.

He led us to the far end of the range to set up. There were a couple of shotguns, pistols, and some autos already waiting for us, but I couldn't take my eyes off the 416 that Spencer was delicately removing from the case.

It could go full-auto, and Spencer had the 20-inch barrel attached.

"Red dot scope?" Cap'n asked.

"Aimpoint CompM4. And AAC silencer. Took this one on my last two deployments. Wanted Nate to see what we're working with in the

Teams."

"Where's my dad's rifle?"

I didn't mean for it to, but the question's tone sounded accusatory; the words hung in the air, compounding the prior strain. No part of me was sorry I had asked it. I knew they didn't have an answer, and I don't know that it mattered. But at one point he did have a rifle like this one, just like he had had boots, and a truck, and a son. And all those were still somewhere on this earth.

Like with the previous tension, Spencer's staccato response was not a brush off. It was its own answer.

"Cap'n, pass me that 5.56 magazine. I'm going to show Nate how SEALs light up a target. You see that beat up Haji truck 400 meters out?"

He shouldered the rifle, flicking the safety, lining the sights, squeezing off a series of rounds in one slick motion, the movement beautiful and clean, no wasted effort, just a single, smooth ballet.

And with the crack of the shots and distant ping of them finding their target, the second round of tension dissipated into an aura of testosterone and cloud of excitement.

After Spencer cleared and made safe the weapon, Cap'n lifted a steel case of ammo, handing it to him. His focus moved to loading a clip – fingers dexterously handling the full metal jackets like a sculptor with clay.

"His gun is with all of us, every time we shoot," he eventually said. His gaze stayed downrange, lost behind dark glasses.

I smirked, kind of snorted through my nose.

"Gimme a break," I scoffed. "That's the best you could come up with?"

"Unfortunately. Now let's see if you can hit a barn door without shooting your ass off."

As previously mentioned, firearms held a significant place in my family. I had shot at traditional ranges dozens of times, but this one was different. For the next two hours we fired at targets – rusted out cars, tires, cutouts of bad guys hundreds of yards downrange – while racing from obstacle to obstacle. It was exhilarating, and the feeling of power that comes with firing a weapon that can expend 800 rounds a minute was overwhelming. The only thing better would have been shooting at actual terrorists.

After we went Winchester, Spencer started breaking the gun down while Cap'n made his gregarious exit, shouting expletives at another group who had just arrived.

"Quite a character, huh?"

"No kidding. I can't believe that's who you guys have been talking about. Doesn't look like much."

Spencer chuckled. "Those are the ones you gotta watch out for. They're the ones in BUD/S that push you harder, make you want to volunteer to be the bowline man or the front position on your boat crew when your arms are screaming and your teeth are chattering. Who you want on your six when you're in combat kicking in doors and clearing rooms. That's who pushes you to be better, to be the best."

He finished collapsing the rifles, the movement pulling his sleeve up just slightly.

"What's that?" I pointed at his right wrist. While already heavily tattooed, there was some new ink on his forearm I had never seen before.

He looked down before slowly pulling the sleeve higher.

There was a picture of a Native American, parachuting out the back of a C-17. He was in full combat gear, assault rife in locked and loaded position, a warrior's yell on his lips. "Geronimo" was the script that ran under the image, covering Spencer's inner wrist.

We locked eyes. No words needed to be said. He lowered his sleeve, and we made our way to his Jeep.

"Something else I wanted to talk to you about." He spit the words out even more sharply than was his usual curt fashion. They seemed serious and carried weight. I turned, wondering what could have him so pensive.

"I'm home on leave for the next two weeks, then will be gone training for nine months."

I nodded – that was nothing new. They were either training or deployed for most of the year.

"Do you know what Green Team is?"

I had overheard the guys talk about Green Team occasionally after a few beers had loosened their tongues.

He explained, "It's the selection course for DEVGRU. I screened before our last deployment and just found out I made it."

"Team 6," I said in awe.

"I also thought you should know your father screened too, and was accepted. He would have been going to Green Team with me."

We sat in silence as I let this news sink in. Naval Special Warfare Development Group, also called DEVGRU, or SEAL Team 6, was the elite of the elite. U.S. Navy SEALs were the undisputed top fighters on the planet, and their all-stars were Team 6. Just to get to Green Team, the 9-month course that was supposedly more difficult that BUD/S, meant you had separated yourself from the inseparable.

"I can't say I'm surprised," I finally said. "About either of you making it. Congratulations."

"Thanks, but I haven't made it yet. Green Team makes BUD/S look like gym class. I wash out, I'll be out of the Teams in a year."

"You'll make it. And Dad would have too."

Chapter 18

I HAD UNCLE SPENCER IN TOWN for a month, and planned to take advantage of it. I PT'd with him, often Bull, and sometimes LT Hagen, every chilly winter morning and they never took it easy on me.

"Look at that beard, man – you look like Paul Bunyan," Bull told me one morning as we ran along the beach. Spring may have been fast approaching, but in this, the first light of dawn, we could still see our breath. "Napoleon, I think Nate here has a thicker beard than you do."

"Yeah, he's a regular Dan Bilzerian."

Spencer was wearing another one of his ridiculous outfits he loved so much. This morning it was jean shorts cut just barely long enough to hide what mattered, but tight enough to accentuate the outline. And don't think that wasn't by design. An extra small tank top landed just north of his belly button, topped with an American flag bandana on his head and black hiking boots. He smiled, squinting at my face.

"Yeah, that is quite the power growth you got going on over there, Nate. But still a little patchy, don't you think, Bull?"

He examined me closer, agreeing.

"A little patchy. No self-respecting SEAL would go down range with his face like that."

"Yeah, I think you're right. He'd need to thicken that up."

"Absolutely he would."

"You know how you fix that, right?"

"Oh yeah, there is one way to get that patchy beard to fill in, Nate. Pretty easy. All's you gotta do is, when you take a leak, drip a little on your finger. Then what you do is, you wipe a little where the hair isn't growing. It'll fill right in for you."

"Works every time."

I kept running, concentrating on my breathing, one foot in front of the other. For them, a four-mile run in the soft sand was a cakewalk. In fact, they would go do a real PT with their platoon mates after we were done. But for me, this was no joke.

"Really? Does that work?" I asked with a serious a face.

"Sure it does, you just gotta remember to leave it on all day," Bull said.

"Cool, I'll start doing that," I said. "Spencer, you know what might work for your beard?"

He looked over at me.

"What's that?"

Me: Calm, cool. Monotone. "If you smear shit on your face you might actually look like your balls have dropped."

Instantaneously, two things happened: First, Bull's surprised howl of laughter shot out like a cannon, legitimizing my joke. Second, the wind was knocked out of me as Spencer tackled me, knocking me straight to the sand. Unable to catch my breath, he scooped me up and ran with me straight into the ocean, screaming like a madman the whole time.

The cold flash upon entry violently sucked out any breath I may have had in reserve. My head went under and I immediately swirled under a small wave. When I came up for air in the chest-high water, Spencer was howling in front of me, splashing around as if he were at a water park in the height of summer.

"What the fuck!" I yelled, sputtering. "You almost drowned me!"

"So return the favor."

"Go fuck yourself!" I retorted.

"Come on, try to drown me!"

"I should," I said, trying not to let him see my anger. "Since we're going to die of hypothermia anyway."

"Fifteen minutes, probably twenty," he said. "The water temp is in the fifties. We could be in here for at least that long before any sign of hypothermia. Try to drown me. I won't use my hands, won't fight back." As if to prove his point he placed them behind his back, treading water easily with just his legs

I shivered, doing my best to keep my head above the water. The weight of my sneakers, sweatpants and sweatshirt made that difficult. The water was now at my chin, waves spraying my face.

I knew that Spencer wasn't going to let me out of this, and it was only a matter of time before he started calling me a pussy. Better to drown.

I decided I would dive at him as quickly as I could, hoping to catch him off balance. I leapt onto his head, pushing down with both hands. It didn't work. He just stood there, like a granite column, not buckling in the slightest. I pushed down with all my might, both hands on his wet head, actually raising myself completely out of the water. He didn't budge.

Until he did. In a flash, he dove into the frigid Atlantic, my confused body tangling and tumbling on top of him. The second we went under I flashed my limbs in all directions, hoping for a lucky headlock or defensive kick. My arms thrashed under the water, searching, grasping. Swimming in circles, my wild swipes connected with nothing but water. Where had he disappeared to?

I rose to the surface, nervously treading water, every sense on pins and needles. He was under there, somewhere. An unseen great white, circling, waiting for the kill. I spun around, trying to catch a glimpse of my attacker. Thousands of sparkling dimples danced on the surface, the sun's kaleidoscopic artwork trance-like. But no sign of him. Not a bubble, a splash, or a ripple. The small waves continued their never-ending march, one after the other, indifferent towards the fish-man skulking beneath them.

There was an unnerving calm in the ocean. I just knew that at any minute there would be a pull at my leg or an arm around my neck. I was freezing and waterlogged, and realized my best shot would be to head for shore.

I began a persistent combat side stroke, learned in these very waters from my dad, swimming with the current nice and easy towards the beach. Nothing but open ocean stretched before me – and no sign of Spencer. For a brief second I almost worried about him before laughing off the ridiculous thought. Even so, he had been under water for a *long* time.

And then, I saw him. Or rather, he showed himself. Barely a speck on the horizon, he raised himself out of the water, at least 100 yards out to sea. The only way I even knew it was him, that it was even a person, was because he was screaming like a banshee, both hands in the air. Although I couldn't see them, I assumed he had both middle fingers extended. Then, just as quickly as he had appeared, he was gone.

Although unable to follow his path underwater, I was still frighteningly confident that he would be upon me before I would be able to react. I turned, facing the beach, and started a frantic swim. Aided by a few decent waves, I quickly swam the short distance back to shore and shook the water from my hair, trembling violently. What I saw next, I couldn't believe.

Spencer was standing next to Bull on the beach, arms on his hips, watching me stagger through the surf line. Instinctively, I spun back towards the horizon, where just moments before he had been treading water in the middle of the sea. But of course Mother Ocean was a SEAL's natural element, and I experienced the shock that enemies of our country had known every time they had gone against this elite fighting unit for the past fifty-plus years.

"Have a nice dip?" he asked, nonchalant.

I made no attempt at hiding my amazement even as I shook violently.

"You have to be kidding me," I said. "Are you even human?"

Bull laughed, answering for him.

"Nope. He's a SEAL."

My wet clothes had nothing to do with the nervous chill that ran down my back.

"Training, Nate," Spencer told me. "Lots of training. Now let's get you out of those wet clothes before you do get hypothermia and your mother kills me."

My anxious brain spun, my worry palpable. That was just one of the many displays I had personally witnessed that made me doubt my dream. And I knew this was just the tip of the iceberg. I decided to voice my fears, to open up to these surrogates.

"What if I'm never that good? What if I can't cut it?" I finally asked.

I examined their faces. Emotionless, just *being*. It wasn't ego. They just weren't like the rest of the men of this planet, much like professional basketball players or concert pianists weren't.

"It's not for everyone, Nate. In fact, it's for very, very few," Bull said. "There's nothing wrong with being normal, with not being extraordinary. It's okay to toe the line, to be a successful businessman or a teacher. The vast majority of people who have walked this earth have been completely happy and fulfilled just being productive members of society. And if that's your path, I'll be proud of you. Your dad would be too."

The thought shook me to my core, terrified me worse than anything I could imagine. "Unfulfilled promise," was something Dad had spoken of with a venom usually reserved for quitters and liars. It was something to be feared, but most importantly, to be conscious of. I was going to be a part of this brotherhood.

"What if I don't want to be like everyone else? What if I have something inside of me, something that tells me that I'm destined for greater things? That I'm not content just following the next man, pulling my weight, and not going above or beyond? What if I want to be part of something bigger?"

"Then you become a United States Navy SEAL."

Chapter 19

I WAS THRILLED when Spencer's Green Team deployment was pushed another month and he stayed in Virginia Beach. Bull had screened for Green Team as well, and they were due later that spring to start the course that would determine whether they would make SEAL Team 6. Until then they were detailed to light training and mission prep in Virginia Beach. I spent as much time with them as possible.

And spending time with them meant PT. Pushing 'em out, chasing rabbits, pull-ups, leg lifts, dips, flutter kicks, long beach runs and more push-ups, all at the gentle urging of Instructor Detse. There was no doubt in my mind that I was training for more than varsity football now.

The sky was just warming one Saturday morning when I slipped out the front door and sat on the front steps with a protein shake, waiting for my training partner. The morning was dewy with a slight chill, which I would be grateful for in a half hour.

"Good morning." I jumped at the unexpected rumble just inches from my ear. After unclenching my butt cheeks I greeted him with a middle finger.

"You should know – I've got my eyes on you," he murmured in the same slow growl. The sunglasses he was peering over had eyeballs painted over each lens. Naturally a pink tutu with black high-top Chuck Taylors completed the ensemble. And it appeared his legs were shaved – I didn't even want to know.

"Why do you have to always have to be so weird?" I asked seriously, embarrassed to be seen with this specimen.

"Weird? I'm a ballerina by trade, you didn't know that? Check my LinkedIn profile."

I shook my head, knowing that he changed his career on LinkedIn monthly. Crash-test dummy, medical tester, cow inseminator – I'd seen them all.

It was a particularly grueling run that morning, followed by 250 pushups and a half-mile swim in the base pool. After, I was resting on the couch when Mom led Tammy into the living room.

She had kept me at arm's length since the night of my foolish adventure, and the as-of-then unfamiliar tinge of regretful decisions had haunted me since. I had just wolfed down a second breakfast and was watching TV when she appeared, blond hair and piercing hazel eyes stopping my breath. A power I was learning girls had in spades.

"Hi, Nate."

"Tammy."

"I was hoping you would be home."

"I'm here. Surprised to see you. I wasn't sure if you got my messages," I stammered.

"I got them. But I needed some time. I'm still not sure what happened that night. And my dad definitely isn't your biggest fan. He doesn't know I'm here."

"Tammy, I can explain."

She cut me off.

"No need. Just tell me it won't happen again, and we'll leave it at that."

"Never."

"Okay, good."

She paused, looking at the TV.

"War coverage?"

"What coverage there is. Sixty-five U.S. troops were killed in Afghanistan last October, the deadliest month since the war began. And they're showing coverage of protests in D.C."

"Yeah, those pesky rights of the American people. Damn First Amendment."

"The rights we are fighting to protect."

"Enough already. My dad's been to Iraq, everyone we know's dad has been overseas. Don't pull the patriot card on me."

"You're against the war all of a sudden?"

"Who is for war? I'm against all people killing other people."

"What if some people have to be killed so more people can live?"

"It's not that simple."

"No?"

"No."

"Well, I think it is. You either stand with it, or you're standing against it."

She paused, gritted her teeth. I can't lie, I liked getting her riled.

"Do you want to debate foreign politics or know why I'm here?"

"Debating foreign politics with a socialist hippy is like shoveling shit upstream," I told her with a smile. I knew she could take the banter, and usually was more than happy to do so. But today it was obvious she was here for a reason. She stopped the familiar debate by reaching into her back pocket.

"I have a surprise for you."

For some reason the announcement made me nervous. There was something about Tammy's confidence, her humble omnipotence that seemed to cast a long shadow. She wasn't worried about what other people thought about her, whether or not she was wrong or out of line. She had a way about her that just exuded aptitude. She actually reminded me of the SEALs I had spent so much of my life with. And that was a bit unsettling on a fifteen-year-old girl. It also could be quite enthralling.

"What would that be?" I asked cautiously.

She rolled her eyes. "Wouldn't be a surprise if I told you. Here."

It was a wrinkled envelope, offered with the indifferent temperament of a cashier handing back change. I took it from her, unsure of what to expect.

Dear Tammy,

Thank you for your note and kind words. It does not surprise me to hear of the character of Chief Butler's son, and my heart breaks for him as it does for my own. That his father lost his life at the side of my husband gives me great sadness, but great peace knowing that two brothers in arms could comfort each other as they made the ultimate sacrifice for the brothers and country they loved.

We are aware of the immense bravery and selflessness Chief Butler and his squad demonstrated that night, and he and his family will always be in our prayers. I hope Nathan understands that his father gave his life for something great, as I know my boy does. While Nathan and Eli have never met, they share a bond that is greater yet more tragic than any in life, and I would encourage them to take strength and solace in that kinship.

*Eli is well aware that Chief Butler had a son his age, and
would be open to a meeting. Our family has since left Georgia,
and are living with my parents outside of Washington, D.C.
Feel free to pass Eli's contact information on to Nathan.*

Sincerely,

Catherine Hawkins

The paper shook in my hands, each letter and word pulsing
through me. I felt something that only can be described as stronger
than empathy, a parallel unity of loss and victimization. Eli. Something bigger than just my sorrow, the understanding and reciproca-
tion of an unfortunate equal. Comfort and additional pain came in
unison, ease in commonality but disconcerting in its equivalence.

I didn't know what to say. It was a gift wrapped in a box of responsibility.

"Spencer."

I nodded, understanding.

"Can't believe you did this." A slow eruption of emotions heated
my face, stretched my skin. I had spent hours thinking of the other
child who had lost his father in the cold Afghan mountains that night,
wondering if his pain matched mine. How his loss had robbed him of
so many pleasures and how many would come to pass. And now I
had a name. Eli. He was real. He was just like me, just like Cheyenne.

"I want to meet him," I finally said. I looked over at Tammy. For
most, an intimate awkwardness would have muddled the interaction,
but not with her. She was laser-focused on my thoughts, my reaction.
I knew no doubt or second-guessing had entered her mind when she
reached out to this family.

"I knew you would. His email address and phone number are there."

I nodded slowly, appreciative and apprehensive. When I looked up again Tammy was gone. It was just me and a letter from a widow in Northern Virginia.

Chapter 20

A SHORT MEMORY can be the only explanation for the events that occurred later that year. Freshman year had just ended, and the promise of a fresh summer to do with as I pleased inflamed adolescent exuberance.

As I imagine all young men are guilty of experiencing at some point, the blowback from a previous mistake sufficiently hid behind the potential of doing it again.

Therefore: another Darren party, another bottle. In reality, it was much more than *a* bottle this time. With some pills, some weed too. But the booze – the same sharp bite, the same blistering track down my throat and into my belly. The same subdued adrenaline, the same numbing result.

"I think Butler's wasted."

The voice took a moment to reach me, and sounded as if it were coming from another room. I looked up from my stupor, smiling, trying to focus.

Gharun and Darren were watching with the same interest reserved for a pouting child.

"Yeah, man, he's definitely wasted."

I grinned, sat up. Show them who's wasted.

"Wasting my time." I was slurring.

"You got something better to do?"

"Sure. Sure I do."

"What's that? Entertain us Butler, I know you have it in you. You're the wild one, right?"

Hopefully making it appear easier than it was, I set both feet on the floor before announcing that everyone should follow me. Curiosity got the better of the group, and before I knew it, several guys were following me up the stairs of Darren's basement. I led them past the people mingling in the living room. To be clear, I had no idea where I was leading them to.

"Thanks for using the front door this time," Darren quipped. He swigged from a Gatorade bottle, handed it off to me.

I blinked some clarity back into my face and looked around the crowded party. No parental supervision again, and the scene showed it. I made eye contact with Doug in the corner. He quickly looked away. His sneer lingered in my memory, and I knew he had no place at one of Darren's parties. I wasn't sure that I did, but I was positive about him. He was not part of the crew that fell out of the front door. A crew on a reckless, juvenile mission that none of us bothered to consider past the moment.

Someone had a car. We piled in, cloudily deciding it was just warm enough for a swim in the nearby rec pool.

A hush came over the car as we eased into the unlit parking spot. The driver (I'm still not sure who it was) killed the headlights, and we sat, silent. The wood frame of the clubhouse stood before us, a flimsy chain link fence the only border between five drunk teenagers and a recently filled pool.

Hesitation, thoughts of consequences, thickened like smoke in the car. We were at a tipping point. Slowly, I saw my hand on the car door. Before I knew it I was out of the car and scaling the fence.

"Crazy bastard, keep it down!" someone hissed, but my excitement had taken hold, and I was over the fence in seconds. I wasn't worried if they followed, I wasn't worried if I got caught. Apparently, I wasn't worried about anything. My clothes flew off, the June air feeling good against bare skin, the impression of freedom that comes with liquid uninhibitedness buoying everything up.

Just as I made the water's edge a dark streak flew past me and a splash erupted in the deep end. Not to be outdone by the sophomore free safety, Gharun had cannonballed into the deep end, fully clothed.

Jealous at him, pissed at myself for not being the first one in, I stood flatfooted and watched him flail, all arms and splatter. Until – wait. He wasn't celebrating. He seemed to be sinking. I paused, making sure I had this right – Gharun couldn't swim?

I dove sharply into the water, smelling the chlorine, feeling the wetness against my skin. In the dark it didn't matter whether I opened my eyes or not; the lack of sight gave the sensation of either vast space or claustrophobia. In a few short strokes I was on him. He thrashed below me, fingers barely reaching the top of the water. He fought me as I got a hold of his waist, trying to tow him towards the side. Finally he realized what was happening and let me take control. I'll never forget the terrified look as his eyes bugged under the water and a single bubble drifted from his open mouth. His face locked onto mine, silently pleading, completely at my mercy. A focused ripple slid across his face and I laughed, easily dragging him to the side.

"Holy shit!" he sputtered, the water sheeting off his head and face. Wide, crazy-eyed, he ran his hand across his hair, gasping.

I laughed again, louder.

"You can't swim, you dumb shit?"

He looked puzzled, like he wasn't sure that he understood the question.

"I guess not," he finally breathed, relief covering his face.

I laughed again, dipped below the surface, glided to the far end. The water was cool and refreshing; I enjoyed the weightlessness and superiority I had in it. When I emerged, the raucous crew was on the deck, removing clothes and pushing each other in.

I took the scene in, my mind reaching. The wooden clubhouse caught my eye, and I popped out of the water, running towards it. My feet slapped on the concrete as everyone stopped to watch. I found a foothold, and hoisted myself against the wall, pulling myself up until I could reach a ledge that ran around the roof. I scrambled to the top, looking down at surprisingly small figures and dark water. Without a second thought and with a running start, I sprinted off the edge of the roof, arms and legs whirling, aiming for that dark rectangle. I don't need to tell you what I screamed as I flew through the air.

The cop looked puzzled as we stood on my front stoop. He hit the doorbell again, and looked at me with confusion when no response came from within.

"We took the bell out," I informed him as obnoxiously as possible.

His cop-glare drilled into me once again before he started knocking briskly with the end of his flashlight.

Finally an upstairs window flashed, followed by quick footsteps on the stairs. The tension increased as each subsequent light and activity dominoe'd towards the front door, until finally it swung open, my terrified mother facing us wide-eyed in her nightgown.

My slouch was rebellious, my sneer indifferent. While both the cop and mother thought my apathy was just for show, truth be told, I really didn't give a shit.

"Nathan. What's..."

"Ma'am, is this your son?" opened the cop.

"Yes it is. What is he doing with you?"

"We responded to complaints of youths breaking into the rec pool, where we found your son with four other boys. They had thrown all the lawn furniture into the pool, and someone had defecated in the shallow end."

I thought my mom's eyes would fall out of her head.

"It wasn't me that took a dump in the pool," I informed her, arms raised innocently in the air.

"You have got to be kidding me," she exclaimed. "Is he under arrest?"

"We did not place them under arrest, but there will be a mandatory court appearance. Community service, I imagine," he told her.

Her lips barely moved as she hissed.

"Nathan, get in the house."

"Here is the notice to appear," the cop said, handing her a piece of yellow paper. Turning to me, he said, "Young man, I hope I don't run into you again."

I glared through him. "Me too, you're kind of an asshole." I then slinked into the house, far from interested in hearing a response.

Chapter 21

IT WAS NOTHING SHORT of divine luck that Spencer had already left for Green Team and wasn't available to mete out punishment in person. I was, however, on the receiving end of an earful via Skype from wherever he was the week after the pool incident. Not for the first time, I was determined to make him proud and not screw up again.

Not that I had much of an opportunity to even if I had so desired. Being grounded for a month didn't leave much room for shenanigans. I was stuck exercising in the backyard and skulking around the house. Cheyenne, at least, was thrilled. Due to a scarcity of resources, we'd become fast friends, entertaining each other while nurturing an already intense sibling bond.

As far as little sisters go, she wasn't bad to be around. Truthfully, Chey was an inspiration. She fully understood her loss without feeling sorry for herself, and appreciated the sacrifice that our father and family had made. She was able to be proud of him – in fact, she was proud to be proud of him – while not abandoning her pain. If anything, it made her stronger. And that had the same effect on me.

I knew there was at least one other person who could empathize. The experience we shared couldn't be explained or shared with anyone else. So I finally reached out to Eli Hawkins.

While I was sitting at home that summer, my already voracious appetite for war coverage had been inflamed, and I read what little I could find on Sgt. Kristoffer Hawkins online. Like all U.S. military KIA, he was apparently a model soldier, father and citizen who gave his life for God and country. There was no mention of a Navy SEAL platoon supporting his medevac. In fact, there was little more than the standard "killed by small arms fire while conducting a combat patrol." Of course, if I wanted to know what club Lindsay Lohan had gotten drunk at the night before, it was only a click away.

The letter Tammy had given me from Sgt. Hawkins's wife was by this time worn and smudged. I had taken it in and out of the shoebox dozens of times, staring at the hand-written phone number, never able to dial it.

I felt connected to Eli Hawkins without knowing him or ever speaking to him. He had gone through exactly what I had, and that meant a lot to me. Our commonality was almost sacred, and I guess in a way I was worried that the sanctity of that bond would be cheapened by meeting or even discussing it.

Tammy hadn't asked if I had reached out to him, and my mother didn't even know the letter existed. But without realizing it, she was the one who finally led me to action.

"I'm getting sick of you lying here day after day, making a mess," she fussed one brutally humid afternoon. I had just finished doing pull-ups in the garage, and was sweating on the couch, sucking down a protein shake.

"You're the one who grounded me!" I exclaimed. "I don't want to be here anymore than you do!"

Her face stretched with anger.

"You're blaming me? You snuck out, got drunk, and broke into the pool! You're lucky I didn't bury you in the backyard!"

"Boys will be boys," I said, knowing that would get a reaction.

"I don't want to hear that crap one more time! Not from you, not from Spencer! That's it, either you find something productive to do, or I'm going to find it for you!"

"Whooo," I mocked without thinking. Bad reaction: challenging my mother was never a good move.

"Okay, smart guy, start with the shed. I want it emptied, swept out and organized. Then you can wash the cars. If there's still daylight after that, you can start on the gutters."

I cringed, knowing I had gone too far.

"But I already mowed the lawn today!"

She paused, thinking. I allowed cautious optimism to creep into my thoughts.

"You know what, you're right. And as always, you did a great job. So forget the shed, forget the gutters. Forget our yard altogether."

Now I knew I was in trouble. That foolish optimism vanished, now it was just a matter of waiting for the other shoe to drop.

She started again, matter-of-factly.

"You're going to go over to the Koch's, and you're going to offer to mow their lawn."

"I am?"

"You are."

"And why am I going to do that?"

"Because Mr. Koch is at sea, and Mrs. Koch sprained her ankle carrying in groceries last week. And there is no one to do her yard. And it looks like crap. AND I told you to."

I felt like I should protest, because that's what teenagers do when their mothers give them orders.

"But I can't leave the yard."

Her smile belied her intentions. "Guess what, pal? You get a reprieve to do the Koch's lawn. And to help her with the groceries when needed. And whatever else she needs. Now move."

I groaned, if only to act like the chore was much more painful than it actually was. Mr. Koch was a boatswain mate on the USS Harry Truman, which had been at sea for the past six months. Truth be told, I liked the idea of helping his family. He had played golf with us a few times and my dad seemed to respect him.

Even so, I made a production of putting my sneakers on and retrieving the mower from the garage, muttering and slamming things loudly. After pushing the mower the few blocks to the Koch's house, I knocked on the door. I scoped the job while waiting for an answer.

Weeds grew tall around the edge of the driveway and sidewalk. The yard was patchy and overgrown and looked like it hadn't been mowed in months. Luckily for me it hadn't been watered either, and the summer heat and drought had retarded its growth. The dullness stood out against most of the other tidy lawns that framed the mostly military-occupied homes on our street. Mom was right, it did look like crap.

"Nate, how are you?" The screen door swung open, and a surprised Mrs. Koch stood before me. One of her young daughters, I couldn't remember which one, stood at her feet sucking her thumb, looking up at me with curiosity.

"Hi, Mrs. Koch. I was hoping, um, I mean I thought that you might like me to mow your lawn. I know that Mr. Koch is at sea and you sprained your ankle, so, you know…"

There was a heavy silence, a long pause. She looked at me so closely I sort of got dizzy. I wiped my forehead, adjusted my stance. Then a vivid wash of appreciation came over her face, and with a sudden swoop, she closed in on me. To my surprise she wrapped her arms around me, squeezing.

"Just like your father, you poor thing. Steve would be so proud of you, Nate."

She pulled back, her eyes finding mine.

"I know you've made some mistakes, and who could blame you. But I see your dad in you, Nate, I see his strength and selflessness. You are a spitting image, and an honor to his memory."

My face flushed. This was the crap I hated.

"Thanks, Mrs. Koch, but I don't think mowing a neighbor's lawn is on par with going to war. It's not a big deal."

She nodded, understanding, lips tightening.

"I know it, Nate, and it may seem like that. But it is. Often the gesture is worth more than the act. Remember that."

That made no sense to me at the time, but I didn't tell her so. I just let her hug me again and listened to her thank me and say that she'd have iced tea waiting when I was done.

As I baked in the heat mowing and sweeping, I took note of the American flags and yellow ribbons that dotted so many homes in the neighborhood. For the most part, the houses were small and close together. But they stood solidly, unified, humble yet proud. Their owners weren't rich – most lived on an enlisted sailor's salary – but they were part of something bigger than themselves. Many had a loved one at war.

When I finished, I declined Mrs. Koch's offer of iced tea as well as the crumpled bill she tried to hand me.

"It's my pleasure, Mrs. Koch," I told her, my face reddening. "Tell Mr. Koch thanks for his service."

I left quickly, avoiding the embarrassment of a prolonged show of gratitude, and wheeled the mower down her driveway.

I had already decided my next destination, and it wasn't back to the couch. A pilot who was deployed to the Persian Gulf lived one street over, his wife alone with their three small children.

The mid-day sun was strong, pushing on me, heating the metal of the mower. My hands vibrated on the grips as I made my way across the bumpy road, a strange sensation that ran up my arms. Several times I paused to wipe the sweat from my forehead and neck.

I rounded Upshur Lane, trying to remember which house the pilot lived in. At least half had yellow ribbons hanging from light poles and mailboxes, proudly designating the household as having a deployed family member or supporting those who did. While this may have been common for my neighborhood, I wondered not for the first time if those outside military communities realized just how many people were putting everything on the line for their freedom. I quickly swallowed the thought; they didn't do it for recognition. They did it out of duty, because it was their job.

Ahead of me, a figure on a bike grew closer. It was Nitin, who I had barely seen since the previous summer. He awkwardly stopped, gave me a half-wave. The smile seemed tense and forced. This wasn't the first time I got the impression he was nervous around me.

"Hey, Nate, whatchu doing?" he asked, straddling his bike on the side of the road.

"Mowing some lawns."

"Community service?"

"Huh?" I asked, confused.

"Oh. Never mind."

"Community service?"

"Yeah. Uh, I heard what happened at the pool, that you guys got arrested and everything. Thought you might have to do community service because of that."

I laughed, knowing how high school and neighborhood gossip went.

"Nah, just grounded for a little. Wasn't a big deal."

"I heard you did a back flip off the clubhouse and into the pool and damn near broke your neck."

I laughed again. It was comical how uncomfortable he was.

"Don't believe everything you hear. It wasn't quite that dramatic – just a little midnight dip."

"I guess people tend to exaggerate. The soap opera that is Landstown High. So you're just making some cash mowing lawns?"

"Just helping out some families whose fathers are deployed. Most of the moms work and they can't afford a lawn service. So I figured I'd give them a hand."

His expression changed from confusion to intrigue, and then: "Want some help?"

The offer was a pleasant surprise. "For sure. You know where that pilot lives? With three really young kids? I know he's deployed, but I can't remember which house is his."

"The Hardy's?" He pointed at a house just down the street. "That's them right there. The mom works at the commissary, right?"

We both looked at the house, which was definitely in need of some yard work.

"Yeah, that's them. Want to bag and rake while I mow?"

He nodded, and we made our way to the small white bungalow.

We stood at the front door shoulder to shoulder, tensely waiting for someone to answer. Bangs and bumps from inside were followed by a woman's yell, then a child's cry. Finally the door opened. Again, a small child stood at the legs of the woman of the house, her eyes mimicking her mother's impatient stare.

"Can I help you?" she asked curtly. A television blared jovial music from a kid's show. A cluttered living room was visible through the screen door. It took a moment until I was able to find my tongue and address this harried woman.

"Yes, ma'am. Um, Nitin and I were offering to mow the lawns of some of the people in the neighborhood whose husbands were deployed. We'd be happy to do the same for you."

"Who are you again?"

"I'm Nate Butler, Mrs. Hardy. I live down the street. We'd like to mow your lawn."

"Chief Butler's son? The SEAL?"

My throat involuntarily cleared and dried.

"Yes, ma'am."

"Well that's nice, Nate, I wish I could, but with baby formula, sitters and bills, who can afford to pay for lawn care? I can barely afford to pay the babysitter so I can go to work."

Nitin chimed in.

"No, Mrs. Hardy, we'll do it for free. Since Mr. Hardy is deployed and all."

She looked at us suspiciously, like we were trying to pull one over on her. I, for one, just grinned stupidly and tried to look as un-threatening as possible.

"If it's free, then I suppose its fine. Just take care not to run over my roses," she finally said, scooping up the child. "I have to get ready to run these kids to day-care so I can get to work on time."

The door quickly shut on us. Our feet stood solid while our faces slowly turned towards one another in entertained confusion. After a lengthy sideways look both Nitin and I burst out laughing.

"Roses?" he sputtered. "Does she mean the poison oak that's growing on her front steps?"

We laughed. It was nice, and usually necessary, to enjoy a moment of levity when dealing with ludicrousness. Then we got to work.

The sun was fast setting by the time we finished. The yard looked good. Salt and sweat crusted over my sunburned neck, arms aching, hands blistered. Corroboration of three lawns mowed that day. An invigorating physical exhaustion earned by hard work.

After thanking Nitin for his help, I struggled along the bumpy road, head held high and soaked shirt flung over my shoulder. I entered the house with flushed cheeks and grandiose ideas, calling to Mom.

"Sorry I'm late, Mom, but I wasn't goofing off!" I yelled, storming into the living room.

"What are you yelling for?" she asked, lowering her magazine just slightly.

"Sorry, but I wanted to tell you. I mowed the Koch's yard, and then after I went–"

She cut me off with a wave of her hand.

"I know where you went," she said simply.

"Yep, we mowed the Hardy's lawn too. How'd you know?" I asked, beaming.

She set the magazine on the coffee table, methodically, as if it were a huge inconvenience. Pursed lips and an unpleased face rotated towards me, uninterested.

"Pretty proud of yourself, huh?" she said.

I was confused. The bite of sarcasm was unexpected.

"Should I not be?"

"You shouldn't waltz in here like you just saved the Amazonian manatees from extinction," she said. "Act like you've been there. I thought you emulated the silent professionals."

I paused, properly put in place.

"Okay, Dad."

She stood up, quickly.

"Yeah, that's right, bud. This is your dad speaking. You think you were the only one who heard his sayings? Who knew his philosophy on how to live this life? I heard them all too, but you're the one who has to live them. You're his son, and you're more his son than you realize yet. But I do, Nate. I realize it. Do you know how hard that is for me? And how scary that is? How much pressure it is for you?"

I nearly laughed. I had never heard truer words. It was as if I had already known these truths but just hadn't recognized them until then. The reality of it was disconcertingly comforting, like the finality of a death sentence, or any unyielding acceptance.

A nod was response enough for us both.

I went upstairs to run a shower. I stared into the steam as it started to slowly build in the bathroom, listening to the rhythmic white noise of hissing water. My mother's words, and their impact, keep repeating in my mind. I peeled off grimy clothes and stepped into the fog. The hot water burned my skin, but in a good way. I thought back to a night a year or so before he was killed, after a training work-up in South America.

He had come back hobbled, Mom admitting quietly to me that he had two cracked vertebrae. He never mentioned the pain or a diagnosis. I wasn't sure what his task unit had been doing on their exercises, but the strain and impact of it was written in new creases around his cheeks and temples. All I wanted to do was spend time with him after not seeing him for a month, knowing well that he first had to decompress and switch back from vampire hours. Finally, with his standard post-deployment routine complete, he was ready to re-join the family. Dinner and a movie – Shoney's and *Harry Potter* on a warm spring evening. The most exciting night my young mind could conjure. All day I had counted the hours until it would be time to go. I remember at school I had looked on my classmates with superiority and pity because they weren't going to get to spend an evening with my dad.

I had followed him out the front door that evening, trying to hide my excitement. I remember I had jammed my thumb playing basketball at recess earlier that day, and I shook it reflexively.

He looked down at me.

"Something wrong?"

"Nah," I said. "Just jammed my thumb a little is all."

"Hurt?"

"It's fine." Then: "Maybe a little."

He grinned and gave a light punch to my shoulder. I jumped back, ready to defend myself. The shot stung, despite my reaction.

"Betcha you forgot about your hand," he said.

I shoved him, hopped into the backseat. "Didn't hurt!"

His smirk didn't dissipate as he opened the doors for Mom and Cheyenne before climbing in.

"Give me a muster!" he called out once we were all loaded into the Explorer. The private wink I secured as he put it in reverse landed like a bear hug. My suspicion that it was forced, the smile too tense, did not have any impact upon my appreciation for it. He had quickly shaved his deployment beard and gotten a regulation haircut upon his return, but superficial cleanness couldn't fully hide an unsettled disposition. It occurred to me that I was becoming accustomed to the growing distance in his eyes after every deployment; it was all I could do to ignore it.

"All present and accounted for," I told him.

Right then my mom suddenly leaned across from the passenger's seat and kissed him on the mouth, hard. It surprised us all. Cheyenne responded with a kissy sound. I watched the scene with interest, inhaling this vision of familial interaction. My father's startled but pleased look, my sister's innocent laughter, my mom's hopeful gesture. I sat back, uninvolved, fully consuming one of those rare moments when you are truly satisfied.

We played our usual "I Spy" game as we drove, Dad spying, "Something black and white. Something round, something long. Something shiny, something wooden. Something powerful and special to our family."

It was clear with the first hint that he had "spied" the Rosary hanging from the rear-view mirror. Mom and I shared a conspiratorial look and she rolled her eyes at his obvious clues.

"The Rosary!" Cheyenne finally blurted out. Together we laughed and cheered for her.

"Good job Pumpkin," my dad said, smiling at her in the rear view mirror. He began to slow the car, pulling over to the side of the highway.

Semi's rattled past as he put it in park, stopping behind an old red Honda Civic with its flashers on.

"Stephen?" My mom's voice sounded more curious than worried. "What are you doing?"

"This guy is broken down," he replied simply. To him, it was as plain as day. He got out of the car, and made his way to the Civic. Without asking for Mom's permission, I hopped out too, following closely behind.

"Car trouble?" he asked the young unkempt man through the open window.

The man looked up with red eyes and a confused expression. He rubbed his dirty, blond hair and stared at my father before answering.

"Not sure what's wrong. I think I'm out of gas," he said slowly.

My dad put his head in the window to get a look the gauge.

"Looks that way. If you wait here, I'll bring you a can."

I looked up at him sharply, worried now about our family's plans.

He met the look, a gentle nod the only reassurance I needed. Even then I understood duty and how it meant different things to different people. To my dad, it meant always doing what's right, and it wasn't even a consideration to not help this man. That was the way he lived his life.

"That would be great sir, but I'm a little short on cash right now."

My dad just nodded, told him not to worry about it and that we would be back shortly.

We missed the movie and ate at Burger King that night. It wasn't the first lesson I'd had in commitment, and by no means was it my last. "That Golden Rule," he called it.

As I stood under the shower, I let the hot water singe my back, my shoulders, my head. I was in no rush, and tried to enjoy the sensation. After all, none of this would matter in a hundred years. I thought of what my dad would do, and what he would expect me to do. Ultimately, I knew he would have reached out to Eli Hawkins, if only to help him cope with the loss of his father. Maybe I could help. If anyone knew what he was going through, it was me.

Chapter 22

ELI WAS MUCH LIKE ME, the obvious notwithstanding, I quickly found as we began to text and talk on the phone. Initially they were exploratory conversations, designed to vet each other, but soon turned into a type of welcome therapy for us both.

I was almost fifteen; him, thirteen. He had struggled in the beginning with the "why," whereas I had been more focused on the "how." We found that we both were jolted awake many nights by the crackle of automatic gunfire and unanswered calls for help.

"I wonder if he was scared," he admitted to me one night. It was our second or third phone conversation and the first time each of us had actually shared honest emotions.

"My dad used to say that everyone was scared, it was how you reacted to that fear that mattered," I told him.

"Courage is being scared to death but saddling up anyway," he replied.

"No shit! John Wayne! My dad used to say that all the time!"

Eli's snicker mirrored my immediate thoughts – our dads were probably pretty similar.

"I bet they would have liked each other," I finally said.

"A Squid?" he joked. "Never."

I laughed. "Yeah, I'm sure my dad wouldn't have been caught

dead hanging with a Dogface." The competition between military branches was ratcheted up even higher in the special operations community, and that didn't escape the offspring. We would have killed an outsider who spoke like this, but the inner-circle enjoyed a respectful rivalry.

Our light, shared laughter ran its course before fading naturally into a period of ease. Any reprieve from reality, even for just a moment to allow the mind to focus elsewhere, was a welcome and indulgent gift. The residual silence wasn't awkward. In fact, I believe the respite that we allowed each other was something especially appreciated, given that few could award it. The facts were what they were and there was nothing to be done about them. The person who understood that the best was on the other end of the phone.

"I've started a kind of, I don't know, charity or something, down here in Virginia Beach," I told him. "Mowing lawns for the families of deployed sailors and soldiers."

"That's great," he said. "Must be nice to be able to give back."

The thought that we had already given so much didn't occur to either of us.

"It is. A lot of the moms work full time, trying to take care of the kids and the house by themselves. It's the least we can do."

"I should start doing that here. We live close to Quantico now, tons of military families here."

"Why did you leave Ft. Benning?"

"After my dad was killed, we had to leave base housing within a year. My mom couldn't get a job in Georgia so we had to move in with my grandparents. It's the five of us and our Rottweiler in their three-bedroom house outside of D.C."

"That sucks," I told him. "My mom is looking for a job now."

"Are you going to stay in Virginia Beach?"

"Not sure. I hope so. Football season just started and I made varsity, but my mom's kind of pissed at me. I've gotten into a few...minor scrapes, shall we say. It's not going to be pretty if I screw up again. Not to mention what my dad's teammates will do. When they're back in town, they're going to hand me my ass as it is."

"Where would you go?"

"Dunno. Pensacola, maybe. That's where my dad was from. As long as I can still surf, I'm cool. But my mom's parents live in Maryland, nowhere near the ocean."

Again, we both went into our silent, reflective shells. There was no need for forced conversation, for small talk. For once, I was just able to have a conversation with someone without worrying about putting up a facade. I wasn't worried what the other person thought about me or what had happened to my family. I usually ended up feeling bad that they felt bad. With Eli, I could just be.

Nitin and I expanded Yard Work for Warriors that fall. Gharun and some guys on the team volunteered, and we recruited a few other kids in the neighborhood to help. The most inspiring part to me were the kids who volunteered and weren't from military families. Their gesture encouraged me; it was a tiny indicator that maybe, just maybe, the general public was not as unappreciative as the media. Despite the slanted and general lack of war coverage, those kids seemed knowledgeable and grateful.

If you asked a sailor, soldier, or Marine deployed to a war zone, most wouldn't say that they were fighting for country first. They'd tell you that foremost, they fought for their buddies. The guy next to them. Second was for themselves. They fought so they and their brothers would come home. Nothing more romantic than that. It wasn't always a blinding patriotic pull that led them to the military and to battle. Love of country was there, of course, but often on the peripheral, along with those other true clichés: commitment, family, duty, honor. And frankly it was a surprise when civilian kids understood and appreciated that. To me, that quantified the fighter's sacrifice, the time away from their families. It's hard to protect those who don't want protection. Appreciation may not be a pre-requisite for what they do, but it certainly makes the cost more palatable.

Eli ended up starting a branch of Yard Work for Warriors in Northern Virginia, while in Virginia Beach we soon had a dozen regular volunteers. Tammy had created a website for us, and between the two braches we mowed 127 lawns that year. Even Doug made a show of volunteering once or twice.

My newfound philanthropic endeavors may have given me some karma points and coverage in the local paper, but it didn't ease Tammy's feelings about why we were needed. Our heated debates about the cost and necessity of war were increasing in frequency, and her idealistic notions were leading to more and more combative discussions. I chalked it up to her affiliation with the fairer sex. Naturally, it didn't go over well when I shared the sentiment.

"*Whose freedom are we saving?*" she asked me late one afternoon after a full day of yard work. We were lying on our backs looking up at a soupy sky, the air thick with moisture and the last gasp of an Indian summer. She said it unemotionally, as if she were asking about a homework assignment or whether a belt matched her shoes.

"Whose freedom are we saving?" I repeated, incredulous. "Yours, mine. Iraqi and Afghan citizens. Not to mention responding to the murder of 3,000 innocent civilians."

"Killing innocent civilians is the answer to killing innocent civilians? We should not have invaded those countries," Tammy said defiantly.

My head spun towards her with anger. Here we go again.

"We were – are – killing terrorists! People who want to kill us and have proven that they will. We should just let the Taliban harbor terrorists intent on killing Americans? Let Saddam Hussein grow an arsenal of weapons of mass destruction?"

"There hasn't been an attack on American soil in nine years! And there were no weapons of mass destruction in Iraq, it was an oil play by the Bushes – oil men from Texas!"

"I'm tired of hearing it was about oil! If it was an oil play, where is the oil? Gas was $1.80 before the war in Iraq. It's double that now!" My voice was gaining volume and intensity. "And tell the Kurds that Saddam didn't have WMDs! It was a necessary proactive strike, before they killed more of our citizens. Or provided sarin gas or anthrax to the millions of zealous Muslims who want to invade our cities!"

"I'm sure they would have invaded our cities."

"I can hear some sarcastic Polish girl making that exact comment in 1938." I stood up in anger – there's only so much you can take, even from a pretty girl.

In a flash, she leapt to her feet, jumping in front of me.

"Allow me!" she shouted, shoving me so hard I actually fell to the freshly trimmed grass. By the time I caught my breath and edited my next statement in my head, her figure had grown small, leaving me to seethe at her back.

Eventually my curses drifted back to earth, heard by only the wind, acknowledged by the trees. Which, incidentally, I imagined to be laughing at my expense. I felt my mouth involuntarily open and close a couple times, searching for the audio to match the considerations darting back and forth in my mind.

I slowly rose to meet the shadows. Slowly, the shock of the interaction began to wear off. Exhaustion suddenly surrounded me like a summer thunderstorm. My days had been consumed with football practice and yard work, and it was taking a toll.

The walk home was slow. Aches I was previously unaware of screamed their presence. My mind swam.

I was sad. There was no other way to describe it, no way to deny it. The waves of sorrow had constantly risen and sunk in the nearly two years without my father, and I remember the ferocity with which that particular one had crested over me.

They usually came with compounding factors, the sum weight of small defeats greatly surpassing their individual pricks. Isolated, the normal difficulties of life would not have such impact, but they were tricky parasites. They attacked the current and unstable pain that was always calling, always begging to be acknowledged. The fight with Tammy was just the ignition they needed to remove the muzzle, freeing them to attack my psyche.

Before I knew it, I was wandering towards Darren's house. Dusk had fallen, and while no longer grounded, I was supposed to be home for supper.

Fuck it, I thought, and rang Darren's bell. An ominous gong echoed throughout the large colonial. The manicured lawn, the lonely windows, the stately columns guarding the porch did a fantastic job of making me feel out of place.

"Is Darren home?" I asked quickly when his mother came to the door. She was a tall, dignified woman who looked at me with suspicion. She was the type who was always asked to speak at the officer's wives club, a by-product of her primness and the status that comes with having an admiral for a husband. I understood, and even took some pride in, my reputation and her worry that I would bring dishonor to the Montgomery clan.

The slain elite warrior's son. The reckless football player who drinks and does crazy shit. But also the kid who started a charity to help families affected by the wars. Truth be told, I liked the dichotomy. The contradiction kept people on their toes. Sometimes even kept their sympathy at bay.

It was obvious Mrs. Montgomery was now trying to figure out who was standing on her front stoop: Nathan Butler the good kid, or the one who broke her fence and got her son taken home in a cop car.

Reluctant but polite, she opened the door slightly and leaned back.

"Darren, Nate is here to see you," she called out.

She didn't budge from the doorway. I smiled awkwardly while trying to find a suitable landing spot for my gaze. It was clear there would be no small talk. After what absolutely could not have been as long as it felt, Darren squeezed by his mom and met me on the front porch.

"What are you doing here, man?" he hissed.

"I didn't know I needed a specific reason to visit, Darren."

"When my mom's home, yeah, it would probably be a good idea to call first. She thinks you're a bad influence. Not the best move for me to be hanging out with you when I'm trying to get a car."

"Just tell her we're going over the playbook."

"She's not stupid, Nate. What do you want?"

I paused, hesitant to ask the question, but emboldened by desire.

"I wanted to buy a couple pills off you," I whispered.

He jumped off the steps and walked past me briskly, closing the door behind him.

"Oxys? What the hell are you mentioning that for at my house? My mom hears you, we're both dead," he hissed.

I stared him down. "That's. Why. I whispered."

He looked at me, deciding.

"Meet me at the park in twenty minutes."

I stood there, watching his back as he hurried back into the house. A wash of guilt hit me briefly, but the cold sweat of excitement pushed it down and I started towards the park.

Chapter 23

NOW WOULD PROBABLY BE A GOOD TIME to mention – admit – that I had starting taking pills a month or two before that visit. Eating and snorting them like Tic Tacs: Oxys, Percocet, Vicodin, Xanax, Alprazolam, whatever we could get our hands on. I had started doing them with Darren, a few other guys on the team. The underwhelming rush of calmness and peace that overtook my body and brain that first time was like an exciting new friend promising peace.

Now I could actually see myself spinning out of control, but either due to stubbornness, indifference, or lack of willpower, I continued ferociously down that path. That night I bought two 20mg Oxycodone pills from Darren and crushed them up right there in the park, snorting them out of an envelope with a dollar bill. This is what it had come to. I sat on a swing, relishing the slide into oblivion.

After, I laid in the clumped sand, mind and body separated and enjoying their time apart. By the time I got home that night, curfew was long since broken and my mother met me at the front door once again.

I was grounded, as expected. By this time the punishments were barely a nuisance, let alone any kind of deterrent. My bedroom window conveniently overlooked the garage roof, and it was a mere scale and leap to the nearest oak branch canopying the backyard. My bike was usually placed on the far side of the garage, which led to easy midnight escapes that winter. They often ended with empty bottles, joints, and any pills available.

In fact, by the new year, I was sneaking out nearly every night to get wasted. Often it was meeting Darren or other teammates at the park, sometimes just riding my bike around alone, high on painkillers or tranquilizers washed down with stolen vodka or wine.

One blurry weekend afternoon my mother asked me to get her some Aleve from her medicine cabinet. She was laying on the couch with a washcloth over her eyes, suffering from one of her increasingly frequent migraines. To my delight, I discovered a weathered bottle with a date from just a few days after my father's death buried in the back. "Alprazolam, 1mg." Grinning widely, I cuffed the bottle before bouncing back downstairs and happily handing Mom her two Aleve and a glass of water.

It was a jackpot for a teenager experimenting with drugs.

"Twenty-two pills," I gloated to Darren, shaking the pill bottle in his face.

It was the middle of the night, and we were swaying gently on swings in the deserted park, passing back and forth a bottle of red wine he had swiped from his parents. They would never notice its absence.

His eyes lit up like silver dollars, almost causing him to choke on a gulp.

"Twenty-two! And they're one milligrams? Blue footballs?"

I nodded, smirking.

"Compliments of Tricare."

"How many do you think you can do without dying?" he dared.

I looked at him closely. He, like everyone else, knew the best way to get me to do anything was to tell me I couldn't do it.

"I know what you're doing there – don't, because you know I'll take one more than you and two more than everyone else."

He smiled, and held out his hand.

"Let's start with two," I said, shaking them onto his palm.

He flung them into his mouth and grabbed the bottle of wine to wash them down.

I made sure he saw the three I was holding, and watched with amusement as he stared, wide-eyed and jealous.

"Down the hatch," I said, grabbing the wine bottle.

He wanted another, to be even with me. I gave it to him. Then I took two more, relishing the unease it caused him.

Someone slurred, "In 100 years, none of this will matter." I think it was me.

A pause settled between the swings; a supercharged anticipation descended upon us. My senses heightened; in the dim tree line behind us, I sensed scurrying squirrels, the falling of leaves. The single light framing the basketball court seemed more brilliant than usual, directed at me like a spotlight. It was focused only on me, communicating somehow, thousands of individual needles of light streaming at me, finding my clammy skin, illuminating my slumping frame, trying to tell me something. I did my best to listen, to respond, but everything slurred in slow motion, my head getting too heavy to keep upon my shoulders.

"Anger is sadness turned outwards," it told me, hollow and plain.

With great effort I lifted my head, forced open an eye. The silver haired bum was back and staring at me peculiarly. Were they his words?

"What the fuck do you know about it?" I wasn't sure if I had actually spoken or if it was just a thought. He seemed to understand.

The light burned brighter, appearing to emanate from somewhere behind him. The effect blinded me, while donning a halo on him. He seemed to be getting closer but farther away at the same time – I realized we were moving with the light. I leaned back, apathetic to the journey, strangely cognizant that we were going somewhere new.

I couldn't tell you how long that trip took, where I went or what I witnessed. I do know that I experienced things I wasn't ready to, and they scared the hell out of me.

My eyes opened with a start, shock and terror leading me from unconsciousness to confusion. I didn't know where I was or what had happened, but based on my mom's face I knew it wasn't good.

"Nathan!" she cried out, touching my forehead. I looked up at her, focusing on hurt and tears, knowing I had done that.

"What happened?" I croaked, taking in the white, sterile room. The smell struck me first. Disinfectant and vinegar burned my nostrils. I clumsily reached to my face, feeling the tubes in my nose and IV in my arm.

"Shh," she murmured, grasping my wrist. "Just rest. You had an accident."

Accident my ass. The pills and wine in the park came rushing back to me. A searing flash of embarrassment and regret jolted through me. My first and only reaction was shame. She had been through so much, and now I was responsible for adding to her misery. I turned my head to hide my tears. Before I knew it, I was asleep again.

When I woke for the second time, a doctor was standing over me, holding my eyelids open while shining a light into my pupils. For a second, I thought I was back in the park, riding the light into the unknown.

The doctor's less-than-friendly voice brought me back to reality.

"You're a lucky young man."

"What happened?"

"You were in respiratory failure with toxic levels of alprazolam and alcohol in your system. No blood or oxygen got to your brain for an extended period of time," he told me while taking my pulse. "You easily could have been brain dead. Someone was looking out for you."

"Wow," was all I could say.

"See you on the other side."

The whisper floated from the far corner of the room. I twisted my neck in an attempt to find the speaker, to respond, but was too weak to move.

My mother's soft words comforted me as they always did, even when I didn't deserve them. "Stay still honey, you need to rest."

Again, I sat up in a desperate effort to source the familiar voice.

Mom spoke again, urgently. "Please, Nate, lie back down."

I squeezed back teardrops at the soothing sound of her voice, tried to swallow. Noticing my pain, she explained: "They had to pump your stomach, Nathan."

I cringed. I wanted to sink into the hospital bed, to disappear with humiliation. I couldn't believe it had come to this.

My homecoming from the hospital later that week was anything but warm. Once I was strong enough to get myself out of bed and perform a semblance of normal daily functions, Mom went about her business with barely a glance in my direction.

I didn't fault her for her attitude towards me; the old saying about it being worse when a parent is disappointed than angry was true. I felt horrible about letting her and our family down but I didn't know how to make it right.

On one of the first mornings home from the hospital Cheyenne had tip-toed timidly into my room. I had been drifting in and out of sleep, still feeling weak and dejected, but lit up when I found her standing at the foot of the bed. She was looking down at me with an intense glare, nibbling on her lower lip. She carried that pose only in her most serious of moods, and I could tell she had something very important to say.

"Hi, Chey," I whispered, cracking a smile. "How you doing?"

"*I'm* fine," she pouted. "How are *you*?"

"I'm feeling better, thanks for asking."

"Well I just wanted you to know that I don't feel sorry for you. I mean, I hope you feel better and all, and I don't necessarily want you to feel crumby, but it is your own fault."

Her words stung, per their intent.

"You're one hundred percent right, Chey," I told her, sitting up to take her hand. "It is my fault, and I don't deserve your sympathy. But let me earn your trust back."

She looked at me wearily, deciding something.

After finally nodding in thoughtful agreement, she told me, "Deal. *If* you promise you will never do drugs again. I may only be nine years old, but *everyone* in my class knows that drugs are bad for you. Didn't they teach you that when you were in the fourth grade?"

"They did, Cheyenne, and I made a big mistake. It will never happen again, I promise."

"You promise?"

"I promise. On everything I love."

"You know Daddy can hear you. You better not be lying, 'cause he'll know."

I pulled her closer. What had I done?

"I'd never lie to you or Daddy," I told her, feeling her tremble in my hold. "I promise."

She pulled herself up, taking deep breaths. Delicate hands calmly smoothed her white and pink polka-dotted blouse before looking me dead in the eye.

"Good. Because I don't want to lose you too."

My father had broken his promise to my mother, and I was destined to break mine to my sister.

Chapter 24

I HAVE BEEN, to put it mildly, anxiously awaiting try-outs all week. Under normal circumstances, the upcoming weekend is unimaginably distant to a fourth grader on a Monday morning. But as this was no ordinary weekend, it had been no ordinary wait.

I am staring at the ceiling well before Dad is scheduled to wake me. When I finally deem the time appropriate, I whip the covers off, retrieving my glove from underneath the pillow.

The smell from the oil is strong. It smells like promise. I quickly unwind the string holding it together, unwrapping it like a highly-anticipated gift. I remove the ball and insert my hand. I flex it, back and forth, back and forth. Spit in it, pound it, raise it to my eyes, blocking the sun and catching flies. A pound of leather defining a childhood.

I don't taste my breakfast and have to be reminded to say goodbye to Mom and Cheyenne. I'm in the pickup before Dad is even downstairs and out of it before it's fully stopped.

A whiteboard shows that I am in Group 2, batting on the Great Neck Field. I Velcro and re-Velcro my batting gloves over and over while watching the coach pitch to other players. They spray balls all over the field. They are good; I am better, I think, just before a beefy kid hits one over the left field fence. Then "Butler" is called by a man with a clipboard, so I grab a bat and head to home plate.

The first pitch is inside. I let it go. The second bounces. Frustrated, I feel my heart beat faster. I twirl the bat, glare at the pitcher, imploring him to send one down the middle. He does. I swing and miss. He does again, I miss again. I grit my teeth, furious. Whiff.

The coach keeps throwing, I keep missing, I keep getting angrier and angrier. I have never hit this badly. My mind spins. The encouragement from the coaches, the other kids, just increases my anxiety. Somewhere behind me, Dad is watching.

After more than enough misses, the coach with the clipboard calls out "Davidson" and I walk off the field. My face is red and I throw the bat at the dugout, narrowly missing Davidson. I make eye contact with Dad just as the bat is spinning through the air and am actually able to witness the transition from sympathy to fury. His eyes widen and mouth opens into a yell, but I am already running the other way. A string of curses flies from my mouth and I run while parents, coaches and players watch, mouths agape. I can hear him chasing after me, and it's not until later, at home, that the embarrassment fully hits.

Chapter 25

THE FLEETING REMNENTS OF WINTER blurred past, as they tend to do. By spring the combined traumas had substantially worn me down and a general discontent left me with a pittance of the prior season's exuberance.

At the urgings of my coach and Spencer, Mom had reluctantly allowed me stay on the football team. Spring practice was fast approaching and the prevailing belief was that football would deliver discipline and something to work towards. I was just happy it got me out of the house, even if my passion for the sport had waned.

But at some point, simple adolescent anger had given way to a deep-seated restlessness and indifference that those around me had to suffer. Whether Tammy wasn't speaking to me or vice versa was irrelevant, and I had missed a scheduled visit from Eli when I was in the hospital. To add to the stress in our household, an unfair but intense distain for my mother had set in, rendering me nothing short of a complete asshole.

To her dismay and my brashness, our own yard had fallen into disrepair. It gave me a rebellious thrill to see dandelions bent over the driveway and shrubbery casting shadows on the front steps.

"You have got to be kidding me." My mother stood in front of me, hands on hips, disgusted-mother look smeared across her face. For her trouble she was met with my best teenage-angst sneer.

"What now?" I groaned.

Anger flashed across her eyes before she paused, collecting herself. After a deep sigh and feature reset, she started a passionate plea.

"Is this how it's going to be, Nate? From now on? I want to know now, so I can prepare myself."

"Know what? Prepare for what?" I practically spat.

She took a deep, pained breath.

"If I've lost you. The drinking, the drugs, the sneaking out, the crazy antics. But more than that, the attitude. The lingering case of the I-don't-give-a-shits. That's what hurts the most. I want to know where my little boy went. And I really want to know if he's coming back."

I swung my legs off the couch and started to stand. I didn't need this bullshit. Screw it. Screw them all.

Her arms shot out, crashing into me violently, sending me back down. In shock, I looked up to find a desperate – but not yet defeated – woman. Pain was mapped in sharp creases that intersected her face, meeting in angry symbols of anguish. Her eyes – those bright, confident eyes – now seemed empty and shallow.

"You don't seem like a happy person," she stated plainly. "I don't even remember what your laugh sounds like. You don't smile. You're not pleasant to be around." The words landed like bullets; because, I realized, they were true, all of them.

"All I want out of life is for my children to be happy. That's what I have left. Yours and Cheyenne's happiness. And you're close to throwing away any chance of a happy life."

I tried to swallow the rock in my throat. "What about your happiness, Mom?"

"My happiness was filled with bullets in an Afghan valley and buried on a warm fall day in Florida two and a half years ago."

"Well, that's pretty fucking hypocritical," I blurted. The response was instant and fierce. Her right hand shot out, palm connecting on cheek with a CRACK.

We held our poses, each more shocked than the other. Staring, until she finally spoke – a whisper really, just audible over the pounding in my ears.

"You have your whole life ahead of you, Nathan. But the decisions you make today will dictate how the rest of your life goes. My job is to help you maximize the opportunities afforded to you. And I will not fail in doing so. So right now, this minute, you decide what is right. I still trust you to do the right thing, and I know your father would too."

My breaths came slowly and steady through my nose, lips pursed in anger and confusion, tasting salt and guilt.

"I'm sick of it! Sick of being compared to him, of being held to his standard! I'm not Dad, I'm just not!"

I turned away from her, making my way to the front door before she could respond. The door softly clicked behind me as I stepped into the dewy morning. A hazy brightness singed my vision. The songs of crickets bounced off the house, adding to nature's symphony.

I walked to the edge of our lawn, surveying the small piece of land where so much had changed. The space was the same. The familiar juniper tree standing isolated in the middle of the yard. The faded white siding connecting with the rain gutters I had cleared of pine needles and oak leaves so many times. The curved driveway, lined with burning bushes now overgrown and shedding their crimson flakes. A flock of the delicate flowers rolled in the wind, floating up and across the street. I watched their journey as they spread out and re-grouped, spread out and re-grouped, like a school of minnows communicating in a language only known to them. The gust died out, they settled back to earth to await their destiny.

I retrieved a broom from the garage to sweep them up. After mowing and edging I swept the driveway again, then the sidewalks. By the time dusk fell I was on my knees, dirt-caked but fulfilled, spreading the last bit of mulch around those burning bushes, their arms extended out towards the heavens and my heart not far behind.

While I'd worked, I had done the math. Eight hundred and fifty days.

Later that night I sat on our front steps wedged between Cheyenne and Mom. There was a scent of early summer in the air. We were quiet and peaceful, licking mint chocolate chip ice cream cones. We sat close together, shoulders rubbing, softly laughing at inside jokes in the warm glow of the porch light. A family.

When headlights snaked their way along the quiet street, three sets of anxious eyes followed. The car slowly overtook the streetlights one at a time before easing to a stop at our curb. Nervous looks were shared; I didn't know that we would ever get comfortable with unannounced visitors. We stared into the porch light's glare, curious and tense. Two car doors shut gently, giving way to the sound of soft footsteps on the sidewalk.

I stood protectively, squinting into the dark.

"Uncle Spencer! Bull!" I called out excitedly, recognizing the confident gait and athletic builds making their way up the driveway.

"There's the Little Warrior," Spencer called out, reaching us. "Gayle," he said, extending for a hug before leaning into Cheyenne. "Well hello, Chey, did you miss us?

His hand swallowed her nodding head. She threw her chin towards the stars, trying to get a better look. She was thinking the same thing we all were, and Spencer and Bull showed their guilt for not being able to deliver it each time they came home.

"What's wrong with you?" I asked suddenly, noticing Bull's right leg was dragging.

"Training accident," my mom blurted out at the same time he did. An uncomfortable laugh followed, the comedy of open secrets absurd. Of course we had had our fill of "training accidents" over the years. The guys were always banged up – broken fingers, twisted knees, separated shoulders. They kept it as quiet as possible, lest they be sidelined or called soft by their teammates.

Cheyenne looked up at us curiously.

"What's so funny?" she demanded. The defiant way of a child.

The fact that I was included in the collective look between the SEALs and my mom was, to me, like admission to adulthood. Soon the laughter increased, changing from uneasy grins to carefree, genuine joy.

"You guys are crazy," Cheyenne told us, shaking her ponytail before turning her attention back to her cone.

Our mother leaned in for an Eskimo kiss and nuzzled against her neck.

"No, yooou're crazy!" she crooned, making room for Spencer and Bull on the steps. "Spence, Rob, ice cream?"

They both lit up and nodded, two big, chiseled kids.

"Chey, would you like to help your mother get these tough Frogmen some ice cream cones?" she asked, taking Cheyenne's hand.

"Is that because they are going to yell at Nate?" she asked smugly before being whisked inside.

Excited and surprised, I turned to Spencer and Bull, grinning broadly.

"So where were you guys? Green Team? You guys in SEAL Team 6 now?" My questions gushed rapid-fire, immediately changing my audience's expressions over to anger and disgust.

"Did you just say Team 6?" Spencer asked, incredulous.

Bull took a menacing step closer, sneering at me. "Sit your butt down, close your mouth and open your ears."

He towered in front of, over me, blocking the street light like an eclipse. The gnarled face did not show an ounce of give, of concession. The calmness, the coldness of the words, amplified each as they rang out, landing as a forceful unit.

"I had better never hear talk like that out of you again. Is that how we operate? Is that how you grew up, with your father talking about what he did? We don't talk about that stuff, and if you want to be around us, you won't either," he spat through gritted teeth.

My face flushed and stomach flipped. I looked down at my feet, ashamed and embarrassed. "Silent professionals" was the expectation of these men, and anything short of that would not be tolerated.

I had screwed up again.

"I'm sorry, Bull. Uncle Spencer. I really am. I was just excited to see you, and..."

But Spencer cut me off before I could finish.

"Don't give me that sad-sack horseshit. Did I hear that you mooned the marching band at a pep rally? And left a burning pile of dog crap on someone's front steps? We haven't even gotten to the drinking and drugs yet. We're going to have a long talk with you, boy, and if you end up with some bruises during the course of those discussions, well, we'll just have to chalk that up to the price of education."

The glare of a SEAL, especially one just back from whatever grueling scenarios they had just endured, has a way of shrinking you into a hole of fear and reflection. In fact, it makes you really wish you could take back whatever action had led to angering said SEAL. I was reminded of just how much I wanted to be on the other end of that steely stare in the future.

Bull was still steaming, and the quiet monotone of his words did not diminish how terrifying he was. In fact, the controlled anger intensified his intimidating presence.

"Are you kidding me, Nate? Is this some type of joke? Overdosing on drugs? Is that the legacy you are following? Is that who you are, who you're going to be? If so, I can tell you we don't want any part of it."

I knew better than to answer these rhetorical questions and tried to look as ashamed as I felt.

"Well, the bad news for you, boy, is that we're not going to let that be who you are. If we have to beat it out of you, so be it. But there is no fucking way we're going to let your father's son grow up to be some junky piece of shit," Spencer said.

I started to open my mouth but quickly shut it, rethinking my strategy. I knew they didn't want to hear excuses, didn't want me to bullshit them or shirk responsibility. Time to take my medicine.

I began again.

"All I can tell you both is that it will ever happen again. I take full responsibility for my mistakes, I sincerely apologize and hope I can earn your trust back. It will never happen again."

It sounded great coming out and I had hoped I had dug myself out. Not quite.

Bull's hand flew out, grabbing me by the throat. Not so hard as to choke me, but more than enough to let me know he was there.

"I don't give a darn about your promises and you can shove your apologies up your rear," he fumed.

Then, just as quickly, he removed his hand from my neck. Tiny footsteps came closer, the front door swinging open. His murderous look seamlessly transformed into a friendly smile just as Cheyenne hopped outside, concentrating on the two heaping cones in each hand.

"Here you go, Uncle Spencer," she sang, little hand extended proudly. Her grin suddenly froze when the green scoop slid off the cone, landing with a plop on the ground in front of her.

Cheyenne's face melted into a pained contortion, her mouth agape. Spencer rushed forward, laughing loudly in an attempt to stave off what were sure to be imminent sobs. Before the first bellow could escape Spencer had plucked the ice cream off the ground with his fingers and popped the entire thing into his mouth.

Cheyenne's eyes went wide with shock while Spencer's cheeks bulged and he worked the ice cream in his mouth, swallowing dramatically.

"Whoa, that's gross," she stammered, forgetting about the brimming tears.

Spencer's hands shot to his head, gripping it violently, his face twisted in obvious agony.

"Brain freeze?" laughed Bull with pleasure.

Mom came back outside. We turned to her, laughing.

"You don't want to know," I told her.

We watched Spencer's antics with amusement until he was able to gather a few deep breaths, finally raising his hands in defeat. I was just glad the focus was off me.

"Whew," he exclaimed, "that did not feel good."

"I thought SEALs didn't feel pain," my mom offered sarcastically.

"We don't. Just enjoying my ice cream. Thank you, Gayle. And Cheyenne."

"Would you like to come in? I'm guessing you could use a home-cooked meal. I have ziti in the fridge, it shouldn't take long to heat up."

Spencer put his hand on my head in what probably looked like a gentle gesture, but in reality his vise-like grip made me empathize with the brain freeze.

"Thanks, Gayle, we'd love to, but Nate was just asking us to run him through some PT bright and early tomorrow, so we'd better get some shut-eye." He turned to me sharply and said, "0500, be ready."

And with that, they walked back down the driveway, smiling at the ladies, shooting darts in my direction.

Chapter 26

THERE EXISTS A REMARKABLE STILLNESS in the hours between the dead of night and first dawn. I eased out the front door the next morning, softly closing it behind me, and stood alone under the porch light. After a moment of acclimating to the dark, I shivered, sat on the top stop, awaiting my instructors. The sound of creatures always near but rarely seen lit up the surroundings. They croaked and chirped in anonymity, evidence of the time of day's limbo.

My adrenaline was already flowing, senses heightened. I could hear the leaves in the trees, feel the slight breeze moving blades of grass. Until, unannounced, a powerful force lifted me off the ground, slammed me back down. My head swam, no identifiable thoughts, breath quickly sucked out of me.

When I finally got my bearings, two callous figures stood over me, towering against the steel gray sky.

"Fuuuuck," I whined, resulted in a New Balance tennis shoe landing on my chest.

"Watch your mouth," breathed Bull. Then, "Let's go."

They let me scramble to my feet just long enough to start a determined and motivated pace. My cold limbs initially flailed in an effort to keep up. And so the day began.

We ran in near silence, the plodding of six feet in occasional unison softly absorbing the concord of first light. Our route led us up Diamond Spring Road towards the Navy Operational Support Center, which was at least six or seven miles from my house. I knew better than to ask for confirmation when no destination was offered.

The pace was faster than I was used to and the ease with which my training partners made each stride and overtook each mile quickly began to wear on me. While each side stitch and labored breath pushed me closer to an undetermined breaking point, Bull and Spencer seemed to strengthen and widen the performance gap.

Still, I did not utter a word or complaint. I tried to focus on Spencer's tight jorts, his Santa Claus stocking hat. Anything to take my mind from the pain.

As expected, we made a left on Shore Drive, running in between Lake Whitehurst and Little Creek Cove. The sun began to make its entrance over my right shoulder, but I barely noticed the muted colors painting the inlet. I was concentrating on my breathing, mind over matter.

I soon fell into an obstinate rhythm, enjoying the pain and challenge to body and brain. It was liberating to be completely under someone else's control; I was at the mercy of Bull and Spencer and complete concession was the only option.

This was more mental than physical. SEAL training is proof that the body can endure more than we can imagine: it's the mind that will give out first. So I relied on a sort of transcendentalism. On each stride, each one-foot section of pavement, each block. Each bounce of that ridiculous hat. Thinking about school, football, girls, whatever. Don't think ahead to the final goal, don't dwell on what has already been accomplished. What's the best way to eat an elephant? One bite at a time.

As if sensing my relative comfortableness, Spencer and Bull suddenly shot off the main road, sprinting towards the marina. I surprised myself by meeting their intensity, gritting my teeth at burning thighs and searing lungs but staying close enough to hear the gravel their feet kicked up.

We stopped at the edge of the cove as quickly as we had started some forty-five minutes earlier. Blood rushed upwards to my face, where it met the line of sweat flowing south from my hairline. I paced, hands on head, enjoying the flurry of endorphins and passing of this first test. I gulped oxygen as swiftly as possible while at the same time trying not to look too winded. This being just the beginning of our day left little room for celebration, although I did allow myself a momentary pat on the back.

"Happy with yourself?" Spencer challenged. He looked like he had just gotten back from a stroll in the mall rather than a six-mile run.

"Not, really," I breathed. Then, cracking a smile, "Instructor Detse."

He ran with it, giving me a "hooyah," before telling me to drop.

I hit the deck with gusto, arms extended and back straight.

"Push 'em out," he said calmly, walking around me as I counted out twenty-five pushups. After completion, I held my pose, waiting for further instruction. Softly, it came.

"Push 'em out."

I began another set of twenty-five, but he interrupted my count with his own.

"Four, FOUR, five, six, seven, SEVEN," he deadpanned, before suddenly erupting.

"All the way down!"

He leaned down, his face inches from mine, screaming.

"If you want to do girl push-ups I'll get you a tampon and we can finish PT when you get back from the gynecologist!"

Spittle landed across my face, but I didn't dare acknowledge it. My arms burned, my body already tired from the run, but I clenched my chin and finished the set. Barely.

"Push 'em out."

I almost groaned, but sucked it back in the nick of time. Instead, I smiled to myself, knowing that it didn't matter to me if my arms were at their breaking point – my mind wasn't, and wouldn't be. I'd do this until I died.

"So you want to do drugs? To drink, get fucked up, is that it?" Spencer started. "You want to be some loser druggy? Well, I got news for you Butler: not on my watch!"

Bull picked up where he left off. "One way or another, we'll motivate you, son. We'll keep you on the straight and narrow if we have to beat it out of you. ALL THE WAY DOWN! Even when we're not here, we're here. We see all, and we know all."

"And if there is one more incident, one tiny misunderstanding involving drugs, we will fuck you up beyond recognition, Butler," growled Spencer. "Just think about doing it one more time, see what happens."

"Advil, Nate. No more than two in a four hour period, not to exceed six in a day. Anything past that and we will be on you like white on rice. Do not test me."

"Twenty-five," I stammered, waiting in the lean and rest, not caring if they made me do another set. I'd do 100 more if I had to.

"Feet," Bull said softly. And then: "Get wet."

I tried to hide my shock, but a sideways glance verified their seriousness. Resigned, I jogged towards the Little Creek Channel, doing my best to turn my brain off before taking an uneasy breath and jumping in feet first.

The cold brackish water jolted my insides. The water was waist deep, leaving my sweaty upper-body exposed to the cool breeze while my lower extremities rattled below the surface. I turned back to my instructors, unsure as what to do.

"It ain't surf torture, but it'll have to do," Bull said, hands on hips. "GET YOUR WHOLE BODY WET!"

I threw my feet back, allowing my upper body and head to submerge. The sour water found its way into my mouth – puking became a real possibility. I rose, spitting, shivering, shaking my head, at attention as best I could with vertigo spinning me sideways.

They put me through a few more iterations of surf torture before bringing me back to dry land and into the lean and rest.

Bull glared at me, disgust plastered across his hard face. "Having fun yet?"

"Hooyah, Instructor Bullin!" I bellowed.

"Good. Push 'em out."

I did what must have been a solid set of pushups, counting loudly, because he recovered me after only one set. My teeth involuntarily chattered while a blend of sweat and channel water leaked from my head. Minutes seemed like hours; I couldn't believe the sky was still lackadaisically completing its transformation to day. My innards begged for the warm blanket of sunlight.

Spencer pointed a finger down the seawall. "That bench. There and back in one minute. Pays to be a winner." He clicked his watch.

I was well aware of that phrase's significance. As good as it was to win, it was even worse to lose. Over a minute wasn't an option. I took off, pumping my arms as leaden legs tried to keep up. I gritted through the pain, slapped the bench, did a 180. Every fiber of me put out as hard as it could, focusing on the two SEALs calmly awaiting my return. I leaned forward as I reached them, like a sprinter does when crossing the finish line, wheeling my head in their direction. I waited for an indicator – did I make it? Faces that may as well have been stone offered no inclination either way. Finally, Bull spat on the ground, simply stating, "Pays to be a winner. Recover."

I allowed myself the faintest of smiles, pacing slowly, living in the simple momentary lack of pain.

"Way to put out, Nate. You get to pick the next evolution," Spencer told me. His expression hadn't changed from when he had been berating me, but didn't need to. Max effort and results were the creed these men lived by, and I had shown them my resolve.

"How about surfing?" I asked mischievously.

They exchanged an amused look, almost lightening the mood.

"Surf torture?" Spencer mocked. "We can sit in there all day."

I shook my head, terrified that I would have to go stand in the cold bay again.

"Surfing. We get the boards and head to the jetty. Nice and small today, I'm sure you land lubbers can handle it."

"Man," exclaimed Bull, smoothing his bald head, looking off into the distance. "You Butlers and your surfing. Your old man made me go once. Bet him he couldn't eat more habanero peppers than I could. Of course the son of a gun wouldn't stop until I started puking fire. A hurricane swell, I think he called it. Barely even made it out past the break, still not sure how I made it back in. I'll happily place a limpet mine on the bottom of a carrier, but you're not getting my carcass back on a surfboard."

Spencer and I laughed. Even though I had been young, I remembered the bet. It hadn't seemed odd at the time, but I remember how mad my mom had been. Dad had barely left the bathroom for days and the house had reeked to high heavens. It was one of the few times she had actually been happy when his platoon had left for a training exercise. "Let the jerks who put him up to that bet sit for fourteen hours on a cargo plane with him," she had said after we dropped him off on base.

Spencer now looked at me quizzically. He had never even seen the ocean before joining the Navy, and while he was half-fish now, surfing was a whole different animal.

"What are you prepared to put on the line?"

I paused. As fast as it came, I pushed out the thought that I very well may have gotten in over my head. There were precious few things I could beat Spencer at. Except...

"Whatever you want," I replied confidently.

"If you lose, I'm going to PT you into the ground. We'll have our own version of Hell Week. We'll call it Hell Weekend, and you'll be with me from Friday after school until Sunday night. And you can leave your jammies and pillow at home."

I actually felt my heart fall into my stomach at the notion, but at the same time I knew there was no way I could back out.

"And if I win, you'll go surfing with me?"

His scoff solidified the deal.

"Done," I said as assuredly as my racing brain would allow. "Now what's the bet?"

"You tell me, this is your evolution."

There was only one thing I could think of to even entertain the possibility of having an advantage. But I wanted us to arrive there carefully.

"I dunno Spencer, you've been through all the training. Pick something."

"Well, at sniper school I had four hours to stalk through the desert and shoot a target from 2,000 yards while two trained snipers sat on the back of a pickup with binoculars trying to spot me. In BUD/S

I had an instructor try to drown me while I couldn't defend myself. At Green Team we – "

He stopped short, knowing he had given away a major secret.

"Ha!" I called out, smiling broadly. "I knew it. You guys screened positive for Green Team, passed and are now in Team 6."

All too familiarly, Spencer's arm flew out and once again I had a hand around my throat. I gagged, tried to pull away.

"Don't ever let me hear those words come out of your mouth again. We should have never mentioned Green Team to you, proven by the fact that you keep mentioning it. If you want to be part of the community, act like it. Do you ever hear the operators you know talking like that?"

He answered for me, swinging my head from side to side.

"Understood, I will never say anything else about Teal Seam Ticks again," I croaked.

To my surprise, they both let out a chuckle. The levity seemed like a good opening for me to make my suggestion.

"How about football? You line up on the goal line, I'll stand at the 50. You try to score a touchdown. I try to tackle you. Best of three wins."

They paused, glaring at me. *Through* me. The stares made it feel like time had stopped. I actually felt my toes sweating. What was it about these men that could make you want to dig a hole and bury yourself with just a hard look?

I could tell Spencer wasn't crazy about the idea, having been a wrestler and never playing football in high school. Bull actually looked somewhat proud – I think he was impressed with my ingenuity. He later admitted as much.

Despite any reservations, there was no way Spencer wouldn't take the challenge. And even better, it got me out of more PT that morning. My clothes were still damp and teeth chattering when he smiled, agreeing to the bet.

Now I just had to make sure to win.

Spencer walked ahead, loosely stretching and cracking his neck. He wasn't looking at us, wasn't talking, wasn't smiling. I gave Bull a nervous look, whispering, "Man, he's taking this seriously."

Bull looked sharply at me, his expression nothing but serious.

"Can you guess why? Second place gets dead in our world. We don't lose. In anything."

It occurred to me, not for this first time, just how focused these warriors were. Not a wasted word, movement or breath. They lived the Teams, and winning at everything they did. Anything else to them was ridiculous, an absurdity. Being anything other than the best wasn't even a consideration or possibility.

As was my custom, I considered the words intimately, letting them soak in on their own accord. Another tick on a growing list of inherited experiences that I hoped with continued nourishment would foster a foundation of self-evolution. Especially since I knew without a doubt where my path was heading.

We crossed Amphibious Drive, heading towards the base football field when seemingly from nowhere and everywhere the deep intones of a bugle surrounded us. Ahead, Spencer stopped abruptly, veering at attention in the direction of a huge American flag being raised by two Marines. Bull and I halted in turn, as did each pedestrian and car. Time stalled, save for the sound and slow ascension of that flag. The air glowed, filled with the hallowed notes of our country's anthem. The auditory memory was all too reminiscent of my own Taps experience on that day since past. Naturally, the expected range of emotions coursed through me. The song spoke to me. It filled me with pride and sadness and anxiety and fear and honor. I stood as tall as a house, my teenage muscles swollen, radiating the same pride we all felt. A beat bookending the last note's echo slid into the measured sounds of early morning normalcy. Only then did I feel the stretched tear fading down my face. I was able to wipe it before Bull noticed, but only because his sleeve was pulled across his own.

Once again I realized that when I had lost a father, they had lost a brother.

We entered dull grounds. The low-budget base field featured more weeds and dirt clods than grass. But the sparse amenities offered to the nation's fighting forces were something we stubbornly took pride in. I was learning that toughness comes from necessity, which military life bred.

Initially, I was amused at Spencer's intensity while lining up on the goal line. But his scowl quickly unsettled me, again making me question the wisdom of the challenge. When I thought back to the cold bay and more push-ups, I figured this couldn't be any worse.

Bull stood on the sidelines between us, calling instructions.

"Spence, you have three chances to get past this tadpole and score twice in the far end zone." Then he addressed me, laughter on his words. "Puke, somehow you have to stop him from scoring twice. Or planting you at midfield. Good freaking luck."

My heels on the 50, I looked over my opponent. We were actually close to the same height by that point, not that that meant anything. The most noticeable of many differences was the challenge his biceps and chest presented to his t-shirt's fabric – mine flitted in the breeze as if still on a coat hanger.

And then it began. He started slowly, straight at me. Leaning forward, I angled in his direction, waiting for him to commit. He continued a methodical path, slowly picking up steam with each passed yard marker. We finally met at the 35. His sudden acceleration was led by a cartoonish shoulder and forearm, both connecting solidly with flesh and cartilage. The impact sent me straight back, lifting my legs until I was parallel to the ground. The world went black save for the bursts of light in my peripheral – the stars could have either been from the shoulder to the face or the bounce of my head on the turf when I returned to earth. By the time I could rise to a knee, Spencer was already dancing in the far end zone.

"Whoo-ee, I bet none of them high school boys hit that like!" he gloated as he walked past me. "That's how a Cornhusker hits. Wanna give? Ring the bell?"

"No fucking way," I spat, rubbing my jaw.

"You poking the bear, boy?"

"The only thing worse than losing is quitting."

"I'll take 'Phrases Your Old Man Used to Say' for 500."

"Just line up," I told him, making it to my feet.

His scowl seemed more real and intense than before. I flexed my jaw to make sure it still worked, then determinedly took my place to wait for the next rush.

This time I flew off my line, straight at him. His tactic was the same; brute force. We sprinted straight at each other, neither making an attempt to avoid the high-speed collision. At the moment of impact I squatted low, my shoulder landing squarely with his thigh.

If I thought there had been an explosion in my brain on the last run, this time seemed like a collision with a semi. The back of my head felt like it had split down the middle. I gasped for air, only able to make out black and bright flashes of light. Time stopped. I could hear myself groaning.

"Get up, boy!"

I could make out the yell, but it was muffled, sounded like someone yelling underwater. I rolled to my side, tasting blood and dirt. Bull stood over me, unimpressed.

"Did he score?" I whispered.

"Nah, he tripped right over you and fell too. Looked like a Mack truck squishing a bug."

"Sometimes you're the bug, sometimes you're the truck. And sometimes the bug stops the truck," I said, trying to manage a grin. "Rubber match."

"Don't get cocky. I'm guessing if he runs you over like that again we're going to have to scrape you off the field with a spatula."

"I'm okay with that," I told him, raising myself to a crawling position. "As long as he goes down with me." Bull sneered at my outstretched hand and walked back over to the sideline.

"Thanks."

Spencer was already lined up and ready to go. Bouncing on the balls of his feet, flexing each side of his body. Luckily I was too concussed to be intimidated. He began an aggressive trot while I was still seeing double. I wagged my head, started towards him. Aim for the middle one.

Stomping feet, grunts and curses were the soundtrack in my groggy head. He tried to turn the sideline and was nearly past me when I dove at him, head first. There was a crunch when I connected with his knee, hard enough to turn everything dark. Slowly, a veil lowered over my eyes. I tried to get to a knee, but dizziness took over. And that's the last thing I remembered.

It felt like a dream, smelled like a dream, tasted like a dream. I certainly thought it was a dream. But when I unclenched my eyes and batted them against the morning glare, I realized the two apparitions hovering over me were real. There was a dim memory of my temple connecting with a leg of solid muscle.

"What the fu-," I started, before a familiar New Balance sneaker landed on my chest.

"Don't even think about it."

My brain struggled to grasp what had happened, focusing most of its energy on the railroad spike that seemed to have been driven through my skull. I made an effort to get some moisture on my dusty tongue, with little success. All the while strangely unconcerned at how challenging it was to fill my lungs with enough oxygen to speak.

"Did. I tackle. Him?" I somehow managed to exhale, trying to focus on one of their faces.

I wasn't sure who said it, but when I heard "pays to be a winner," my smile couldn't have been removed with a belt sander.

Chapter 27

NEEDLESS TO SAY, the resulting surf session with Spencer the following weekend was one of the most fun times I ever had in the water. SEALs innately believe they are superior at everything, especially anything related to Mother Ocean, so my carving and his wipeouts made for a morning of bliss. He did make me pay the man during PT later that afternoon, but each additional evolution just legitimized the triumph.

It was great having the guys in town for such an extended period of time. I cherished every meeting, even though often it meant they were kicking my ass. I knew the call could come and end it at any time. Touching pills or booze was a consideration less likely than becoming a Gators fan. Their scowling faces and gnarled bodies were a daily deterrent, impossible to ignore.

It is debatable whether or not one should take pride in doing what is inherently expected of him. That being said, I did allow myself some personal gratification that May when I declined Darren's invitation to a party at his house. Even though Spencer had unexpectedly cancelled a camping trip and I hadn't spoken to the guys since a sudden departure two weeks before, I still refrained. Their presence never seemed far away, no matter what corner of the world they may be in.

Instead, I exhausted myself cutting lawns that weekend. The

seemingly never-ending rotation of local servicemen fighting in Afghanistan and Iraq all had yards that needed attending to. I remember I was especially tired that Sunday night, my eyes leaden as I laid on the couch with Mom and Cheyenne watching *The Simpsons*. Mom had led me into my bed sometime soon after, too tired to even brush my teeth. When she woke me up several hours later, any lingering drowsiness vanished with the thunderbolt that she delivered.

"We got Bin Laden."

It took some time to gather my thoughts. Once I felt the news had appropriately settled in, I shuffled, in somewhat of a daze, out of bed to join her in the living room. It was the middle of the night, although I wasn't sure of the exact time. Cheyenne was half asleep on Mom's lap, the television flicking bright flashes across the wall. The scene had the aura of a hospital waiting room after a family has been given serious but hopeful news.

The sudden ring of the phone seemed louder than it should have, quickly bringing each of us out of our individual trances. Mom answered, giving short, muted replies before hanging up. Immediately, it rang again. Her arm shot out, taking it off the hook. We tried to smile at each other while she scooted over, making room for me on the couch.

"It's true what they say."

"What's that?"

"All actions do have an equal and opposite reaction."

Her comment brought a wry smile to both of our faces. Cheyenne barely stirred as I lowered myself next to them.

I still wasn't sure how to react to the news that the man responsible for indelibly turning our lives inside out had finally been brought to justice. A chapter had undoubtedly been closed, but still I felt oddly unsatisfied. There was a glee, no doubt about that, but something was missing nonetheless.

I had once overheard Dad and Spencer drinking beers in our garage, discussing the impact 9/11 had on them.

They were under the hood of his pickup, the job in progress unfathomable to my young mind. I had held my breath at the top of the stairs, the door just showing enough light for me to hear the crack of beers and smell their cigar smoke.

"I didn't know what to think." My dad's voice had sounded colder than usual, detached. "In a sense, I was almost grateful. I had always known what I was put on this earth to do, and now I would be able to prove it. The sheer focus, the privilege of being the men who were going to get that eye was an honor. I'd had my Budweiser for almost four years, and I was finally ready to earn it."

"Shit, I was a half-assed rodeo clown drowning in pussy and Natty Ice. I didn't know my ass from my elbow. But when I watched those towers go down, I knew I finally had a purpose. I joined that day. The Army recruiter was closed for lunch and I couldn't get to the Marines' 'cause I had left my pickup at some honky-tonk the night before. The next closest recruiter in the strip mall was the Navy's, so I walked in and told them I wanted to kill ragheads. There was a poster with a Frogman exiting the ocean in the middle of the night, M16 locked and loaded, face painted green, looking like Chuck Norris fucked Chuck Pfarrer. I told that black shoe to sign me up for the SEALs, I wanted to blow shit up. He stifled a laugh and egged me on. I'm sure he never thought for a second I'd make it." Spencer chuckled. "Had no idea what I was getting myself into."

"You were a SEAL then, you just didn't know it."

Spencer paused, mulling the words. "Every SEAL starts as a tadpole, I suppose."

Those words had hit me hard that day, and their impact had never dissipated. I sat silently, thinking back to that conversation and how different the impact of 9/11 had been on our family than on the rest of the country's.

The television showed the Presidential Podium, empty. The newscaster said President Obama was due to speak any minute. Mom's expression soured when he strutted across the screen.

"Tonight I can report to the American people, and to the world, that the United States has conducted an operation that killed Osama Bin Laden, the leader of Al Qaida," monotoned the President of the United States. Despite the messenger, his words lifted me up, gave me an increasingly rare sense of pride and patriotism.

The word that it had been Navy SEALs came shockingly fast. That it was them wasn't a surprise to me – but that the administration had admitted who it was and even specifically mentioned SEAL Team 6 blew my mind. I couldn't begin to imagine the outrage the operators were experiencing knowing they had been outed by their Commander in Chief.

I thought back to the last time I had spoken to the guys. Per usual, they hadn't offered any details as to where they were going. Could they have been involved? I knew it was possible, and I knew they would never tell me. And I for damn sure would never ask.

I read whatever I could find online over the following weeks, and was shocked at how much information Obama and his administration had revealed about Operation Neptune Spear. I didn't have to speak with the SEALs to know what their reaction would be to putting a face to the mission. *Their* face. The Vice President, to the horror of the special operations community, had actually admitted that the SEALs who had completed the raid were from the secretive Team 6. And as far as I could tell, LT Hagen, Bull, and Spencer were all now members of DEVGRU, even if they couldn't admit it.

"Why is it okay to be happy that someone got killed?"

I was not terribly surprised to get this question. Cheyenne had been silent but introspective ever since the news, and now that she seemed to have her thoughts in order she was ready to discuss.

To start with, she made it clear she was confused about everyone's reaction in the days after the Bin Laden mission. Not just our family's reaction, but the swarms of people who had flocked to the streets in celebration and the general joviality surrounding his killing.

Slowly, I removed the headphones blasting Dropkick Murphys, wiped my forehead. I had just gotten home from a workout when she poked her head into my bedroom, that serious face making it clear this wasn't just a social call.

Again I cleared sweat, more as a mechanism to buy time while considering a response.

"Because he was an evil man who was responsible for killing thousands of innocent people. If it weren't for him, Daddy would still be alive."

Her mouth tightened and she thoughtfully looked to the ceiling. A decision had been made. She said simply, "Then I'm glad he's dead too. At least now he can't kill any more people."

I grinned and put my hand on her head. "You're a smart little girl, you know that?"

She nodded knowingly while telling me that I could be a smart boy if only I tried. Feigned incredulousness forced my eyes wide as I scooped my insulter into the air and bounced her upside down. She giggled so hard that she ended up tooting right in my face. By the time our laughter had subsided we were laying shoulder to shoulder against the rough carpet, exhausted.

Chapter 28

THE GUYS RETURNED to Virginia Beach a few days later. Superficially, it was like nothing had happened. It would be hard to say whether the underlying tension was invented by a hopeful, adolescent brain, or if the perceived paranoia was real. But their aggression did seem to be boiling over, daring me to ask the unaskable.

When Spencer took me to TGI Fridays to make up for cancelling our camping trip, the conversation was strained, steering clear of current events. We didn't even acknowledge that there *was* an elephant in the room, let alone what it was.

The truth was, as I began preparing for football practice, I still had no idea if they had been involved in the mission. Not that I didn't spend a significant amount of time wondering. But before I knew it, two-a-days started and it was business as usual in the Butler household.

On the last Friday of August they got back from a short training mission. It just so happened to be our first game of the season, and when I looked up in the stands that night, my breath quickened with exhilaration and nervousness.

To call that evening's conditions muggy would be a disservice to swamplands throughout the Southeastern United States. The stadium lights bore down steeply from above, highlighting gnats and optimistic high school eyes. The atmosphere buzzed with hormones and promise, of kids living in the moment and the shedding of stress that comes each Friday. Gharun was stretching us when I made out Spencer, Bull, and LT Hagen perched like gargoyles sprinkled in the stands. The three SEALs loomed next to Mom and Cheyenne. Their presence always relegated those in their wake to the shadows, despite their best efforts at anonymity. Mangy beards and hair paired with sunglasses and collegiate wear couldn't hide their muscle tone, or the air of confidence and power radiating like a halo. There was no mistaking the fact that they stood out in the half-full stands. However, my excitement was tempered knowing there was a good chance that warm-ups would be the only time I would touch the field that night.

The guys, ever vigilant in their quest to preserve public decorum, knew better than to wave and cheer, lest they embarrass me. My mother seemed to not be aware of this social contract. Her hearty cheer when she caught me looking into the stands had the expected result. And because they knew better, the guys decided in some psychic show of oneness to stand at the same time and start chanting my name and number.

"Woo-hoo, Nate Butler, that's our guy! Let's go, number twenty-four!" The outburst collected looks not only from their fellow spectators but also my teammates, who had no qualms about joining in the mocking cheers. Before I knew it half my team and the crowd were serenading a junior bench warmer stretching muscles he wouldn't be using.

I wish I could tell you that extended cheer before the game was the most awkward part of the night for me, but that wouldn't be true. The worst part was coming out of the locker room after the game with a clean uniform and dry head, where my fan club was patiently waiting with the other families in the parking lot.

"Good game, Butler," Darren said, passing me by with a pat on the butt. The ambiguity of the comment was extra insulting.

My mom greeted me, as only moms and good dogs do, with an affection disassociated from success or failure.

"Hi, honey," she said, wrapping me in her arms the best she could. "Better luck next time."

Next to us, Darren was shaking the admiral's hand as they discussed a third down play in the fourth quarter. Mr. Montgomery thought his son should have audibled to a hot read, while Darren explained that coach wasn't giving his first year starter audible powers just yet.

"Well, that coach doesn't know his ass from his elbow," he snapped, snatching Darren's helmet and turning towards their car. "It would've been six."

LT Hagen made a face at their backs before gripping my neck. "Yeah, what he said."

Spencer cleared his throat – the air was thick with sympathy.

"I know better than anyone that you can lower your shoulder and make tackles, bud. Keep working hard and you'll be starting before you know it. Every member of a team has their role, remember that."

I nodded, appreciating the sentiment, although in reality it was little solace. I was uncomfortable with the whole thing, the whole night. I just wanted to get in bed and read a book. The scene struck me as strange, being surrounded by these three men. It was a drastic difference from my teammates' post-game gatherings around us.

"I know. Can we just get out of here?" I said sharply, walking towards Mom's car. Cheyenne fell into step with me, and for once even her presence didn't ease my anxiety.

The two of us walked ahead quickly, climbing into the Explorer with no further conversation. From the front seat I could hear a muted exchange between my mother and the SEALs in the parking lot. I didn't bother trying to listen, sighing impatiently while waiting for her to get in.

"Could you have been ruder?" she finally said, starting the car.

"Technically, I think it's 'more rude,'" Cheyenne chirped from the back, eliciting a glare into the rear-view mirror.

"Don't you start, young lady," was the angry reply. "I get enough lip from him."

I was appreciative of the gesture but uncomforted nevertheless.

"I just want to go home, mom. I'm tired and embarrassed, and really wish you hadn't dragged the guys to watch me stand on the sidelines all night."

"I didn't drag anyone anywhere. Those men just got back from God knows where, and how do they choose to spend their first night back home? Going to your game, that's how. Show some appreciation."

"I just want to go home." Intentionally or not, it came out as a whine.

"Well tough, because we're going to a barbeque on the beach. There's a pre-deployment send off for another task unit, so I'm going to need you to lose the attitude."

The thought of facing the guys after such a public humiliation was a kick in the nuts. Generally this opportunity would fill me with excitement and anticipation. It was rare that the whole team and their families were able to get together, and the occasions we could were better than any holiday. For me, it was like a regular kid getting to hang out with their favorite NFL team. These guys were my heroes. And now I'd have to be subjected to their jokes about being a bench warmer.

We pulled up to the beach on 89th Street next to Ft. Story, a huge bonfire greeting us. Bright orange flames danced against an obscure backdrop of ocean sky, licking stars and moon alike. The night was perfect, the mood a restrained cheeriness, the only option to ignore the brimming undercurrent of future menace and shared loss clawing at the edges. But for the moment, just the moment.

Silhouettes with obvious personality danced around the fire's reach. Large men held babies while toddlers ran in between legs. Wives and girlfriends stood to the side, sipping wine or beer while watching their overgrown children play with the actual ones.

I followed my mother onto the beach, if only because I had to. Here, in the dark, at least I could maintain anonymity. Cheyenne loosely held onto my shorts for guidance and support. I helped her out of her flip-flops, in turn flexing my bare toes in the cool sand. Several operators quickly greeted us, offering burgers and drinks.

Westhead saw me first, and let out a loud whistle. I remembered him from Jaco's. My heart rate picked up but I stepped towards him anyway.

"That's Mo's kid, Little Warrior? Damn, boy, you got big. You look just like your daddy," the tall Texan called out. They never feared the obvious, and rather than shying away, embraced it. "How old are you now?"

"Almost sixteen," I told him, raising my chin. He looked older too.

"Almost sixteen, huh?" He spat dip into the sand. "You know you're still young when you say 'almost.' When you're old, you round down."

His dark eyes continued to scan me. "Looks like you've been hitting the gym. Ol' Bull and Spence been PT"ing you?"

I nodded like it was no big thing to be working out with SEALs. In truth, it was extra gratifying to know that Westhead knew about my training.

"Good, that's real good stuff, Nate. Those long beards'll prepare you for a warrior's life. Keep at it, you'll be in the Teams in no time." He swigged beer and together we watched Bull walk up.

"This boy's going to college before he decides on any career path, that you have my word on," Bull sternly told us both. Westhead's sideways glance indicated a cautious deference to the experienced operator.

"Shiiit, that boy has special operator written all over him. I say get him orders to BUD/S day after graduation."

A just-discernable flicker of anger adjusted Bull's expression – if you didn't know to look for the change, you'd have missed it. Until it was too late, I imagined. "Go get me a water, Pig, and leave the boy alone."

Westhead leaned back and let out a throaty laugh, winking at me while starting to walk away. "Give you a hundred bucks if you can get him to curse."

"Don't be a cheapskate," Bull called to his back. "I know the pool is up to 600 bucks."

I shook my head, knowing it was probably true. When my dad had been on Team 4 he had once split a thousand dollar pool for the guy who went the longest without bathing. He and another operator had both made it over a month – through daily PT, training work-ups, ocean swims, and who knew what else without washing anything other than their hands. Their OIC at the time had finally called the contest a draw after deciding that two SEALs who smelled that bad would be unable to sneak up on even the most undisciplined enemy. The other guy had been single, which Dad said should have allowed him odds. Mom made him sleep in the garage after the second week of that bet. Maybe it doesn't always pay to be a winner.

Bull led me to an unoccupied spot on the edge of the bonfire. We took a seat in the sand, facing the flames. I looked out over the water, hearing its gentle call better than I could see it. The days were getting shorter, and sadly I thought back to early summer when each day squeezed out just *that* much more light. There was something special about early summer's optimism; each day's growth gave you something to look forward to. After the summer solstice it was a series of slow steps back to darkness and the drudgery of winter.

"Don't emulate that lunatic, bud. He only has one speed, morning, noon and night."

I took a fistful of sand and felt the cool pebbles fall through my fingers. "So what did you do to your hand?"

His swollen fingers flexed in the firelight. He shrugged.

"Changing a tire. Just scraped the knuckle a little, is all."

I laughed. "Funny, I read that a bunch of SEALs in West Virginia got into a bar fight with some amateur MMA fighters. Busted them and the bar up pretty badly."

He looked at me with genuine surprise. "You read that? Where the hell did you read that?"

"Internet, Bull. Everything's on the internet."

"Is nothing sacred anymore? Jiminy cricket. Bar fights and SEALs go together like peanut butter and jelly. I'll tell you this – you better be happy there wasn't this internet craze when your daddy was coming up. He put his brand of whoop-butt on many a deserving jarhead in his day."

I smiled, suddenly very interested.

"Yeah? How bad?"

He leaned back in the sand, a soft snicker just rising above the pops and cracks of the fire.

"There was one I heard about – mind you, I got this second hand, and you know how stories go, especially with some of these guys." He motioned abstractly, encompassing everyone around us. "Some of these guys just like to hear themselves talk. But what I *heard* was, his task unit got into a pretty good dust up with some local boys after a training work-up, way back when he was still an FNG."

I was rapt, leaning forward, silently urging the story to continue. Of course, once Bull sensed my excitement he took his time, making a show of pulling the details.

"Hmm, I'm trying to remember if they were in Twentynine Palms or Camp Pendleton…" He rubbed his gravelly chin, looking to the stars. I rolled my eyes and sat back. Any additional evidence of discomfort or impatience on my part would only encourage further delay.

"Yeah, I believe it was 29 Stumps. Well, there's only like one bar within twenty miles of that dustbin, in Yucca Valley, I believe. Anyway, after this work-up was over, the boys headed out there, some place called Terrapin Station. It's since been closed, just some dump in the middle of nowhere. I actually made it there once. Terrible food, if I remember correctly. But great service. The service was impeccable."

I breathed deeply, determined not to acknowledge the stall tactics. I could feel his grin in the dark.

"Oh, but back to your old man. So, they all head out to this bar after some grimy two-week work-up in the middle of the Mojave Desert. This was in August, if I have my story correct, 120-degree-day after 120-degree-day, finding sand in cracks you didn't even know you had. Being a new guy, your dad was the designated driver. So he's sitting at the table with the guys, sipping Cokes or whatever, while everyone else is tying one on. And of course, they're getting *after* it. Well, one by one, guys keep popping into the head, taking longer and longer each time. It gets so bad with guys waiting to drop deuces they have to take over the women's bathroom. While all this is going on your dad notices one of the bartenders dropping something into the drinks he's making. So Mo makes his way to the edge of the bar, casually reconnoitering this bartender. Some long haired hippy type, tight with the locals and apparently not a fan of the United States military. Because when your dad jumped over that bar and knocked out every tooth in that kid's head, a bottle of Visine flew out of his hand. One of the other bartenders tried to hide it, but no dice. Once the boys figured out they were messing with their drinks, it was on. They beat the crap out of every male employee and patron in that place. At least the guys who weren't still in the shitter did."

The night cleverly hid the drop of my chin and the shock associated with it. Story over. Bull raised his large frame, wiping the sand off his butt. I couldn't see his features in the dark, but I had no doubt he was once again grinning at me. His version of a gift, although no one would believe it. I thought about looking for Westhead, but decided I'd keep this our little secret. I smiled to myself, feeling like – well, like a kid with a secret.

"Did they get in trouble?"

"Shooot… First rule of bar fighting is to not get caught. The team leader had those boys out the back door and down the road before the last redneck hit the ground. We don't wait for the MP's."

I laughed, appreciating not just the story but Bull's trust. His outline made its way down the beach, shrinking, never turning back. Eventually I rose, wandered towards the sound of kids playing. Cheyenne was following a boy her age around the fire, poking at it with a stick. She was imitating him, seeing how close they could get to the flames. Nothing like supervised fire to illustrate the perceived indestructability of youth.

Locked in child-like focus, she paid me no mind, so I turned to find my mother in the muted chaos. I found her standing in the shadows of the receding waterline, alone, staring into the sea. Her shadow stretched across the calmness of the water's edge, a distorted reflection in the moonlight. I didn't want to disturb her comfort and solitude, so I turned away, listening to the soft roar of each wave rolling to shore.

"Nathan." The firm, confident voice took me by surprise. Unnoticed, LT Hagen had made his way to my side.

"Hi, LT."

"Mind if I stand with you?"

I gave my standard apathetic shrug.

"How are you doing with everything?"

I wasn't sure what "everything" he was referring to, so I just shrugged again.

"You seemed angry tonight after the game."

"It's embarrassing. You guys come all the way to our stupid game, and I don't even get to play. I know you're not used to failures."

His eyes wrinkled in confusion and maybe disgust.

"You think you're a failure because you didn't play tonight? Nah, Nate, you're only a failure if you never tried. If you didn't give it your all. And while God knows you've had your share of screw-ups, I don't see you as a quitter. None of us do."

"Have you ever failed at anything?"

Without missing a beat, he answered simply. "No."

I nodded, not surprised.

"That doesn't mean I've never lost at anything, or couldn't do something. But I've never quit at anything. And I don't care how cliché this sounds, they're clichés because they're true. Losers quit, it's that simple.

"Life isn't easy, Nate. You know that better than anyone. Doesn't matter if it's school, football, whatever. No one is going to hand any-thing to you. And drugs, that shit is for losers. That's quitting. Quit-ting on your family, quitting on yourself, quitting on us. And we won't let that happen."

My face flushed, half in anger, half in humiliation. I'd heard this speech before.

"I know, LT Hagen, that's over."

He nodded. "Good enough for me."

I turned to him in appreciation. It's rare to hold something so fa-miliar in awe, but even with proximity I held such reverence for this man and what he represented that I felt lucky to simply be in his presence. Which made these conversations more difficult. And sur-real.

"Was he really as good as they say?" I asked him quietly.

LT Hagen turned, his hard features outlined mystically in the full moon and distant fire.

"Do you even have to ask that question? Don't you already know?"

I stammered, trying to put my feelings into words. "Do you think you can miss something you've never had? I feel like – well, I feel like he was the greatest man I've never known."

He let out a rumble, an exaggerated laugh that at first pissed me off.

"How is that funny?" I asked aggressively.

He put his muscular arm around me and pulled me close in his firm, caring way. "You are a Butler, that's for sure. That sounds like something he would say. You don't decide what you miss, Nate. We all miss him, for his selflessness and fearlessness just as much as for all the little nuances that annoyed the hell out of us. You know his greatness, Nate – in fact, you know it better than anyone does. Be-cause it's in you."

I took the words for what they were. I was used to versions of them, and surprisingly I found the expectations were becoming more of a welcome challenge than a burden.

"What do you tell people?" I asked.

His face belied his confusion. "Huh?"

"When people ask you what you do? What do you tell them for a cover story? I know my dad used to say he was a cat-whisperer. People would believe him too."

LT Hagen chuckled and looked to the sky. "Classic. He also used to tell people he shoveled elephant crap at the circus."

"What about you?"

"Me? Hell, I just tell 'em I'm a janitor. It's the truth, sort of. We're usually cleaning up other people's shit."

It was supposed to make me laugh, so I did. I was still laughing, louder than I should have, when a yell came from the shoreline. We squinted our eyes to see at least a dozen SEALs stripping to either their boxers or less, sprinting into the surf.

Spencer explained, "Midnight races. New Senior Chief in Bravo Platoon challenged the Echo NCO's to swim out around the horn into Broad Bay and run back through First Landing State Park. Don't even want to think about what happens to the last man back."

I was shocked. "That's like a three-mile swim and six-mile run through swamps and the woods! In the middle of the night! For no reason!"

He calmly answered, "There's plenty of reason."

I let that settle.

"Do you think that things happen for a reason?"

He turned, confused again. "What do you mean?"

"You know, when people say 'Everything happens for a reason.'"

He sighed. "I personally think that's horseshit. If you want to believe there is some all-encompassing reason that your dad got killed and it makes you feel better, then I'm not going to tell you not to believe that. But I sure as hell don't think there is some genie pulling the strings and that what happens to us is for some greater good."

"You don't believe in God?"

"I don't know how I could, the stuff I've seen. That's what makes guys like your dad and Bull so rare in the Teams. That Christian stuff isn't for me, but if it helps people cope with what they have to do, I'm all for it. Anything to get us through this life with our sanity intact."

"Easier said than done," I told him, staring through filtered moonlight into the expanse of ocean. "Sometimes I feel like swimming out there and never stopping, just to see where it ends."

"That's loser talk, bud," he said, squeezing my shoulder before walking away.

I stood, alone, motionless, thinking what it would be like to drift away into the nothingness. No more worry, no more pain. What my dad and Sgt. Hawkins felt. Or didn't feel. I imagined it would be just like before I was born.

"Nate, Mom is looking for you. I couldn't find you anywhere! What are you doing anyway?"

Cheyenne ran up behind me. The air had cooled by the water, and I could see her breath when she spoke. I leaned towards her, zipped up her jacket, then realized how cold I was.

As if reading my mind she asked, "Where's your sweatshirt?"

I looked down at her and tried to smile, taking her hand.

"Guess I left it in the car. Want to go with me to get it?"

Chapter 29

AND THEN IT WAS THREE YEARS. I almost missed it, the anniversary.

When I banged through the front door that evening, I found Mom and Spencer on the couch. Darren had just dropped me off from practice, and I let my gym bag fall loudly to the floor. Seemingly startled, they popped up.

"Spencer! What are you doing here? Thought you guys were out of town."

He found a coaster for his beer then rubbed his hands through stringy hair.

"Work-up's over. Full deployment in two weeks so we have some downtime."

I didn't bother to ask location or mission, but I knew a full deployment meant combat in either Afghanistan or Iraq.

"How was practice, honey?" my mom asked, walking into the kitchen.

"Fine," I told her. "I practiced with the seconds. Davis still has a tight hamstring, so I'll probably get some playing time tomorrow." I turned to Spencer. "Can you guys make the Bayside game tomorrow? Last home game of the year."

He and my mom traded looks. Apparently he received some silent approval.

"I'll be there," he said. "LT is working around the clock finalizing mission prep, but me and Bull'll be there."

I nodded, confused as to the awkwardness circulating the room.

"Take a quick shower, dinner will be ready shortly. You don't mind if Spencer stays, do you?"

Puzzled, I answered, "Why would I care? He always eats here." I dropped my gym bag, and headed upstairs. "I need my Under Armour shirts washed before the game tomorrow, please."

After starting the shower, I took a good look at my dirt-and-sweat-streaked face. Some scruff was actually starting to fill in on my chin, and I rubbed it proudly. I decided I'd try to shave, and headed into my mother's bathroom to find a razor and shaving cream.

The top drawer held nothing but standard women's beauty supplies. Makeup, cotton balls, lotions and gels I didn't even want to identify. Same in the second. The third was a jumble of soap, band-aids, an old hair dryer and something wrapped in a frayed towel. Intrigued, I reached for it, and was surprised by the weight. My fingers explored the shape, finally meeting metal. I unfolded the towel, realizing I was holding my father's Desert Eagle .50 AE pistol. I had seen it often when he was alive, even shot it once, but had forgotten all about it since his death. I felt the heft, the cool metal, the power weighing in my palm. The safety was on, but the clip was full. And suddenly I remembered the date, and realized that exactly three years to the day a chaplain and Navy SEAL officer had rang our doorbell.

I stood, unmoving, holding and contemplating the weapon in my hand. I turned it over, looked directly into the barrel. Flicked the safety: on, off. On, off. Cold, powerful metal. Damaging, liberating, powerful. Suddenly a flash of electricity surged through my spine, rushing through my body until it was all concentrated in my finger.

My index finger, my trigger finger. Quickly, gingerly, I put the gun back exactly as I found it, folded in the towel, tucked in the bottom of the drawer. Pale and light headed, I made my way back into the steam of my own bathroom, ready to shave and shower before dinner.

I dabbed a bit of shaving cream directly on the razor and harshly scraped at the hair above my lip. It immediately started bleeding, as did my chin when I tried the same thing. I realized I had no idea what I was doing. Trying to think back to when I would watch Dad shave didn't help. The truth was, I couldn't remember. A fog, a whisper of a vision rattled in the back of my mind. Him swishing the razor in a sink full of water? I tried, but that only stained the water pink. No matter what direction I moved the razor in, I seemed to take off more skin than hair.

I bandaged myself the best I could with toilet paper, and went downstairs. The smell of spaghetti sauce greeted me as I held reddening tissue to my face.

"What happened to you?" came Mom's shocked response.

Embarrassed, I reached up, felt the half dozen pieces of toilet paper held to my chin and neck with dried blood.

"Tried to shave. Guess I didn't do a very good job."

The belly laugh that came from Spencer sitting at the head of the table left me embarrassed and angry. I pulled off the toilet paper.

"Nate, stop that! It's starting to bleed again," my mother called out, approaching me with a paper towel extended. "Let's blot it with this."

"Guess it's time I teach you how to shave, bud," said Spencer, still laughing. "Or you're going to need a transfusion. Good thing I was a corpsman."

I didn't attempt a response, just took my seat at the table, seething. Cheyenne ran in from the kitchen and slid out the chair next to me with great production.

"Nathan!" she yelled after seeing my face, "What happened? Are you okay?"

I tried to cover my face with my hands and told her to shut up.

"Mom, Nate told me to shut up!"

"Honey, leave your brother alone. How much spaghetti do you want?"

I kept my head down and tried not to cry.

The depression lingered, growing, eating at me. While I couldn't tell exactly what was wrong with me, I knew I wasn't right. My mind raced, I couldn't sleep past dawn, and my emotions swung back and forth from violent anger to a piercing sadness. I didn't know what to do.

To make matters worse acne had attacked my face, and not just in the typical teenage fashion. To me, the breakouts were unbearable, and I was embarrassed to go in public. I tried every cream and medicine available, with no relief. To add to the cruelty, our health insurance had changed with my dad's death. I was unable to get an appointment to see a dermatologist in network for almost six months. Mom and Cheyenne told me my face really didn't look that bad.

The usual joy and excitement of Christmas completely missed me that year, and I doubt I cracked a legitimate smile this side of the new year.

Mom and Cheyenne were on the receiving end of my despair, as unfair as that was. Initially, they both tried everything they could to cheer me up. The unappreciated attempts soon stopped. When Mom suggested a therapist the subsequent blow up was such that I was forced to go.

I was surprised to learn from Eli that he went to a psychologist too. He didn't laugh when I told him I was going to screw with her and say I could talk to the dead. Instead he let me know that he actually felt better after each weekly session and that I should give it a shot.

So with just enough bitching and venom to make it appropriately difficult, I agreed to visit Dr. Linda Farmer, adolescent psychologist and Ph.D.

"Why are you here?" was the first thing she asked me.

I was seated on a cozy beige love seat in a cramped office, facing a woman I didn't know who was expecting me to share my most private thoughts.

"'Cause my mom made me."

She nodded, slowly, proof we were simpatico. On the same team.

"I can understand that. Why do you think she wanted you to talk to someone?"

I stared back into bright eyes, suddenly softening at her kind face and motherly persona. It was either make this difficult on both of us, or just acquiesce and get it over with. To my surprise, I felt my face go warm with a surge of emotion. I blew my nose.

"Probably because my dad got killed and I got caught drinking and doing drugs and I'm so fucking sad it feels like my chest is going to explode," I finally blurted out in a single breath because that's the only way I could get it all out before my voice cracked and the tears flowed.

She leaned back, sympathetic. "That's a lot for a sixteen-year-old to handle, isn't it?"

"I guess. Nothing that people all over this country aren't going through every day."

"Okay," she said. Paused. "Do you think you are a smart person?"

I thought that was an interesting question, and told her so.

"It's important to understand how people view themselves. Often, it's much different than the rest of the world does," she explained.

I thought about it before nodding.

"I suppose I am. I mean, I'm not like engineer or scientist-smart. But common sense-wise, I'd like to think so. Although there's no real test for that. Maybe that's just what dumb people tell themselves to make them feel better."

"I would think you would have to be somewhat intelligent to come up with that, wouldn't you?"

I shrugged. "Or a sociopath."

She laughed. Sincerely.

"Okay. How else do you see yourself?"

"What do you mean?"

"What are your impressions of yourself? Are you a good person, a happy person? What kind of person are you?"

I thought carefully before answering.

"I'm hard on myself, I can tell you that. I'm not one of those people who blame other people when bad things happen to them. I know they're my fault and I'm really hard on myself about that. Most people go around making excuses for why they're shitbags, but I refuse to lie to myself. Everything that happens to everyone is their own fault."

"Was it your fault your father was killed?"

"Of course not. But everything I did after that was my fault. All the bad stuff, getting in trouble. I have no one else to blame for those failures."

"Do you think you are a failure?"

"You said *a* failure. I had said I had *some* failures."

"Doesn't answer the question."

I grabbed a nearby tissue, raising it to my face. Choking, I answered honestly.

"Not necessarily a failure, not yet. I realize there is time to turn this around. But there's a lot I've done that I'm not proud of. And I wish I could stop dwelling on it, could move on. I feel like I'm walking under a long shadow that I can't get out from under."

"Your father's shadow."

I nodded silently, feeling the force of rising tears and knowing there was no way to stop them now.

"I'm just so fucking lonely," I stammered before breaking into sobs.

It got worse as winter wore on. Every day the sun would set a little earlier and I would miss what had been and become more hopeless for what would be. I started to miss a lot of school, and while it depended who you asked whether or not my illnesses were legitimate, there was no ignoring the corporeal pain inside my chest.

Although still forcing me to see Dr. Farmer, I could tell my mom had for the most part given up on me. Spencer's squadron was deployed, and I was basically uncontrollable. While she had caught me drunk and high several times, she didn't know the extent of it. Or maybe she did, I don't know.

I usually kept a bottle of vodka taped to the bottom of my bed, and most days started with a few warm swigs. If I went to school at all, half the day was skipped and spent smoking weed in the woods or drinking and doing pills at someone's house.

That was basically how one cold morning began. An angry wakeup yell from the hallway, followed by chugging what was left of a half pint of Burnett's swiped from the base package store the day before. It left me bleary eyed and angry (which I had found was better than sad) before I trudged out of the house. Not much different or similar than many blurry mornings during that time.

Cheyenne walked ahead of me to the bus stop, by this time embarrassed of her brother. She wasn't sure exactly what I was up to, but she knew it was wrong. It was impossible not to notice that I was always in trouble, at school, at home. I let her go ahead, deciding I would rather spend the morning in the park, smoking the blunt I had in the front pocket of my sweatshirt than sitting at a cold desk while teachers talked at me.

When I arrived Darren was already there, sitting on the benches with a few other kids. They were smoking cigarettes and talking loudly when I walked up.

I made my way towards the group, surprised to see Tammy with them.

"Tammy," I blurted out, trying to hide the blunt behind my back. "What are you doing here?

My heart still skipped a beat when I saw her, although we rarely hung out any more.

"Looks like the same thing as you," she replied in that imperturbable manner she had perfected. "You gonna share that blunt, or let it burn a hole in your ass?"

I laughed, surprised, and extended it to her like a prize.

"Didn't know you smoked."

She took a deep puff, turned to Darren, leaning forward. He met her half way, letting her blow the smoke into his mouth. He received it hungrily, his mouth moving closer to hers until their lips met. After an exaggerated kiss, they parted, smoke trailing from each mouth.

"Lots of things you didn't know."

Darren smirked at me, reached for the rest of the blunt.

I felt empty, hollow, my head spinning. I couldn't catch my own thoughts. The sight of them together sickened me. I turned away, started walking.

"Where you going, Butler? We're going to party at my house today, you don't want to come?" Darren called after me. I walked faster, no plan or thought as to where I was going.

The morning's blend of vodka and Valium churned in my otherwise empty stomach. I lurched over the cracks on the basketball court, feeling them make an early exit. I moved quicker, managing to reach the tree line before throwing up.

And there I stood, out of view but not earshot, suffering while they smoked my weed. Their laughter and assumed insults rang in my ears. I leaned against a wiry pine tree, saliva and phlegm stringing from mouth and chin, watering eyes burning and unfocused.

As soon as the shock wore off, embarrassment hit.

And then as it was wont to do, my brain took me in another direction, reeling, fixated on her loss of innocence rather than my dearth of idealism. She was one of few pure things to me, an untouched and rare commodity. And now she was soiled. I knew what Darren, star quarterback and dirtbag, did to the girls he hung out with. And the last virtuous thing I knew had vanished.

My fingers kneaded my temples in an attempt to calm a throbbing head and heart. School was not in the cards that day. I looked at my watch. 8:39. Mom would soon be leaving for work. I headed down the familiar path through the woods, acutely aware of how unchanged the beaten trail was in the years I had been using it, yet just how different its occupant was. I followed it blindly and instinctively, navigating the turns and clawing branches until reaching our backyard. I paused; again, while *it* hadn't changed, the yard seemed different. The picnic table, the small lawn covered in pine needles and oak leaves, the white siding and rain gutters, all the same as they ever were. It was me, my viewpoint that was different. Understanding that was little consolation.

There was movement in the kitchen window – I watched as my mom hustled into the garage. The vodka under my bed called me. I was hoping I still had some Valium or Percocets stashed around my room. I felt strangely sharp, clear-headed, maybe because I had thrown up my earlier buzz. Maybe not. What I needed was something to dull the pain, to numb.

When I heard the garage door close and was sure she was gone, I entered through the back door, stopping in the kitchen. The house seemed especially quiet, as if it was holding its breath, afraid of what I might do.

I moved quickly, dropping my book bag and grabbing a bottle of orange juice en route to my bedroom. Once upstairs I reached under the bed to that familiar hiding place, frantically untwisting the caps from the vodka and orange juice bottles simultaneously. I pulled hard, fast and deep on the first bottle, leaning my head back, eyes closed, feeling the current of warm fluid sail past my tongue, singeing my throat and warming my belly like a bolt of lightning.

It didn't relieve the pain. It was overwhelming now, intense and physical. I felt like I was trapped in an elevator. No way out, no relief. I bounced up and down, my body on fire.

"There is no hope, no help in store." The voice was familiar – the old man again. From somewhere, his hollow words reached me, embodied me, spoke from deep within me.

"There is no way out," the words either mine or his or both. The despair crested, enveloped me, the past, present and future. My hair stood on end, my organs tried to escape their shell. I found pills, any pills, but not enough. I threw them in my mouth, crunching them with my teeth, not tasting the bitterness, begging for their deliverance. But there was none.

"Why, why, why?!" someone shouted over and over. I sobbed, although I did not know what I sobbed over. I yelled, but at no object. Punched, at no target.

The light-headedness was a welcome respite, a deadening sensation taking me out of my pain.

"When there is no hope, all hope is lost," the voice said plainly.

"Then what is there left to do?"

I found myself standing in the doorway of my mother's room. Frozen, both numb and feeling every sensation heightened at once. My legs carried me into the bathroom. I went to the bottom drawer. My arms opened it, my hands lifted the towel. They cradled the heavy steel, they massaged the metal grip. I'd never held a gun in this direction before. It was terrifying, intimidating. My eyes looked deep down the barrel, into the chasm that all know will meet them eventually but none understand until it does.

Contemplating may not be the right description, but it's not inaccurate either. Somewhere a clock clicked seconds away loudly, *tick, tick, tick*. I felt it in my chest, heard it in my ears, lived it in the atmosphere. The scariest part was not knowing.

I still have no idea if I was going to or not. I had one foot in eternity and one in reality. And by the grace of God I'll never truly know where I would have landed.

"Nathan! Christ on the cross, Nathan, what are you doing!" my mom's shriek snapped me from my trance. The gun clattered on the linoleum below. She fell on top of me, wailing.

"No, not you! Not you too! I won't allow it!"

The words came in rapid-fire through the heartbreak. Her arms wrapped me in a vice-like, protective embrace. Spasms shook my body, tears soaked my neck. Over the past year I had a lot of reasons to harbor a guilty conscience, but never before and not since have I ever felt so horrible about myself.

I moaned, tried to turn over, sick. Face down, I bawled into the tiled floor, wondering when and how it had come to this. She was doing the same.

We lay there, exhausted, for how long I don't know, until her grip relaxed and we fell back, drained and crushed. I started to speak but she shushed me each time, over and over, running her hands through my sweaty hair. I was in a trance-like state, afraid to think, to acknowledge my position. But somewhere deep inside me, a forgotten sensation was growing. To my surprise I felt relief, that fleeting, rare warmness I had unknowingly been seeking.

Chapter 30

THE IMMEDIATE REPURCUSSIONS were numerous and quick. Fortunately, Dr. Farmer was able to convince my mom that it wasn't an actual suicide attempt. She proposed I was merely probing boundaries. I didn't have an opinion one way or another, but the theory did keep her from having me committed.

I did cringe when I heard Dr. LaFata, our family physician, refer to the incident as a "cry for help." He said this to my mother and me at an appointment where my prescriptions were changed yet again. That was bullshit, I knew. An over-simplification. I had no intention or lack of, just a series of actions that led me to where I was now and not to the alternative.

My state at that time was fluid, undefined. The new meds helped, I think, but I still hadn't turned the corner. I ended up back in front of a familiar window, familiar thoughts and fears racing through my mind.

The look on Tammy's face when she peeled the curtains back was nothing short of disgust. I ignored it, braced myself.

"Talk to me," I pleaded.

"There's nothing to talk about. You – this – can't happen."

"I just need to talk, Tammy, that's all."

She paused and whispered, "I know what happened. We all do."

"I don't care. Call it the cost of the human condition."

"I call it fucking nuts. You scare me, Nate. You scare everyone."

"I'm leaving."

"Good."

"No, I mean I'm – we're – leaving Virginia Beach. We're moving to Maryland to live with my grandparents. Next week."

"So what do you want from me?"

I thought about it before answering. It was a good question.

"I guess for you to care. You're the only one who gets me, Tammy. Who ever has. Who knows what makes me tick. I don't want anything *from* you. I just want you in my life. Visit me. Take my calls. Send a fucking email when I'm gone."

"Well, that's not going to happen, Nate. Now go home. If my dad catches you here, he'll kill us both."

With that, the window slid to a close and the curtains met back in the middle, effectively shutting me out of her life. I figured I would never speak to her again.

As I slunk away into the darkness, I saw movement in the window next to hers. Doug, the rat bastard. I thought about putting a rock through his window, but for once exercised restraint, and headed home.

And just like that, we packed up. There was no anticipation, no excitement about the move, just another incident we all had to deal with. A date that would come and go before the guys came back from their deployment. It was unnerving knowing that when they returned we wouldn't be there, that there would be no evidence we ever had. At least I would escape the lectures. The long looks, the venom. I was able to Skype with Spencer once and his disappointment could not be exaggerated. There is no need for specifics; I'm sure you get the gist.

Cheyenne didn't take the move very well. In her young life she had only known Virginia Beach and our home and couldn't understand why we were leaving either. The more tantrums she threw, the deeper my guilt. *Because your brother is a fuck-up.*

But the truth was, it wasn't just my troubles forcing us to leave. While my antics were a leading factor, unbeknownst to me we were having trouble with the bills. The military casualty benefits were fast dwindling, and we had only received my dad's housing allowance for 365 days after his death. The reality was, although we had lived a humble lifestyle before his death, without my dad's salary and benefits we couldn't afford to stay in Virginia Beach.

So just like that, we were gone. With little fanfare my grandparents came to help load the truck and move us to Laurel, Maryland. I didn't know that side of the family well and it felt like we were moving in with strangers.

I found my grandfather cold and my grandmother strange. Much older than my paternal side, they had an ancient aura about them. Like they were waiting to die. The house was old and airless and the floorboards creaked when I tiptoed across the living room or up the stairs. It smelled funny. Cheyenne and I shared a room filled with furniture from a long-forgotten era. My anxiety and sadness waned, if only to come back as anger, hot and intense far inside me.

Starting a new school in the middle of junior year wasn't ideal, but the list of people I could complain to was small. The first day came before I was ready. Barely a word was spoken on the ride that morning, until my grandfather grabbed my arm as I opened the car door.

"Be good," he advised before releasing me. I softly shut the passenger door and entered my new school.

Walking through the busy hallways, careful not to make eye contact with anyone, I scanned the room numbers as casually as I could, searching for 113. Homeroom, according to my already-wrinkled schedule. The halls were filled with normal high school clatter, friends shouting greetings, practical jokes and curses. Optimism, room for growth. Fresh opportunities. Not anything I identified with. I found the half-empty room and took the first seat I saw, purposefully slumping anonymously.

"My seat." It wasn't a question, or even a demand. I looked up at a large kid standing over me lazily.

"'Scuse me?"

His eyes skimmed past me, now alert, although his body language showed no sign of aggression. In fact, to the casual observer it could appear that he was merely asking my name, or where I was from. He chewed calmly on a toothpick, making it hard to recognize the antagonistic undertone.

"Bitch, I said that's my seat. Get the fuck up."

A wash of anger seared my forehead, freezing me. As my adrenaline subsided I thought of my grandfather's warning. *Unbelievable*, I thought. *My first day and this is going to happen.*

Using all the strength I could muster, I slid out of the chair, clutching my empty book bag in my right hand. I didn't look at him, but didn't look away either. What I did do was take the seat behind and try to swallow the sharp sting of backing down. Not to my surprise, he followed me to that seat.

"My seat."

I half-smiled and shook my head. It was a relief, really. There was no choice, and that was a therapeutic feeling. I performed the same action, sliding out of my chair, but this time I let the backpack fall to the floor. Once I got to my feet we squared off, and he soon realized that whatever end result he had been expecting, this was not going to be it. The room erupted into shouts and crashing desks, but I was immune to it all. I pounced on him quickly, and we both went to the floor. I was on top and felt my fist connect with his face. A great feeling, exerting your physical power over someone who just seconds before had felt himself superior. As more punches traded, I felt a crushing blow to my left temple that left me breathless and seeing white. Everything moved in slow motion and I felt myself sliding onto my back. Then everything went black.

I don't remember when I came to. There are glimpses of being led down the hallway, seeing blood caked in the webbing of my fingers, an ice pack wrapped on my swelling head. Curses and moans and adults trying to take order and the shocked yells of girls too close to violence and blood, and finally my mother's worried voice and my grandfather's angry one and then the soft, honest words of Cheyenne when I finally opened my eyes for good.

"Huh?" I asked, confused.

"I was telling you how worried Ma is about you. I told her you'd be fine."

"And how did you know that?"

"I knew. I *know.* Do you want some ice cream?"

"Why would I want ice cream?" I tried to sit up, but that just sent a jolt through one side of my head. A lack of saliva made licking my cracked lips pointless.

"Why *wouldn't* you want ice cream?"

"Good point." I looked around, dejectedly realizing I was in what was now my room. It's a sad state of affairs when you aren't even comforted by your own home.

"What happened?"

"You got in a fight, you dumbass. First day of school and you already got suspended."

I rolled over, feeling the pressure on the side of my face. "Watch your mouth," I told her. With effort. Then, "I did?"

She nodded matter-of-factly. "That's gotta be a record, even for you."

"Any idea what happened to my face?"

"We're pretty sure someone kicked you, seeing how there's a shoe print on your cheek."

I put my hand to my cheek and was horrified at the size of it.

"Let me see a mirror."

"I don't know if you want to do that, Nate. It's pretty bad."

"I can handle it."

"Okay."

She came back with a handheld mirror; what it revealed was indeed gruesome. I looked with curiosity at the circular lines that ran from temple to chin. It truly was the exact imprint of a sneaker, decorating a distended half of human face I barely recognized. My right eye was the color of a ripe cherry and was nearly swollen shut. Dried blood cracked against my lips and around my ear, which was bright red in its own right.

"Kind of cool, huh?" I said, trying to manage a smile.

Cheyenne rolled her eyes. "Something wrong with you, brother. I'll go get Mom, you need to ice it."

"Don't forget my ice cream!" I called out.

I recovered the best I could that weekend. I didn't have the most sympathetic of caretakers – only Cheyenne would talk to me past basic conversation, and even she was less than friendly. I was tired of feeling guilty, so I did my best to numbly shelve the latest disappointment to the recesses of my brain. I did, however, allow myself some pleasure thinking about the beating I know I administered before being cheapshotted.

The swelling had gone down significantly a couple of nights later, although the whole left side of my face had turned into a colorful array of yellows and blues. I remember sitting at my window, listening to the rain, wishing I had a Xanax or Valium squirreled away to help me rest. I planned to get to sleep early and enjoy the last night of my suspension.

It had poured all day, which suited me just fine. It was still coming down in buckets with no respite in sight when I climbed into bed. I sat in the quiet dark, staring into the backyard. Raindrops streaked the window, and I tried to not be reminded of thousands of tears. The glittering flashes soon put me into a trance, a dream-like state just this side of consciousness. A voice snapped me back into reality.

"Got a minute, Nate?"

I flicked the light on my nightstand, looking to the doorway. My grandfather was standing there uncomfortably, which made me uncomfortable.

"Sure."

He cleared a towel off the back of the desk chair, and sat down stiffly. We both looked at Cheyenne, breathing heavily in her bed, the comforter up to her chin. She didn't stir.

Grandpa whispered for her benefit. "Back to school tomorrow, right?" The soft drawl was fragile, slow, almost like he wasn't sure his audience could speak the language.

I nodded, anticipating but not blaming him for the lecture I knew he had to deliver.

Instead, he started by saying, "I'm not here to tell you what's expected of you. You already know that, and me telling you again isn't going to make it register if you don't."

"I know, Grandpa, and I can't tell you how sorry I am. I know everyone is tired of hearing me apologize, and believe me, I'm tired of having to. But I'm not going to screw up again."

His arm raised, motioning for me to stop.

"I'm not interested in apologies or promises anymore. Your mother isn't, your father's teammates aren't. But that's not because we don't believe you. We do, in fact. I know that deep down you're a good kid, Nate, and I know you'll figure it out. I just hope it's sooner than later."

The sympathetic tone was a bit of a surprise. I wasn't sure how to react, so I stayed silent. He wasn't done and seemed to be getting to the reason he was here.

"Have you heard about the first time I ever met your father?"

I shook my head, surprised I hadn't. Grandpa had been a cop in Pensacola before retiring to Maryland.

"It was before he and your mother started dating. Before they even met, I believe. Being a local cop I had heard about him, the crazy daredevil football player always toeing the line between boys being boys and criminal mischief. Like someone else I know." He took the opportunity to attempt a smile, I guess, to try to relate.

"Well, one night after a game, we got a call about a one car collision back in Gulf Beach Heights. I was the first officer on scene and found a car wrapped around a light pole, on fire, the engine sparking. A crowd had already gathered, mostly drunk high schoolers from a party across the street. They were keeping their distance, afraid the car was going to blow. As I'm putting my cruiser in park, some kid comes sprinting through the crowd, pushing his way to the car. Without looking at me, without asking anyone for help, he runs up to the burning car. Like everyone else in the crowd I start yelling at him to stay back – by this time the flames from the engine were shooting a foot or two in the air. I was sure that car was going to blow, and I didn't want this crazy kid going with it.

"So I ran over to grab him, to pull him back. As I got closer, I could see that the driver of the car was trapped. The flames were getting close, and it was clear he was going to be severely burned or worse if he didn't get out soon.

"By this time the other kid had taken his shirt off and wrapped it around his hands. He peeled the driver's side door back, bending it against the hinges. I reached out to help him, but the door was so hot I had to let go. I could barely see inside the car with all the smoke, so I tried to grab this crazy kid and pull him back before the car exploded and killed all three of us."

His voice quieted here.

"When I put my hand on his shoulder, he shoved me and I flew back, landing on my ass. I hit the ground hard. So hard, my head snapped back and smacked the pavement. Knocked me out cold. When I came to, I was sitting against a tree about fifty yards away. The driver of the car was propped next to me, out of it. And there was the other kid, shirtless, looking about as terrified as if he'd seen Satan himself. He didn't know whether to shit or go blind. I realized it was Stephen Butler, who had scored the game winner against Escambia with a pick-six earlier that night. When I was able to get to my feet I told him to turn around and put his hands behind his back. I handcuffed him and arrested him for assault on a police officer. Toughest arrest I ever had to make. We never discussed it even after he married your mother, but we both knew I had done what had to be done. So had he."

Grandpa hadn't looked up once as he spoke and I now saw the emotion in his face. I wondered why I had never heard the story before, and why he was telling me now.

"It's a fine line between hero and screw-up Nate. And often the designation is subjective.

"One more thing about that story. Because I was out cold when your father pulled the kid out of the car and I never actually saw him behind the wheel, we couldn't arrest him for drunk driving. But the DA decided to prosecute anyway, based solely on Stephen's testimony. It just so happened that kid was the school's starting quarterback and one of your father's best friends. But when his defense attorney addressed the courtroom on the morning of his trial and asked if Stephen Butler was present, your dad stood up and told him he was. He told him that yes, he would testify that the quarterback was the driver that night. Knowing that, the kid pled guilty and got thirty days in jail and his license suspended for a year. The University of Florida rescinded his scholarship, and some people called your dad a rat after that. But he never regretted what he did. And for what it's worth, he was voted team captain his senior year."

"What's right is right," I said.

"Indeed. That's the way your father saw everything, no matter how hard being right was."

I am happy to report that upon arriving in homeroom the following day, the teacher was the first person in the classroom and had assigned seats for us. Mine was on the opposite end of the room from the kids who had jumped me. I made it a point to make eye contact with each one of them before settling into my seat.

To everyone's surprise (including my own), I was able to keep my head down and actually focus on my grades for the rest of the semester. Being a loner (but not lonely) was the easiest way I knew to stay out of trouble.

And then, as they were inclined to do, Bull and Spencer appeared. The last remnant of winter was making its presence felt and a light layer of snow coated mine and Cheyenne's shoulders. We had been walking home from the bus stop, our steps barely making a sound in the fresh powder. I was being told bossily why German Shorthaired Pointers were better dogs than Labradors when I noticed the rental car parked at our curb. A jolt of adrenaline and nerves shot through my body, as it always did for unannounced visitors. I squinted through the snow and saw my grandmother opening the door for them.

Cheyenne saw our guests at the same time and pulled my hand as she began to run. "It's Uncle Spencer, Bull! They're safe!"

We made our way up the driveway and into the house on the double, relieved and excited to hear deep voices politely accepting tea from Grandma.

"Bull!" Cheyenne called out, running straight into his hard thigh with a thud.

Bull feigned injury and exaggerated a groan.

"Goodness Cheyenne, have you been PT'ing with the SEALs?"

She looked up at him, grinning.

His eyes went wide with shock. "Or have you been fighting with them? Who knocked your tooth out? I'm going to get them, you just tell me who!"

She pulled her cheek back to give him a better look. "It was my last molar. Got two bucks from the Tooth Fairy too!"

"Was it Nate?" He grabbed me in a headlock. A firm, tight head-lock. "Was it this ruffian who knocked out those teeth? Just give me the word, I'll teach him a lesson for you."

"He could use one," my mother said, walking up behind us.

Bull let me fall abruptly. I grabbed my throat. I didn't dare gag, but slurped air as discreetly as possible until I caught Spencer's death stare from across the counter.

"So we hear. Hello, Gayle, how are things?" Bull asked, reaching across for a quick hug. I looked over the giant man, registering the normal changes that always accompanied them after deployments. They had been at war for the past six months. I wondered if I looked as different.

"As good as they can be, I suppose."

My eyes went to Spencer, noticing the same superficial changes. They hadn't lost much weight, which they often did when the op pace was fast, working mostly nights and relying on MREs at remote outposts with no access to a gym. His dark eyes seemed to be set even farther back than normal, the protective shadow not revealing much. I could sense an unease and tenseness about both of them.

"Lucky for Nate, we're only in town for the night, so we won't get a chance to fully debrief him on this trip. We have some business in D.C., then have to head back to Virginia Beach in the morning. But there's always next time."

Embarrassed, I tried to put on a fearless face and remained silent.

"He's been really good since we moved Uncle Spencer, I promise," Cheyenne said protectively. "He may have gotten in one fight, but it wasn't even his fault."

Bull lifted her, and raised her above his head. The stock smile seemed forced, his emotions strained like other things were pressing on him.

"Don't you worry about that stuff, Princess; Nate can take care of himself."

She squirmed, seeming angry. "Put me down please. He's *my* brother, I can worry if I want."

Bull actually seemed offended by the rebuke. He set her gently on her feet, and returned to his tea in silence.

An awkwardness hung in the air, a topic left unspoken, still, after all these months. We continued the small talk for a while, dancing around the obvious until eventually I went upstairs to do homework. When I came down for dinner, the house was quiet.

"Where'd did the guys go?" I asked Mom. Her small outline framed the stovetop as she made dinner.

Her shoulders tensed at my voice but she didn't turn before answering. "They had to get back to D.C. They have an early meeting in the morning."

I accepted that; it was the nature of their business.

"So I'm guessing you didn't ask them."

"Of course I didn't ask them. You're assuming I want to know."

"Don't you?"

"It doesn't really matter, does it, Nathan?"

I thought about that – does it matter who scores the winning run as long as the team wins? I knew at best that would be the response I could expect. At worst, a punch to the throat.

"I guess not. But I would like to know."

"It's like they told the president when he asked them – they all pulled the trigger."

Chapter 31

MUCH LIKE AFTER the first life-changing event we endured, our family fast grew into a routine in Maryland. The house was cramped with the five of us, but it was cozy and could even have been perceived as happy. Mom had decided to go back to school, and was working full time while taking classes online at night. I actually made honor role that spring. Naturally, Cheyenne took home her standard report card filled with A's.

Although Eli now lived only a short way from us, we still hadn't had the chance to meet in person. We exchanged emails and the occasional phone call, but for whatever reason our schedules hadn't aligned. Like most people in my life, he seemed to be genuinely happy to hear I had had no issues with alcohol or drugs since the move.

That was around the time when the nightmares began. It was as if my consciousness, beaten into an unwitting satisfaction by its waking health, needed an outlet for its demons, which it found each nightfall.

It reached a point where my anxiety exponentially increased as the day grew shorter. In the mornings, while exhausted, I was relieved to see daylight and comforted in the knowledge that bedtime was a speck in the distance. As school got out, that speck grew bigger. The anticipation of night closed upon me like a curtain. After dinner, the curtain began to fall, the stress and anxiety washing over me and starting the vicious cycle of fear begetting terror. By the time I was huddled over the sink brushing my teeth I was a basket case. The thought of relief that a Xanax would provide was not lost on me.

I would start out reading in bed, my eyes quickly gaining weight until Hemingway or McInerney rested undefended on my chest. Then, as quickly as slumber found me, it suddenly pulled away, leaving my heart pounding, eyes tunneled into the ceiling and the sheets cool to the touch with sweat. In a panic, I would gasp to catch my breath while simultaneously racking my brain for the source of angst. Close, but always just out of reach, hiding like a child in an orchard. Just out of view, a breeze against my outstretched grasp.

I suffered in silence. I didn't want any more therapists, any more pills. I was normal once again in Maryland. I didn't get in trouble, did my schoolwork, didn't tell the few acquaintances I had about my father. There was comfort in solitude and anonymity.

I was aware enough to know I had turned a corner in my life and in how my brain worked. Apathy, I found, was a wonderful comforter.

I may have been unhappy, deep down, but I was not willing to trade unhappiness for unawareness. I was beginning to take notice of how the rest of the world coped: by simply lying to themselves. Ignorance may be bliss, but it's weak. And I decided then that I would take informed suffering over unwitting head-up-your-assness any day of the week.

So while I was miserable, it was an optimistic misery. An accepted misery. I didn't feel sorry for myself, didn't dwell on it. I didn't blame anyone else or expect anything from the world. I just accepted it, knowing it was my lot in life. That made it easier, understanding that I was just meant to be unhappy. If there was a God, He made me like this because He knew I could take it. It was like the SEALs; they got the hard jobs because they can handle them. And God knew I could take the pain and hopelessness that He threw at me. I didn't blame Him. In fact, I took it as a compliment.

So the nights tormented me, the days tolerated me. It went on like that for some time. My head was in such a fog from exhaustion and depression that the days melded together into one long exercise in tolerance. I was just waiting for high school to end so I could start the next chapter of my life.

One afternoon while I was waiting, Grandma picked me up from school, her sweet though reticent smile an easy greeting. She was a quiet woman, content to be around the action while not immersed in it. She politely asked me – more so because she should than out of any real interest – how school was. When I told her it was fine, she merely smiled and nodded, my words maybe registering, maybe not.

My heart skipped a beat when she pulled onto our street. The telltale signs of the presence of our SEALs called out as loudly to me as if they were standing in formation in the front yard. A non-descript American sedan was parked by the curb, backed in so it faced the neighborhood's exit. The front door to the house was open, letting the storm door reflect light and activity behind it. Like rain in the air, I could feel their presence.

Often I was filled with worry, or at least apprehension, when they dropped out of the sky. While that was my initial reaction that day, I quickly shed that fear, knowing that for the first time in a while I had not done anything that they would be mad about. In fact, I had something important to discuss with them. I was excited, an emotion I hadn't even realized had been missing for some time.

I thanked Grandma for the ride and jumped out of the car, slamming the door behind me. I moved up the walkway as swiftly as I thought acceptable and casually went inside. Two heads alertly turned in the direction of the creaking door, anxious looks on both their faces. I froze, the earlier anticipation leaking from my body. Was something wrong?

"Nate, how was school?" My mom popped up from the couch, smoothing her hair. She seemed unsettled, uncomfortable.

"Ah, it was good. Got an A on my English paper," I said, surveying the room. I made eye contact with Spencer, whose stone face gave away nothing. My hand went to my forehead again, wiping sweat that wasn't there. It was a nervous tick recently developed, and more than likely was having the opposite effect of its intent.

"Where's Bull, the other guys?"

Finally, he spoke. "I'm not enough SEAL for you? I even came bearing gifts."

I was intrigued, but knew not to show my interest.

"Yeah? I'm not pulling your finger."

He feigned a smile then looked at my mom. After more than a beat she pulled her gaze from him.

"I told Spencer he could take you to the Dropkick Murphys show tonight at The Fillmore. And he WILL have you home by 11:30. It's a school night." She looked back at him, expecting acquiescence. Which she received with a nod.

"You good with that, bud?"

I focused on breathing in through my nose, out slowly through my mouth, just like the SEALs had taught me. That would control my adrenalin and emotion, calming me. The last thing I wanted was Spencer to see how excited I was. Another emotion that as of late had been absent, a feeling I knew existed but that my mind had relegated to mere recollection. Suddenly it was back.

But I played it cool. Of course, Spencer knew I was playing it cool.

"If you have schoolwork or something, I'm sure I can give the ticket to someone on Team 4. They have a few operators in town training with Secret Service snipers this week, and I know they're bored."

I shrugged my shoulders as casually as I could, sporting an embellished look of indifference before a huge grin cracked through. "Awesome!" I blurted.

"Good. Hurry up and get ready, doors open at 7:00."

Fifteen minutes later we were in his Jeep, racing towards Silver Spring with "The Warrior's Code" rattling the car's tiny speakers. Together we drummed on the dashboard, singing along loudly with complete disregard as to how bad we sounded. The decibel level negated any conversation while we merrily sped through rush hour traffic. Occasionally I had to discretely grip the door handle during particularly dangerous passes, but that only added to the excitement.

We arrived at the venue in plenty of time, and settled in at a table by the bar while the opening act went on. Around us, I could feel eyes on Spencer. Aside from the tattoos and muscles, there was something about a SEAL amongst civilians. It was an aura that most couldn't put their finger on but inherently seemed to recognize. Like always he was aware of the attention, but didn't acknowledge it.

"You seem to be doing good, Nate, I must say." Spencer drank quickly from his beer. He was fidgety, couldn't seem to keep his attention on one thing. "Can't believe you'll be graduating high school next year. Any idea what you're going to do? Still looking at colleges?" His short-sleeved shirt rose and fell with his hyperness, the motion continually catching my eye and drawing it to the tattoo honoring my father.

I chose to ignore the question, at least for the time being.

"You seem strange, fucked up," I told him. I wasn't afraid of offending; directness and brutal honesty was a way of life with these guys, and was becoming a part of who I was as well.

"Shit has been tough, I'll tell you that," he finally admitted.

"How so?"

He called the bartender over and ordered another beer. He caught me eyeing the fresh one and half smiled.

"Want one?"

"What?"

"A beer – you want one?"

"I'm underage, they won't serve me."

"Have some of mine, what are they gonna do?"

I took in the bubbles, the color, the syrupy smell. I could almost taste it, the bitterness, the warmness that would flow through my body. It had been a long time since I had last had a sip of anything. Before I realized it, Spencer's face was an inch from mine, and I could smell the alcohol on his breath.

"Trick question, dipshit," he spat.

I met his stare and sneered back.

"Did I say yes? Did I try to take a sip?"

Satisfied, he leaned back and tried to look relaxed. I could tell otherwise. For one thing, his right eye kept blinking. Involuntarily, it seemed. And he still couldn't sit still. His fingers either tapped the sticky tabletop or ran through his now-shaved head. He cracked his neck half a dozen times and his knee wouldn't stop bobbing.

"So was that how you try to avoid the question? You don't want to talk about whatever it is?" I challenged him.

His eyes narrowed. There was no doubt something was weighing heavily on him. The stress leaking from the corners of his mouth, the bags under his eyes, the cloudy distant stare – they all added years to his weathered face. He had recently turned thirty-one.

"What are you looking for, Nate?"

"Don't people usually want answers when they ask questions?"

He leaned back, replying, "Not always they don't."

I sipped my Coke and thought about it. There were about a thousand things I wanted to ask him, that I wanted answers to. I wanted to know what it was like to kill someone. I wanted to know how many men my father had killed. If Spencer had been on the Bin Laden mission. I wanted to ask him what I was missing growing up without a father. What didn't I know about becoming a man?

And I definitely wanted to ask him more about the night my father was killed. About everything that he had done, that he had said that day. And the day before, and the day before that. Because it was getting harder to remember him, to really remember him. What he looked like, what he sounded like. How his aftershave smelled, how he climbed stairs. Did I only know him from pictures, from home movies, from stories? Or was he still a part of me, a sketch on my soul rather than a regurgitated image from family photos and legendary tales? I hoped our relationship was kept alive somewhere, despite the years he had been gone.

I wanted to know all these things, but couldn't bring myself to ask. There was nothing to say, nothing to do. There were no answers, and if there were, what would they solve? Talking about it wouldn't change a thing. I stared back at Spencer, my chin jutted, teeth clenched. His jaw stuck out too, the hard, sharp lines of his jagged face connecting with mine across the table. We stayed like that, communicating silently. He knew. He understood.

It occurred to me that he had been dead for twenty percent of my life. After the age of twenty-six, every year would be one more than I had with him. The thought terrified me, and I thought I was going to lose it. I was sure I was going crazy, right there while the walls of a bar in a music hall slid closer and closer, sitting across a sticky table from Spencer as soft bass and muffled cheers diluted my hearing and racing thoughts sped up my head. I was suddenly aware of Spencer's hand on my arm and when I looked up to meet his hard eyes they told me everything was going to be alright.

"I gotta take a piss," I finally told him, standing.

When I came back, there was a commotion near our table. I pushed against the crowd, swarming with other bodies, feeling their heat and sweat. Trying to get a look. Shouts lifted above the general din of the room. Spencer's voice, to be sure. But cracked, frantic, like I'd never heard it before.

"Alright! Alright! Back up! That's enough!"

His orders were almost desperate, pleading. I saw his face, agitated, painted red with rage. Then the crowd shifted and I lost sight of him.

"Everything's fine, he's fine, your buddy is fine," his voice called out, trying to sound calm. "Just relax, everybody back up!"

I turned sideways and pushed hard into the crowd. A man was lying at Spencer's feet, not moving. He had another one by the shirt collar, arm extended, holding him at bay.

More shouts, more pushing, and I almost fell under the crowd. Wild, I shoved back, able to squeeze forward.

"Spencer!" I called out, reaching for him. He looked over, found me. His arm relaxed and dropped the other guy. He held his hands up, palms facing me.

"Nate! Just stay there Nate, everything is fine!"

The crowd shifted once more, this time towards me. Again I felt my feet lifted off the floor. I grunted, pushing back hard, forcing my way forward. Two bouncers beat me to the table, reaching Spencer before I did.

He turned, faced them, arms raised, urging caution and restraint. They paused, deciding.

"Be cool, man," one said to him, just out of reach.

"These guys had it coming, man, they had it coming," he kept saying. "I didn't want to, but they had it coming."

His eyes were wild, his shirt soaked with sweat. Even in the chaos, he radiated calmness, order. The bouncers continued to eye him wearily, not sure what to do. The defensive posture he had taken did not put them at ease.

I looked to the floor, and saw a badly beaten man. His nose was sideways, his face covered in blood. His buddy, who Spencer had just let go, was now on one knee, his left arm hanging loosely at his side.

"Fuck this guy man! He had no right, it was none of his business!" he was yelling.

Spencer continued to back up, ignoring the pleas. I froze in place, shocked at what I was seeing. Spencer wasn't Spencer, I didn't know who he was, he was crazed, he shot forward, a jumble of screaming, grunts, body parts rolling around, the crowd collapsing on us. Possessed, I fought and clawed my way towards him, getting pulled and thrown away from the battle. Then it was over, and I watched Spencer being dragged by four bouncers towards the exit, his eyes wide and accepting, resigned to his fate.

And then we were outside. It was hot, bright, and unnaturally silent.

In my admittedly limited experience, I've found that once a thought is created, once it's been formulated and begins to fester in one's head, it's only a matter of time before at least some semblance of that notion is put into practice. Whether or not acting on it was even part of the initial agenda is, in general, inconsequential. It can start as an inkling, an unrealistic concept one isn't even fully aware of, or just an idealistic desire. It percolates. That seed sprouts, the desire grows. It becomes a possibility before transforming into potential. And that is a near step to action.

I let Spencer in on my plans on the drive home. We were calm, if not subdued. There was no mention of what had just happened. He seemed normal again, upbeat even, aside from a ripped shirt. And the eye that still wouldn't stop twitching.

He watched me for some time, managing to steer the car while focusing in my direction.

He was looking through me, into me, and I knew what he saw. True self-awareness is a powerful tool when honestly acknowledged, and while rare, at that moment I was one with my external impression. We both knew I could do it.

"I don't know if you can do it," he finally said.

"Yes you do."

"I don't. And neither do you. No one knows until they go through it. Tougher men than you have tried, and failed. Some of the toughest men on the planet."

I nodded, agreeing but unflinching.

"All the studies that have been done, all the research on trying to determine why some make it and most don't – they've overlooked one thing. And I know what it is. And I have it."

He snickered. "You know what makes a SEAL a SEAL?"

"I know the trait that no one talks about, but that every person who graduates from BUD/S and gets their Trident has."

"Enlighten me, smart guy."

"Desperation. For whatever reason, they cannot fail. They cannot ring that bell, they cannot quit. Because whatever pain and punishment is meted out in training or anywhere else cannot match the alternative. Giving up and not making it would be a fate worse than death. And that's me. I'd rather die than not make it. So no matter how bad it is in BUD/S, I'll make it. I'll make it, or I'll die."

The car's dials illuminated Spencer's face through the shadows. He was still staring at me, and again I was sure I knew what he was thinking. But I didn't gloat, I took no pride in knowing that I was one of the few that could become a Navy SEAL. It was just a fact, and one I had known was my destiny since – well, since before I had known it.

"Then I'll tell you this, Little Warrior. Be careful what you wish for. You want the glory, do you? The status? You don't understand the sacrifice. Maybe more than others you do, but you still don't fully understand. You want a wife, a happy family? Forget about it. Ninety percent of SEALs are divorced. Why do you think I'm still single?"

I opened my mouth to answer, but thought better of it.

"They don't write books about the shitty food. The brochures don't talk about the boredom, the bureaucracy, the shitty pay and crummy lodgings. Your recruiter doesn't mention that you are no longer a person who owns his own life. The Navy owns you, heart and soul, body and mind. You are already dead, and you only begin the transformation into a warrior when you accept that. You are not afraid of death, you're only afraid of failure.

"They tell you in the beginning of BUD/S that it's the easiest part of being a SEAL. That if you make it you will spend your career cold, wet, and sandy, and in more pain than even when you're in Coronado. And it's true. But that's just the physical toll.

"Being away nine months a year isn't conducive to a happy home life. Your old man was probably the only happily married SEAL I know. And that doesn't mean it was perfect with him. How many of yours and Chey's birthdays did he miss?"

Rhetorical question, but I shrugged anyway. Although I did know the answer.

"Well trust me, it was worse for him missing those birthdays, holidays, and anniversaries than it was on you guys. Believe me, I saw him staring at your pictures before missions, in whatever shithole we happened to be in. It drains a man, lying to his family and friends all the time. Telling them you're training and won't have cell phone service when you're actually on a mission that you can never tell anyone about. Coming back to the real world after killing and nearly being killed, when you've already accepted your own death. Swerving your car every time there's a paper bag on the side of the road. Night terrors, when you can sleep. Forget about sleep, about a true, honest to God, full night's sleep. Ever again. Guilt may not keep you from falling asleep, but it sure wakes you up. Guilt about what you've done, guilt about what you weren't able to do. And then you have to pay bills and go to the grocery store? We may put up a good front, but you'll never be normal, spending your life rotating from training, war, home, training, war, home. That's all you know, and it's damn hard to live a normal life after that."

"Is it worth it?"

"Every second," he said without missing a beat. "A price can't be put on the brotherhood, on being a part of something bigger than yourself. I wasn't wired to sit at a desk and sell software, no matter what happens to me."

That was the last time I ever saw Spencer. Three months later he and Bull were dead.

Chapter 32

IT WAS AUGUST 6.

As much as our family had already been through, as much pain as I had already experienced, this day was beyond comprehension. It felt like a dream world, a locked nightmare with no escape, no matter how hard I wished it away. It wasn't happening, couldn't be happening. I was as close to going crazy that day as a person can be while still aware of the slide.

When I walked in the door my grandparents were sitting on either side of my mother, rigid and motionless on the living room couch. They were silent, riveted to the television, which blared ominously. Mom leapt up as soon as she saw me, throwing her arms around my shoulders but not speaking. I untangled myself, asked what they were watching. I paused to look in each face. Horror and pain stared back. Then to the newscaster, who was reporting from Afghanistan, and once again back to them. It couldn't be. And then a sob escaped from my mother, and I was taken back to the day it happened. The first time. It couldn't be.

My head spun and stomach soured instantly. Shots of electricity tingled my legs. I reached out for an end table for support. My head waved from side to side, seeking activity.

"Where's Cheyenne?" I pleaded, finally catching Grandpa's attention. Sad eyes flicked towards the hallway, at our bedroom. I sprinted in that direction, terrified of what I would find.

"Hi Nate."

She was seated on the floor, Indian-style, calmly writing in her notebook. She looked up. My pale face and wide eyes clearly startled her. A nervous look washed across her face.

"What's wrong?" she asked immediately.

I took a deep breath. A gust of wind swirled the bright green curtains against the open window, drawing my attention. I looked over with curiosity and watched the heavy fabric shoot out. The wind whistled and danced, curtains flapping purposefully. The sudden action startled Cheyenne, and her apprehension visibly grew.

"What's going on?" she demanded. Mesmerized, I watched the shades continue to bounce and flutter. The heavy breeze seemed to have a physical existence, living in the fading light that shone green on the wall, the floor, my sister. I felt a peace come over me. I calmly turned back to her.

"I don't know. Nothing. Whatchu writing?"

"A letter to Uncle Spencer. I want to see if he can come to the Fall Recital. I'm doing a reading from a poem that Ms. McCabe found. Want to hear it?"

I smiled and took a seat next to her. I couldn't think of anything else I'd rather hear, and told her so.

She stood and started reading deliberately from a laminated sheet.

Golden and red trees
Nod to the soft breeze,
As it whispers, "Winter is near;"
And the brown nuts fall

At the wind's loud call,
For this is the Fall of the year.
Good-by, sweet flowers!
Through bright Summer hours
You have filled our hearts with cheer
We shall miss you so,
And yet you must go,
For this is the Fall of the year.
Now the days grow cold,
As the year grows old,
And the meadows are brown and sere;
Brave robin redbreast
Has gone from his nest,
For this is the Fall of the year.
I do softly pray
At the close of day,
That the little children, so dear,
May as purely grow
As the fleecy snow
That follows the Fall of the year.

After finishing, she looked up proudly, awaiting my reaction. "Think he'll be able to come?" Then: "Nate, you're crying!"

My hand brushed my cheek, and sure enough it came back wet. I forced a smile, and reached for her.

"You just did such a good job, I'm so proud of you," I said. The tears were really flowing. She approached me, confused and scared; with one hand she wiped my face and with the other gripped my fingers tight. And then came the sound we hoped we would never have to hear again.

We stood slowly, sordid imaginations not able to conjure what was waiting on the other end of that doorbell.

We went through it all over again. In some ways, it was worse this time – we knew what to expect. Experience can help a person get through most things, except of course when it makes it worse. Feelings that one can't fathom they will ever re-experience, and never should. Then it can be an anchor, multiplying the pain as anticipation augments reality.

There were the same unanswerable questions, the same constant loss of breath. Floating sensations. They were gone, they were all gone, and it was truly unimaginable.

There wasn't a notification team this time. Technically, it wasn't family. And those who would have notified us were gone. In one fell swoop, in one stroke, all gone.

Commander Hagen, who was in the process of retiring and hadn't been on the deployment had arrived with the news. It was the greatest loss of life in special operations history – that was the statistic that had greeted Mom when she turned on the television that afternoon. It had overtaken Operation Redwing for that title, which I had read about extensively. I had even met Marcus Luttrell, the Lone Survivor, a couple years earlier when Spencer had taken me to the Army/Navy game in Philadelphia.

Special operations meant a lot of things to a lot of people, and while it could have been Green Berets, Rangers, Delta, Marine Recon or any of the couple thousand other Navy SEALs on active duty, Mom later told me that she never had a doubt it was DEVGRU. And that they were *our* SEALs on the Chinook that went down very near the same spot in Northern Afghanistan where my father had been killed.

This time there was a glut of news online about the crash, mostly because it was the same group who had taken out Bin Laden, even if they weren't the same men. I learned specific details from CNN.com and the Navy Times about the mission that took thirty American lives. Bull, Spencer, and twenty other SEALs, plus Navy support personnel, airmen, soldiers, the pilots, a military dog and Afghan soldiers.

I contemplated the horror they must have felt as their helicopter was shot out of the sky by a well-placed Taliban RPG. They were en route to reinforce a Ranger platoon that had fallen under heavy fire during a raid on a high value Taliban target. I knew that would have been the way they wanted to go, helping their brothers.

And now, like my father and so many others before and after, these men were gone. One day they were here, pushing me on runs or yelling at me to get my legs higher on flutter kicks. Cursing me out or congratulating me over email. Comforting my mom, teaching me how to shoot fireworks. Tickling Cheyenne and changing the oil in the Explorer. Now they weren't. In a way, it was hard to believe they ever were. That was the hardest part of all.

There were more funerals than I wanted to imagine or thought that I could. Two were all I could handle: Special Warfare Operator, First Class Spencer R. Detse and Command Senior Chief Special Operator Robert Bullin. My mother attended them all. She made it her mission to travel the country, paying her respects to the families and honoring the elite who had fought side by side with her husband. We hadn't known all of the fallen, but more than we ever would have believed.

Ms. Dotty, Bull's ex-wife, stayed with us the night before he was laid to rest in Arlington National Cemetery. I recognized the same glazed, numb look I saw behind so many eyes during that time. I knew it well and could now stomach it with experience.

It was inappropriate, the weather. How could the sun shine, birds glide, and a soft breeze move branches, ruffle black dresses? How could cleanliness be so dirty, shininess so clouded? The universe didn't care. It didn't have rules or a conscious. Everything was the was the way it was and there was nothing anyone could do about it. God? Mother Nature? A Higher Power? Everything just was; it didn't happen for a reason, it just happened. That, I was convinced of. The sun doesn't care about sorrow any more than the hurricane cares about a tin-roofed shack.

I actually found strength in the pain; embraced it, swallowed it, let it churn and grow inside. It festered while I observed. Silent mourners, tears hidden behind sunglasses. Black cars reflecting dark ties and blue uniforms. White gloves, the front row, the sickening thud of metal pounded into wood by calloused fists. Six men, a folded flag. A single voice, echoing across silent crowds, making personal contact with all. Then another. Then another. Then another. The feats, the selflessness, the duty, the honor. The sacrifice, the commitment, the stream of banalities. All true, but no matter.

Bugles, Taps, Amazing Grace, the familiar notes wafting across my face like that soft breeze. The glint off the instruments bright across my naked eyes. A lawnmower, barely audible in the distance, proof of gravity's continuation. I inhaled its refuse, the sweet smell, the same as it was in my backyard as a cemetery as a golf course.

Cracks of thunder filled the air. Again and again, shoulders involuntarily lurching at each noise, each symbol. For where we are and why we are here.

Rows of graves, rolling across the landscape. They were there yesterday and they will be there tomorrow. More of them. Knee-level now. They used to reach my waist. I feel bigger around them, as one usually does with familiarity and experience. The stone doesn't care either way, it doesn't reciprocate. Like the birds or the sun or the hurricane it is just there, doing what it is supposed to do. It doesn't change with emotion, no matter how significant or impactful. It just is.

And, I realize, so are we. I know what I can change and fully understand what I can't. It's a nice thought, maybe offers some comfort. But more than anything, it allows me to just be. And that's not so bad.

Then there was one more to go. The last one. I hoped. I stood before the bathroom mirror, face lathered thick with old shaving cream. At sixteen I still didn't have much of beard.

"Here, let me help you with that."

Grandpa appeared in the reflection behind me. He looked old. It occurred to me just how much death he'd seen over the years. I dropped my hands and stiffened slightly when he reached over my shoulder and picked up the razor.

"There's your first problem. How old is this razor? It could barely cut butter."

I paused before answering. "It was my dad's."

He set it down gently before opening a drawer. "Well we can at least give it a new blade." He changed out the blade and offered a soft smile. "I think you've used enough shaving cream for a dozen shaves." He took a hand towel, thinning out the lather before handing me the fresh razor.

"Start here," he said, motioning just below my sideburn. "You want to shave down, with the grain. Careful, don't press too hard. There you go. Now rinse the blade, get the hair and cream off – look at that, there actually is some hair there. Now go up from the bottom of your neck, like this."

"Grandpa?"

"Yes?"

"Did you ever wish that Mom didn't marry Dad?"

The question didn't shock him as I expected it would. I wasn't even sure why I had asked it.

"Why would I wish that? You think because he died young and left my daughter alone with her pain? To raise two children on her own?"

"Dunno. I guess."

"Nate, I would give anything for my daughter to not have to go through the pain she has had to endure. I would happily have given my own life, that goes without saying. But the one thing I wouldn't take back – not that anyone is making me the offer – but the best things we have out of that pain are you and Cheyenne. Those are the greatest gifts and legacy he could have left, and even with Gayle's broken heart, we wouldn't change a thing. Not that anyone's offering. Now splash your face with cold water and slap a little of this on."

I did, and recognized his smell on me. A large hand clamped down on my neck. He led me from the bathroom. I took a deep breath, and headed for the car. One more to go.

Chapter 33

THIS WOULD BE THE HARDEST ONE yet, there was no doubt about that. Honestly, I was just ready to get it over. I had made my peace, said my own goodbyes, on my own terms. I was over the pomp and ritual of the formal send-offs. Wherever Spencer was, it wasn't in that box, that I was sure of.

Everything looked the same. It felt the same, sounded the same. As it had at my father's, at Bull's. It pained me to think that I was so conditioned to this that they felt familiar. Common, even. What a strange and unfortunate sentiment.

With more than a tiny stab of guilt, I conceded that Spencer's funeral was going to be harder on me than even my father's had. Shock, youth, and denial had shielded me that day, which seemed like both a lifetime and a moment ago. Now, while I had grown calloused and hardened to these tragedies, I was more aware of what they entailed.

We walked anonymously with the other mourners, murmuring to each other in the summer sun. The different levels of sacrifice struck me yet again, and once more I was awash with something resembling anger at the oblivious patriots lining the streets, dabbing eyes. We were the ones suffering, who knew real pain. At least the SEALs in attendance, whose bright Tridents mesmerized me as they graciously shook hands and accepted thanks for their service from housewives and city council members, at least they would be able to get some payback. Some time ago Spencer had made it clear that they could not properly grieve during wartime, that this was the time to destroy the enemy in the name of the fallen. That's what they were trained to do. The real reflection would come year later, with night terrors and anxiety and guilt. With failed relationships and road rage and too much drink and sleepless nights. But for the present, they had to remain hard knowing that soon enough they would be back on cargo planes with their kits and rifles and explosives and take it right to the sons of bitches who had killed the people we loved. And invariably some of them would come back in the same shiny, wooden boxes as the one in front of us, the one all these people had taken half days from work to see lowered into the ground. And they fully accepted that. I sucked back tears, tried to extinguish the fire in my chest. Cheyenne's grip tightened. She didn't look over at me but didn't have to. Her focus translated through sweaty palms. Right now, there was no doubt who was consoling who.

Spencer had not been close with his parents. They divorced when he was young and while his dad lived in the same small town in which he had grown up, he had not been a part of his life. His mother had been an alcoholic, her presence scarce both physically and psychologically, eventually leading the angry young man to turn down a baseball scholarship from a small Christian college to join the Navy. *See The World* was the promise. *Adventure. Blow Shit Up.* Sounded great to him, just what he was looking for. That first meeting with the Pacific had been a rude one on the first day of indoc.

"Nate," he once told me, "When I first looked out across that expanse of water, I couldn't believe what stretched before me. I thought the fields of Nebraska were endless. To me, that Pacific Ocean may have been outer space itself."

Having grown up mostly in Virginia Beach, I had laughed, thinking I actually had something on him. "You must have shit your pants the first time you did surf passage!"

He had looked at me with that sagacious stare that could electrify hair follicles, nodding, unembarrassed. "I was scared, that's for sure. I remember the sound of the breakers were what really got me. TV doesn't do justice to the sound of the ocean. It sounded like thunder, regular and cyclical, but with no end. I realized that without fail, those breakers always rolled in, one after another. Always had. They would never stop, never pause. It was the enormity of it that got me, I think. The finality. But I like scared. I feed off scared. I may have been terrified by those six-foot waves and freezing water, but I knew I would beat it. And I made every timed swim and was the Smurf crew's bow man for night rock portage during Hell Week. Shit, scared means nothing. Some guys say they aren't scared, which is bull. Fear is what kept me going during BUD/S. Fear just lets you know that the obstacle is worth beating."

I thought back to that conversation while watching his mother receive her flag, the commanding officer of SEAL Team 6 kneeling before her. I smiled, realizing that I didn't have anything on him just because I grew up around the ocean. He had something on everyone else, the same thing all SEALs had.

The honor guard played Taps, the salute cracking across fluorescent skies. We wiped away more tears. Like those waves in the ocean, always more.

I was just able to mumble a "how are you doing?" to Mom as we wound our way towards the exit. We were in the middle of the procession leaving Arlington National Cemetery, a small ceremony on Ft. Meyer the next stop for teammates, family, and close friends. The Arlington County police had blocked Route 50 from both sides. People stood outside of cars paying respects and rubbernecking. An end-less line of headlights eased down the highway, mostly made up of concerned mourners heading back to grateful existences.

She sighed, and leaned her head against the glass. Cheyenne had her head on her shoulder. They both looked so weary.

"As good as can be expected, I suppose. How about you?"

I didn't know how to answer, so I didn't. We rode in silence until reaching the base, following the other cars to a remote parking lot, MP's screening those who entered.

"Gayle, Cheyenne, Nate, our deepest condolences from the entire special operations community. I know how close Spencer was to you and your family. He was a great operator, man, and brother." I turned to identify the friendly voice, and after a moment of confusion, fi-nally placed the face. Westhead, the young SEAL who had told me stories of my father in the restaurant the night before his funeral and I had joked with at the beach barbeque the year before. Tall, fit, and respectable in his Dress Blues, starched lid and polished Trident, he was from SEAL central casting.

I can't say that he necessarily looked older than I remembered, mostly because he still didn't look much older than me. I guess it was experience I perceived, a wisdom and maturity behind colder, darker eyes. He was doing everything he could to make them friendly and welcoming, but I saw right through that. Like all of them, he had seen and done things we couldn't imagine. It was a miracle he was able to put that aside and act the role of soother, a healer when the time called for it. That's what he wanted to play now. After a beat I realized that's exactly what I needed.

"Pig, right?" I asked, macho. It could be that I was out of bounds, but if there was ever a time I could get away with a little disrespect, it was a day like this.

"Yep. You can call me Dan if you want. Pig was when I was a new guy."

The crow with multiple chevrons on his upper left sleeve came into focus.

"Guess you're not a new guy anymore, huh?"

"Guess not." He put his hand on my shoulder and with an instructive nod led me inside, away from the crowd. The proffer, for whatever reason, seemed natural. I didn't hesitate to follow.

"First off, I have something for you." He reached into his jacket pocket, and pulled out a large sealed envelope. "It's from Spencer. He wanted you to have this should he make the ultimate sacrifice." His arm extended forward. Slowly, robotically, I accepted it, clutched it tightly in my fist.

"I didn't know you were that close to him," I finally stammered.

"Before he left for DEVGRU Spencer was like an older brother to me. He mentored me, much like your father did for him." He chuckled, remembering something.

"Saved my ass from the guys more than once, that's for sure. In fact, saved me from your old man's wrath right after I got my Budweiser. My first week officially in Team 2, and we have a night shipboarding exercise. The full platoon jocks up, loads in the helos, heads out into the Atlantic. The guys were fresh off a deployment and subsequent leave, and no one was thrilled about spending their first night back cold and wet. The guys just wanted to complete the exercise and get back to a warm bed.

"We reach the ship, an old decommissioned freight Maersk sold to the Navy for just this purpose. We board, fast and with the proper violence of action, everything's going smooth. I'm in the stick that's supposed to fast-rope onto the stern, blow a door leading to the cargo bay and clear the bay. The Senior Chief was this short red-headed dude from Boston named Lucky. Lucky was a mean bastard, at least twenty years in the Teams, with the biggest Napoleon complex I'd ever seen. He *hated* new guys, was the worst hazer out of anybody. Well, as the breacher my job is blow the door, so I set the charge, prime and time it, and step back to wait. Nothing happens. Everyone's looking at me, this FNG, and I'm racking my brain, trying to figure out why the charge didn't blow. And of course knowing there's a possibility that the second I go check, it could blow. Long story short, I forgot to dual prime the charge. I went back and attached a new initiator, dual primed that bitch, and it blew right on time.

"To my surprise, no one said anything to me on the trip back to base, or even once we were back in the ready room. It was a new guy mistake, and while I felt terrible about it, it would never happen again. Lesson learned.

"So I thought. We debriefed with the Master Chief over a couple of beers and a bucket of fried chicken. As soon as we were done, guys started to trickle out, heading home. I thought I had escaped punishment – believe me, I was beating myself up worse than anyone else could, or so I thought – until I felt a hand on my shoulder. I turned. Mo, with a gentle touch to remind me it was alright. Yeah, right. That gentle touch clamped onto my collar bone, bringing me to my knees. Before I knew what happened they dogpiled me, beat my ass. Punches, kicks, my face slammed into the linoleum. I got choked out, thankfully, and when I came to I was in what they call 'a tapeworm.' Meaning I was buck naked and wrapped from head to toe in duct tape, with only a slot for my nose and mouth.

"When I came to, I heard Lucky call out 'Let this trial come to order.' Kangaroo Court. I knew I was in for it. They quickly found me guilty of many offenses, ranging from, I think, sodomizing a panda bear to watching *The Kardashians*. Both serious offenses, with steep consequences.

"The guys felt they needed to be drunker before passing sentence, so they stuck me in an ice bath, while they headed to the strip club to get adequately lubricated. For the next hour I froze my balls off in that slushy. I was almost relieved when a light finally came on and the muffled sound of my pissed and drunk platoon mates got closer.

"For the next hour I was force fed Jack Daniels and Texas Pete's hot sauce until I was puking fire. We reviewed the proper process for dual-priming a charge about twenty times, once for each shot I took. Finally around daybreak they ran out of steam and bourbon.

"The process of pulling the tape off was as painful as you think. Not much body hair was left when they were done, they made sure of that. The pile of spent tape looked comical, covered in pubes and blood. Lucky then took permanent marker to my face, leaving me for the next week with caricatures and phrases not suitable to be repeated. Then they tied me to the flag pole and left me. To die, I thought. I was in and out of consciousness, feeling pretty damn sorry for myself, when I heard a car pull into the lot. I figured they had come back to finish me off. It was Spencer. He cut me down, and brought me to his cage to get me some clothes. Of course he gave me nut-hugger UDT swim shorts and a sequined Brittany Spears sweatshirt, but that was what you would expect to find in his cage. I was still dry-heaving so he gave me an IV, and then drove me home. We barely talked on the ride, but we didn't need to. The point had been made – you fuck up in a normal job and the company loses a sale. You fuck up in the Teams, people die. He picked me up the next day on the way to work and by walking me into the team room, he let the rest of the guys know I was alright.

"When we got in, your dad was sitting at a table, reading the paper. He looked up at Spencer, then to me. He nodded at me, and I knew that my new guy mistake was now forgiven. Those two taught me more about being a SEAL that night than BUD/S, SQT and any training op combined. And I'll never be able to thank them enough."

In many ways I was moved by his story, but also disgusted by his failure. He wasn't looking for sympathy, not then or now. My dad and his teammates had done what needed to be done, like they always did. And Spencer had done what he felt was right. *What's right is right.*

The crowd buzzed, a single entity. Its momentum carried us inside. Independently but together, people began to take their places inside the cavernous auditorium.

On a small stage fifteen individual memorials greeted us. Fifteen well-used rifles stood upright, with fifteen sets of dog tags hanging from them. Fifteen weathered helmets rested on each stock, fifteen pairs of dusty boots at the base. And fifteen framed 10x15 photos of smiling, youthful, exceptional young men. Men when they were alive. Smiling, in Dress Blues and tuxedos, on happier days. Rosy cheeks and white smiles. The DEVGRU 15, Gold Squadron. A tragic loss of life of an elite fighting force sworn to protect this country. And the public barely noticed, even after the unwanted attention on SEAL Team 6 after the Bin Laden operation. Too busy twerking and catching up on DVR'd reality television.

The funny thing was that this lack of attention would have been fine for these silent professionals. Would have been refreshing. By their nature they did not yearn for recognition or accolades and certainly not crocodile tears.

I still couldn't believe they were gone. I stood listening to Westhead and found myself wondering if he could be next. His tight smile made me think that just maybe he could read my mind.

With no bravado he explained, "You never know if the next ticket punched could be yours. If it is, so be it. But you can't think that way. We have a job to do, we do it, and then we go home. And if I *am* next? Know I had a blast on the way out." He actually winked.

There was nothing more to say. I stood up. I was grateful for what Westhead had shared. All I could offer was an optimistic expression that I hoped articulated the intended sentiment.

The room was now filled. Subdued conversations made the space hum with restrained emotions. At least half the mourners were in military uniform, many wearing the Trident, more not. It wasn't just Team 6 – these fifteen fallen had made their mark in Teams on both coasts, and those not deployed were here grieving over their fallen brothers.

A confident voice, crackling through worn speakers, brought the room to attention. The captain who had presented Spencer's mother with her flag was standing crisp and proper in his Dress Whites at the podium. He looked surprisingly average, save, of course, for the glistening pin on his left breast. He was normal in stature, a thin mustache and scanning eyes completing the picture of military aptitude. He had walked with a pronounced limp earlier, but was now standing ramrod straight, a serious man. I had heard that he had lost the leg in a parachuting accident and had made the decision to amputate the leg and get a prosthetic so he could stay in the Teams. And now he was the commander of DEVGRU.

His message was not unfamiliar for these events, which didn't make it not true, just me bored. Maybe bored was too harsh. Resigned and all-too-aware of the theme. I was well familiar with the sacrifice these men had made. Of their bravery, dedication, no-quit attitude, etc., etc. I had been reminded of it every single day since the first time it happened, and now once more. I didn't need to hear it again.

So I slipped out a side door, finding myself in a small gym. I could hear the muffled words of the skipper in the other hall, but save for echoes and two shiny orange rims I was completely alone with my thoughts. And Spencer's package.

It took some time to get open. The large manila envelope was taped securely, my name written curtly in small block letters across the front. I examined the script:

NATHAN BUTLER. J.I.C.

Just In Case. Basic, formal, direct.

I took my time opening it. A single page came out first, yellow legal paper, covered in a surprising amount of blue ballpoint ink, the same simple script as my name. I gently put the letter to the side, feeling a wash of déjà vu.

Next came a dusty Trident patch, well worn, still showing the frayed edges and thread where it had been cut off his uniform. The patch Spencer had worn and had died wearing and protecting. He knew that no other symbol had more meaning to me, that nothing else symbolized the weight and burden of the warrior duty/battle call than that Trident, thus he had made sure I received his. I set it on top of the letter, anxious fingers reaching back into the envelope. I nearly pricked my finger.

The third item that slid out of the envelope was a Silver Star. I thought that curious, since I knew he had a laundry list of medals and awards that he had never told us about. In fact, his medals had only been discovered by his family at the viewing, where, laid out in his Dress Blues, his SEAL brothers had painstakingly ensured every medal and ribbon he had rated over a decade of warfare was displayed. So why had he included a Silver Star?

I pondered that as I reached back into the envelope. Something slid to the corner that my clammy fingers couldn't grip. I turned the envelope over, and out flew a shiny, cylindrical object. Its single clang on the basketball court seemed deafening; I caught it in mid-air on the bounce.

It was a shell casing. From a large-caliber rifle, clearly. One of the casings, I would learn from the letter, that had come from my father's weapon as he fought that day almost four years ago.

The letter also let me know that the Silver Star was not Spencer's. It was, in fact, the one awarded to my father posthumously. Spencer wrote that he had worn it pinned on the underside of his body armor ever since the mission that had killed my Dad, a reminder of the tradition he was responsible for upholding.

There was one more item. It felt heavy and hard in the bottom of the package, threatening to rip a hole in the bottom at any second. Even after pulling it out, I was unsure of what I was holding. When it came to me in a flash I began laughing uncontrollably. Relief washed over me, a reassurance I hadn't felt in a long time. Everything was going to be okay. I looked around, made sure there were no witnesses. Gently placed it back in the envelope.

I've given much thought about this, and have decided that it wouldn't be right to share the final object bequeathed to me by Spencer. If ever I change my mind, you'll be the first to know. Suffice to say it was something that only he could provide and will give me great comfort for years to come.

Then it was time to read his letter, which ended up being the hardest part of a very hard day. The paper shook in my hands, the words blurred by tears. Soon I was lost in his words, in his wishes. Those, too, I have decided won't be shared here. It could be argued that the personal and private thoughts of a man so aware of his mortality that he put pen to paper to share his final feelings while still very much alive should be kept private. We all walk the earth knowing that one day we will leave it, but most of us assume it will be far in the future, after the proper amount of time and experience. These men don't live with that comfort or expectation.

Then again, I don't know. Maybe I'm just being selfish. Maybe I just don't want to share this piece of Spencer with anyone. Maybe I just want something to stay between us.

What I can tell you is that while he knew he could not be a father to me, I was a son to him. And he loved me, Cheyenne, and my mother very much. We were his family. All things I, and the reader, already knew. He didn't, and didn't need to, tell me that he willingly gave his life for his country, but even more so, for his soldier brothers fighting next to him. We had that talk countless times, and it would have been redundant to waste his final words telling me what I already knew. Instead, he included some revelations that shocked but didn't surprise me. Those too I'll keep between Spencer and myself. Mission secrecy and all.

When I realized that the blue ink was blotting, I wiped my face, took a deep breath, and tucked the letter away, if only to salvage the quality of work. Then I slowly placed the remaining items back into the envelope, re-sealing it tightly for safekeeping. The fluorescent lights from the gym were beginning to make me dizzy. But I was at peace, somehow, and my eyes instinctively went to the sky. I wondered what pranks my dad was playing on Bull and Spencer.

When the gym door groaned open, I didn't have to turn to tell who was there. I blinked a few times, rolled my shoulders, and with a deep breath and upbeat smile turned to face my family. It was time to go home.

Chapter 34

THE MONTHS WENT BY, as they tend to do. They didn't go slowly, didn't go fast. Just passed the way time does, in this case in a less remarkable fashion than I sometimes was accustomed to. Gun to my head, I'd guess I'd describe the period as lonely – but not in the context you're thinking, not traditionally lonely in the bad, depressing way. More of in a quiet, somber way. A semblance of normality?

There may or may not have been a few instances of casual juvenile drinking, maybe even some recreational drug use my senior year. Whether there was or wasn't is inconsequential, as any episodes were minor and would fall under the category of normal high school activities. Maybe that characteristic alone makes them notable.

Somewhere along the way my voice stopped cracking and my face cleared up. My body continued to fill out, a result of hard work and hormones. Slowly – or maybe all at once, who could tell – my mood, for the most part, stopped sucking. While I may not have realized it when it was happening, looking back I can say with confidence that others did.

Mom got a full-time job at Navy Federal Credit Union while finishing her degree in Human Resources. The money from my father's life insurance went towards a down payment on a small rancher down the street from my grandparents, who often watched Cheyenne after school and in the evenings when Mom had class. We moved in that fall, just as senior year began.

At my mother and grandparent's behest I had applied to the University of Maryland and Towson and gotten into both. I had no intention of attending either.

And then the week before school started I got an email. From Tammy. Her dad had retired and taken a job at Ft. Meade. She and Doug would be attending Laurel High. And she "couldn't wait to see me."

I stared at my phone, not conceding anything – a thought, a reaction, an emotion. I didn't allow myself any of that for about as long as you can tell yourself not to think of something before you think only of it. Notions of Tammy had certainly entered my mind from time to time since our last antagonistic meeting in Virginia Beach, but I wasn't sure how I felt about her now. She had abandoned me when I needed her the most, hadn't she?

Of course it didn't matter. Age and desire easily superseded past transgressions, and the best I could muster was to force (hopefully) an appropriate delay before an enthusiastic reply. Even the blatant effort to minimize my eagerness was, at best, obvious.

We were to meet at the mall after the first day of school. The day when students start the morning with the best of intentions and outfits, freshly coiffed hair and new sneakers a clear sign of their intent to win the day. For those still in that mindset by the final bell, it was a win. My collection of nerves didn't start making themselves known until last period.

Tired of being a chauffeur, Mom had bequeathed me the Explorer, which I parked well ahead of the scheduled meeting at Five Guys. For the next hour I wandered the mall checking my reflection in anything that would return it.

I didn't realize the interest that the CVS pharmacy would pique in me until I found myself passing it for the third or fourth time. I hummed, "We could all use a sedative," and thought how a Xanax would be just the thing to calm the nerves, and I also thought it was a good thing that I didn't have any, because I would probably have taken two or three or four footballs and either fallen asleep in my burger or OD'd. I took calm, purposeful breaths and took solace in my likeness: a tanned, muscular young man. A future Navy SEAL. How could she not like me?

Finally the time came, and I made my way to the food court, full of energy and optimism. I saw her before she saw me, an image as only such an eager imagination can conjure. Her hair shined, her confident pose radiated as mall-goers buzzed around her. I steadied myself, and approached Tammy for the first time in almost a year. I made sure to wipe my hands on my jeans before I spoke.

"Hey."

She looked up, quickly. When our eyes met I wondered if I saw more eagerness register across her face than mine.

"Nate." She stood to offer a hug. I met it, turning sideways to avoid bumping heads. I hoped she hadn't felt me shaking.

"Tammy." Her hair had a strong scent. Perfume? Conditioner? I extracted it from my face before figuring out where to sit.

Pleasantries completed and seats selected, it quickly became evident that something in our dynamic had changed. Before long I was leaning back confidently in the booth, picking at her fries, monosyllabically answering her questions. To my surprise, I discovered that I was at ease.

She droned, "The last thing we wanted to do was change schools before senior year, but when Dad retired he got this gig with the NSA, so we really didn't have a choice." She bit at her thumbnail, explaining their arrival in Maryland. I smoothed my hair, making sure to flex a bicep when I did it. "Doug put up a fight, but really he just wanted to make a scene. He's more of a drama queen than ever now, really." She leaned forward, her breasts actually pushing the fry bucket towards me in what I could only assume was an attempt at seduction.

There it was again. Something had definitely changed. It could have happened that night at her window, or over time, or more likely since I had sat down at this dirty plastic table fingering greasy fries and scanning the crowd for hotter girls.

She had grown into a striking young woman, there was no doubt about that. But something about her was different. Of course it could have been me that changed. But whatever had happened, her mystique was gone, and I wondered if it had not transferred to me.

Can two people co-exist with dual enigmatic auras? I thought not, now even more confident that the power had shifted. I rested my foot on her bench, chewing, half listening while pondering this change.

It occurred to me that two people get together when they each believe their counterpart to be better than themselves. A little inferiority to make it feel like you're getting a bargain. If you think you can improve on your partner, naturally you look elsewhere. And rarely does anyone think their partner is on the *exact* same level as them. That's why they break up: one begins to see themselves as better than their mate, when previously under the impression they were inferior. The balance tips. That's why me and Tammy hadn't worked, and the same reason we wouldn't now. The tables kept turning, and damn, it felt good to be on this side.

"So he's even more of a bitch now, huh?" I said antagonistically. The adrenaline of first sight had waned and I was feely awfully superior.

Her face reddened as she lowered it. "I always felt bad about the two of you. I don't know why we couldn't all hang out together."

I laughed, unintentionally cold. "Always thought it strange that you guys weren't closer. Aren't twins supposed to be inseparable?"

"We've always been competitive. Guess that just bled over into our social lives."

I shrugged.

While finishing her fries I told her about a back-to-school party that weekend. Rumor had it there would be a keg, and I'd be happy to introduce her around. She (too) readily accepted, and we ended up getting pretty drunk on warm beer and Jell-O shots in the woods behind the athletic fields.

She touched me every time she had a chance that night. Barely left my side, in fact. Excuses were made to grip my shoulder, feel my chest. It was laughable, and I can remember thinking that I'd never felt so cool, so in control. Tammy Simmons, the girl of my dreams, was now throwing herself at me. Well, dreams of nights past. And she was doing it in front of the whole school, no less. I had never really known where I stood in the social pecking order, which isn't to say I hadn't given it a good deal of thought. Many times I had mulled over how great a power it would be to actually see yourself as others did, an impartial third-party view from a first-person perspective. At that party, for the first time, not only did I know that omnipotence, but it revealed a view from the top.

I lost my virginity that night, in the backseat of the Explorer. Something made me think she hadn't.

Chapter 35

THINGS THAT HAPPENED senior year: four more Navy SEALS died – two in combat in Afghanistan, one in a training accident in Arizona, one by suicide. Cheyenne found out our father had missed her birth. An email from Westhead told the story about what his teammates had done to my dad the night before his wedding; my mom, still unable to hide her anger at it, confirmed. I made out with three girls and kind of had sex with another. Tammy and I traded months of thinking we were better than the other, meaning, of course, that we still couldn't work. I alternated between not caring and thinking my heart was going to explode out of my chest when she didn't return a text. It was the coldest winter on record and me and Naom, a kid from Seattle who I had started hanging out with, decided it would be a good idea to jump into the Chesapeake Bay on New Year's Eve. Surprisingly we were sober since Naom didn't drink and said an altered state of mind impinged on his creativity. He was a writer and under his influence I found that I too liked to write – short stories and the occasional poem that he had a way of editing without being critical or at least without making his critiques sound like criticism while actually encouraging my writing, even though spending so much time with him probably didn't help my social standing, but I found that didn't matter as much to me anymore, and besides, being an awkward artsy jock was supremely unique, and I had to think that at least I had that going for me.

He had completed a novel that he was going to self-publish, which I thought was really good but for some reason had trouble imagining that he had written it, even though I knew he had written the book about a boy who had a pet elephant and took him everywhere he went, but it turns out in the end that there was no elephant, had never been an elephant – sorry for the spoiler if you were planning on reading *The Elephant in the Room*. I tried mushrooms with Naom, which I know goes against his edict about mind-altering substances, in fact goes as far against that edict as possible, but that was Naom, a contradiction, which is a nice way of saying a hypocrite, I guess, although it didn't seem that way. They didn't do much to me, the shrooms, I mean I saw some lights and crap, I think, but mostly I just had to take a shit and eventually threw up after listening to a lot of Pearl Jam, and sang "Elderly Woman Behind the Counter in a Small Town" at the top of my lungs while listening to it on my headphones walking home from 7/11 after buying Big League Chew, a Charleston Chew and Vitamin Water, not noticing or caring that people were looking at me like I was crazy, not minding because I was really into that song and in my experience if you like that song, you *really* like it, it *inspires* you, which is what I told Westhead in one of our more frequent emails. He's a big Pearl Jam fan.

Westhead had transferred to a West Coast Team, but as far as I could tell the mission and deployment frequency had calmed down since we had left Iraq and were in the process of turning Afghanistan over to its Army, and he was more than willing to send me workouts and advice on how to prepare for BUD/S since I was secretly spending a lot of time at the Navy recruiter's office in the Pink Oak shopping center talking Special Ops with Petty Officer Dan Patton, who had actually met my father a few times, although he hadn't known he was a SEAL. We watched recruitment videos together, discussed the wars. He was a smart guy, Petty Officer Patton. He treated me like an equal. I would still be seventeen when I graduated, but could enlist with a parent's signature. There was obviously only one option for that signature, and I was unsure if I would get it or not. If not, I planned to work out until my eighteenth birthday and then promptly head off to Great Lakes with orders to BUD/S after A-School. If I washed out of BUD/S or SQT then it would be the fleet for me, a possibility that never crossed my mind.

I sat with Petty Officer Patton on many an afternoon, him asking me nearly as many questions about my dad and the SEALs I knew as I asked him about joining the Navy. A definite squid. But I realized my experience being around the Teams my whole life was something special, something that would be invaluable as I began the hardest journey any man can volunteer for, especially when compared to some sailor from Iowa who's only read about BUD/S and talked shit about becoming a SEAL in a jarhead bar in Rota but met a SEAL once and he wasn't impressed, said that he didn't seem so tough so he does a shitload of pushups and swims laps at the MWR pool yet has no real idea of the commitment it takes to make it like I did, which I expressed in the journal I started, whose entries quite honestly alternated between expressing my excitement about joining the Navy and highlighting great workouts to pissing and moaning about Tammy to half-assed teenage philosophies on human existence and analyzing the reason for my random bouts of sadness. My mood drastically depended on the month. When I was happy I couldn't imagine the state that I had been in when I wrote how depressed I was; when depressed I couldn't picture myself happy again. Eventually I reached a point where I didn't mind being sad, and if you are content to be sad, are you really?

I stopped taking my meds, which never really did much for me, and started smoking cigarettes. I stopped smoking cigarettes, tried dip. Once, I got drunk and threw up the dip, so I tried chew after that. Most of the SEALs I knew dipped or chewed, and that was good enough for me. I saved Doug from getting beat up by a couple of guys on the football team after he turned one in for cheating on a typing test (I'm still unsure how ones cheats on a typing test). I didn't want to, really, but I decided to save him anyway. Ox, the guy who he turned in, was pretty pissed at me, and as you can imagine you'd rather not have a guy on the football team named Ox mad at you. We didn't come to blows, but it was close. I think once he realized I had no problem fighting him and in fact might have wanted the fight more than he did he decided to back down, something I've found that's often the case. I was disappointed, I think.

Tammy had been there that afternoon out front of Shake Shack, and unless I'm mistaken it was admiration I saw in her face. She texted me later that night, at least. I didn't return it. Saw movies and read books and articles about SEALs, some by SEALs. Enjoyed most of them, but was angry that people seemed to be capitalizing on their blood and our tears. Flash floods, lightning bolts, cicadas, new friends, old friends, blowing smoke rings, eating onion rings, yearbook pictures, fender benders, a part-time job, too many parking tickets, not enough free time, sadness, happiness, depression, hope, concerts, life, discomfort, which I think I thrived on...hearts and thoughts they fade

Chapter 36

THEN I FIGURED it was time.

"Ma? Can we talk?"

A haunted look instantly flashed across her face, a look that will forever be ingrained in my consciousness. She stiffened at the interruption, casually drying her hands with a black and white checked kitchen towel. A shadow crossed over her forehead, and it was obvious in her eyes that she knew what this was about. Like she always knew.

It was a month before graduation.

I escorted her out of the kitchen, motioning for her to sit on the loveseat. A lot of work had been done since we had moved into the new house, on a limited budget. Grandpa had painted this room a cool, muted blue with bright white trim. Grandma had found the fabric and together they had reupholstered our old couches, transplanted from Virginia Beach. We had ripped up stale carpet, finding rough wood floors that shone brightly after I spent hours sanding and staining them. Yard sales and discount stores had provided the rest of the décor, and maternal creativity and care had perfected the motif.

I ran my hands down my thighs, smoothing my jeans. I wasn't nervous, because I recognized that as a wasted emotion, but there wasn't going to be anything easy about this conversation.

The beginning, which I had expected to be the most difficult, was anything but.

"You want me to sign a waiver so you can join the Navy." It wasn't a question, or even a statement. In fact, the lack of emotion made it sound like she was reading a billboard or a menu. Blankly, I nodded.

"Well, it's not going to happen."

Again, I nodded, as much a reflex as anything. Like I said, I knew it wasn't going to be easy. Nothing worth doing is.

"And now you're going to convince me of why I should. You're going to tell me that in six months you'll be eighteen and you're just going to sign up anyway. That's it's in your DNA to be a SEAL, that you want to carry on the family name and a Butler doesn't ever give up. That you have a duty to your father. Do I have it right?"

Needless to say, I was somewhat taken aback. She did, in fact, have it pretty much dead-on. I decided to start with humor.

"You make great points, Mom. You've got me convinced," I said, mock-smile hopefully disarming.

She sighed, looked up at me sadly. "Sit with me, Nate."

Once I did, she continued. "It's a noble thing that you want to do. I've worried about this day since you were in diapers. But it's different now. To you, this is still a fantasy."

I cut her off. "A dream, not a fantasy. Big difference."

"You're right, there is a big difference. And knowing the difference is difficult. Do you remember when you were a kid and you wanted to be an astronaut? And then a professional basketball player?" I didn't. "Well, your father told you that you could be any of those things, that you could be anything you wanted to be. He fed the fantasy."

"Isn't that what parents are supposed to do?"

"No, Nate, it's not. We're supposed to prepare you for life. For you to have the happiest and most successful life you can. Not to live in a fantasy world. If every kid who wanted to be an astronaut ended up being one, we'd have more people on the moon than in Los Angeles. It's just not realistic."

"It's realistic for me to become a SEAL. I know I can do it."

"I have no doubt that you *can* do it, Nate. I have no doubt that you could be an astronaut if you wanted. I just don't think you *should* do it. That's the fantasy instead of the dream. I want you to dream, I just don't want you to chase a fantasy. And until you're eighteen, I can still keep you from doing so."

My face flushed in anger. I stood quickly.

"What kind of a mother says that? Doesn't want her child to fulfill his fantasy? You ask me, that's terrible!"

"I want you to be happy, Nate. To be comfortable. I know what the Teams do to men, to their families. The lifestyle. I don't want that for you. You should know a comfortable life."

"Comfort?" I spat. "Comfort? Comfort is bull! Comfort is stifling and suppressive. It makes you weak and satisfied. I don't ever want to be comfortable! I want to achieve great things, to push myself and those around me. One thing you said earlier was right. It's in my DNA. And yeah, if you won't sign the waiver I'll have to wait until November to join. But we both know I'm going to do it. It's just a matter of whether it's with you or against you."

"Haven't I been through enough!" she yelled. "Don't I deserve a good night's sleep?"

Shaking, I reached into my back pocket and unfolded a single sheet of paper. I couldn't meet her eyes while gently placing the waiver on the coffee table. Too upset to speak, I left the room before her sobs reached me.

It happened to be one of the rare occasions when Tammy and I were speaking, so I gave her a call after the conversation with my mother.

"I'm not surprised that was her reaction," she told me.

"I guess I'm not either. I just can't believe she actually wants to stifle my dream."

"Fantasy."

"What?"

"Fantasy. She's right, a fantasy is a far cry from a dream. Or maybe it isn't, I don't know."

"Well, which is it Tammy?" A vicious pause, then: "What's your fantasy? Your dream?"

"Why does everyone have to have a dream? Everyone's always looking for the next best thing, for what they don't have. Can't I just be happy living in the moment?"

I wanted to tell her no, that was the stupidest thing I had ever heard. Miraculously, I held back. Instead I told her, "Those aren't mutually exclusive." Maybe I was maturing.

She sighed. Loudly. She was the one frustrated? "I just came across a quote on my newsfeed: 'In the end, we only regret the chances we didn't take.' What's your take on that?"

I thought about it for a second before answering. I smelled a trap.

What I *didn't* say was "I think that people who make life decisions or base their philosophies on Facebook memes should slit their wrists." I *did* say, "Cheesy, but true. No regrets, take chances. What we all should be doing."

I thought the responding howl was a bit excessive, but I didn't give her the pleasure.

"It's the dumbest thing I ever heard," she said. "How often do you really regret *not* doing something? I bet you regret od'ing on Xanax. I bet you regret getting arrested. And before you even think about say-ing some bullshit about how you don't regret those things because they made you who you are today, *don't*. Next you'll tell me every-thing happens for a reason, too."

"You better be careful, your pinko liberal cronies are going to boot you from the hippy club if they hear you talking like that."

"I'm not interested in being placed in a box, Nate. I'm interested in being happy, centered. And I realize that everyone can't run around following their dreams. We love the stories about Julia Rob-erts taking the big leap of faith and taking her beat-up Beatle across the country to become a movie star. But there are about a million waitresses and failures who took the same highway. There's nothing wrong with being a nurse or a government contractor. Nothing wrong with stability. If everyone goes out on a limb, there's no one on the ground and all the branches will break."

I stifled a laugh. "Such imagery, Tammy. You should write, really you should." Then, before the next speech: "So you don't think I should be a SEAL either?"

"I'm not saying that, Nate. I'm saying if you do I hope it's for the right reasons. I just think that people often think they're following their dreams but are actually living in a fantasy world."

Chapter 37

FROM UP HERE, everyone kind of looked like ants. They weren't though, they were people. They were my classmates and their families, some of them friends, looking very tiny from so far away.

I watched the throng, neat rows of royal blue gowns walking one by one towards the stage erected in the north end zone. Subconsciously I counted the first ten or so, knowing that "Butler" would have been called with no response from somewhere within that group.

From my perch at the top of a rise overlooking the field I had the best seat in the house. To tell you the truth, sitting there, I kind of felt like Holden Caulfield, I really did.

I knew my mother, sister and both sets of grandparents were sitting somewhere in those bleachers, expecting me to follow the line and accept my diploma. They were unaware that I had decided not to.

I told myself it was because she wouldn't sign the waiver, that was why I wasn't attending my own high school graduation. My own small, personal protest. And, in part, yeah, that was why. But there was more. There's always more.

I suppose I had always felt alienated from my classmates, especially since the move to Maryland. People not like me, who hadn't been through anything like I had. But even in Virginia Beach, surrounded by other Navy brats, I didn't always identify with my peers. Even when I hung out with Naom, or Gharun, or Doug, or Tammy, or Darren, or whoever. I was always different from them, and we all knew it. It wasn't a good different or a bad different, it just was. And this symbolic stand against the dog and pony show had its roots somewhere in that realization. I didn't know how or what I was trying to accomplish with it, only that some statement be made.

So I stayed away. And in doing so caused my family more anguish. I took another swig from the pint of Jim Beam and wiped my nose. Right then I hoped that my dad couldn't see me, because I knew he wouldn't be proud. With that thought I examined the bottle, chucked it into the woods. I may be a prick, but if possible I'd rather stop being a self-destructive prick.

Later that night, a relatively passive graduation party where I found myself making eyes at Tammy from across the room:

"That again?" asked Naom.

I looked over at him, surprised he had noticed.

"Dunno," I told him. "We'll see."

I was feeling as close as I could to content, sipping keg beer disinterestedly. There was a slight tug on my mood, of whose origination I couldn't place. It wasn't necessarily negative, just *there.*

We were sitting at the kitchen table with a few other kids, more Naom's friends than mine. Tight black jeans were the go-to fashion statement, scruffy beards on those who could grow them, even a couple of wallet chains. Stereotypes abounded. Football players wouldn't be attending this event, which is partly why I agreed to go.

There was a tame game of hearts being attempted, but two of the guys weren't drinking, and even after all I'd been through I still didn't trust someone who didn't drink, or at least fake it like Naom did.

"I'm on an all soup diet," one of them was saying. "Four times a day. Barley, tomato, chicken noodle, whatever."

"Chicken soup for the soul," someone muttered.

I whipped my head around to get a better look at the kid speaking. Auden or Aiden or something. I think I had German with him. Rail thin because he thought it made him look "above," skinny jeans and a deep V-neck. The kicker: a wool stocking cap perched on his head.

"It's June," I breathed, tired.

"'Scuse me?"

I turned to him, not attempting to hide my disgust.

"I said, it's June. It's hot out."

He shrugged. "Sometimes I eat it cold. Doesn't really matter."

"I mean your hat, your freaking beanie. It's June."

"Oh." He shrugged again, still not getting the point.

"Hipster doofus" came to mind, and I stood up, not knowing where I was going but knowing I needed to exit this scene.

"Where you going?" the guy called out. "We're in the middle of a game!"

"Need a beer?" I asked Naom, already knowing he would only hold the one he had as a prop all night. I didn't wait for a response, making my way to Tammy.

She saw me coming, and leaned into Colin Harpers, whispering secretively – all part of the game. Inwardly I smiled, enjoying it, embracing the threat as a kid does on a roller coaster.

"What's up, Colin?" I said, playing my part.

"Butler, what's up man?" He turned to me, a very specific and knowing glean to his eye. A purposeful look, I thought.

Hoping we were still making small talk, I told him, "Ready to be out of this shithole, that's for sure."

"I, for one, need a beer," Tammy interjected before slinking away.

Colin turned back to me, looked up from his phone.

"So I heard something about you. Looks like it's true."

Just like that, the mood got hard.

I gritted my teeth, having a feeling what was coming.

"And what's that?"

"Your dad was some type of hero? A Navy SEAL and shit?"

"Who told you that?" I asked. Rhetorically, of course. A reaction.

Instead of answering he held his phone up. My father's smiling face stared back at me, a picture from Iraq I was already familiar with. His standard desert props – M4, beard and sunglasses – dominated the frame.

I wasn't as taken aback as I would have expected. It wasn't something I would ever volunteer or wanted to talk about with my classmates, but it happened and was out there. And Tammy, for whatever reason, had felt the need to tell them.

"That's my father, if that's what you're asking."

"That's badass, man, why didn't you tell us? A Navy SEAL? Don't lie, did he cap Bin Laden?"

And that was exactly what I wanted to avoid. I searched for a proper response, but finding none, turned to walk away. Behind me, a small group had gathered, blocking my path.

"Hey, ya'll, it's true! Butler's dad was a SEAL!" A low but powerful murmur rippled at those words, and the crowd drew closer. I found I was in exactly the position I was least comfortable in: the center of attention.

Amid the din, Tammy's face came into focus across the room. I couldn't read it and sure couldn't figure her motivation, but I knew she disgusted me.

I thought back to the time in Virginia Beach when her and I had smoked a little pot in my basement and had one of our talks. It was right when things got really bad between us, and looking back, probably marked the beginning of the end.

Anyway, we were a little stoned, and feeling somewhat philosophical. Flexing intellect. And she had asked me if I ever thought that my dad had died in vain. That maybe his death had accomplished nothing but bringing pain to two continents. The loathing I had felt that day was rekindled many times over at that graduation party.

The thing about being modest is, if people *think* that you're being modest then they automatically think even worse of you than if you were bragging. Backpedaling, I tried to deflect the crowd's questions as best I could. They came rapid-fire, leading to few cogent answers but much sweat and not a small amount of vertigo. They finally started to lose their steam after Colin read the Wikipedia page out loud. They seemed satisfied by that trite synopsis, which to me was ridiculous, an insulting oversimplification. But they were appeased and amid the backslaps and respectful gestures I was finally able to make a quiet exit and go home.

Chapter 38

SUMMER USUALLY MADE ME THINK of yard work and football and surfing, none of which were applicable to my life now. My football career was over, the nearest beach was three hours away, and Yard Work for Warriors had run its course back in Virginia Beach. I had a one-track mind.

I still had five months before I could enlist, and I wasn't going to let them go to waste. BUD/S would be the ultimate test of body and mind, and I used the time to prepare myself. Already isolated, I rarely turned my phone on, let alone return the few calls and texts I received. I was on a mission.

My physical routine has been well documented, but I had to turn it up a notch. I ran, swam, and did pushups like my life depended on it, although I had no qualms about the physical aspect of this challenge. The fittest men in the world regularly rang the bell – getting through BUD/S was more about conquering mind than body. So I focused on preparing for the mental torture I would endure. "Success is when opportunity meets preparation," he always said. I knew that with all things equal, I'd be more prepared than every other candidate.

So I subjected myself to fun trials like baths of ice water. I would lay submerged until my skin burned, holding my breath until purple lips sputtered. I would exercise for hours on end with only a few hours of sleep. Twice I stayed up for two days straight, pushing myself on long, near-delirious runs and countless pushups, imaginary instructors' bellows pushing me forward.

To simulate drown-proofing, I tied weights to my feet and jumped in the pool. That exercise nearly had an unintended result after I struggled to untie one of the barbells.

I drove to the Shenandoah Mountains for a twenty-eight-mile march, a backpack filled with thirty pounds of sand leaving my shoulders bloody and raw, my back bent.

"The best advice I can give you is to lose the word 'can't' from your vocabulary," wrote Westhead in one of his emails. "It sounds cliché, and it might be, but the men who make it through BUD/S are the ones who want it the most. The ones who won't quit, would die before quitting. The truth is there is no way of knowing if you are one of those men until you try. When you haven't slept for four days but still complete a four-mile ocean swim. When you're doing somersaults in mud pits, or are near hypothermic in the Pacific, or doing timed runs in the sand with compound fractures in your legs. When your rashed groins are hamburger meat and you know that at any point you can make the pain stop. That there is a donut and cup of hot chocolate waiting for you, that you can get under a blanket in the cab of that pickup for quick a ride back to the barracks and a warm bed for twelve hours of peaceful sleep if you just ring that bell. But you choose not to quit. There's no one that can make that decision for you."

I sat at my desk re-reading that email, and I'd be lying if I said it didn't give me goose bumps. I just knew I would be one of the few to make it, I had to be. But I also knew that no matter how hard I pushed myself now, there was no way to truly prepare for the test that was the six months of BUD/S. "How do you eat an elephant? One bite at a time."

"Wanna do something, Nate?" I turned from my laptop, greeted by Cheyenne's toothy grin.

I returned the smile and invited her in.

"Whaddcha have in mind?" I asked her.

Her eyes went to the ceiling before brightening. "How about ice skating?"

"That would be nice," I said.

And so we went ice skating that afternoon. I helped her tie her skates and took her hand when she needed it, and watched her from the other end of the rink when she didn't.

Chapter 39

"Ready?"

I'm not, but I can't show it. Directly below my feet a sheer drop stares back.

He's looking at me, waiting, testing. Behind the Oakley goggles it's impossible to tell whether his eyes show patience or frustration. He shifts his weight on the snowboard, making me think it's the latter. There's a tension between us, and I'm mad at him for putting me in this position. I'm scared, but worse than the fear of the mountain is the fear of showing it.

I'm jealous of Cheyenne, down on the bunny slopes with Mom, standing sturdy on two skis, probably going into the lodge soon for a hot chocolate. Not standing at the lip of a double black diamond being scrutinized like a term paper.

Despite the cold and altitude, sweat forms on my brow. My face flushes with panic at the realization that I can't do this. I can't.

Dad drops in, bombing down the mountain with not even the consideration of a backward glance. My panic turns to anger and with a clenched jaw I leap forward, my thoughts on violence.

I am twelve and just conquered my first double black diamond and will have my dad for less than a year.

Chapter 40

IT WAS BRUTALLY HOT, especially for May. Summer seemed determined to shoehorn its way in, as apparently spring had relinquished its God-given territory with little opposition.

I focused on the heat. There was much more on my mind, but the heat was there and I was grateful for it. For any distraction. I was fiercely aware of each bead of sweat as it formed on my forehead. I stepped lightly on the crisp, even grass. I didn't wipe my face.

I found that if I didn't focus on any one marker, if I just let my eyes wander without agenda, the white tombstones would mesh into the grass like a soupy blur. Which was helpful, because I still wasn't ready to enter the frame of mind I needed to be in. It was mental procrastination: waiting to do something until the circumstances presented gave you no option. I would wait until I *had* to pull my shit together, and then I would. But for the next few precious moments I would maintain numbness and only acknowledge superficial sensations.

That escape only lasted another hundred yards. I had arrived in Section 60, home to the many young men who had made the ultimate sacrifice in Iraq and Afghanistan.

The air was thicker here, the heat more oppressive. Row after crushing row of simple memorials intimidated me, overwhelmed me.

It was hard to believe that each marker not only represented but actually held an extinguished life. Slowly, I counted the too few years from 1986 to 2012. 1984 to 2003. 1978 to 2014. Joshua Micah Mills, U.S. Army, 24. Travis L. Youngblood, U.S. Navy. Jeffrey C. Bland, United States Marine Corp. Matthew Philip Wallace, Brian Matthew Bunting, Alan Dinh Lam. I couldn't help but read each name, calculate their ages, all too aware how many weren't much older than me when they had died.

At the back of Section 60, the markers stopped suddenly in the middle of a row. That empty land was particularly disconcerting, knowing what it represented. The earth was still brown and newly torn up in front of the last few plots, while the unclaimed land was still virgin and green. The realization that sometime soon that earth would be disturbed sent a shockwave through my body, forced me to continue moving. What were its future inhabitants doing right now?

I avoided the other grievers, many of whom were young women with very young children. They had laid out blankets with sandwiches and fruit and juice packs for the crawling toddlers. They were the lucky ones, not yet aware of what this visit to Arlington meant. I envied their indifferent smiles and oblivious play. In their mothers I recognized the pained expressions.

I saw platoon mates drinking beer with their buddies, fathers having quiet talks with their sons, friends leaving shot glasses of Jamison, kids' laminated poems authored with love. Rosary beads and birthday balloons, birth notices and love letters, bobbleheads and photos from happier days. Flowers and American flags.

I looked again at my phone for the site number of my first stop. I soon found it. Sgt. Kristoffer Hawkins, Army Ranger, Purple Heart. Loving father, husband. I did the math: thirty-nine years old.

On top of his grave was a rock painted red. In white lettering, someone had written "I miss you Daddy." Jasmine, Eli's younger sister, no doubt. A baseball sat at the base of the tombstone, and I knew that Eli had left it there.

In the ground before me lay the man who had bled with my father. Had not only been there with him at the end, but had left the earth with him. I couldn't help but picture cartoons of the two of them rising to Heaven together. It made me chuckle, and my upturned cheeks caught tears. Between the sweat, snot, and tears, the back of my hand was quickly a wet mess. Embarrassed, I lowered my sunglasses and my head, hoping no other visitors had noticed. I wasn't a kid anymore.

I stood before the grave, contemplating. Wondered when the last time was that Eli, the kindred spirit I still hadn't faced in person, had visited. After a proper amount of time, I made my way to the next plot on my list, four rows over.

"Spencer Detse. SOCS. Afghanistan. April 3, 1981. Aug. 6, 2012. BMS W/VALOR & 3 GS. Purple Heart."

Most of the SEALs lost on that Chinook two years earlier were buried here, together, in this nondescript row. Too many markers reading Aug. 6, 2012. I knew all their names, though not all of them personally. It looked the same as the thousands of other rows, those which held men killed in WWII and the wives of generals or career airmen who had suffered strokes at age ninety.

Bull was next to Spencer. Just the way they would have wanted it. An operator I hadn't known was laid to rest next to them, another next to him. I walked along the row. It was strange, reading the names. I felt connected and disconnected all at the same time.

"You a SEAL?"

I turned to the soft voice, unaware the question was directed at me.

"Uh uh," I said even softer, not really looking up.

"Oh. You kind of look like one, that's why I asked." Then: "I knew Bill. He's down there. I actually knew a bunch of them. They were all on Team 6 and were killed when their helicopter was shot down in Afghanistan."

"Mm hmm," I agreed, pulse quickening. I managed a better look: She was pretty, mid-thirties, blond. She looked like the kind of woman who hung out with SEALs.

"Anyway. They were good men. They'd be glad to have the company," she said before walking away.

Suddenly I was struck with an urge to leave. I wouldn't have stayed for anything. After a final salute at Spencer's grave, I made my way to the Explorer as quickly as I could.

It was packed with all my possessions, which didn't fill it even halfway. I hoped the old SUV would make it across country.

It had been a week since I had graduated boot camp and left Great Lakes for Mom's house. My hellos to my family had occurred three days ago, the goodbyes in the past hour. My SEAL contract had been waiting for me after boot camp; next stop, BUD/S.

Soon I was on Route 66, headed west. The excitement and nerves increased exponentially with each passing mile. Grains of sand falling through fingers, barely discernable until a pile rested at your feet.

I enjoyed the solitude of the road, the mental challenge of putting as much distance between myself and the East Coast as possible. I didn't sightsee, didn't stop to stretch my legs, just moved forward as quickly and efficiently as possible.

Civil War battlegrounds casually turned into tobacco fields turned into the rolling hills of Tennessee into the depressing Memphis sky. A rusted bridge carried me over the Mississippi River. By the end of that first day I had crossed the unofficial end of the eastern United States. I stopped at a Hampton Inn in Little Rock for what was left of the night.

I was back at it before sunrise. The green highway-scape soon browned. I sped over flat fields holding acres of unidentifiable crops and bales of drying hay. My eyes bleared and glazed over through Oklahoma and the Texas panhandle. The two were indistinguishable without the staggered green highway markers, scarred with bullet holes and serving as perches for watchful crows and buzzards. The plains gave way to desert, where heavy eyelids told me it was time for rest.

That stop the second night was in Albuquerque, an impressive distance for two days of disciplined driving. Back on the road just as daylight crested, the destination that much closer.

Colorful canyons which appeared to have been formed by giants dripping wet sand onto the earth, the long stretch of pavement only limited by the human eye. A sky like I had never seen before, the power of the blues and strength of the whites. More desert, leading to the California state line.

My foot grew heavier as the finish line neared. Those grains of sand had added up, and my intensity grew. A different emotion would appear each mile, running the gauntlet through excitement, self-doubt, nervousness, self-realization, uncertainty, disbelief, excitement. And then I was there. Coronado.

Chapter 41

THE SUN WAS MAKING its final descent at an angle I was not accustomed to. I squinted into it, tasting the salt water on my lips, enjoying the chill through my wetsuit. Ensign Brock Carter, a wiry California kid, paddled in front of me. A wave lightly tossed my board, splashing cold Pacific water over my head. I shivered, but not from the cold.

Carter and I both would be starting BUD/S with Class 289 next week. We had met at Corpsman school – if we failed out, four years of sticking dependents and running sick calls awaited us. He had been honor man in San Antonio. Guess who he just edged out.

Although I had only just met Carter, so far I liked him. And he seemed to like me well enough. But it didn't matter. We both knew every time we went for a run or grabbed a beer, went surfing or talked to chicks, we were sizing each other up. Seeing if the other had what it takes. Because the truth is, you are only as strong as your fellow shipmates. The last thing you wanted was someone weak in your boat crew. And as an officer, there was a chance Brock would be the OIC of our class, which would put even additional scrutiny and pressure on him.

He looked the part and had the pedigree, that was for sure. Brock's dad was a retired SEAL Commander, and like me, he had grown up around these men. As much as you could without actually going through it, we knew what to expect.

He was barely 5'10", probably 155 pounds, but he radiated self-confidence and awareness. He had been a cross-country runner at the Naval Academy and like me, had been training for the upcoming six months since before he could remember. At twenty-two he was a lot older than I was, and that maturity showed. I decided it was something I would emulate.

"Nice right coming!" he called out. I turned to get in position, but as soon as it formed, the wave fizzled. That's the way it goes sometimes. We paddled close together, starting to feel the bond that men do when they know they will soon be experiencing something few will. I shielded my eyes with my hand, letting my mind wander peacefully with the evening horizon. The colors on the water were unworldly, bouncing off the ocean like natural strobes. It was hard not to be mesmerized by the natural beauty, although soon that seascape wouldn't be so friendly and inviting.

Behind us stood the famed Coronado Hotel, a symbol of luxury and comfort right next to the beach where we would soon be tortured. I laughed, and tried to clear my mind of the thought. *Focus on the now.*

"Pretty intimidating, huh?"

I nodded and splashed the cold water on my face. While we were in wetsuits today, we wouldn't be come Monday, when indoc began.

"It feels cold now, doesn't it? Just wait until..." he trailed off, realizing the morbidity of the comment.

"It's gonna be a blast!" I called out, the words getting lost in the wind. I turned, faced an oncoming wave. It was a beauty, a head-high left barreling with power. I lowered my head, began to paddle. It caught me in its graceful grip; I was one with the water. I popped up effortlessly, enjoying the rush as always. I yelled to Brock, to the wind and waves, "Geronimo!" and rode it back to shore.

Glossary

160th SOAR Nightstalkers – The U.S. Army's Special Operations Aviation Regiment. The best Army helicopter pilots and crew make up this group, based at Ft. Campbell, Kentucky.

A-School – Technical training after boot camp that each sailor must attend in their area of expertise.

Apache – An Army attack helicopter.

Bagram – The largest U.S. military base in Afghanistan.

Black shoe – A derogatory term used by aviators in reference to ship drivers in the Navy.

Blowout kit – Medical supplies taken into battle.

Boat crew – The men assigned to the same boat in BUD/S.

Boatswain's Mate – A Naval rating that encompasses many jobs on a ship, including its upkeep.

Bowline man – The person who jumps out of the boat during rock portage to secure the boat on top of wet rocks. This dangerous evolution takes place in front of the famed Hotel del Coronado.

BUD/S – Basic Underwater Demolition/SEAL Training. Divided into three phases, this is considered the hardest training in the U.S. military.

Budweiser – Another name for the Trident.

C-130 – Large military troop and transport plane.

C-17 – Large military transport plane.

CACO – Casualty Assistance Calls Officer. A sailor tasked with assisting the families of deceased service members with arrangements and benefits.

CAS – Close Air Support. Aircraft fire called in that is to land near friendly forces.

Chief Petty Officer – Enlisted rank of E7.

Chuck Pfarrer – A famous retired SEAL who is now an author.

Click – Kilometer.

CO – Commanding Officer.

Combat side stroke – A modified version of the side stroke used by special operators.

Commissary – A grocery store on a military base.

Corpsman – An enlisted sailor trained to give medical aid.

Cracker Jacks – Dress Blues uniform for junior enlisted sailors.

Crow with Chevrons – The patch worn on a Navy uniform designating the sailor as a Petty Officer.

Danger close – In artillery and naval gunfire support, information in a call for fire to indicate that friendly forces are within 600 meters of the target.

DEVGRU – United States Naval Special Warfare Development Group. Also known as SEAL Team 6.

Dogface – Term for an Army foot soldier.

Dress Blues – Formal uniform worn by members of the U.S. Navy in the colder months. Commissioned officers and chief petty officers wear a double-breasted black coat and trousers, while junior enlisted wear Cracker Jacks. Dress Whites are worn in warmer months.

Evac – Evacuate.

Exchange – A department store on a military base.

Fast-rope – A technique for descending from helicopters when the helicopter cannot land. A thick rope is thrown from the helicopter and operators slide down it.

First Phase – Phase One of BUD/S is seven weeks long and is the physical conditioning portion of the training. Hell Week comes in First Phase.

Fleet – In general, a large formation of warships. Represents a job on a ship.

FNG – Fucking New Guy.

FOB – Forward Operating Base.

Frogmen – An early nickname for Navy SEALs. Goes back to WWII, to the Underwater Demolition Teams who were the SEAL predecessors.

Ft. Benning – Large Army base outside Columbus, Georgia. Home of the 75th Ranger Regiment.

Ft. Meade – U.S. Army base that houses the NSA and many other intelligence agencies.

Ft. Meyer – A small Army base in Arlington, Virginia.

Great Lakes – Naval base in Michigan that houses the Navy's boot camp.

Green Faces – Nickname given to SEALs in Vietnam after they would paint their faces before missions. The enemy could only report that they were attacked by "men with green faces."

Green Team – The selection and training program for SEALs to join DEVGRU, or SEAL Team 6.

Grinder – The asphalt area at BUD/S where students do calisthenics.

HAHO – High-Altitude, High-Opening. Used to airdrop personnel at high altitudes when aircraft are unable to fly above enemy skies without posing a threat to the jumpers.

Head – Bathroom, in the Navy.

Hell Week – Five and a half days of constant physical training during Phase 1 of BUD/S. Students are given a total of four hours of sleep during this time.

HESCO Barrier – A semi-permanent wall built of wire mesh and heavy duty fabric, filled with sand or gravel.

Hindu Kush mountain range – 500 mile long mountain range that stretches from Northern Pakistan to Central Afghanistan.

Honor man – Recognition for the top man in a training class.

Hooyah – Battle cry SEALs use for everything from "yes" to "okay" to show general enthusiasm. Origin unknown.

HVT – High-Value Target.

Indoc – A three week orientation before BUD/S to get students acclimated to the rigors of SEAL training.

IR lights – Disposable infrared lights which only can be seen with night vision devices.

J'bad – Short for Jalalabad, a city in Eastern Afghanistan with a U.S. Army base.

Jarhead – A derogatory term for Marines.

JOC – Joint Operations Center.

KIA – Killed In Action.

Lewis Burwell "Chesty" Puller – Famous Marine Corps general who fought in WWII and Korea.

Little Creek – Referring to the Naval Amphibious Base, Little Creek, Virginia. This is where Naval Special Warfare Group 2 (East coast SEAL teams) are housed.

LZ – Landing Zone.

Marine Recon – The United States Marine Corps' Special Operations unit.

Mark V – Small boat used by Special Operations forces.

Master Chief Petty Officer – Enlisted rank of E9.

Medevac – Medical evacuation.

MH-60 Black Hawk – Highly modified Black Hawk helicopters flown by the 160th Special Ops Aviation Regiment.

Midrats – Nighttime meal for sailors on late-night or early morning watches.

MP – Military Police.

MRE – Meals Ready to Eat. Dry, sealed meals troops eat when away from a base and hot food.

NCO – Non-Commissioned Officer.

Night rock portage – A dangerous evolution in BUD/S where each boat crew has to paddle their rubber boat through the surf and onto a large group of rocks in the dark.

O+ – Blood type.

OIC – Officer in Charge.

OIC of the class – BUD/S is one of the few training schools where enlisted sailors and officers go through the same curriculum, side by side. The Officer in Charge of the class is the highest ranking student.

Operation Redwing – The 2005 mission where a four-man SEAL patrol fought hundreds of Taliban fighters in the Afghan mountains. Three of the four SEALs were killed and a book and movie were made called Lone Survivor.

Overwatch – Sniper support for ground troops.

PJ – Air Force special operators, also called Pararescuemen. Operatives tasked with recovery and medical treatment of personnel in combat environments.

Platoon – Navy SEAL platoons are made up of sixteen SEALs plus support personnel.

PT – Physical Training.

QRF – Quick Reaction Force. Another unit or platoon on standby to assist in battle as needed.

Quarterdeck – Technically, the area on a ship where the captain stands. Used in the Navy to mean an open area where people gather.

RGP – Rocket-Propelled Grenade.

Roll back – When a student at BUD/S is injured or can't meet certain requirements, the instructors can send him back a phase, where he will graduate with another class if he completes training.

SAW – Squad Action Weapon. A portable but heavy machine gun. Usually the biggest or most junior members of a platoon will carry the SAW.

SDV – SEAL Delivery Vehicle. A fully submersible vehicle that can be launched from a submarine, aircraft carrier or airdropped to deliver SEALs underwater for clandestine missions.

SEAL – The U.S. Navy's Sea, Air and Land commandos.

SEAL Team 2 – An East Coast-based SEAL team. Officially, SEAL teams are broken into two groups: Group One (SEAL Teams 1, 3, 5 and 7) is based in Coronado, California, and Group Two (SEAL teams 2, 4, 8 and 10) is based in Little Creek, Virginia. DEVGRU (Team 6) is housed in Dam Neck, Virginia.

Senior Chief Petty Officer – Enlisted rank of E8.

Six – Having your back, as in the six o'clock position on a clock.

Slushy – An ice bath. A way to haze new SEALs and BUD/S students.

Smurf crew – The name for the boat crew in BUD/S where the shortest candidates are assigned.

SQT – SEAL Qualification Training. A four-month advanced course SEALs must take after BUD/S before earning their Trident.

Squid – Derogatory term for a sailor.

Squirters – Enemy combatants trying to escape the battle.

Sugar cookies – Another BUD/S evolution, when students are sent into the ocean and then told to roll in the sand until they resemble a sugar cookie.

Surf torture – A favorite of BUD/S instructors, consisting of sending students to lay in the freezing Pacific Ocean, pulling them out just before hypothermia sets in.

Swim buddy – A fellow BUD/S student who you must be with at all times.

TAD – Temporary Additional Duty. Essentially the equivalent of a business trip for military personnel.

Taps – A song usually played on the bugle at military funerals.

Task Unit – When more than one SEAL team or platoon deploys together for a specific mission.

Tricare – Health benefit program for the military and their dependents.

Trident – The Special Warfare Insignia worn only by Navy SEALs after completing BUD/S and SQT. One of the few badges in the Navy that is the same color for both officers and enlisted men.

UDT – Underwater Demolition Teams. The precursors to the SEALs, they cleared beaches and conducted maritime missions in WWII.

UDT Swim shorts – Very short swimming trunks popularized by UDT swimmers in WWII and still worn by SEALs today.

Warning order – A preliminary notice of an order or action which is to follow.

Winchester – Out of ammunition.